SURVIVE

TOM BALE

978-1-913419-57-8

ALSO BY TOM BALE

The Stone Song

One Dark Night

Each Little Lie

All Fall Down

See How They Run

The Catch

Blood Falls

Terror's Reach

Skin and Bones

Sins of the Father

For Niki

PART I

SELECTION

1

The runway is in sight when the plane appears to stall. They all feel it, the descent interrupted, and the engines if they're still working can't be heard over the whirr of the air circulation and the whine and hiss of pressure in their ears.

Jody Lamb, sitting between her children in the middle of three seats, gasps as the aircraft lunges to the right. She can see past her son to the dipped wing, pointing like an accusing finger at the scrubland and glinting blue sea of the bay.

She smiles down at Dylan but he is absorbed in the view from the window: the solid earth so close, but probably not survivably so. The wing judders and flexes like a plastic ruler about to snap. Jody feels warmth against her skin; her eight-year-old daughter Grace has clutched her hand and Jody knows she must play the grown-up. Unlike her younger brother, Grace is scared.

They tip sideways again, and a ripple of anxiety spreads through the plane.

'What's happening, Mummy?' Grace has to shout the question, because their ears are blocked.

Jody makes sure to exaggerate her lip movements when she says, 'Nothing, honey. We're just coming in to land.'

A glance across the aisle at poor Sam, a first-time flyer, and she can read it in his face, the same prayer: *Don't let my children die.*

It's their first foreign holiday as a family – the first time ever that Sam or their children have been on a plane. Only Jody has flown before, in her own childhood, and it was Jody who calmed their fears, promising them all that it was safer than crossing a road.

Until now Sam has been making a decent job of keeping the plane in the air by willpower alone, but he's starting to doubt whether that will be enough. By leaning slightly he can see one of the cabin crew, strapped into a seat that faces the passengers, and she looks... not calm so much as blank faced, like she's put on a mask for their benefit. If she was about to die, wouldn't she tear off the mask and scream the name of the person she loved most?

Maybe not, he thinks, given that we're English. But when he looks over his shoulder, he sees that in several rows there are people holding hands across the aisle. Families, like his, that have had to be seated in separate groups.

It's tempting, but he's worried it will upset his daughter if he suggests it. Dads aren't supposed to be afraid of anything, are they?

He presses his palms together between his legs and bows his head, staring at the safety card. Before take-off he studied it for so long that the couple next to him began to snigger – and if Sam was his brother or in any way like his brother, he might have gone off on one.

But he isn't like Carl, thank God. So he doesn't react when

the bloke mutters something to his wife. They must think Sam's praying – though maybe that isn't so far from the truth.

When the man taps on his window, his wife leans over to look, and Sam can't help but turn. He catches a glimpse of something moving past, and despite the painful blockage in his ears he hears the man say, 'Gulfstream G650. Magnificent!'

'Is it meant to be that close to us?' his wife shouts.

'It'll have priority to land. The VIP on board won't want to wait behind a cheap package tour!' Then a sniff, as if the man – in his own head – has far more in common with whoever's on the other aircraft.

Maybe he does. The couple are a lot older than Sam and they look sort of well-fed and pleased with themselves, like they've found a secret supply of cake in a world where everyone else lives on porridge.

The aircraft shudders, there's a loud clunking noise and a few people cry out. When they tip to the left, Sam can see the private jet is about to touch down. Lucky bastards.

Someone taps him on the arm. It's Grace, with a question. Even though he doesn't hear it properly, Sam makes an effort to nod and smile. He gestures at her to make sure the belt is tight across her lap, then turns away, and now he *is* praying. Praying that, if it does happen, it's over quickly.

A sharp pain in Jody's ears is followed by a pop, and her hearing is restored. She focuses on the sound of the engines – thank God they're still functioning – but as she does, the pitch changes and she knows this is it.

Other passengers are thinking the same, she can tell by the murmur of worried voices. The aircraft tilts sharply to the left and she looks out of her window, expecting to see that the wing has sheared off. But, no, it remains intact, shuddering against a backdrop of pure blue sky.

On Sam's side there is land in sight, but they seem to be alongside the runway rather than approaching it. A crawl of trees is proof they're still moving, although it feels like little more than a walking pace: Dylan goes quicker than this on the way to school.

The middle-aged man in Sam's row is talking in a confident voice. The man becomes aware of Jody's scrutiny and for a second his gaze switches to her, his eyes widening a fraction. Then Sam leans across and says, 'He reckons we're coming around, landing from the other end of the runway.'

And so it proves. The plane banks and descends, and from the windows on each side they see rows of trees, a villa or two with terracotta tiles on the roof, a scattering of goats grazing in a field; all of it as close as if they were observing it from the upper floor of a building.

Grace's hand tightens on her mum's in the final seconds. Dylan, meanwhile, is joyfully oblivious to their feelings. How wonderful, Jody thinks, to be five and fearless, savouring every moment of what she has come to regard as his second life.

2

Sam's ears are still blocked. He's opening and closing his mouth the way he was told to do, but stops when he realises the smug couple have noticed. He must look a right knob.

For most of the flight they've been acting as if he didn't exist, though he caught a few disapproving glances when he ate the food Jody passed to him – it was his idea to bring sandwiches from home rather than pay the rip-off prices at the airport. The Smugs, on the other hand, ordered the full in-flight breakfasts, a couple of brandies and even a small bottle of champagne.

Now Sam can feel the plane coming down. He tenses, but the landing when it happens isn't much more than the jolt you get from driving over a pothole. It's only as he lets out a breath that there's a sudden roar from the engines. The plane seems to lurch as if caught on something – Sam pictures a tripwire stretched across the runway, snagging on the wheels. He grabs the arms of his seat and for a second goes rigid with fear. Talk about bad luck, to crash now–

'Don't panic!' says Mr Smug with a mocking snort. 'It's only the reverse thrust.'

'To slow us down,' his wife explains. 'But I'm sure it would give you a shock, if you're not used to it.'

'It's certainly done that.' Clutching his seat, the man mimics a terror-stricken face.

Sam offers a weak smile, then turns to Jody. She's holding hands with the kids, the three of them pressed back in their seats like they're on a rollercoaster. The deceleration is pushing against Sam's chest, too, but he can feel it easing.

They're down. They're safe. *Oh thank Christ...*

'Textbook landing,' says Smug. 'Couldn't have done it better myself.'

'Oh, please, Trevor. You had one lesson, for your fiftieth, and that was in a light aircraft a fraction of the size.'

Sam tunes them out and tries to relax. From now on, he tells himself, the holiday can only get better.

The plane slowly turns, treating them to a distant flash of sea. All through the cabin there's the rustle of movement. The buzz of conversation seems to rise – though maybe it's just his hearing returning to normal – and the atmosphere seems a lot more cheerful. Sam guesses they'll never know how close they came to disaster.

Once they're at a stop it's suddenly manic. Overhead lockers pop open and people are jumping up, stretching and jostling for their luggage, and queuing for the exit before the doors have even opened. The cabin crew look on in amusement, like they're overseeing a bunch of chimps at feeding time.

Sam meets Jody's eye and smiles with gratitude. He's been trying so hard to feel good about this holiday, because he knows all too well how much it cost and what it means to her. And he *is* excited about it, of course he is. But this scare is another reminder of how the love he feels for his kids, which he always assumed would be a light and giddy sensation, so often takes second place to *anxiety* about them, which has the exact opposite effect – it makes him feel heavy, almost crushed by the knowledge that he can't protect them from all the dangers in the world.

Sometimes he finds it impossible to crawl out from under that weight and appreciate the good things while they're happening, even though he knows he'll almost certainly look back one day and regret what he missed.

The first passengers are filing out, vanishing into the glare of the Adriatic afternoon, when Dylan abruptly bursts into tears.

'Darling, what's wrong?'

'I don't wanna go out there. It'll eat me.'

'What?' Jody glances at the doorway again, and realises that from Dylan's perspective it must appear that the passengers are stepping into a furnace.

She caresses his cheek. 'Oh, darling. It's very hot outside, but it's completely safe. I promise.'

Sam squeezes in beside her to offer encouragement; as a result they lose their place in the queue. The older couple from his row push past without a backwards glance.

'Come on, Dyl,' Sam says. 'We're here now, mate.'

'And we're going to have a fantastic time!' Jody takes her son by the hand and they head for the exit, where the cabin crew are doling out good wishes. One ruffles Dylan's hair and says, 'Cheer up, dude, you're on holiday!'

Then they're out of the plane, dazzled by the brightness, and it's like they've walked into a steam room.

'Now, isn't that lovely?' Jody asks.

'Oh my God, it's amazing!' Grace exclaims. 'I am going to get *such* a good tan!'

'Breathe the air, too. It's so different from home. What does it taste like to you?'

Dylan sniffs. 'Petrol,' he says, and there is laughter.

Three buses are lined up, waiting to ferry them to the terminal building. On the nearest one, the couple from Sam's row are staring triumphantly in their direction. But the doors shut before they reach the bottom of the steps, causing Dylan to sag. 'Ohhh...'

Jody quickly points to the next bus. 'We'll get that one, look.'

'But I wanted *this* one...'

'They're all the same,' Grace snaps, and Jody is determined not to get cross because she knows how weary they all are, dragged up at four in the morning so her dad could drive them to Gatwick for a five a.m. check-in. Beside her, Sam isn't much help, casting fretful glances at the plane as though he's already worrying about the journey home.

Jody sighs. This is only the third time they've gone away as a family, and the last occasion – an ultra-cheap voucher holiday at a caravan park – was not an experience she wishes to repeat. Five days on the Suffolk coast with torrential rain and winds that could strip the flesh from your bones. Grace caught a vomiting bug, and because Sam vetoed paying for an upgrade they were stuck in a static home with all the comfort and appeal of an old sardine tin. Afterwards Jody vowed that the next break they took would be a proper holiday, even if that meant saving up for years.

And here we are, she thinks. *So could we all be a bit bloody happier?*

The second bus fills to bursting point, then trundles across the apron to the terminal building, pulling up beside a covered walkway leading to a set of wide glass doors. A line of passengers from the previous coach are still waiting to go inside. As they take their place in the queue, there's a sudden yelp from Dylan.

'What is it?' Jody asks, but his hand has slipped from hers and he's running.

Neither of them has done anything to encourage it, but from somewhere their son, at the age of five, has developed a fascination with guns and weaponry. What he's racing towards looks at first like a shop dummy; then Sam realises it's a soldier in uniform, positioned beneath a small awning that protects him from the sun. He has an automatic rifle slung across his chest.

'Wanna see the gun!' Dylan cries, and does a convincing impression of automatic fire: *czhczhczhczhczh*. The soldier twitches at the noise, his grip on the rifle seeming to tighten.

Then Sam grabs his son, heaving him up to shoulder height. 'Come on, Dyl.'

'Daddy put me down!'

'Nope. We've gotta go inside.' Aware that the soldier is watching them closely, Sam backs away. He takes out his phone, intending to head off a tantrum with a couple of photos. But as he starts to frame the shot, there's a shout from behind him.

'Wouldn't do that if I were you.'

It's a young man in the queue. He has the carefree look of a student: long hair and a scruffy beard, lots of beads and leather wristbands. His girlfriend has braids in her hair and braces on her teeth. They're probably only three or four years younger than Sam and Jody, and yet he's struck by the gulf that separates them: a whole great ocean of experience, hardship, responsibility.

'Won't hurt, will it?' Sam wonders if this skinny kid is trying to pick a fight with him.

'It's prohibited to photograph anything military,' the girl explains. 'They get, like, really uptight about it.'

'Yeah?' Scowling, Sam carries Dylan over to Jody and Grace, who are queuing just ahead of the students.

'It's a police state, is what it is,' the skinny kid says. 'One wrong move and you'll wake up in a cell with electrodes strapped to your b–'

'Ssh!' the girl hisses. 'Not in front of their kids!'

She laughs apologetically. Sam realises he is still glaring at the couple, and Jody gives him a warning glance: *Cool it*.

So Sam relaxes. Or pretends to, at least.

3

Sam finds it odd to greet the chill of an air-conditioned building with pleasure. For most of his life he's associated cold rooms with draughty windows, poor insulation and a lack of money for proper heating. Even in their current home, which has double glazing and a modern boiler (and costs them eleven hundred quid a month in rent), the heating has to be rationed in winter: an hour in the morning, two hours at night.

'It's not too cold for Dylan?' he asks.

Jody meets his eye. 'Dylan is absolutely fine. Aren't you, kiddo?'

The boy shrugs. 'I'm hungry.'

'We'll get something soon, once we're through this bit. We have to show the men our passports first. Look.'

They do look, which is probably a mistake. The queue is long and messy, splitting competitively into three channels at the security kiosks. Some travellers are waved through almost immediately; others are kept for two or three long minutes. Trevor Smug and his wife are way ahead, of course.

A sudden rattle of applause catches Sam's attention. It's coming from a small crowd clustered round a doorway at the far side of the hall. Is someone famous passing through, he wonders – maybe from that private jet?

He goes on tiptoe to get a better view, then realises he's drawn the attention of one of the grim-faced men in the kiosks. Sam quickly turns away.

It occurs to him that all the staff are men, and many are vaguely similar in appearance: short and stocky, with black hair and dark stubble; lots of moustaches but no beards. It's a look that reminds him of TV clips from the olden days – dodgy adverts for aftershave and cigars. What's odd is that he can tell they're foreign. But how?

Further down the room there's a glass partition, and beyond that another sprawling queue of arrivals. Again he's pretty sure they're not British: probably German or maybe Swedish, something like that. He wonders if those people can tell he's English just from his face, and thinks they probably can.

And do they also get a feel for his background, what social class he's from? Can they tell that he's from somewhere near the bottom?

His own view is that he has battled his way on to the first rung of the ladder and now has the second rung in sight. He and Jody are both twenty-six. After more than ten years together they've got two kids, the eldest already at junior school, and yet they don't own a home and they have no chance of getting a mortgage or saving up for a deposit – not when there's the crippling rent to find every month.

So a holiday like this one – high season, all-inclusive – it feels like they're broadcasting to the world that there's loads of cash kicking about. And there isn't.

I virtually gave up smoking for this, he reminds himself. No new trainers for over a year. Two Fridays in three he didn't go to the pub after work, and Jody gave up even more than that, as well as working all the extra hours she could at the shoe shop.

No new clothes, cheap make-up rather than the nice stuff from Boots, walking instead of taking the bus.

Three years of scrimping and saving (he's used the phrase many times but still has no idea what 'scrimping' means) and this time next week it'll be over, just like that. Two thousand, seven hundred and fifty-eight pounds: gone.

It scares him, if he's honest. He doesn't see how this holiday can ever live up to their expectations, or justify the money they've spent. Jody disagrees. She says it's about giving the kids an experience they'll be able to treasure for the rest of their lives. And as she keeps reminding him, after what they went through with Dylan, they all deserve something a bit special.

It takes another hour to clear passport control and retrieve their luggage from the baggage area, which has become a bear pit containing over a thousand weary, irritable holidaymakers from four different flights. At Jody's urging, Sam fights his way through the crush and returns with both of their cases, hard shell Samsonites borrowed from Jody's parents. They load them on to a trolley, endure a mini-tantrum from Dylan when he's prevented from clambering on top, and make their way to the arrivals hall.

Jody spots a couple of English girls from their tour operator, Sheldon Travel. After a clipboard consultation they're directed to the main car park: coach number fourteen.

Outside, it's even hotter than it felt when they got off the plane. They stop on a wide marble concourse and Jody shields her eyes with her hand, surveying row after row of coaches.

'There's Eleven,' Sam murmurs, and then Grace says, 'Fourteen! Over there, look!'

This lifts their spirits until Dylan starts crying again. 'Mummy, *I* wanted to find it!'

'You did, in a way. And you're helping now, by being such a good boy.'

That doesn't work as well as Jody hopes, so she rummages in Sam's rucksack for the emergency stash of Haribo. Smiles on the kids' faces at last.

Crossing one of the access roads, there's a bus swinging round towards them but they're looking right instead of left. Sam has stepped off the kerb when Grace grabs his arm. 'Dad!'

He jumps back, standing completely still until the bus has thundered past. There's a familiar blankness to his gaze. Jody is only too aware that Sam's way of coping with stress is to withdraw into himself, and although he doesn't intend for his reaction to make everyone tense, it nearly always has that effect.

For a second, nobody moves or speaks. Then, to Jody's relief, Sam breathes out slowly and summons a grin for the kids. 'Looks like you two had better teach me how to cross the road.'

The coach driver is short and stocky, with greying hair and a moustache. He wants the name of their hotel but Sam's mind has gone blank. He has to call Jody back just as she's trying to herd the kids aboard.

'The Adriana Beach,' she says, a bit tetchily.

'Sorry.' Sam starts to repeat it but the driver has already snatched up a case, which he slings into the luggage bay with an impatient sigh.

Hurrying the trolley back to the terminal building, Sam feels disorientated, not just because the traffic's on the wrong side, or because of the heat, or the unfamiliarity of his surroundings. It's more to do with a suspicion that everyone else knows the rules – what to do, where to go, how to behave – as though there's a set of instructions that was handed out to them but withheld from him.

The signs don't help. He knew the country had its own language, but he hadn't imagined that the writing would look so different. The meaningless squiggles bring back painful memories of all the years he struggled with reading, feeling like he was shut out of everything. There was talk of dyslexia, but his mum never did anything about getting him tested.

He still burns at the memory of the humiliation, having to attend remedial classes in the first year of secondary school. That's when the truancy got out of hand and his life so nearly went off the rails, just as it had done with his brother a few years before. But whereas Carl had been beyond help from the start, in Sam's case his uncle Paul had stepped in to save him.

Jody and the children are at the back of the coach. Sam settles next to Dylan and takes a fistful of Haribo to share. The driver's got the engine running, thank God, so the aircon is working.

Dylan is chewing on the gooey sweets while chattering away, and Sam feels guilty when his eyes keep drifting shut. Each time it's a tougher challenge to open them again, and suddenly he's in the middle of a weird kind of waking dream. They're on the plane as it falls into the sea, but it doesn't break apart. People gather at the windows, pointing at the exotic foreign fish as the plane slowly sinks towards the bottom. Sam is sure they'll all die once the oxygen runs out but no one else seems the slightest bit worried.

Then Jody says, 'Isn't that your friends?'

Sam rubs his eyes, leans forward and spots Trevor Smug and his wife wheeling a trolley in their direction.

'Oh, *ff*–'

'Ssh. They weren't that bad, were they?'

Sam pulls a face. 'Really up 'emselves.'

'Did they say where they're staying?'

'I didn't ask. Won't be at ours, though. We're only three star.'

Jody looks hurt. 'Don't say "only". On TripAdvisor it's voted the number two hotel in our resort.'

'I know. But a bloke like that'll want number one.'

The middle-aged couple climb aboard with a lot of huffing and puffing, making it plain that they're furious about the 'disgraceful inefficiency' of the airport. Both of them notice Sam but pretend they haven't, dropping their gaze as they shuffle into the nearest available seats. Jody wonders if they resent the fact that she and Sam made it on to the coach ahead of them.

Thankfully a Sheldon rep turns up, introduces herself as 'Gabby' and announces, to a few sarcastic cheers, that their departure is imminent. She sounds friendly and enthusiastic, speaking in a warm accent that Jody thinks might be from Leicester or somewhere like that. After running through a quick headcount, Gabby signals to the driver who shuts the door and eases the coach on to the access road.

Before settling back, Jody conducts a quick 'family assessment'. Grace has her head against the window and is almost dozing. Sam, bless him, has come back to life and is earnestly discussing missiles and tanks with Dylan. Now Jody can stare straight ahead and focus on nothing...

Except the rep, Gabby, is coming along the aisle, summoned by the middle-aged grumps. She's in her early twenties, pretty in an over-made-up way. Long blonde hair in a side parting, which swirls as she turns her head, resting in a spray on her shoulder. She's wearing the Sheldon uniform of a patterned shirt (white with red and blue palm trees) and a plain blue pencil skirt; nothing particularly fashionable, but close-fitting enough to see that she has a *very* good body.

It can't have escaped Sam's attention, either, and yet he

doesn't seem to give the woman more than the briefest of glances.

The middle-aged couple start to protest about the time it took to retrieve their luggage. The man appears to be talking directly to the rep's chest. She seems well aware of this, leaning closer as if to make it easier for him to perv. Within seconds he's nodding and smiling, *thank you for listening, not your fault at all, blah blah blah...*

Jody sighs, hoping Sam is right about their choice of hotel.

4

The five-star resort is their first stop, about twenty minutes in, and the only people to disembark are two elderly women in large sunhats. Sam starts to think he's tempted fate.

Another ten minutes till the next stop, then two more in quick succession, by which time there are only three groups left on the coach, including the Smugs and Sam and Jody.

'Okay,' says the rep, 'Adriana Beach is next, and then the Sunrise is our last drop-off today.'

Jody beams at him. 'Us next, thank God.'

On the first part of the journey they learned a bit about the island – though it was a struggle to stop Dylan from talking over the rep. It's sixty kilometres end to end and fifteen kilometres at the widest point, the second largest of some twenty-odd islands in a… here the rep used a word that sounded like 'archie-pele-go'; then she giggled and admitted she could never pronounce it properly.

The part they're in is the south-west corner, which has some of the best beaches and the larger resorts. The island is notable for its limestone, olive trees and pine forests. Other than that it's mostly the scrubland he noticed as the plane came down. Small trees and rocks, a lot of mud and dust: nothing like the rich greens and rolling hills of Sussex.

Still, it's the beaches that matter. And the climate. Gabby jokingly agreed to guarantee them temperatures of around thirty degrees over the next week, no rain unless they're really unlucky – 'Even then it's likely to be a quick thunderstorm at night; the lightning's *incredible* here sometimes!'

There's a bit of history, stuff like when the island was first inhabited, and then Sam has to focus on keeping Dylan distracted, pointing out of the window at the rocky landscape and wondering if there could be any soldiers hiding out there.

'Are there, Dad?'

'Might be. This is probably the kind of place they use for training.'

'Oh, wow!' Dylan gets up on his knees, nose pressed against the glass. Jody goes to say something but Sam shakes his head. He's just bought them some peace and quiet – not to be sniffed at, now the Haribos have gone.

Jody's first impression of the hotel is far from encouraging. After driving past an orchard of sickly looking trees, they see a sign for the Adriana Beach and take a sharp turn into the approach road. The grounds are fenced off with barbed wire, enclosing yet more scrubland. They pass a dilapidated building that resembles a lock-up garage. The area around it is strewn with discarded equipment: rusting patio umbrellas and broken sun loungers; a coil of red hose pipe like a sleeping snake.

Then over a slight ridge, and the main building comes into sight. Five storeys high, dull grey in colour, at first it reminds Jody of a block of council flats. This isn't a view that appeared on the website. Her whole body seems to crumple with disappointment, not just for herself but because she's anticipating how Sam will react.

Gabby the rep is leaning forward in her seat, murmuring to the driver. Jody wonders what the woman will do if they refuse to get off the coach. *This isn't good enough. We paid a lot of money and we deserve something better.*

Jody's mouth goes dry as she imagines saying the words. If a complaint is needed, she knows she will be the one to make it. Sam has no stomach for dealing with authority, even in the form of a holiday rep barely out of her teens.

Earlier, when Gabby invited questions at the end of her introduction, there was some general grumbling about the chaos in baggage reclaim. Then a woman asked about the landing. Gabby didn't seem to understand the question, and a man with a strong Lancashire accent chipped in: 'No problems with our flight.'

'This was from Gatwick,' the woman said. 'Third year running we've come here, and today we're all set to land when the plane suddenly swerves and goes round to the far end of the runway. I think it was because a private jet had come past and got permission to land before us.'

'Overtook you, like?' the Lancastrian joked, and someone else muttered, 'Boy racers!'

Gabby continued to look baffled. 'I'm sure there was never any danger, but I'll see if I can find out any more...' The way she trailed off made Jody think she wouldn't be trying too hard.

Now, taking a deep breath, Jody summons the strength for what might be a vigorous argument. Then a gasp from her daughter: 'I saw the pool!'

'What?'

'Between the buildings. It looks really nice!'

The coach eases into a layby directly outside the hotel

entrance. Hanging baskets offer a splash of colour, and there are potted palm trees spaced at intervals like a guard of honour. Jody can see movement within the lobby: a waiter carrying drinks on a tray. She spots a long bar glinting with optics, comfortable sofas and attractive lighting. Perhaps it's cowardly, but she decides not to say anything, at least until they've had a look around.

The middle-aged couple are already on their feet, their flight cases blocking the aisle. The rep ticks their names off the list, then beams at Jody as she leads Grace forward.

'Happy holidays! Don't forget the welcome meeting this evening!'

Once they've assembled on the pavement, Sam heads round to fetch the cases. Dylan wants to go with him and has to be restrained. His frustrated cry draws a wince from the middle-aged woman. Her husband appears, wheeling his cases, and sneaks a glance at Jody's body. Sam comes up behind them, wearing a sheepish grin meant only for her: *Look who we've been lumbered with.*

As the coach moves away, the woman's gaze drifts from her husband to Jody as she says, 'Are we set? Got all your stuff?'

The questions are delivered as if they're together in a single group, and the woman is treating her like a child. But Jody makes the effort to smile politely. After all, it's not this woman's fault that she and Sam had kids too young, or that they still react badly to any suggestion that they can't cope.

Jody is well aware that they're both far too prickly about it, the result of feeling for years that they have been unfairly judged, looked down on, for the bad luck and mistakes of their youth.

Right this second, Sam doesn't care what the hotel's like – he just wants to get to their room and crash out for a while – but first there's the check-in to survive.

Trevor nods in the direction of the departing coach. 'Didn't tip him, I hope?' Sam shakes his head but Trevor carries on complaining: 'Outrageous, the way everyone expects something for nothing these days.'

Sam hesitates at the entrance, only for Trevor to wave him through. Ironically, this is one occasion when Sam would have preferred to let the other man go first and watch what he did; now he has no choice but to approach the reception desk and introduce himself.

He's dreading the thought that the staff will speak no English, or that their accents will be too strong for Sam to understand. But as it turns out, the man who greets him has very good English. He's young, dark-haired, and looks a bit like an Italian footballer, Schelotto.

Sam has to fill in a form, and fights off his usual panic, thankful that it's all simple stuff: name, address, nationality. He puts 'English', then adds 'British' as well. He can never remember which one you're supposed to use.

There's some confusion when the man refers to Jody as 'Mrs Berry.' Sam has to explain that she's Jody *Lamb*, not Berry, and the man turns away to check the booking details on a computer. Feeling vaguely ashamed, Sam wants to explain why they're not married. It's partly the expense of a wedding when there are so many other priorities, partly a ridiculous problem over surnames. Sam knows she doesn't like how 'Jody Berry' sounds, and 'Jody Lamb-Berry' is even worse: *A very peculiar flavour of jam*, as she's often joked.

It doesn't cause a problem, but there's another worry when the man requests their passports. Luckily they're in Jody's handbag, meaning Sam has to ask for them. The Smugs are within earshot and don't react, so Sam has to assume it's not some kind of scam. He hands them over and is told they'll be kept safe until they check out.

A couple more minutes and it's done. Each of them has a white plastic wristband fitted: proof they're entitled to the all-inclusive package. Then Sam is given tokens to exchange for beach towels, as well as two plastic key cards which not only open the door but also operate the electricity in the room.

Taking a case each, and a child each, Sam and Jody head across the lobby and through a set of double doors which lead outside. Another blast of that stunning heat, like someone's turned a blowtorch in their direction. Feels pretty good now he's adjusting to it.

This side of the hotel is a different world; everything nicely laid out, lots of well-watered grass and flowers. A network of pale stone paths run through the gardens, leading to a pool and a large patio area filled with sun loungers, paired off beneath huge white umbrellas. There's a pool bar with a thatched bamboo roof, half a dozen people sitting on stools and sipping drinks.

As they trundle the cases along the path, Sam feels the hairs prickling on the back of his neck. Several people have glanced up from their sun loungers; one or two in the pool are turning in their direction as well.

'We're getting eyeballed,' he mutters, feeling sweat pour from his face. In his experience, coming to someone's notice usually means trouble, but Jody only laughs.

'Because we're the newbies, all pale and sickly. A few days and we'll be doing it too, checking out the latest arrivals and staring in pity at the leavers.'

Dylan can hardly contain his eagerness to explore, so they end up making all sorts of promises just to hurry him past the pool and into a separate accommodation block. Their room is on the ground floor, along a wide corridor with tiled floors and unglazed windows. The air feels surprisingly cool, the walls throwing clever shadows that prevent the heat from building.

Room 109: they're here at last, at the end of a long, hard journey – planning it, saving for it, then the travelling itself – and Sam is nervous. *Nearly three grand.*

He fumbles with the card and finally has it. The door opens with a click but it's heavy. A fire door. The room is dark, warm and stuffy. Sam leaves the cases and walks in, as if he needs to make sure it's safe for his family – and there's a man in the corner, completely still–

What the hell?

'Here,' Jody calls. Sam missed the slot by the door. She places her own card into it and a couple of lights come on. The man who just scared the shit out of him is actually a big old-fashioned standing lamp. Sam laughs, feeling like a fool.

The room is gloomy because the blinds are shut. There's a low grinding noise and the air begins to stir as the aircon gets to work. Now that he can see the room clearly, his first thought is that it's a mistake. This can't be theirs.

It's larger than some of the flats they rented as teenage parents, and the furniture and decoration are a hell of a lot smarter. Tiled floors, and deep maroon walls with a kind of gold flecked pattern where a dado rail would be. Pale oak-effect furniture, but solid looking: not self-assembled.

There's a big double bed with a silky cream-coloured bedspread, and some kind of fancy arrangement of towels lying on it, shaped to look like a swan. A couple of chairs and a table, a low unit with a small TV, then a wide open space and an alcove off to the side with two single beds for the kids. There are even curtains to pull across for some privacy.

He glances at Jody, who is pinching her nostrils together and blinking a lot. For a second, she won't look in his direction.

'So, kids,' he says, 'what do you reckon?'

'It's really cool!' Grace inspects the alcove and points to the right-hand bed. 'I'll have that one.'

Dylan immediately flings himself on that bed. 'I want it!'

'Oh, I'll have this one then.' Grace sneaks a sly look at her parents: *Outwitted*!

Jody chuckles. Her hand goes out to Sam, her fingers curling between his. He's still struggling to find the word that describes how he feels, but settles on *delight*. It's a sensation like being wrapped in a thick, warm towel, and his thinking is suddenly clear and straightforward.

They worked bloody hard to save for this holiday. It cost them more than they could afford, to be honest, but now it's done, and whether they enjoy it or not is pretty much in their own hands. So either he goes on fretting, ruining it for himself and probably for his family as well... or else he puts his worries aside and focuses on having a good time.

He pulls Jody into his arms, and when they're squashed up together, he says, 'Sorry I've been such a dick. You were right.'

'Was I?'

'Yeah. We need this, don't we? A proper break.'

He kisses her on the cheek, then on the lips. The kids are peeking out of the alcove, and seeing this embrace through their eyes, Sam is aware that he doesn't have a single memory of his own mum and dad like this: cuddling, laughing, showing affection for one another.

5

The blinds are opened to reveal a sliding glass door that leads to a small patio area, divided from its neighbours by a low wall on each side. There's a table and two chairs, and a lovely view across the manicured gardens to the nearest of the three pools, less than fifty metres away.

The en-suite bathroom doesn't have a bath, just a complicated-looking shower, but the room is large and clean, with plenty of space in the cabinet for their toiletries. Jody is inclined to get started on the unpacking, but she can't find it in her heart to disagree when Dylan insists they should go straight to the pool.

She changes into her new bikini, excited but also apprehensive about how she'll compare to everyone else around the pool. At least they all have plenty of new clothes, courtesy of her mum. A few weeks ago she admitted that she'd been saving up, secretly, on Jody's behalf. Two hundred pounds, which she, her mum and Grace had spent in Primark, New Look and TK Maxx during a fantastic girls' day out in Crawley.

She hadn't told Sam about the windfall until afterwards,

when she showed him the chinos, shorts and T-shirts she'd bought him. His reaction was oddly subdued; not ungrateful or angry, not going on about all the practical things they could have got with the money. Instead he'd sunk into one of his moody silences for a day or so.

But he wolf whistles when she emerges from the bathroom, which almost makes her blush.

'Don't. Is it all right?'

'You look great.'

'You really do, Mum,' Grace adds, as if she already knows that a partner's verdict can't be taken at face value.

'My thighs, though...'

Sam shakes his head. 'Don't be silly.'

His turn in the bathroom. He changes into a pair of swimming shorts and a Brighton & Hove Albion shirt. She'd prefer him to wear one of his new tops but it's not something to make a fuss about. At twenty-six Sam still has quite a narrow, boyish frame, but his job as a painter and decorator has given him good muscle tone. The sight of his pale spindly legs makes her smile, though – as does the fact that he's left his socks on.

He bends over and hooks a sock with his thumb, flicking it off in her direction while giving her a knowing look. *Later*, he's saying, and the thought makes her stomach muscles clench for a second.

I'll ask him tonight, when we're in bed.

Before they head out, she insists on slathering them with sun cream. 'No one's going home burnt, and that's a promise.'

It's nearly three o'clock when they step outside. They collect swimming towels from a cabin by the pool, then find a group of unclaimed sun loungers and make camp beneath a couple of umbrellas. Sam accompanies the kids to the pool while Jody adjusts the lounger to sit up and watch them.

She lets out a brisk sigh, as if to say, *Right, what's next*? And realises the answer is: *Nothing*. After all the packing and preparing, it's a difficult transition to make. For weeks she's been carrying a mental checklist inside her head, and now it's complete. There is literally nothing she has to do. Nothing but relax.

That thought brings a tremor of doubt. Can she still remember how?

Sam's never been one for swimming, although he and Jody regularly take the kids to the local pool. Grace is already a confident swimmer, and Dylan is fearless even when he's floundering. To stay afloat he kicks and thrashes, never minding if his head goes under and he catches a mouthful of water: he just spits it out, laughs, and starts again.

From the safety of the pool, Sam studies his fellow holiday-makers, hoping for pointers as to how he and Jody can blend in. There seems to be quite a mixed bag: young couples and family groups and a few older people. No one's wearing much, which adds to the challenge of guessing nationalities. What he takes to be the Germans (maybe Danish or Swedish as well) seem more evenly tanned, with better skin. The men have longer hair and wear rings and necklaces and dodgy sandals, while the women are more likely to be fit – *elegant*, perhaps, is a better word, even when they're only wearing a few scraps of fabric.

The Brits, on the whole, are paler, flabbier, and have far more tattoos – his own are pretty understated compared to some – although there's one guy with a massive white gut, a shaved head and ink all over his arms and chest who, when he calls to his wife at the bar, turns out to be Russian or something. Sam had him down as a solid Essex geezer.

Lots of people are smoking, and the drifting aroma of

tobacco makes him dizzy with longing. He set out to quit nearly two years ago, channelling the money into their holiday fund, and since then he's only lapsed on a handful of occasions, but it's going to be much harder to resist temptation in a country where smoking isn't banned – or even disapproved of, by the look of it.

Once he's got out and towelled off, and the kids have announced that they're starving, Sam volunteers to investigate what's on offer at the pool bar. He's happy to go alone but the other three tag along, curious to experience what all-inclusive really means.

The bar is staffed by two young guys, dark-skinned and cocky in a way that doesn't rile Sam like it would at home. They're serving a man who's ordered a load of complicated-looking cocktails, and knocking back a beer while he waits. At one end there's a glass cabinet with fresh fruit, pastries and various filled rolls, then a chest freezer with three flavours of ice cream. And it's self-service, which the kids cotton on to with broad smiles.

'So we can get ice cream whenever we want?' Grace asks.

Jody shakes her head. 'Only when Dad or I agree. Otherwise you'll burst.' A negotiation follows, the deal being that they can have ice cream now, as long as they choose a roll and some fruit to eat afterwards. 'Back to front, but what the hell?' she says to Sam.

While they're sorting the food, he orders drinks. Out of habit he reaches into his pocket, then remembers and lifts his wrist-band into view, although the barman seems uninterested. Even so, Sam can't help patting the empty pocket of his swimming shorts, still a bit doubtful that he'll be given the drinks and not asked for money in return.

But that's what happens, and it's weird in a nice way. After a happy little picnic, Jody makes the kids play games for ten minutes, then she takes them for a swim. Sam stays where he is, feeling pleasantly full and lazy. He admires Jody's body as she walks across the paved area around the pool – only that causes a stirring, so he switches his attention to a large group wandering across from the direction of the restaurant, chatting and laughing together. He counts four couples and eight or nine children. It makes him think of his own extended family, and how they would never come away together like this – not even if someone won big on the lottery.

Sam is one of six kids, including three half-siblings, ranging in age from nineteen to nearly forty. He's uncle to eight more, and there are various step-parents and cousins, though the only ones he feels close to are his Uncle Paul and Aunt Steph, and their girls, Nina and Zoe. That's who he'd bring with him, and with his eyes shut and the sun warming his body, Sam drifts into an enjoyable daydream where his sudden good fortune puts him in a position to repay the generosity Paul and Steph showed to him. He pictures their faces when he says he's treating them all to a holiday: anywhere they want to go.

Trouble is, Nina's in the second year of her law degree, while Zoe has recently returned from travelling in South East Asia. That causes his daydream to stutter a little, but he can't take it personally: when kids nowadays get such amazing opportunities, it would be crazy not to take them...

Kids nowadays, he thinks ruefully. As though he's forty rather than twenty-six.

Almost without noticing, Jody rediscovers her ability to relax. Suddenly two hours have passed, and she decides that this is enough exposure to the sun for the first day. Back to the room for a nap, she decrees, and no one protests – although that sly chancer Dylan wangles another ice cream out of them first.

Her gut reaction is to refuse, but when she opens her mouth, she hears herself saying, 'Go on then.' Because that's the point of holidays, isn't it? That's what she hopes to lay down in their memories to relish for years to come. The treats. The not saying no.

In the room, Grace and Dylan sit on their beds and read the comics they were allowed to buy at Gatwick. Jody makes a start on the unpacking, kneeling beside the open cases on the cool tiled floor. Sam helps, obediently placing clothes and toiletries in the homes she allocates for them.

It takes a while to register how quiet the kids have become. They exchange a glance, then Sam tiptoes to the alcove and has a look round. He waves her over. Jody slips her arm round his waist as they stand for a moment, cherishing the sight of the children zonked out on their beds, Dylan snoring gently, Grace faintly smiling in her sleep.

'Beautiful,' Jody whispers, and Sam nods and whispers back: 'Thank you.'

'What for?'

'This,' he says, and kisses her, and carefully they draw the curtain across the alcove and close the blinds before creeping between the half-empty cases, discarding their clothes as they go, and slip into the spacious double bed.

'We can't,' Jody hisses. 'Can we?'

Sam shrugs. 'Just a cuddle.'

Jody's full-throated laugh nearly ruins it. She has to clamp a hand over her mouth. They push off the top covers, leaving only a sheet, wriggle down beneath it and embrace. The mattress feels cool for a few blissful seconds; their bodies are warm and quickly grow warmer, their touch soft then softer; the sun has already heightened the sensitivity of their skin, so all that's needed is the lightest of caresses. They make love with hands and mouths, fingers and lips, with slow and slippery teasing, tasting salt and sun cream, alcohol and chlorine, and the feel beneath their fingertips is of silk, the wetness silky and hot, their movements slow and smooth, fingers pressing hot and harder, fierce and fast then faster, gripping, gliding, gasping; finished.

They sleep.

6

Until Sam snaps awake. The room is unfamiliar, dark but with the threat of a terrible brightness straining to reach them. He senses someone watching from the corner, then remembers the floor lamp and with that he knows exactly where he is and how he came to fall asleep.

'What time...?'

Jody stirs, then jerks upright. 'Welcome meeting's at six!'

Sam checks his phone. 'It's five to.'

'Shit.'

'Do we really have to go?'

'We ought to, if we're going to make the most of this holiday.'

Sam says nothing. He would dearly love to lie here and drift for a while, but he can't later complain that he's missing out on information if he doesn't bother to turn up for the meeting.

They dress quickly. Sam feels guilty about waking the kids, until he pulls back the curtain and finds Grace reading a Lemony Snicket book while Dylan is staring at the ceiling, as if thinking deep thoughts about life and the universe.

Five minutes of musical chairs in the bathroom and they're ready to leave. The heat and light are dazzling after the cool dim cave of their bedroom, but it helps to rouse them. Walking briskly, they retrace their route to reception and this time no one around the pool gives them a second glance.

The welcome meeting is underway in the far corner of the main lounge. A dozen or so people sit at a cluster of tables, listening to the rep. It's Gabby, from the coach, holding a plastic folder bearing the Sheldon logo. Spotting her, Jody lets out a tiny snort. Sam knows the sound means something but he isn't sure what.

Gabby glances round and breaks into a smile, meeting Sam's gaze for a long second. She looks ridiculously pleased to see him, and he has to remind himself that her wages probably depend on how many people show up for these talks. Jody has already warned him that the reps push you to sign up for their trips.

Sorry, Gabby, he thinks. *You won't be fleecing us.*

To Jody, the look on the rep's face seems to be one of relief. Which is odd, given that there's already a respectable turnout. The middle-aged couple from the plane are among the group, but keep their gazes fixed on their laps.

Gabby, however, interrupts her spiel to say hello, then consults her list. 'Now, it's Sam Berry and Jody Lamb, yes?'

The rep invites them to take a seat, and Sam instinctively selects a table at the back of the gathering. It's close to the tray of complementary drinks: either white wine or orange juice. He picks up juices for the kids, nothing for himself. Jody considers the wine, then she too opts for juice.

She feels oddly ill at ease as she sits down; grimy from the heat and disorientated from sleeping so unexpectedly. They also had sex, and she wonders suddenly if they might smell. With a clutch of panic, she glances at the middle-aged couple just as the man looks up and stares straight at her. Jody turns to listen with exaggerated concentration to what Gabby has to say.

While she speaks, the rep hugs the folder to her chest, which to Jody seems like poor body language – until she realises it's to prevent people from staring at her boobs. Aside from that, Gabby has a confident, attractive manner, and doesn't seem bored to be repeating the same information for what must be the umpteenth time.

'So, welcome, once again, to the beautiful island of Sekliw.' She pronounces it 'Sekley'. 'In a minute I'll tell you about some of the brilliant places you can visit, but first a bit more about the island itself. There are six main settlements, all on the coast, two each on the east, the west and here, near to where we are, on the south.'

From a group of two couples with several children between them, a bald man with a Yorkshire accent says, 'What about the north?' The other man in their group, pretending to sound aggrieved, says, 'Yeah. Don't forget the north!'

Gabby gives them an indulgent smile. 'I'd never do that, guys! No, the north of the island is much less developed than the rest. Apart from one or two private estates, there's a nature reserve that might one day be turned in to a major tourist attraction.'

It's possible to hire jeeps or mountain bikes to explore the interior, she tells them, but most leisure activity takes place on the coast. She runs through the official excursions, which include jet skiing, scuba diving, island tours, dolphin hunting – '*so* amazing to photograph' – and some speedboat rides.

'And they're all safe, are they?' someone asks.

'Absolutely. At Sheldon Travel, we take health and safety very seriously.'

'But wasn't there a crash last year? Quite a nasty one.'

Gabby seems irritated but hides it quickly. 'I know the incident you're talking about – a tragic collision between a speed-boat and a fishing vessel. But on that occasion the boat was a private charter, and the people on board had been drinking and, uh, taking illegal substances. All our trips are run by qualified crew.' She regards the group with a sombre expression. 'That's one of the reasons why I'd recommend you arrange your excursions through Sheldon Travel.'

A hand goes up. 'What about terrorism? Haven't there been protests against the government?'

Again the rep looks uncomfortable. 'On the mainland, yes. But let's face it, that's the same almost anywhere nowadays. Here on the islands it's very peaceful. In fact, the president's son has a home on Sekliw. You can hardly get a better recommendation than that, can you?' She giggles, but cuts it short when no one else seems amused.

'One more thing... I don't know how many of you have had a chance to "peruse" the information pack in your room, but this week there's a special prize draw to attend a VIP champagne reception at the Hotel Conchis.'

For those who don't know, Gabby explains that this is the most exclusive hotel on the island, a favourite with the jet set, including movie stars, music icons and royalty. The reception takes place on Thursday afternoon and offers the winners a chance to sample the delights that the Conchis has to offer.

'In return for attending this welcome meeting, Sheldon Travel thank you by entering your names into the draw, which takes place tomorrow–'

'What if we're in a group?' asks the bald Yorkshireman. 'We're here with my brother and his wife.'

Gabby tuts regretfully. 'It's limited to the one family only. But don't forget that your party has several rooms, so you get more than one entry into the draw.'

'Guess we'll have to scrap over who goes, then,' his brother says, to general laughter.

Gabby hands out the brochures – booking form included – and thanks them for listening. For a second she's staring at Sam again. Conscious of Jody turning in his direction, he quickly looks away.

She shows him the brochure. 'I know I said these are usually overpriced, but the boat trip sounds nice.'

Sam pulls a face. His only experience of boats was a day-trip to Dieppe when he was fourteen. He was violently sick on the ferry – though, to be fair, cider played a part in that.

Grace is leaning in to look. 'I'd *love* to see dolphins. Can we do it? *Please*?'

'On a boat? Yeah!' Dylan has a glint in his eyes that guarantees tears and trouble if they don't agree.

'How much?' Sam says, wishing that just once this wasn't the question he had to ask before any other.

'Twenty euros a head.' And as he's wincing, quietly, Jody adds, 'But I think it's less for the kids.'

They stare at each other for a second: their telepathy is pretty finely tuned when it comes to money. Sam's problem is that he'd rather die than look poor in front of other people. If he's put on the spot in any way regarding the price he'll sign up just to avoid the embarrassment.

He can sense Gabby monitoring them. A moment later, she pounces. 'Hi, guys. So glad you made it to the meeting. Anything you fancy?'

To Sam's ears it isn't said with any sense of double meaning, but Jody's expression goes cold.

'The boat trip, maybe.' With Jody bristling, Sam is reluctant to meet the rep's eye, but equally worried about looking at her body. He ends up addressing the floor. 'With the dolphins?'

'It says there's a reduced price for children,' Jody adds.

'Half-price, although for this handsome feller,' – the rep grins at Dylan – 'there won't be any charge.'

'Oh, right. So, fifty quid – sorry, euros – in all?' Sam says. Before Jody can interrupt he nods decisively. 'We'll do that one, then.'

'Brilliant. That's Saturday...' She falters; for a second it's as though a shadow has crossed Gabby's face. Then the smile returns, a pen is magicked up. 'Best do the form now. How are you paying?'

'Credit card,' Jody says.

Sam nods reluctantly. They've only had the card a couple of years, and it's rarely used. Sam knows all too well how dangerous it is to live on credit. One of his cousins owed more than thirty grand by the time he went to prison, and he'd never borrowed more than a couple of thousand to begin with.

Jody hands over the card, and while Gabby is filling out a receipt, Sam says, 'Did you find out what happened with that other plane?'

At first it's like she hasn't heard. Then she blinks a few times and finally nods. 'The airport staff said it was a straightforward landing. Sometimes they change the direction you come in, because of the wind.'

Several more guests are waiting to speak to the rep, but Jody gets in a question about the kids' club, and Sam becomes aware of Grace, laughing and saying something behind him. Because of this, the thought that's just popped into his head dissolves as he turns and discovers that one of the waiters is crouched down, chatting with Dylan and Grace. It's a sweet gesture, even though Sam's first reaction is that someone's moving in on his family.

'I'm getting a drink,' Dylan says proudly. 'From the man.'

The waiter glances at Sam, then straightens up and says to Dylan, 'One Coke with ice, no lemon!' He gives a sharp salute. 'Yes, sir!'

Dylan runs after him as the waiter returns to the bar. Grace follows, then Sam, and it's too late to change direction when he sees who else is there.

7

Jody can't work out what it is about the rep that makes her uneasy. During the talk, there were a couple of times when she seemed to be looking at Sam a bit too intently. On the other hand, there were times when she was doing the same to Jody. It weirded her out, frankly.

Now it comes as something of a relief to see, at close range, that Gabby isn't quite as perfect as she had imagined. There are pimples on her cheeks, covered in foundation, and a couple of her teeth are slightly crooked.

Other holidaymakers are competing for the woman's attention, so Jody thanks her and joins her family at the bar. The snobbish couple are standing less than a metre away, but they and Sam seem to be engaged in a determined ignoring competition. Jody clears her throat so that the woman glances round, then smiles and says hello.

Introductions are made – 'This is Trevor, and I'm Kay, Kay Baxter,' – and Jody asks if they're going to book any of the trips.

Kay shakes her head in a dismissive way. 'We may rent a jeep to explore the island. We prefer to go alone.'

With obvious reluctance, Sam turns towards them. Only

now does Trevor's face light up. 'Who's this?' he says, and rears back, his mouth gaping open in a silent, terrified scream. 'That reverse thrust can really catch you out, eh?'

Jody freezes inside, while Sam issues a pretend chuckle. 'I haven't flown before,' he says.

'Genuinely?' Kay couldn't sound more shocked if Sam had just announced that he used to be a woman. Fortunately Dylan chooses this moment to contribute, using a forearm to wipe off his Coke moustache before declaring: 'We're gonna see doll-things!'

'Dolphins,' Grace corrects him.

'Oh, how lovely for you!' Kay gushes, overdoing the enthusiasm.

'Just remember they can't guarantee the creatures will make an appearance,' Trevor cautions. 'If they don't, all you've done is paid to look at the sea!' And he guffaws, seemingly oblivious to the hurt he might have caused.

His wife is slightly more perceptive. 'I'm sure you *will* see some,' she says. 'And we're all entered into the prize draw, of course.'

Sam gives a snort. 'Dunno why they think we'd want to go off to some other hotel, when this one's got all we need.'

The Baxters look at him as though he has duly met their low expectations. After a moment, Trevor says, 'The Conchis has an extraordinary reputation – though granted it's not for everyone. Horses for courses and all that.'

By now Sam's got a scowl so fierce you could toast bread from it. Jody puts on a big fake smile and says, 'It's been lovely to meet you, but we need to go and feed these two hungry kids.'

'Three,' says Sam, and unexpectedly gets a laugh. 'I'm starving.'

. . .

'What a couple of total–'

'Mm. No need to say it.'

Sam checks the kids aren't listening too closely before imitating Trevor's deep and phlegmy voice: '"Not for everyone." Not for the chavs, that's what he means.'

Jody glares at him. In their house there are two forbidden *c*-words. Fortunately the sight of the restaurant brings an end to the conversation. It's a vast room with dozens of tables and a serving area in the middle. While they're taking it in, a senior-looking man in a grey waistcoat approaches and gives them a quick once-over. 'Your first night?'

Jody nods. 'Yes.'

The head waiter, or whatever he is, goes on staring at Sam. 'For the evening our dress code is for trousers. Smart clothes. But as it is your first night...' He winks at Grace. 'Come, I find you a table.'

Sam feels about six years old as he's led across the room and seated next to a pillar that hides them from most of the people nearby. The head waiter takes their order for drinks, then explains that they can simply help themselves to whatever they like. 'Enjoy,' he commands, and Sam isn't sure whether he detects a certain bitterness.

It's probably not necessary, but now they've been allocated a table, Sam doesn't like the idea of leaving it unattended, so he and Grace wait while Jody and Dylan go off.

'You've been really good today,' Sam tells Grace. 'Thanks.'

She shrugs. Although pale and tired, she still looks extraordinarily pretty and grown-up. Sam can't ever quite believe that he's allowed to take any credit for how she's turning out.

'It seems really nice here, but... I dunno. I'm not as excited as I thought I'd be.'

'Probably because we were up so early. A good night's sleep will help.'

Jody and Dylan are back sooner than he expected. He peers at Jody's plate: a bit of salad, a bread roll, something that might be fish.

'That's hardly anything.'

'It's my starter. I'm going back for more, and so are you.'

He'd forgotten about having different courses. On the rare occasion they eat out, it's usually a pizza, a burger, a curry. But she's right – even if he's not feeling particularly hungry, he ought to make the most of it.

He and Grace find where the plates are stacked, then choose some food. In the centre of the room it's very noisy, with the constant sharp clatter of crockery and steel echoing off the tiled floor. He discovers that you have to be on your toes, dodging through a busy stream of kitchen staff collecting empty trays and bringing fresh ones. And some of the other diners are a pain: it isn't all good manners and 'After you, my dear chap,' but sharp elbows and an urgent every-man-for-himself attitude, as though they're competing for the food instead of sharing far more than they could ever eat.

In fact, both the choice and the sheer amount of it is staggering. Sam wonders how much is wasted. Do the staff get to take the food home to their families? And how would that feel, night after night, eating the lukewarm leftovers of the rich?

The rich. It shocks Sam to include himself in that category, but here it's true. He's sensed it already in some of the looks he's had from the waiters – a mix of fear and respect, envy and contempt that he knows all too well. *My job depends on you, but don't expect me to grovel.*

Jody had fears about the quality of the food, given the challenge of catering on such an enormous scale, but it turns out to be delicious. And the beauty of this system is that you can sample several dishes, then go back for more of what you like best.

Not tonight, though. They're simply too tired to overindulge.

Outside, they get lost on the way back to the room, but it turns into a lovely experience, wandering around the main part of the hotel complex. It's dark now, and the buildings and even many of the flower beds are floodlit in warm colours. The air is rich with fruity, unfamiliar blossoms and the heat, which is still noticeable but no longer oppressive, adds to it a taste like burnt sugar. The only disappointment is a sign forbidding use of the pools at night. In Jody's view this would be the perfect time for a swim.

By the main pool they discover a thriving bar area with twenty-five or thirty tables, nearly all of them occupied. The focus is on a makeshift auditorium at one end, where a young man is playing what sounds like traditional music on a violin. Not the sort of thing they'd normally go for – the kids especially – but in this setting it's an enchanting sound.

They all stop to listen, and Sam gestures at the bar. 'We could get a drink.'

She looks at the children, who actually seem to have revived a bit. It's Jody who is ready to drop. 'Do you mind if we don't?'

Back in the room, they take it in turns to use the bathroom. The kids investigate the TV, but all they find is an ancient episode of *The Simpsons*, dubbed into some incomprehensible language. Grace reads for a while, and Dylan is allowed to play games on Jody's phone. At nine o'clock it's lights out for that end of the room, and within minutes they're both sparko.

Thirty seconds later, Jody and Sam are in bed, too. The air-conditioning's up high and it's cooled the room enough for them to snuggle together without discomfort. They laugh about how early it is, bemoaning their own lack of energy. Sam says he's as tired as if he'd spent the day painting ceilings.

'This has been more fun, though, hasn't it?' Jody asks.

'Yeahhh.' He sounds doubtful. 'No, definitely.'

'Really? Because at times I felt you were regretting it.'

He shrugs, his smile fading to something more complicated. 'That's just me, I suppose.'

He's been stroking her stomach for a minute or two. Now he moves upwards, tracing a soft line over her breasts. Jody yawns, but he doesn't take offence. He's yawning himself.

'That Trevor and Kay,' Sam says. 'Sniff a lot, don't they?'

'Mm. As if nothing's ever quite good enough.'

'Yeah. Or maybe they're cokeheads.'

It's such an unlikely image that Jody splutters with laughter, and Sam has to shush her, for fear of waking the children. He's still caressing her, and when she reaches for him, it's a friendly contact rather than a sexy one – which is surely the best you can hope for after more than ten years and two kids.

Or so *she* believes. But is it enough for Sam?

'What do you think of Gabby?' she asks.

He makes a face. 'Do we have to talk about her?'

'Thought it'd get you in the mood.' She squeezes him, playfully, but he winces.

'Why?'

'Oh, come on. You must have checked her out.'

'Not really.'

Her snort of disbelief resembles a whale expelling water from its blowhole. And now she can't decide whether to laugh or cry.

Oh, Jody, only you would choose a moment like this to liken yourself to a bloody whale.

Slowly, over the course of several weeks, Sam has come to understand that there's something bothering Jody. At times he's wondered if she knows – or at least suspects – what it is he's hiding from her. He prays she doesn't.

No, he thinks. She'd confront him straight away. She's a lot braver than he is.

They make love again. They're pretty sure the kids won't wake up but still it affects them. They move together and find a rhythm that's slow and intense but makes no sound. The silence adds something to the experience, makes it seem *holy*, almost, though Sam has no idea why he thinks that. He's not religious; never goes to church apart from weddings and christenings; a couple of funerals.

Jody is first to fall asleep. She issues a tiny snore, and he smiles, realising that they've already had a fortnight's worth of sex in one day. He takes this as a good sign.

It's only when he's drifting off to sleep that he recalls what he should have queried with Gabby at the welcome meeting. When they got off the plane, the air had been completely still. So how come they had to land differently because of the wind?

8

The next day is like a rebirth. Cooled and calmed by the whirr of the air conditioning, they sleep heavily for more than eight hours. It is, by a long margin, the best night's sleep Jody and Sam have had since becoming parents.

By seven a.m. they're dressed and ready to explore. This time they go further afield, checking out the whole complex on a meandering path towards the beach.

At the shore they discover that theirs is the middle of three hotels, each with its own section of private beach, complete with a bar and dozens of sunbeds. They're close to the eastern boundary, where an armed guard is wandering back and forth on the boardwalk that runs between the beach and the hotel gardens. He has a gun, holstered on his hip like a cowboy. An identical guard patrols the western boundary. Recalling how Gabby assured them that the island is completely safe, Jody wonders if they were told the whole story.

They steer Dylan on to the beach before he notices the gun. He and Grace need no excuse to go dashing down towards the water. Sam and Jody slowly follow, holding hands.

'Isn't it lovely?' she says.

'Perfect,' Sam agrees.

The beach is mostly sand, with patches where large rocks are showing through. The sea is a beguiling shade of turquoise, flat and calm as far as the eye can see. The sound of it slurping against the shore is practically the only thing she can hear, although far out towards the horizon a couple of speedboats are darting back and forth. Jody remembers the accident mentioned at the welcome meeting: drink and drugs, a violent collision. How terrible for such a tragedy to happen in a place as beautiful as this.

She shivers, and Sam gives her a look. 'Okay?'

Jody nods, reminded of that weird saying her mum uses, about someone walking over your grave.

Strolling back, they find the hotel coming slowly to life. Not many guests about, but plenty of maintenance staff in grey boiler suits, silent as ghosts. The gardens are being watered and the warm wet smell coming from the concrete transports Sam to a moment in his childhood. He can't remember the exact circumstances but he knows it was the school holidays and he was stupidly happy; dawdling along a pavement after the rain, sweets in his pocket and no one on his case...

He smiles. Memories like this are what he and Jody want for the kids. Little nuggets of sheer joy to carry into adulthood.

Machines have been set to work in the swimming pools, droning noisily as they clean the water. There's a radio playing somewhere, a news bulletin with a man ranting and bawling. The words are more like grunts and growls than any language you could understand, though when he pauses a crowd starts cheering as if it makes perfect sense.

Sturdy middle-aged women in pink tunics are starting on the rooms, pushing carts full of cleaning equipment. One or two nod in greeting; others won't meet their eye. At the main pool they spot a sleepy-haired man tucking towels around a group of sunbeds.

Sam laughs out loud. 'People really do that?'

'Oh yeah. Even when there are loads of places spare. The Germans are supposed to be famous for it.'

'He looked English to me,' Sam says, and Jody gives him a sideways glance: *And you're the expert, how?*

They enter the restaurant with a little more confidence and choose the same table they had the night before, then go to inspect what's on offer for breakfast. Bread seems very popular here; bread and cake, biscuits and pastries. And people say the Brits are unhealthy, Sam thinks.

He's tempted by the idea of a full English, but the bacon's not cooked the way he likes it (burnt to a crisp) and the scrambled eggs look pale and watery. Instead he takes what he thinks is an omelette, as well as a couple of croissants dusted with icing sugar. Jody steers the kids towards the fruit, encouraging them to sample some peaches and pears.

It's not as busy as last night, but still reminds Sam of a school canteen. A couple of times he has to rein in his temper when someone barges in front of him. It makes him think of the fights that used to start in the queue for lunch, when he was mocked for being eligible for free school meals.

Once they're eating it's all fine again, talking about how to fill the coming day. They'd noticed a stack of kayaks and pedalos on the beach, and the resort offers a host of water-based activities – paragliding, banana rides and so on – though these, unfortunately, aren't part of the all-inclusive deal.

He gets up to fetch a second cup of tea and maybe some

toast. The kitchen staff are gliding back and forth, already such a familiar sight that Sam barely notices them. But one waiter catches his eye, perhaps because his face is as smooth and pink as a child's. He's moving quickly, balancing a tray loaded with glass tumblers for the fruit juice.

Crossing the centre of the serving area, he lifts the tray to shoulder height, neatly side-stepping a small boy with a brimming bowl of cereal. But he hasn't noticed the milk that's dripping from the kid's bowl. His foot slides out on the tiled floor and he tries to keep his balance but it's hopeless. Sam watches the accident in what feels like slow motion, the tray leaving the man's hand and taking on a life of its own, tipping up and over, the glasses stacked four deep and lined up in rows, sliding like deckchairs on a sinking ship and then falling, falling...

The noise when they strike the tiled floor could be a bomb going off. The whole room comes to a halt, even as the waiter himself lands with a hard slap on his arse. Cries of shock and alarm as many of the glasses shatter, sending fragments in all directions. Others stay in one piece, spinning like props in a fancy magic trick.

The waiter isn't badly hurt, but tears come to his eyes as he stares at the chaos. Some of the guests are shaking their head in sympathy; others are grinning, reaching for their phones to take pictures. There are urgent shouts from the kitchen and the head waiter who seated them the previous night comes striding out, followed by a couple of men in chef's whites. They're all gabbling away in their own language, and Sam can tell it's not a happy discussion.

For a second, the senior guy seems to forget where he is. He hauls the waiter up and starts yelling in his face. One of the chefs mutters a warning and the mood changes at once, the head waiter nodding apologetically to the guests, urging them to continue their meals. More staff race in with cloths and brooms and rubbish sacks. The young waiter is hustled away.

Back at the table, Jody tuts. 'That poor boy. I wonder if breakages are deducted from their wages.'

Sam shrugs. Judging by the look on his boss's face, that's the least of the guy's worries.

9

Jody didn't actually see the incident – only the aftermath – but the sound of the glasses breaking sent a bolt of panic through her body. She immediately thought of the question at the meeting the yesterday, about the threat of terrorism.

She makes a deliberate effort to shrug off the fear, but she's aware of a nervous undercurrent in the room, like the subliminal buzz of a TV on standby. Sam seems really unsettled, though he does his best to act normally.

It's with a sense of relief that they hurry back to the room to get sorted and then head for the beach. They're early enough to take their pick of sun loungers, and invariably the kids want to be right at the front.

That's fine with Jody. After slapping lotion on them all, she has a blissful half hour while the others play in the water. It's only when they come in for a drink that Jody remembers the kids' club.

She checks the time on her phone. 'It starts in twenty minutes.'

Sam pulls a face. Dylan is busy digging a channel in the

sand. Grace is lying face down on her towel, iPod on, lost to the world.

'Shall we forget it for today?'

'Are you sure?' Jody has been cherishing the thought of getting some quality time with Sam, but maybe, she thinks now, he isn't as keen on the idea.

Then again, he's right that it seems selfish to palm the kids off on other people when they're so obviously having a good time. This is a *family* holiday, after all: the pleasure is in experiencing it together.

'They can go tomorrow.' Sam frowns. 'Is that Thursday, or Friday?'

'Thursday. I think. Yes, it's Wednesday today.' She laughs. The first full day and they're already losing track. That must be a good sign.

The beach bar opens at ten. On the dot, there's a small crowd gathering to fetch the first beers of the day. Jody can see Sam reacting, and she has to remind him that different rules apply on holiday. 'Like eating cake for breakfast,' she says.

She encourages him to have a beer but he insists on holding off till eleven, as if to prove to himself that he can. When Jody fetches it for him, she throws caution to the wind and tries a rum-based cocktail called a Hurricane, served up by a charming waiter who seems to be giving her the eye. He probably does it to all the women here, but it's a welcome boost to her confidence just the same.

The morning passes in a warm and wonderful blur. She and Sam take it in turns to switch off while the other watches Dylan. It's about as safe as it can be – the beach shelves gradually, and there's barely any swell – but the boy is often too daring for his own good.

Grace, as usual, places no demands on their time. She

sunbathes, reads, listens to music. She swims a lot, and there's a touching moment when she encourages her dad to venture into deeper water. Jody remembers how reluctant Sam was when they first went to the beach together in their teens. Now, anxious not to look like a wuss in front of his daughter, he makes a determined effort, and seems to gain in confidence under her instruction.

They eat a late-morning snack, then go back to the room. Today nobody can sleep, and by two o'clock they're outside again. Dylan is still hungry, so he and Sam head off to the restaurant while Jody and Grace laze by the pool.

'We're going to be good,' Grace has told her dad, and although Jody laughed, it's left her worrying about the pressures her daughter will face to keep her weight down, the preoccupation with body image and dieting that she and her friends are already exhibiting.

The pool area is almost deserted, although most of the loungers are draped with towels. Jody finds a vacant umbrella and drags a few spare sunbeds over. Then it's time to lie back, sunglasses on, eyes shut. She borrows Grace's iPod and listens to Post Malone, keeping the volume low so as not to miss the tranquil chorus of holiday sounds: the backstroke splash of a lone swimmer, the rhythmic slap of sandals on the baking-hot path, the clink of glasses behind the bar. Jody feels incredibly relaxed and can let herself indulge in memories of the previous night; the way they made love so gently, the erotically charged silence–

Maybe she'd started dozing, for she jumps as if electrocuted when someone taps her arm.

'Mrs – ah, Miss Lamb. Jody, isn't it?'

Jody blinks and half sits up. Gabby the rep is crouching beside the sunbed.

'I've got such *brilliant* news for you,' she says, and without quite knowing why, Jody's heart sinks.

. . .

Dylan loads his plate with chips, pasta tubes and meatballs in tomato sauce. Sam has the same, even though he's not really hungry. He can't believe how quickly he's adjusted to this weird new way of life – eating and drinking whenever you want; never having to stop and think about whether you can afford it. If you fancy a snack, you have one. If you want another, you have that too. Feel like trying something different? Well, take a bite and if you don't like it, put it aside and get something else.

This is what it means to be rich, he realises. And while it's a good feeling, it also makes him uneasy. If you can have everything you want, whenever you want, how do you decide what's too much?

Dylan has tomato sauce dribbling over his chin. Sam wipes it away with his finger and Dylan, taken by surprise, giggles as he grabs a chip and holds it out like a gun, shooting at his dad. Sam pretends to duck, using a fork to fire back.

It's a fun moment, reminding Sam that he shouldn't take things too seriously, but soon comes another worry. Now the kids have experienced luxury on this scale, what if they start comparing it to the way they live at home?

Perhaps that's why he says no to Dylan's request for more chips. Unafraid, the boy fixes him with an evil glare. If Sam had ever looked at his dad like that he'd have been slapped round the face.

'Dyl, you're full up. Any more and you'll burst.'

'*Daddy*, I want some–'

'Hey, I know – let's go and see what Mum and Grace are doing.'

'Go in the pool?'

'Maybe.'

'And then ice cream?'

'We'll see. But later on, yeah?'

With peace restored they take a slow walk back, pausing in a shaded area where a small crowd has gathered to watch two Russian men playing table tennis with brutal determination. Sam hoists Dylan on to his shoulders for a better view. It feels good, the weight of him up there, his tiny hands pulling on Sam's hair.

He's proud of the stability he and Jody have given their children. At five years old, Dylan is a real character, bright and cheeky and confident. There's no reason he won't do well at school and even go to university one day. Same with Grace, who's already talking about becoming a scientist. When Sam was her age, he probably wouldn't have known what the word meant.

With lunch over, a lot of people have returned to the pool. It isn't easy to find Jody and Grace among the bodies lying out under the umbrellas. In fact, it's Gabby he spots first. She's talking to Jody, who is frowning slightly, one hand hovering by her sunglasses as if she can't decide whether to take them off.

Then the rep turns and gives him one of her big beaming smiles. 'Congratulations!'

Jody is still frowning and Sam, for a moment, takes offence. Is she taking the piss? *Congratulations on having a holiday that's meant for richer, classier people than you.*

Seeing his confusion, Jody says, 'We've won the competition.'

'That's right! Your name was picked, so you and your lovely family will get to enjoy a VIP reception at the Hotel Conchis.' Gabby seems to be melting with excitement on their behalf. 'Oh my *God*, guys, just *wait* till you see it...'

Sam nods. He doesn't want to be rude, but the Adriana is like a palace compared to anywhere he's ever been. How could this Conchis place be so much better?

Gabby's smile fades as she picks up on the tension. She brings an envelope into view and thrusts it forward. 'Here's the formal invitation. You just have to be in reception for two p.m. tomorrow. You'll be collected and brought back, door to door.'

'What time?' Sam asks.

Gabby seems thrown by the question. 'Two o'cl–'

'No, at the end. What time are we back here?'

'Uh, it's usually a... loose arrangement. If you're having loads of fun, you can stay late.'

'And if we need to go earlier?' Jody says. 'I mean, say the kids get grumpy?'

'Oh, yeah,' Gabby says, nodding. 'Earlier, later, it's up to you.'

10

Jody has the impression that Gabby is relieved to have offloaded the envelope. The rep hurries away, low heels clicking on the path, attracting a lot of attention from the guests around the pool. When someone wolf-whistles, Gabby strikes a pose, playfully sticking her tongue out at a group of young guys near the bar.

Sam sits down heavily enough to make the sun lounger creak. Jody can feel him bristling, and suggests to Grace that she might want to take her brother to get a drink.

'Why?'

'It's good for you – to get some practice.'

'I don't need practice, Mum. It's not hard to ask for a drink.'

'Then for Dylan's sake. Make him feel grown up.'

Grace sighs dramatically, before leading her brother away.

'Growing up so fast,' Jody murmurs.

'They're good kids,' Sam says. Then: 'You sound sad.'

'It's like my mum warned us. The time goes so quickly – before you know it they'll be adults and won't need us anymore.'

Sam only grunts, as though he believes this might be a good thing. He's right, really. And yet...

'Typical, isn't it?' he says. 'The one time we win something, it's when we don't want to.'

'Don't we?' She tries to sound amused, not irritated.

'Okay, don't *need* to, is what I mean. And the way she was so excited – like this place is a dump.'

'I'm sure she doesn't think that. It's just, if this Conchis is very exclusive...'

'So what? It's the same sun overhead. Same sea, the same water in the pool.'

Jody sighs. He's beginning to remind her of her dad, the way he goes off on these rants.

'Posh food, I suppose,' he goes on, 'but, I mean, anyone who takes a look round the restaurant here and doesn't think it's enough needs their head testing.'

'Sam...'

'And champagne is well overrated. That stuff at Trude's wedding tasted rank.'

'That wasn't proper champagne.' Jody raises a hand before he can respond. 'Sam! Calm down, please.'

She gives him her sternest look. This always works, because it only takes a second for him to be reminded of the way his own parents used to rage at each other.

He takes a deep breath. 'All I'm saying is, it's not gonna be that special. And then there's the stress of keeping the kids on their best behaviour–'

'So you don't want to go, I get that. I think the real problem is that you feel we don't belong there. But why shouldn't we go anywhere we like? Who cares if a lot of snobby people think we're... you-know-whats?'

Sam wants to go on arguing but he knows she has a point. He also knows this is one of the things Jody loves most about him –

that he'll listen to another point of view, and if he's wrong he'll be man enough to say so. His dad and his brother Carl have never, to Sam's knowledge, admitted they were wrong about anything – and certainly not to a woman.

In his head, that makes Sam smarter than them. But the way he's handled this hasn't been very smart.

Because he can't shake off the idea that he *is* a chav. The same goes for his whole extended family. He hates his parents for the upbringing they gave him, and yet, if they were attacked or criticised in any way, he knows he would feel driven to defend them. Even his dad, who's dicked around his whole life: not sticking at anything, always taking the easy option and running away, leaving a fresh set of victims to pick up the pieces. And his mum, the pisshead who never bothered if he was up for school because she couldn't get out of bed herself. His mum, who blamed him for the fact his dad had buggered off, then blamed him again, years later, when her relationship with his stepdad went sour.

All that shitty unfairness and yet still he can't *not* feel something for them. He's tried, many times, but there always remains a tiny seed: something that threatens to grow and bloom if it's treated right. For years he's fantasised about one or both of them asking to meet him, then begging his forgiveness for all their failings and swearing that they love him, truly – the way Sam loves his own children: that they love him so much they'd die for him.

The proof of his own feelings are there in the tears that blur his vision when he watches the kids coming back from the bar, Dylan proudly gripping a Coke in both hands, Grace fussing over him with motherly concern while also taking quick sassy drags on a long straw. He turns away from Jody, rubbing his eyes.

'I know how you feel, I really do,' she says. 'A holiday like this... it's meant to be about freedom. But tomorrow's a chance to have a new experience – maybe something we'll never get to do again.'

'I s'pose.' His attention is on Dylan, who's trying so hard not to spill the Coke that he ends up spilling a bit. The boy stops, takes a gulp then carries on, his tongue poking from the side of his mouth like a counterbalance.

Jody caresses his arm. 'Good or bad, it's only a couple of hours. If we really hate it we'll just say one of the kids is ill and make a quick exit.'

It's a deal, then, Jody thinks. But she's conscious of a lingering resentment that something so trivial has threatened to come between them.

For an hour or so they shift the loungers in and out of shadow, according to how much direct sun their bodies can take. Dylan sleeps in the shade, and Sam is virtually dozing, too. Grace is engrossed in her book so Jody, feeling restless, wraps a sarong around her bikini and takes herself off for a walk.

She strolls through the gardens, parallel to the main building. It's siesta time and the paths are quiet. She is mentally rifling through the suitcases, trying to decide if the clothes she brought will be impressive enough for the reception the next day. If not, are there shops near here?

She cuts back inside, vaguely intent on asking at reception. A warring voice tells her it's silly: they can't afford to be buying new outfits now. She'll have to make do.

She grins. Can't be many guests at the Conchis sporting the latest lines from Primarni.

And now a woman is smiling back at her. It's Kay Baxter, sitting alone in a dim corner of the bar, dressed in a long skirt and tailored jacket. Jody wonders if the Baxters ever put on swimwear or venture into the sun.

'Hot out there,' Kay says.

'Sweltering,' Jody agrees. 'Nice, though.'

'Rather too much for me.' She reaches for her glass, a cocktail of some kind. 'It's Jody, isn't it?'

This feels like an invitation to stay and talk, so Jody nods, moving closer to one of the vacant chairs.

'Thought I'd have a wander. Bit of time to myself.'

'Well, it's a busy life as a mother. Never a spare moment.'

Kay's eyes take on a slightly regretful quality, but Jody doesn't register the change until it's too late. 'Do you have kids?'

'No. It wasn't to be, I'm afraid.'

'Sorry to hear that.' Aware that her ability to dislike this woman has been compromised, Jody looks around the room. 'Where's Trevor?'

'He's had to complain about the noise from the room above us. Music and laughing till well after midnight.' She sniffs. 'Russians, I think.'

Jody almost repeats herself: *Sorry to hear that.* She's preparing to say her farewell when Kay asks, 'You wouldn't have seen our rep today, by any chance?'

'She was here earlier,' Jody says, assuming the Baxters want to involve Gabby in their complaint.

'Oh.' Kay purses her lips. 'I wonder when we'll hear about the prize draw.'

The comment seems to hang in the air like a small but potent thundercloud. Jody feels heat rushing to her face. It's an absurd reaction, as is the sense of guilt when she says, 'Actually, we've won.'

'You've...?' Kay places a hand over her mouth, clears her throat and finally offers a smile. 'That's wonderful for you.'

'Sam doesn't think so. Typical man – he has to be dragged kicking and screaming to any sort of formal gathering.'

'Trevor's usually quite...' Kay tails off, and a moment later Jody understands why.

'Did I catch my name being taken in vain?' His voice, deep and droning, reminds Jody of someone irritating on TV, though she can't place who it is. Trevor is wearing a crisp white shirt, tucked into tailored shorts with a brown leather belt, and matching leather sandals over white socks.

He ignores Jody completely, letting out an exasperated sigh. 'They're suggesting we give it another night. I informed them that if we're disturbed again, I'll be insisting on an upgrade.'

'Goodness, I hope it's better tonight.'

'I still intend to register a grievance with the rep. Then we can put in a claim when we get home.'

He sits down next to Kay, exposing bony white knees, and frowns as he realises his wife is trying to tell him something.

'... was here earlier. They've been chosen, from the draw.'

Only then does Trevor acknowledge Jody's presence, his gaze hovering at breast level for a moment. 'What? Who has?'

Kay indicates Jody. 'These– I mean, they... Jody and...'

'To the Hotel Conchis?' Trevor pinches his lower lip and starts to twist and pull on it. Jody has a feeling that he wants to stuff a fist in his mouth and scream at the injustice, but this has to make do instead.

After waiting in vain for him to respond, Kay fills the silence with a fluttering laugh of almost total insincerity and says to Jody, 'And well done, you!'

11

When Sam hears about the conversation, his first reaction is to savour the victory, but it doesn't make him any keener to go. That afternoon, at Grace's request, they give tennis a try. None of them can play properly, but chasing down the ball becomes such a challenge that Sam ends up soaked in sweat, and the swim he has to cool off afterwards is the most satisfying of the holiday so far.

Tonight they take their time over dinner, having several courses. Sam keeps an eye out for the poor bloke who dropped the tray but there's no sign of him. He wonders what other jobs you'd find on an island like this, if the tourist trade kicked you out.

It's nearly half eight before they're done, and when they step into the sweet warmth of the evening the live entertainment is in full swing. Naturally enough Grace is desperate to take a look, and if ever there's some back-up pestering to be done, well, Dylan's your go-to guy.

'But aren't you both tired?' Jody asks, and the kids shake their heads with perfect comic timing.

Laughing, Sam says, 'A late night won't hurt.' In his own

childhood he regularly stayed up beyond midnight, though in very different circumstances to this.

They manage to find a table, and Sam troops off to the bar for drinks. It's only when he returns that he realises the Baxters are sitting less than two metres away. The woman, Kay, glances over and nods at him. Sam nods back, but leaves it at that.

The music is performed by a group of four young women: two singers, two acoustic guitarists. The women are dark-haired and attractive, and their songs have a kind of twisty, twinkly sound that Sam thinks might be Spanish.

Before long the kids have drifted off to join a group of children sitting on a low wall at the edge of the little auditorium. A couple of the animation team are with them, and Sam remembers that they're supposed to be doing the kids' club tomorrow morning. And then this thing in the afternoon. The Conchis.

When the musicians take a break, their songs are replaced by piped-in Euro disco. Sam goes to the bar and waits his turn. Trevor comes alongside, trying to signal to a barman even though the staff are busy serving the people in front of them.

'Quite good, those Iberian fillies,' Trevor says. 'Very easy on the eye.'

Sam isn't sure who he's talking about – the band, presumably – but he nods anyway. He gets served first, so it makes sense to order for Trevor. A whisky and a G&T. Sam passes the drinks back to him, and although he hasn't handed over a tip or been pressured to leave one, something sets Trevor off on the subject again.

'Beggars belief that it's taken for granted. I mean, no one tips me at the end of the day, just for doing my job.'

This could be an invitation to ask what Trevor does for a living, but Sam ignores it. They move away, Sam trying hard not to spill the four drinks he's holding. He's reminded of how

Dylan met the same challenge earlier, and has to check his tongue isn't sticking out.

In his usual sarcastic tone, Trevor says, 'Hear you got lucky today.'

'I suppose.' Although Sam has pictured himself gloating in front of the Baxters, now the moment's here he can't bring himself to do it.

Jody accepts her drink, feeling hugely relieved that Sam and Trevor are managing to be civil towards one another.

'All set for your big day tomorrow?' Trevor asks her.

Jody is able to nod quite confidently. 'It's only a couple of hours in the afternoon.'

'You know who might be there, don't you?' Trevor is only too keen to answer his own question. 'Borko Radić, son and heir of President Dragan Radić. I take it you know who he is?'

Jody's nod is more convincing than Sam's. Once they'd booked the holiday, her dad set about researching the country's recent history, though what he learned was so depressing that she tried not to pay too much attention.

'Warlord turned oligarch,' Trevor says, with what sounds like approval. 'He's ruled for years, even though they supposedly have elections. Siphoning off wealth like there's no tomorrow, lucky bugger.'

'So what would his son be doing at a reception for foreign tourists?' Jody asks.

'A PR exercise. Borko's being groomed to take over. He was quite the playboy after he left Oxford – starlets and cocaine and all that. Fancied himself as an adventurer, delving into the jungles of South America, trekking across deserts. Very keen on safaris, too.' Trevor leans forward, eyes gleaming with enthusiasm, the whisky rancid on his breath. 'If you get a chance you ought to ask him if the rumour's true.'

'What rumour?' Jody asks.

'It's said that he shot a western black rhinoceros, which is now officially extinct.' Before they can react, Trevor guffaws. 'My God, there was an uproar from the animal rights brigade! They wanted a criminal investigation, but no chance of that, of course.'

Jody tries not to recoil; the man sounds repulsive. Fortunately they're interrupted by Dylan, who has run up with another boy in tow. He's about the same age, round-faced and blond, and holding a toy fire truck.

'I want him to share but he doesn't listen,' Dylan complains.

'He speaks a different language, that's all.' Jody suggests that Dylan could set an example by having a drink, then offering the glass to his friend. The experiment is a success, and soon they're kneeling on the path, rolling the truck back and forth.

'How sweet,' Kay says, and Jody is reminded that her dad believes strongly that overseas travel is a civilising influence – even a holiday in a setting as artificial as this.

Ironically, she tunes back in to hear Trevor busy documenting the failings of the various nationalities present at the hotel: '... Russians are just pig-ignorant gits, frankly. They make the *Germans* look polite by comparison!'

Kay issues one of her high-pitched laughs, which seems to be an attempt to soften the impact of what he's saying. 'We're no better, really,' she reminds him.

'Valid point,' Trevor says, wagging his finger. 'Some of the knuckle-draggers on that Manchester flight... it's all fifteen-stone monsters with nose rings, football shirts and tattoos,' – the punchline is telegraphed by a pause – 'and that's just the women!'

12

The crack about football shirts and tattoos cuts deep. Sam wonders if it's intentional. Certainly Kay looks embarrassed, distracting them with a garbled enquiry about how the children are settling in to the holiday. While Jody answers, Sam remembers that he wore his Albion shirt to the welcome meeting. Then again, he doesn't think the Baxters have been anywhere near the pool, where they might have seen his tattoos – an eagle on his chest, roses entwined in Jody's name on his right bicep and the kids' names in Celtic lettering on his shoulder blades.

So take a deep breath, Sam. Trevor's a fuckwit, but you don't want to ruin your holiday by laying him out in front of dozens of people...

Grace brings Dylan back, tears streaming down his face: he tripped over on the path. There's a graze on his knee, bleeding lightly. Normally a tissue and a hug and he'd be good as new, but on this occasion they're grateful for an excuse to leave.

'You know what Carl would do if someone talked to him like that?' Sam mutters once they're out of earshot.

'I do, yes.' Jody links her arm with his, bumping hips in a friendly way. 'Which is why Carl's not in a position to have a holiday like this. And he wouldn't have a partner as wonderful as me.'

Sam can only laugh. It amazes him how she's able to level out his moods so skilfully. Like skimming froth from a beer.

'So, basically, you're saying: grow up. Be the bigger man?'

'Why not? Okay, they're a couple of pompous snobs. But from what Kay told me this afternoon, they wanted kids and couldn't have them. Now they're turning into a sour, lonely old couple with nothing to look forward to. Think of what we have, compared to them.'

Instead of speaking, Sam finds her hand and squeezes it. The kids run ahead, Dylan's injured knee already forgotten. Grace spots some kind of lizard on the path and they stop to examine it. The heat builds around them, and from the plants and bushes comes the urgent buzz and click of insects: crickets, is it, or cicadas?

Jody isn't sure either, but Dylan laughs explosively when she explains how they make the noise. 'Rubbing their *legs* together? That's silly, Mummy!'

As they move away, Jody murmurs to Sam, 'You've been so uptight lately. It's worrying me.'

'Have I?' To his own ear, Sam sounds mystified, but he's not sure if it's convincing. 'When?'

'For weeks now. Months.'

'Oh.' They walk on. 'I could probably say the same about you.'

'So there's nothing wrong? Nothing... out of the ordinary?'

'No,' he says, as if it's a silly question. 'What about you?'

'I've only been tense because you've been tense.'

'Right.' He isn't sure what to say. 'Sorry.'

They walk the rest of the way in silence. Sam's had an idea, and considers telling Jody, but at the last moment he changes his mind.

Back in the room, he checks the fridge and says they could do with some more bottled water. 'I'll pop to the bar. Bring you a proper drink, if you like?'

Jody says no, but smiles warmly. 'You get one if you want.'

And then he's out of the room, easy as that. She didn't see him take the envelope and slide it beneath his shirt.

The Baxters are still at the bar, Trevor nursing a fresh drink and staring into space, Kay reading something on her phone. They don't look up until Sam is looming over them. He drops the envelope on to the table. 'There you go.'

'Pardon?' Trevor says.

'For the thing tomorrow. I, um – Jody and I think you should go, instead of us.'

Trevor is frowning fiercely, like it's some kind of trick. Kay is quicker to take it at face value.

'You don't want to attend?'

Sam shrugs. 'There's plenty to do here.'

Without hanging round for more questions – or a word of thanks – he turns and walks away. He feels pleasantly proud until he's almost at the room, and then the doubts creep in.

The kids are tucked up in bed, Grace with a book, Dylan doing a drawing. Sam kisses them goodnight, and finds Jody in the bathroom. Her hair is tied back and she's applying some sort of cream to her face. Smells like seaweed or something. Nice, though.

'I, er, hope you don't mind,' he begins, and she reads the seriousness of his tone and stops what she's doing, turning to face him.

'What?'

'I gave the invite to Trevor and Kay.'

Jody stares at him, coldly. 'Why did you do that?'

'Because of how Trevor was going on about the president's son... and, I mean, it's not like we're that bothered–'

'*You*'re not. What about *me*?'

'I thought you'd be pleased. It's like you were saying – be the bigger man, and all that.'

She nods unhappily, as though he's throwing her own words back at her as a tactic, and not because he agrees it's good advice.

'Come on, Jode. If we went to it we'd just be worrying sick about saying the wrong things, or Dylan breaking something. And it's brilliant here. Why waste a whole afternoon somewhere else?'

To Jody, it feels like a breach of trust, and that festers while she's preparing for bed.

When she joins him, the room is dark and the children are fast asleep in their curtained-off alcove. Jody slips into bed and listens to the whir of the air-conditioning, the pitch of the motor rising and falling until it begins to sound like a wearisome voice: *Oh yes, don't mind me, slaving away to give you a comfortable night's sleep...*

'I'm just,' she begins, but her mouth is dry and she needs to moisten her lips before trying again. 'I'm annoyed that you didn't discuss it with me first.'

'Yeah, I should've. I'm sorry.'

'Well, it's done now.' She reaches out and finds his hand in the centre of the bed, waiting to make contact. 'We're not gonna let it spoil the rest of the holiday.'

'No.'

A long silence, then the mattress creaks and she turns her head and Sam is staring at her in the dark, an impish grin on his face.

'Do we need to make up?' he asks.

'You want to make up?'

'Wouldn't mind.'

She pretends to mull it over. 'Mm, I suppose you can *earn* my forgiveness if you like.'

13

Jody wakes early and immediately starts to wonder if she let Sam off too easily. What's hard to work out, without the benefit of hindsight, is how much she wanted to go in the first place.

It had been playing on her mind that they'd be fish out of water, but now, when she knows they're not going, she finds herself dwelling on what they might have missed. The picture she summons up is like something from a glossy romantic comedy of the sort she loved when she was thirteen or fourteen. Handsome men in evening dress, women in ballgowns: all very pure and sweet and wholesome.

Then she recalls her dad's warnings about the country. Practically a fascist state, he said, ruled over by a president who had murdered his way to power and now clung to office through a combination of bribery and vicious persecution of his opponents.

'It's too late to cancel,' she'd responded, 'unless you're saying it could be dangerous?'

Dad hadn't backtracked, exactly, but he did try to reassure her. 'From what I've read there's no real trouble on the islands. Precious little meaningful opposition anywhere, now the international community have given him legitimacy. It's all, "Take a bow, Mr President! Of course your elections were fair and free. Of course we'll ignore the reports of intimidation and torture. Now give us your lovely oil, your copper, your zinc!"'

Her dad was like that when he went into one: angry and sarcastic and so passionate that no one else got a word in edgeways. Sam often appeared to be torn between taking him on or running away, but Jody and her mum knew it was best just to tune him out. These days it took less and less to get him ranting about injustice in the world, not least because of what he called 'the curse of the internet'. You no longer had the excuse of not knowing about massacres, poverty, exploitation in some far-flung corner of the world.

'Because nowhere's far flung anymore,' he'd say. 'It's all up close, right here. So the people who do nothing have to face the ugly truth. It's not that they don't *know*. It's that they don't *care*.'

Jody would disagree. She's perfectly aware that she and Sam count among those who do nothing, but it's not because they're indifferent. They simply have too many other priorities: children to raise, an income to earn. They're too busy trying to survive.

Beside her, Sam is beginning to stir, a modest little ranter-in-training compared to her dad. Jody can't help going back over the other moment that upset her – when Sam denied that there was something bothering him. She knew straight away that he was lying, but couldn't bring herself to confront him.

Many times she's rehearsed the scene when he reveals his secret. She's tried to picture how she will agree to forgive him, strictly for the sake of the kids. But the pain, the pain she'll be feeling...

Is forgiveness possible, when someone has torn your heart out?

Soon, she tells herself. *I'll do it soon.*

.   .   .

It's a while before Sam lets on that he's awake. First he wants to reflect on last night. He knows he was wrong not to talk it through with her, but in his eyes the most important thing is that he showed generosity towards people who basically think he's a piece of shit.

He and Jody had made love before going to sleep, but even that hadn't helped much: it felt more like two people having sex on their own. So when he finally opens his eyes and turns in her direction, the first thing he does is apologise again.

'I was an idiot. Sorry.'

'It's all right.' She gazes deep into his eyes and seems to be on the verge of a question, but there's a rattle from the alcove and the curtain swishes aside, Dylan up and eager to start another day.

Wednesday, Sam thinks as he reaches for his shorts and a t-shirt. No, *Thursday*. What should have been the posh reception is now another long and lazy day of freedom. And it begins, on a spur-of-the-moment decision, with a swim.

The pools are out of bounds this early, so they go to the beach instead. A nod in greeting to the bored security guard, and then a staggering discovery: there isn't a single other holidaymaker in sight. The sea is flat, without the slightest ripple. On the surface there are streaks and patches in different shades of blue, some deep like the Chelsea colours, others a sort of milky blue, like Man City's. The sand is cool beneath his feet, and it's a lovely sensation to scrunch it with his toes. A single bird twitters away, as if welcoming them to paradise.

And that's it. No traffic noise, no voices, no dogs barking. And that sugary hot taste to the air: incredible.

Plunging into the water, gasping even though it's not really cold, Sam twists and kicks on to his back, surveys the rows of deserted sun loungers and says, 'It's like we're billionaires or something.'

'What?' Jody is swimming alongside him, creating almost no wash at all.

'The whole place to ourselves. Hey!' Sam calls out to the kids. 'We've got our own private island, you all right with that?'

Grace and Dylan laugh with joy, but when he turns to check on Jody's reaction, she is head down in the water, swimming like she's trying to get away from him, and he doesn't have to be the sharpest knife in the drawer to realise he isn't yet in the clear.

14

Grace is enthusiastic about the kids' club, but Dylan reacts with determined resistance. He wants to go swimming with his dad, and Jody can tell that Sam has little appetite for a battle.

Once they've got Dylan into the main building, Jody suggests it'll be better if she takes them on her own. Sam looks grateful, and jabs his thumb towards a room that has books, games and computers available for the guests. 'Gonna look something up. I'll meet you at the pool.'

Jody nods, but shuts her eyes for a second at the clumsiness of the man. They've just been assuring Dylan that no one was going to the pool until later.

And why, exactly, does Sam need to go online?

The kids' club meets in a small function room with several tables set out for painting and other craft-based activities. Jody lingers for a while, edging away from the table where a young Scottish woman is encouraging Dylan to draw her a picture. There are two other staff, a Dutch girl and an Italian man, all of them exuding a carefree manner that can't help but make Jody wonder what might have been if her life had taken a different turn – college, travelling, a few make-do-and-party jobs before succumbing to a responsible adult existence.

Finally she escapes. There's no sign of Sam in the computer room. Two of the three PCs are in use, which is probably a good thing – otherwise she might have been tempted to search the internet history to find out what he was up to.

You're assuming he won't simply tell you.

On the way out through reception, she happens to glance at the lounge area and spots the Baxters. Kay half rises from her seat, beckoning Jody over. Kay's wearing a floral dress and a pashmina shawl, while Trevor is in razor-sharp slacks, a check shirt and a tie. Are they dressed for the reception already?

'We wanted to thank you, personally,' Kay says. 'Such a kind gesture.'

She turns to Trevor, her expression as stern as any parent training their child in good manners.

'Uh, yes. Very kind.' He gets up, hands fidgeting. 'Would you excuse me? I just have to...'

Run away from me, Jody thinks. Sure enough, Kay is shaking her head in exasperation.

'Believe me, I do my best to smooth off his rough edges. Thirty years and counting.'

'A lifetime's work,' Jody says with a smile. This is the first time she's felt any sort of kinship with the woman, and it makes Jody feel like a proper adult, rather than a child pretending.

'Sometimes I think–' Kay stops abruptly, eyes glistening.

'Are you all right?'

'Yes – no, it's just–' She swallows, tries again. 'We almost split up, two years ago. Well, no, actually I nearly left him.'

Jody nods, cautiously. She has an intuition that Kay isn't accustomed to confiding in people.

Barely whispering, and with frequent nervous glances in the

direction Trevor has taken, Kay says, 'I had an affair. A serious one, not a fling. I was ready to make a new life with him. *Peter*.'

Her voice wobbles on the name. Jody feels her stomach churning; it's as if she has been presented with a possible future version of herself.

'I suppose we both thought Trevor would be the one more likely to stray. He's always had a wandering eye.'

When Kay pauses, as if inviting a comment, Jody struggles to maintain a neutral expression.

'Anyway, Trevor found out about it – about Peter – before I was ready to tell him. And he...' Kay shrugs, flopping a hand into her lap. 'It was like I'd pulled a plug on him. He begged me to stay, said he was nothing without me.' She gives a start. 'I'm so sorry. I don't know why I'm telling you this.'

'Because after this holiday we'll never see each other again?'

'Perhaps that's it. And I suppose I wanted you to know that Trevor isn't... well, he's more vulnerable than you might think.'

Jody manages an awkward smile. 'I hope you both have a wonderful time at the Conchis.'

'Thank you. I know you were more eager to go than your husband.'

As Jody turns away, she realises she can't leave it there. She turns back to see Kay dabbing at her eyes with a tiny lace handkerchief.

'Do you regret it, not going off with Peter?'

Kay stops what she's doing and stares at Jody. 'Every single day.'

Sam has collected the towels and he's getting settled on a lounger when Jody joins him. The first thing she does is lean over and kiss him on the lips.

'What's that for?'

'Nothing, really.' She lies down and stretches out, luxuriously, like a cat. 'Just... I think you did the right thing last night.'

'Okay.' He's curious to know what has caused this change of attitude, but decides not to push his luck. When she asks what he was online for, it's easy enough to fob her off with rumours of a big signing for the Albion.

In fact, his plan was to arrange a little treat – a way of apologising for causing her to miss out on the reception at the Conchis. He was looking up boat trips, hoping to find something with dolphins guaranteed, after Trevor's snarky comment. He found several local charter companies but their prices were ridiculous, and what you got for the money was no better than the trip they'd already booked.

He came away undecided, but also distracted by what else he found. The search brought up news stories about various accidents around the island. One was a fire on board a boat full of environmental protestors, dating back to when the airport was built. The protestors argued that the airport wasn't needed, as the island was only twenty minutes by ferry from the mainland, and the construction threatened the habitat of all sorts of protected wildlife. When the fire broke out, most of those on board managed to escape, but two people died. After that the protests faded away and the airport went ahead.

Then there was the tragedy that Gabby had mentioned: a case of reckless high spirits on the part of three young Danish men, whose yacht had slammed into a fishing boat. It was hard to tell from the rough internet translation, but the fisherman didn't seem to be hurt, and for some reason the bodies of the tourists weren't recovered from the water until a week after the collision.

From that article Sam spotted a link in the sidebar to another incident. Three years ago a young German couple went missing after hiring a boat to go scuba diving. The boat was eventually found, drifting far off course from the approved safe areas for diving. The likeliest explanation, according to the news report, was that the couple had been eaten by sharks.

Now, with a shudder, he says, 'The kids' club don't take them swimming, do they?'

'I don't think so. There's painting, trampolining, archery... probably no time for swimming.'

'Good. And Dylan went off okay?'

'He was fine.' There's a pause, in which he almost tells her about the internet search, but then Jody lets out a sigh and says, 'Perhaps it's Grace we should be worried about.'

'Grace? Why?' Sam thinks of his daughter as far more level-headed than Dylan, quietly in control of her life – and nothing like he was at that age, thank God.

'Because it's Dylan who gets about eighty percent of our attention. Who knows what effect that's going to have on Grace, always feeling her brother's the top priority?'

'But she understands. I mean, she was as scared as we were when–' He stops short of saying, *When we thought we might lose him.*

'Yeah, but he's fine now. So it's probably time we got that into our heads and stopped... mollycoddling him, or whatever it is we do.'

'"Mollycoddling"?'

'Yeah. It means treating him like a baby. Wrapping him up in cotton wool.'

For some reason it's given Sam the giggles. '*Mollycoddling.* Who comes up with these words? It sounds like you could swap it round and no one would notice. Collymoddling! Isn't that just as good?'

15

Somehow he's found a way to make her laugh, even when Jody is smarting over the secrets he's keeping. Why else would he sneak away to use the internet and then give her some nonsense about football?

Okay, so it doesn't make a lot of sense that he mentioned the computer room in the first place. He could have gone off for a drink and she'd have been none the wiser.

'Do you want anything?' he asks, as if he's picked up on the change in her mood.

'No thanks.' Jody turns to stare at the underside of the umbrella, the sun beating down on it with an intensity she can feel through the fabric.

Sam is lying in the same position. After a minute he performs an elaborate yawn. 'Wondering if we should go back to the room...'

'Not now.'

'Sure?'

He sounds disappointed. She can't blame him. That's the whole point of kids' club, isn't it? Mummy-and-Daddy-shag-time.

'It's not that long till they finish. And it's nice to lie here and relax.'

From Sam, there's a short, defeated sigh. 'Fair enough.'

Sam can't work out if she's still annoyed with him – and if she is, he's not sure why. He tries to forget it, and takes her advice. Even with his eyes closed he can see a kind of burning orange glare on the inside of his eyelids. He stares at the little flecks, like crawling insects, that drift across his vision. It lulls him so much that he nearly dozes.

By the time Jody stirs, and suggests a swim, the pool is almost deserted. Probably because the restaurant's about to open. After breakfast Sam couldn't imagine wanting to eat anything more for the rest of the day, but now the thought of a few chips is quite appealing; and maybe a bread roll with ham or cheese. Or ham *and* cheese.

He snorts. *Greedy bastard.*

Jody swims a few lengths, and encourages him to do the same. The pool's not that deep, so he sort of cheats to keep up with her, touching the bottom on tiptoe and springing forward. On the far side, when they swim beneath a footbridge that leads to the bar, Jody stops and they embrace, pressing their bodies close and kissing. *All is forgiven*, he thinks, and the relief is even sweeter than the kiss.

'Should have gone to the room,' he murmurs.

'Never mind. We'll have a nap after lunch.'

They dry off, and then it's time to collect the kids.

Dylan is delighted to see them, although it's also clear that he has bonded with the girl who took charge of his age group. Sam is listening to Dylan's breathless description of the morning's action when Sam recalls what Jody said and makes sure to ask how Grace got on.

'Bit boring,' she says, 'except for archery. I got a bullseye.'

'That's brilliant,' Sam says. 'Maybe you'll be in the Olympics one day.'

'I'm not good enough for that!'

'If you practice lots, it could happen,' Jody tells her. 'We'd better see if there's somewhere you can go for classes, back at home.'

Grace looks thrilled by the idea, and Sam realises that, if not for this holiday, she'd probably never have dreamt of trying something like archery.

The restaurant is heaving, so they opt for Dylan's idea of swimming first. On the second attempt, at about ten past one, it's a little quieter. They have a pleasant meal, though there's an odd moment when Sam catches a member of the hotel staff looking intently in his direction. It riles Sam a bit: he's wearing a perfectly good T-shirt, and loads of other people have shorts on. What's the problem?

Nothing, as it turns out. He's all but forgotten it when they get up to leave and find Gabby hurrying towards them, looking stressed.

What now? Sam thinks.

Then he sees the envelope.

Jody frowns as the rep almost skids to a halt in front of them.

'Oh, there you are!'

'What's the matter?' Jody notices the envelope, and thinks: *Isn't that...?*

'The reception, at the Conchis.' Gabby is gasping for breath.

'We're not going. We gave the tickets to someone else.'

'I know. But you can't.' Gabby doesn't sound cross as much as overwrought. 'Once you've been chosen, it's your names on the guest list. It's not transferable.'

'Why not?' Sam asks.

'There are some genuine VIPs there – the president's son often attends. It won't go down well if other people turn up in your place.'

Sam snorts, but before he can respond, Gabby says, 'Luckily there's still time. The transport isn't here until two.'

'*Two?*' Jody echoes. 'Ten minutes isn't long enough to get ready.'

She glances at Sam, expecting him to agree, but suddenly he's Mr Chilled Out. 'Won't hurt if we're a bit late, will it?'

'It's not ideal, but...' Gabby shrugs, meaning *okay*.

Jody feels betrayed by this change in his attitude. *He's only doing it to avoid an argument with Gabby.* 'I thought you didn't want to go?'

'I'm not fussed, really. But I thought *you* wanted to.'

He's right: hasn't she been sulking ever since he told her what he'd done? Though now, when it's been sprung on her, she's having second thoughts.

Gabby looks on in desperation. 'Please, guys. I know it might seem a bit... I dunno, *intimidating*, but you'll have such an amazing time, you really will. The Conchis is *so* beautiful.'

Jody is shaking her head, trying to stop the onslaught. 'But we'll have to dress up. I'm not sure if we've brought anything formal enough...'

'You'll be fine in a dress and sandals, like you wore to the welcome meeting.'

Jody's mood isn't improved by the way Gabby looks her up and down as she says this. Meanwhile Sam is gazing at her with such an innocent, easy-going expression that for a moment Jody wants to throttle him.

Unlike many of his extended family, Sam isn't a big believer in fate. All that *Everything happens for a reason* – it's bullshit. Life is full of luck and hazards, split-second decisions that can change everything. There's no grand plan to make sense of it all, as much as people might wish for one.

But right now, this feels near enough to fate, especially as he got nowhere when he looked for a boat trip.

They hurry back to the room, urging the kids on without fully explaining what they're doing. Sam can't work out why Jody seems so unhappy, and hardly dares to ask her. He's unlocking the door when she makes a sucking noise, like a wince.

'Trevor and Kay...'

'What about them?'

'Gabby must have asked for the tickets back. Can you imagine how gutted they'll be? And now that I know–' She breaks off, won't tell him what she was intending to say. 'There's no time.'

Grace is first in the bathroom to freshen up. Dylan is told to choose a small toy to take with him. Jody kneels by a chest of drawers, digging through it to find clean outfits for the kids. And for Sam: his chinos and a white linen shirt get tossed over her shoulder and he snatches them out of the air. All the while she's muttering to herself: things like, 'Why are we doing this?' and 'I must be mad.'

'Jode, it's okay.'

'You've changed your tune, now your friend Gabby's put the pressure on–'

'Hey! She's not *my* friend any more than she's yours.'

'I didn't mean...' Then she tails off, because it sounds a bit feeble and they both know it.

'The reason I agreed wasn't to get Gabby out of trouble. It was because I made a mistake last night. Because of you, being so disappointed when I said we weren't going.' Sam forces a grin. 'Anyway, it's something a bit different. And it's free!'

'Everything's free here,' Jody reminds him. 'And you were dreading it.'

'Yeah, but finding out now means we haven't been worrying in the run-up to it.'

'That may suit you . I could have done with time to prepare.'

'Fair enough,' he says, and apologises while she frets over the lack of proper shoes. Sam only brought trainers and a pair of Nike sandals; the sandals will have to do.

She regards the wardrobe in dismay. 'If this really is some super-posh place, and I'm gonna turn up looking like–'

'You look beautiful, whatever you wear. I mean it.'

Jody raises one eyebrow – he doesn't often do this sort of gushy talk – but he can tell it's had the desired effect.

'Get a bloody move on, then!'

16

Somehow they all manage to wash and change in less than fifteen minutes, though Jody still can't quite believe they're going ahead with it.

Normally Grace would welcome any excuse to dress up like a princess, but she insists on wearing her black pleated skirt and a pink top. A cheerleader outfit, basically, but Jody doesn't have the strength to argue.

Dylan, in khaki shorts and a polo shirt, looks very presentable, but his eyes are blank and puffy round the edges. What with kids' club, an hour in the pool and a big meal, he is wiped out.

'You can have a nap on the bus, okay?' Jody says.

'Don't wannoo!' he cries, throwing down the small action figure he's chosen.

Grace makes a sarcastic noise. 'He'll probably be sick.'

'No he won't.' Jody sighs. 'Thanks, Grace.'

They walk the now-familiar route around the pool, trying to maintain a rapid pace without breaking into a sweat. Jody has gone for a knee-length lemon print dress and low-heeled sandals. As well as a small leather bag, she's carrying a cream cardigan. It's a smart, slightly demure look; overall she feels reasonably satisfied with her appearance, even while resenting the influence that Gabby had on it.

Stepping into the air-conditioned lobby, who should they see but the Baxters. Kay registers their presence but won't meet Jody's eye. Trevor, meanwhile, is glaring furiously at Sam, as though he's convinced the whole thing was a set-up, designed to humiliate him.

Sam doesn't pay much attention to the Baxters. Dylan is getting fractious, so Sam scoops him up and past reception. He finds Gabby waiting on the pavement, tapping at her phone. She almost bursts with gratitude at the sight of them.

'Oh, well done, guys! Thanks for getting ready so quickly.'

Before Sam can speak, Dylan wriggles and calls out: 'Max! Max!'

Another family are standing at the kerb, among them the blond boy that Dylan had befriended the previous evening. Sam puts his son down and Dylan dashes over to greet him.

'That's the Fischers,' Gabby says, 'a German family who also won a place at the reception. I hope you don't mind but it looks like you'll be travelling together.'

'Yeah, okay.' Sam is assuming they'll be in a minibus, so it comes as a shock when they hear the distant rumble of an engine, and what rolls into sight is the high square bulk of a Hummer.

Then he gets a side view and discovers it's a *stretch* Hummer. He's seen these before, usually transporting drunken hen parties around Brighton on Friday nights.

He laughs in disbelief. Dylan comes running back, brimming with new-found energy. 'Dad, are we going in that? Are we?'

'You sure are,' Gabby answers for him. 'It's VIP all the way!'

Even Jody is smiling, and Grace says, 'Can we take a picture? I want this on Instagram when we get home!'

'We'll take lots of pictures.' Sam catches Jody's eye and winks; her nod in response says, *Yes, we've done the right thing.*

The big car pulls into the layby. The driver is wearing a full chauffeur's uniform. He gets out, greets them with a salute and opens one of the rear doors.

With Jody gesturing for the Fischers to go first, Sam turns to Gabby and says, 'Sorry about the, er, mix-up.'

'Don't worry. All's well that ends well.'

She looks so pleased he almost thinks she's going to kiss him. He feels embarrassed, and then a question pops into his head: 'This president's son. He doesn't happen to have a private jet, does he? A G650?'

Now it's Gabby's turn to look awkward. 'Y-yes, he does. Why do you ask?'

Sam shakes his head. 'No reason.'

To Jody, the inside of the Hummer looks like a nightclub on wheels: rich leather upholstery, deep blue carpeting, strings of multicoloured lights along the ceiling. There are three different sets of seats, so plenty of room for the two families.

The Fischers are probably in their late thirties, not unfriendly but a bit severe-looking. As well as Dylan's friend, there's an older boy, perhaps ten or eleven, so engrossed in a game on his iPad that he doesn't seem to have noticed his surroundings.

There are two TV screens in the back, playing pop videos at low volume. The driver also points out a clever little cabinet, which houses a fridge full of miniature bottles of champagne as well as beer and fruit juice.

'Oh my God!' Jody exclaims, and the Fischers nod and smile, sharing the same kind of incredulous delight.

Once they're moving, the drive is fast and smooth and very quiet – the cabin must be soundproofed, Jody guesses. Drinks are selected, and then they raise their glasses in a toast, suggested by the German father.

'To the Conchis!' he says in English, and before the glasses reach their lips, Jody adds, 'And to us!'

She's persuaded Sam to try a bucks fizz, and watches with amusement as he swallows, grimaces, takes another sip and grudgingly admits that it's 'not bad'.

Savouring the bitter-sweet flavours, the tickling pleasure of the bubbles on her tongue, Jody rests her head back and shuts her eyes. *This is the life, eh?*

Sam says quietly, 'D'you reckon Trevor and Kay saw the Hummer?'

'Probably.' Jody tuts. 'I feel so sorry for them.'

'Even after the looks they gave us?'

'I pity them. Have you noticed how often they're just sitting there, not saying a word to each other?'

Sam is silent for so long that she finally gets the joke, and playfully swats him. But then he says, 'Maybe that'll be us, one day?'

'Maybe.' It's a scary thought, but Jody's also touched by the idea that he's imagining them still together in their fifties, or older. She takes his hand. 'So we ought to count our blessings.'

The Hummer has two rows of two seats facing inwards, and the narrow side windows are heavily tinted, giving only a dim impression of the passing countryside. What Sam can see of the scenery is nothing special: fields, trees, low hills. The occasional crumbling cottage.

After a second drink, they're all nicely relaxed. The German couple aren't saying much, though at one point the man yawns, catches Sam's eye and says, 'Siesta!' Sam grins, then finds he also needs to yawn.

But it's Dylan and his friend Max who are making a real effort at international relations, sitting tightly together to play some sort of game on a Nintendo Switch. The older brother is similarly glued to his iPad, though he's also sneaking glances at Grace from time to time. This brings out the protective father in Sam. He sits up straighter, throwing his shoulders out, until Jody realises what's going on and gives him a little jab with her elbow.

It's a sort of sad-happy moment. Only a few more years and he'll have to be on guard against the boys who will come sniffing round his daughter, the way he once did with Jody – not that her parents could have done anything to stop what happened there.

Grace, he reminds himself, before he gets bitter about it. *Grace* is what happened there. And for all the stress and trouble when the pregnancy was first discovered, Jody's parents – just like the rest of them – wouldn't be without their grandchildren now. Not for anything.

Sam goes back to gazing out of the window. Fields growing some sort of vegetable, green leaves resting on dry, pale earth. Between the rows, a farmer leans wearily on a fork as he watches them pass. He's middle-aged, with grey hair and a hard weathered face. His eyes seem to bore through the tinted glass, and Sam feels a stab of guilt, almost wishing he could explain that it's not his car, that what they're doing this afternoon has no connection to the life they normally lead.

I graft for a living, the same as you.

More crops in the next field, but here the leaves look bigger, greener. Either it's something different or else these are just healthier and more successful for some reason. Sam knows practically nothing about nature: you could take him round a supermarket and he wouldn't be able to say what grows on trees, what comes out of the ground and what gets cooked up in a factory. It came as a shock the first time he learned that tuna was this great big fish. He'd vaguely assumed it was about the size of the tin it came in.

This part of the island strikes him as very different from their holiday resort. Poorer, more basic. He can imagine the locals living simple lives, digging their own wells for water, maybe using horses to pull a plough. It makes him wonder if the Conchis really will be all that special.

17

They've been travelling for nearly an hour when the Hummer makes a right turn and ascends a long steep hill. The terrain here is rocky and barren until the summit, when they pass through a wood of tall pines, growing so densely that they seem to exist in darkness.

Jody hears a gasp. The German woman is sitting at an angle which gives her a view into the driver's cab, and as such she's the first to set eyes on the hotel.

The building lies below them, alone in its splendour on a rocky coastline with trees on three sides and a sparkling sea lapping at it on the fourth. The hotel has been designed to resemble an ocean liner, perched on a low cliff as if awaiting the high tide to float it off. Jody counts five storeys, each one a slightly smaller replica of the floor beneath. A mast-like tower completes the impression, strung with thick cables that are fixed to railings that encircle a walkway on the upper floor. The frame – she wants to say hull – is painted white, but a good seventy percent of the exterior is made of glass.

The road descends into an olive grove and reaches the hotel grounds, where the Hummer drives beneath a triangular steel sculpture, fashioned to resemble a pair of giant anchors propped together. For some reason it makes Jody think of two lovers sharing a drunken kiss.

They join a line of vehicles pulling up at the entrance to the lobby. The guests are being met by a small army of young men and women in stylish black uniforms. When it's their turn, Jody finds herself gripping Sam's hand. She feels absurdly like a bride, arriving at the church on her wedding day.

'Ready?' Sam says, and there's a nervous tremor in his voice because he too is light years out of his comfort zone.

'Let's go,' she says, and then, in a whisper, 'Thank you.'

'What for? I gave the tickets away.'

'But you also persuaded me to take them back.'

The staff member who greets them looks like a young Cillian Murphy. After taking the invitation from Sam, he ushers them into a vast atrium. This is where Sam's argument is tested first – how can the Conchis manage to be so much more majestic than their own hotel?

Jody wouldn't have thought it possible, but somehow this place makes the Adriana Beach look like a rundown guest house. It's something to do with the scale of the place, the height of the atrium, the way the sunlight floods in from every direction, enhanced by subtle artificial lighting and thin, gauzy shades to eliminate glare.

And it's the interior design. She's often heard people on TV use phrases like 'clean lines' and 'simple elegance' but this is the first time she's witnessed what those things mean in practice. And it's astounding, unreal – like a movie set enhanced with CGI, though the only special effects here are money, money and more money.

They file into a large elevator, along with another British family who Jody vaguely recognises from the plane.

'Mummy,' says Dylan in an earnest voice. 'Does a king live here?'

There's affectionate laughter from the other family, and Jody can't help but join in.

'Not exactly. But it's where a king would stay, if he came on holiday.'

Even the lift is padded and mirrored and cleverly lit, like a luxury apartment all of its own. Sam's first impressions have left him stunned and a little confused. Is he thrilled, won over, or is he angry about the money that's been spent on this place? All this marble and gold. There's a word he's trying to find: op... opulent?

He isn't totally sure, but when he whispers to Jody, she nods. 'It is. Though *decadent* is what my dad would say.'

The lift arrives on the top floor and they're escorted into a function room that seems larger than the arrivals hall at the airport and nearly as busy. There's a long bar curving around one end of the room, a stage at the other end, and the sea-facing side is mostly open to a wide timber deck with rails like those of a ship. Beyond that, nothing but glassy blue ocean and just a misty smudge on the horizon that might be the tip of a neighbouring island.

The other British couple are similarly impressed. The mum's already talking to Jody, and Sam can tell the dad is psyching himself up to speak to him. At least these two don't look as snobby as Trevor and Kay – and they're a bit younger, fortyish or thereabouts. They have a teenage daughter with them, a surly-looking girl with garish make-up and an outfit so brief it looks more like she's going pole dancing.

As well as maybe a couple of hundred guests, there are dozens of hotel staff, all of them virtually identical in age and appearance. On the stage there's a band playing with such casual expertise that Sam wonders if they're famous. Given the surroundings, it wouldn't surprise him if it was bloody U2 or somebody.

A lot of people are drifting on to the terrace. Despite the room being open to the elements on that side, the air-conditioning system is pumping out cooled air to mix with the sea breeze, and the result is a perfect temperature. For practically the first time in three days, Sam doesn't have a sheen of sweat on his forehead.

He takes a cold beer from a passing waiter, then plunges into conversation with his fellow Brit. The man's name is Gareth Dowd, married to Michelle, and he's a self-employed plasterer. They're from Sevenoaks, and Gareth supports Crystal Palace. Sam quickly relaxes. He can talk easily about the building trade, and what Seagulls supporter doesn't relish a bit of sarcastic banter with an Eagles nut?

The women are chatting together, involving Grace and the couple's daughter where they can. Only Dylan is ignored, but he doesn't seem to mind. Sam makes sure to glance round every few seconds, tracking his son's confident exploration of the room.

More drinks arrive, and plates of strange finger food: little pastries, lots of things with fish, some dubious-looking stuff that Gareth reckons is caviar.

'You like to try, sir?' a waiter asks.

Sam shakes his head. 'Maybe later.'

Michelle overhears and offers her opinion in a loud whisper – 'It's hideous!' – and the two pairings link up to form a single conversation.

'You know, this place is *really* amazing,' Jody says, already sounding a bit tipsy, 'but the weird thing is...' She breaks off, giggling.

'What?' Michelle asks.

'It sort of reminds me of...' Jody shakes her head at Sam. 'You're gonna think I'm bonkers.'

'Go on.'

'The De La Warr pavilion.'

'In Bexhill?' Sam thinks about it, then he laughs too. 'Yeah, it is a bit.'

Gareth starts nodding. 'I think I know where you mean. That art deco place on the front?'

Jody splutters: 'Can't see many movie stars or royalty heading to Bexhill-on-Sea for their holidays, can you?'

What a lightweight, Jody thinks. *I'm drunk already*. Then again, what does it matter if she is? They're on holiday. And this couple are fun to be with, not all snooty and prim – although Michelle has been trying to prise out the reason why she and Sam had children at such a young age.

Steering the conversation away from personal stuff, Jody indicates the waitress who has dispensed yet more drinks. 'Is it me, or are all the staff here drop-dead gorgeous?'

Gareth rocks back on his heels, surveying the room as if sizing up for a quote. He's a tall man, with long arms, narrow shoulders and a thin neck: the perfect shape for plastering ceilings, Jody thinks, and swallows down a burp of laughter.

'Yeah, you're right,' he says. 'Every single one of 'em.'

'She means the fellers as well,' Michelle points out.

'And not just physically,' Jody says. 'They all look bright – intelligent, I mean – but with the bodies of...'

'Porn stars?' Gareth suggests.

'I was going to say *athletes*.' She's teasing him with a strait-laced tone. 'Isn't that a bit annoying for the guests, though?

Paying all that money to be surrounded by people who'd make you feel inferior?'

Gareth and Michelle nod thoughtfully but Sam has another view of it.

'If you can afford to stay here, you're not gonna feel inferior to anyone. They probably get an extra buzz from getting all these "gorgeous" people to run round after them.'

'Good point there,' Gareth says, which has Sam swelling with pride. He can do this stuff, Jody realises: socialising, small talk. If only he'd believe in himself a bit more.

She drifts out of the conversation for a moment, wanting to savour how mellow she's feeling. Grace looks star-struck in the presence of Gareth and Michelle's daughter, Alice. The girl is showing off her iPhone, something that Grace desperately wants for her next birthday; and no doubt before long her brother will be pestering–

Looking round, Jody gasps. 'Where's Dylan?'

18

Jody sees that the pitch of her voice has grabbed Sam's attention. It's a tone they both associate with panic. *He's gone all floppy. I can't get him to wake up. I think there are spots appearing...*

This, for a moment or two, feels just as terrible. There's a gut-wrenching fear when Jody considers how high up they are. Of course he'd be drawn outside, and the railings are easily climbed: a challenge for a boy who came all too close to death and now seemingly knows no fear.

Sam is already moving; Jody instructs Grace to stay put and hurries after him. She realises that the band has stopped playing. The atmosphere in the room has changed, the buzz of chatter reduced to a low expectant murmur. More and more people are drifting towards the decking, as if drawn by some irresistible curiosity.

Ghouls, she thinks, and her heart is ready to break even as Sam, momentarily hidden from sight, straightens up to reveal a small lost boy in his arms.

Oh thank you thank you...

'Went exploring, didn't you?'

As Jody hugs her son, a man in evening dress steps up to the microphone and says, 'Ladies and gentlemen, if you will please make your way outside for the next stage of today's entertainment. *Meine Damen und Herren...*'

He runs through a few other languages but everyone's got the gist. They and the Dowds join the throng, milling around in the glare of the afternoon sun. The staff continue to circulate, replenishing drinks, while another small team is busy preparing something.

Oddly, they bring out three long metal plates that look like girders, which they attach to the outside railings, a couple of metres apart. Jody and Sam work their way closer and see that they are narrow platforms, extending way beyond the deck. Heavy-looking steps are wheeled out and bolted on at one end to provide a counterweight.

By now, the crowd is starting to grasp what this could mean. There are exclamations as those closest to the railings peer over to see what lies below. Although the building is stepped, the difference between the floors looks greater from a distance: a clever optical illusion to enhance the impression of an ocean liner. But there's no illusion when it comes to their height. They're at least fifty or sixty metres above the level of the sea.

Three slender figures thread through the crowd: two women and a man in black lycra suits. In perfect unison they climb the steps and then stop, possibly to allow for dozens of phones to be set to video. Sam lifts Dylan on to his shoulders, and Jody immediately warns him not to get too near the edge.

'Ladies and gentlemen,' the MC says. 'Let us count down together. Five, four, three...'

The divers tense on *two*, drop into a sprinting stance on *one*, and take off a moment later: two measured strides and then a leap, coming down heavy and bending the boards below the level of the railings, springing up with all the momentum of their weight and speed to launch into the air. Their bodies straighten on the ascent, then fold and fall and straighten again, arrowing down towards the water, and not a single spectator dares to take a breath – because surely they'll never be able to clear the rocks at the base of the hotel?

To Sam it feels like a suicide mission: three lives sacrificed purely to entertain a load of boozed-up tourists. At first he backs off, not wanting Dylan to witness the bodies hitting the rocks, and so he hears the gasps of amazement before he sees what causes them.

The divers came prepared. Hidden within those lycra suits are flaps of material that fan out like wings. The divers spread their arms and sweep outwards as well as down, giving them the few extra metres they need to avoid the rocks. In the final second their arms point downwards again and they cut smoothly into the water, to whoops of celebration and relief from the watching crowd.

'Batman!' Dylan is clawing at Sam's face in his excitement. 'They were being Batman, Daddy!'

Cutting through the cheers is a strange hissing noise, like gas leaking from a pipe. Sam wonders if the air conditioning is playing up – if it is, there'll be hell to pay for the poor bastard who fitted it.

The sound seems to be getting louder. Rising. And now there are more gasps and laughter, more heads shaken in disbelief, for someone – not one of the divers, but a man wearing a helmet and a black bodysuit – is flying through the air towards them.

'Batman *and* Superman,' Sam mutters. The man has a jetpack, which looks like a set of gas tanks strapped to his back, controlled by a joystick in each hand. He zooms up past them like a rocket, and Dylan isn't the only one to let out a squeal of pleasure at the sight.

With real skill, the man eases downwards, slowing as he glides towards the terrace, clears the railings and nudges forward, hovering in mid-air while people spill backwards to give him room, finally landing as effortlessly as if he'd stepped out of a limousine.

Inside the lounge, the MC's booming voice announces: 'Ladies and gentlemen, may I present to you our most esteemed guest of honour, His Excellency Borko Radić.'

There is thunderous applause. The staff who set up the diving boards cluster around the president's son, removing his helmet and the jetpack while he steps out of his bodysuit. Beneath that he's wearing the full dinner jacket, white shirt, bow tie: like James bloody Bond.

True to that image, two beautiful women approach him. One hands him a glass of champagne, then they link arms and escort him into the main room. Sam and Jody exchange a look.

'This place...' she says, and laughs.

'Unbelievable,' he agrees. Her earlier comment about the attractiveness of the staff has got Sam idly wondering if there's some unfortunate part of the country, perhaps on the mainland, where the only inhabitants are thin, fat, ugly – whatever – because all the perfect people have been rounded up and brought here to work, like that old fairy tale about the guy who gets rid of the rats.

For a second, Sam sees Borko in a different light. Not Superman or James Bond, but the Pied Piper. And he can't help shivering.

There's an electric buzz to the air as they head back inside, Sam only just remembering to duck down because Dylan is still on his shoulders. The way everyone is smiling and chatting, you can tell this is an event they'll be talking about for years to come.

Thank God Gabby gave them another chance to attend.

. . .

The women all want to fuck him; the men want to be him. Jody can't remember who that was originally said about, but she suspects it applies to Borko Radić, pretty much.

The president's son isn't how Jody had pictured him – the reckless, law-breaking big game hunter that Trevor Baxter so admired. She would have imagined him to be a shorter, burlier man than this, somewhat rougher around the edges. He and his dad might run the country, but by the sound of it they came from fairly basic – if not to say savage – beginnings. And that kind of background has to leave a trace, doesn't it?

Well, not if Borko is anything to go by. He's tall, slim and athletic, his dark hair just long enough to be mussed up from the helmet he was wearing. He's a fair distance away, but she gets the impression of olive skin and strong features, along with the two-day stubble that seems to be obligatory on this island.

Certainly there's no missing his charisma; as he takes to the stage he looks suave, relaxed, graceful.

The MC steps back, bowing respectfully. Borko stands at the microphone but says nothing for a few seconds. He wants to let the room settle, let them appreciate who he is.

Then, in a suitably dry tone, he says, 'My apologies for the method of transport. I was running late.'

There's laughter, most of it completely natural. Borko's voice is rich and powerful, and his English is spoken with hardly any trace of a foreign accent. Even more impressively, he goes on to repeat the joke in German, and then in Russian.

'Before I continue,' he says, 'we have arranged for your sons and daughters to be entertained elsewhere. Children and speeches do not make for a good match!'

This time the laughter's slightly muted. As he translates the message, a group of what look like circus performers enter the room. They are wearing dance outfits, and have faces painted to resemble various wild animals. Some are juggling as they walk while others perform acrobatic tricks, climbing and flipping over one another. They move through the crowd, accompanied by waiting staff bearing trays of confectionery, and collect up the children as they go.

'We have many surprises in store,' Borko says to convince those who are wavering. And to the parents: 'I assure you, they will be perfectly safe.'

Alice does that teenage huffing and shoulder-jerking to her parents. 'Do I have to?'

'Oh, go on,' Grace begs her, and the Dowds look relieved when their daughter gives in.

Dylan, who has never been a clingy child, does seem to hesitate at first. Then a young man with the face of a leopard brushes a hand against his ear and produces an egg from it. Dylan touches his ear and grins, enchanted by the trick.

'Do it again!'

The man nods his head to one side: *Come this way.*

'See you in a minute. Be good!' Jody calls, but they're already oblivious to their parents. She watches them go, and doesn't notice that for a second Sam looks absolutely stricken.

19

I can't say anything. Jody will think I've gone nuts.

Sam tries to rid his mind of the Pied Piper story. Of course they'll be safe.

He takes a sip of beer but doesn't really like it. He has developed a fine understanding of his limit where alcohol is concerned, and knows he's nearly there.

With only the adults present, Borko starts by explaining how his country enjoys good international relations; his father regularly meets other presidents, prime ministers, financiers and chief executives.

'Myself, I am a frequent visitor to your countries. I love to spend time in the clubs and casinos of the West End, or skiing in the Alps, sailing in Denmark, hunting in Siberia. And now, when it is your turn to visit *my* country, I wish to leave a good impression with, uh, people of all backgrounds. Unfortunately it is not possible to offer a reception on this scale to everyone who visits Sekliw, so instead we hold the competition at each hotel.'

He translates swiftly, and when he resumes again in English, Borko's eyes seem to narrow slightly.

'Some might believe there is an ulterior motive at work here.'

A little chuckle. 'Not true, though it is my sincere wish that afterwards you will tell your friends what an inspiring holiday this has been.'

He moves on to the issue of the nation's troubled past, and the tough challenges his father had to face in order to make the country stable. As a result it has become, in Borko's opinion, 'a glorious place to live, to work, to take a vacation.'

He pauses, scanning the audience as if daring anyone to disagree. Sam notices that some of the waiting staff look slightly nervous.

Finally Borko winds it up, urging his guests to enjoy the party. 'If there is anything you require, you have only to ask. Today, we are at your service.'

It seems a bit over-the-top to Sam, but most people around him are clapping enthusiastically, Jody and the Dowds among them.

A flare of light catches Sam's attention, coming from the terrace. All he can see above the heads of the crowd is a jet of flame. He grabs Jody's arm, wondering how quickly they can find the kids and get out of the building, but stops when he hears whooping and laughing.

Then a gap opens up to reveal yet another incredible sight: fire-breathing stilt walkers.

Sam has to blink a few times before his brain will accept what he's seeing. Three stunningly fit women dressed in what is basically bondage gear – skimpy leather bikinis with various straps and studded belts around their neck and wrists – marching along the terrace on stilts while twirling flaming torches in their hands. Their bodies are gleaming as if coated in oil, six-pack stomachs rippling as they walk.

'Wey-hey,' says Gareth in a low, hungry voice. 'Now the *grown-up* entertainment begins.'

· · ·

The women share bemused glances at the way Sam and Gareth are leering at the stilt walkers, but Jody can't really blame them. Her own attention is frequently drawn back to the stage, where Borko is shaking hands with the returning musicians.

She loses sight of him as he steps down. The crowd as a whole is moving towards the terrace to get a clearer view of the stilt walkers. She hears a furnace-like roar as one of the girls sprays a jet of flame into the air.

Then there's a disturbance nearby: Borko is coming her way, flanked by a couple of bodyguards. People shake his hand and clap him on the back and he nods, absorbing their compliments with a dutiful smile. An elderly woman makes a comment about the hotel, and Jody hears him reply, 'In a manner of speaking. I own the company that owns it!'

Now he's almost within touching distance. His gaze alights on Jody and doesn't veer away; for a long moment he is looking directly into her eyes and she thinks: *He knows me.*

Impossible. It lasts only a second, and Michelle is standing right next to her but doesn't seem to notice anything untoward. By the time Sam and Gareth turn to look, Borko is already striding past, his attention focused on other guests; and no doubt some of them are falling for it, too.

It's a trick they teach politicians, Jody realises. The ability to make you feel like you're the only person who matters to them.

All the same, she feels a little shaken. When she mentions needing the toilet, Michelle says she'll come, prompting a snigger from Gareth.

'Why is it you girls always have to go together?'

'To complain about men with their eyes out on stalks,' Michelle says, gesturing at the fire breathers.

Sam leans close and murmurs to Jody, 'Check on the kids, will you?' She gives him a questioning look but he only shrugs, as if embarrassed to show how much he cares in front of the other couple.

Jody and Michelle fight their way against the flow, following a sign for the rest rooms, and it's a relief when they come to a wide hallway with a marble floor and several easy chairs. The aircon is so effective that Jody decides to put on the cardigan she's carrying.

The Ladies is as sumptuous as every other part of the hotel, with an array of toiletries in little glass jars lined up on a shelf above the sinks. Michelle alights on them with glee, while encouraging Jody to do the same. 'They'll be gone by the end of the day.'

Jody takes a couple of soaps, and says that's all she can fit into her handbag. She's never felt comfortable helping herself to anything: it feels too much like theft.

They go on chatting while they're in the cubicles, Michelle becoming less and less discreet.

'You know how, with some men, you can tell they're gonna know what they're doing – between the sheets, I mean? Wouldn't you bet that Mr Borko scores highly.'

'I daresay he gets plenty of practice.' Jody can't help shivering as she recalls how he seemed to peer into her soul.

'He could practice with me any time. I'd even let Gareth have his fun with one of those fire-breathing hussies in return!'

Jody laughs, but the conversation is making her uneasy. This feels like an alternative glimpse of the future: would-be swingers like Gareth and Michelle or lonely husks like Trevor and Kay. Is there any hope that she and Sam can avoid either fate?

After washing her hands, Jody says she wants to see how the kids are doing.

Michelle is dismissive. 'They'll be fine.'

'I know. I'm paranoid. It's–' Jody stops, but knows she has to explain. 'Dylan was quite ill, at the start of the year. In hospital for a while.'

'Oh dear. What was it?'

'Uh... meningitis.' Jody hates saying the word; not just because it's a reminder of the agony they went through, but because all too often people rear away at the very mention of it – as though she or Dylan might be carrying the disease right now.

But Michelle briefly rests a hand on Jody's shoulder and says, 'How awful for you. I'm sure I'd be paranoid after a thing like that.'

There's a corridor at right angles to the hall. Jody can hear exuberant shouts and screams from a doorway at the far end. A couple of the staff are huddled outside, as if taking shelter. When one of them spots Jody, he moves clear of the doorway, and Jody realises she was half expecting to be barred from entering.

The noise level is deafening, which is partly down to the acoustics of the room itself, and partly because the kids are running riot. At first she can't make sense of their costumes, the sinister blank faces. They're in a space the size of a sports hall, complete with a sprung timber floor and a high vaulted ceiling. The narrow windows are covered by heavy shades, blocking any natural light. About a third of the space is taken up by a gigantic soft play area on three levels, complete with various tubes and climbing bars. Two steep slides drop into a ball pit large enough for about fifty kids.

The rest of the room is bare, except for a row of tables at the back groaning with soft drinks and snacks...

And guns and ammo – because most of the children have put on thin coveralls and masks, and they're charging around firing paintballs at each other.

No. Not at each other. Jody sees that their targets are four or five of the staff, who are dressed as waiters but also have painted faces and long rubbery clown shoes that hamper their move-ment – to the delight of their assailants.

It takes Jody a minute to identify her own children. Dylan, of course, is enthusiastically taking part in the paintball game, brandishing a gun almost as big as he is. Grace and Alice are also kitted out, but have found a quiet spot on the far side of the ball pit and are doing more chatting than shooting.

The other staff, including the entertainers who led them here, are standing at the far side of the room, close to the refreshments, in what is obviously a designated safe zone. With a distinct air of relief, they watch as the poor waiters are pursued through the play area and shot mercilessly, their smart jackets and trousers splattered with bright red paint.

One of the men gets cornered at the top of a slide. He endures a couple of shots at point-blank range, then, with a convincing cry of desperation, he hurls himself into the ball pit. With the red and white makeup, it's hard to tell for sure, but he seems oddly familiar. Jody is denied a second look because the man is submerged beneath hundreds of plastic balls, while more shots rain down from above.

Then he reappears briefly, and recognition brings a gasp.

It can't be.

20

Somehow Sam has become trapped in a conversation with Gareth about foreigners, and how there are 'too fucking many' of them in the UK. He's praying they move on to safer ground before Jody comes back.

It started with a comment about how 'they don't seem as bad in their own countries.' This was in relation to a holiday to India a few years back, which Gareth and Michelle enjoyed far more than they expected. 'Filthy, how they live, and poor as buggery – but doesn't mean we want 'em coming over here, does it?'

Suddenly he's in full flight, and Sam can't do anything except keep his expression neutral and wish he was somewhere else. Until now Gareth had seemed like a nice enough bloke, happy to eye up the stilt walkers. At one point he whistled sadly and said, 'I'd give ten years off my life for an hour in bed with her.' Sam was tempted to joke that, if his wife caught him at it he'd probably lose far more than ten years.

He wonders if that sense of disappointment is what has turned Gareth's mood. Now he's raging that 'they all need to be sent back, not just the blacks and pakis. Everyone foreign.'

There was a time when Sam might have agreed – this was

basically what his own parents had brought him up to believe – but for the past couple of years they've had a Romanian working with them, and he's turned out to be a really top bloke: hard-working, reliable, gets his round in. It was Jody who pointed out that, before they got to know him, Sam and his workmates would have wanted the guy kicked out of the country. So it's complicated. Surely Gareth must realise that?

Sam is gearing up to say so when Michelle returns. Jody's gone to take a look at the kids, she tells him, and Sam pretends this is news to him. It's also an opportunity to change the subject. He asks about their hotel, praying this won't spark off another rant.

Then Jody appears, her brow creased with anxiety. Sam's heart lurches.

'What's up? Are they all right?'

'Yeah.' Her eyes say otherwise. 'Just something I want you to see.' She flutters a smile at the Dowds. 'Won't be a second.'

'Jesus, thanks,' Sam says as she leads him away.

'Boring?'

'Racist. Like you wouldn't believe.'

'Oh, that's awful.'

'The kids are okay, aren't they?'

'Yes. Having a whale of a time.'

'So what is it...?'

They escape the main lounge and hurry along a corridor towards the ear-splitting noise of the children's party. Sam is cringing even before he takes in the sight of kids in facemasks swarming over a gigantic soft play structure, armed with realistic-looking guns. The whole room looks like the site of a massacre, and it takes him a moment to process the fact that it's not a bloodbath, but paint.

That lessens the shock a little. But he's been paintballing

himself, on a stag weekend, and it's definitely not suitable for kids as young as Dylan.

Sam looks around for evidence of supervision. Three or four of the waiters are standing at the back of the room, keeping their heads down. The only other adults in sight are a couple of tough guys standing by a door in the opposite corner. They remind Sam of nightclub bouncers.

Jody lets out an exclamation: 'It's getting worse! There were more staff than this a minute ago.' She clutches his arm. 'Look over there.'

She means the ball pit, where the kids have trapped a group of men with clown faces.

'You see that one, second from right?'

'Yeah. Looks shit scared.'

'Isn't he the waiter from our hotel? The one who dropped that tray?'

The children are still firing at the men, but most are running out of ammunition. Some throw their guns down and make for the food and drink. Grace is among them, leading Dylan away from the chaos with a protective arm around his shoulders. Jody feels both proud and slightly pained to see Grace taking on the role of mother; already she's developing a sense of responsibility towards others and won't put herself first.

Both have removed their masks. Dylan looks horribly overheated and possibly a little tearful. They haven't yet noticed their parents.

Then, in the ball pit, someone hurls a ball at one of the clowns, striking him full in the face. With frenzied cries, the other kids follow his lead, joyfully bombarding the men, who twist and writhe but have nowhere to hide.

It's out of control, Jody thinks. Why doesn't someone stop it? Why are the men putting up with this?

The second question is answered when one of the clowns struggles to the edge of the ball pit and starts to clamber out. Jody registers that a couple of thuggish-looking men have taken a few steps in his direction. Grimly, he slips back and surrenders to the onslaught.

'Grace!' Jody raises her arm to get her daughter's attention. The children approach at a run, and Jody realises they have been spotted by the guards – or whatever they are. One of them raises a wrist to his mouth and appears to speak into it.

The wildest of the kids, having helped themselves to food, run back to the play area and start lobbing pastries and cakes at the hapless clowns. A boy who has been dry-clicking his gun observes the food fight for a moment, then ploughs through the ball pit until he's behind the clowns. He reverses the gun and swings it by the barrel, catching one of the men on the back of the head. There's an eruption of blood as the man pitches forward and vanishes beneath the plastic balls.

A girl screams, loudly enough to cut through all the other noise. The children around her stop throwing food and look up as if emerging from a trance. The Dowds' girl, Alice, sidles away from the ball pit with a suitably angelic 'It wasn't me' expression on her face.

'I don't like this, Mummy,' Grace says.

'Neither do I.' Jody soothes her daughter with a stroke of her hair. 'But it's all right now, darling.'

'I wanna go home,' Dylan cries. Sam kneels down and strips off the protective clothing, then lifts his son up. Grace removes her coveralls, tossing them away with a look of distaste.

'It was fun at first,' she says, 'but they let everyone go mad.'

As they turn to leave, they find a man in a suit marching along the corridor towards them. He's grey-haired, with a neatly trimmed beard and eyes as dark as buttons. Jody thinks she saw him earlier, with Borko. The hotel manager, perhaps?

'My dear lady,' he says, in excellent English. 'Something is wrong?'

Jody tries to explain, Sam chipping in to help. It would be easier, probably, to show him the aftermath, but Jody senses that neither of them wants to go back in there.

The man introduces himself as Naji Hussein, but doesn't say what his position is. He listens with a grave expression, nodding rapidly before they have finished.

'A case of, uh, "high spirits", possibly?'

'Worse than that,' Jody says. 'They're being allowed to run wild.'

'Mm. The play room allows for freedom, and that, perhaps, awakened their inner savagery?' He looks faintly amused by the idea.

'They were attacking the men in the ball pool,' Sam tells him. 'One of them is a waiter from our hotel. The Adriana Beach.'

Hussein gives a frown that Jody feels sure is fake. 'I think you are mistaken.'

Sam shakes his head. 'It's him. Yesterday morning he dropped a tray of glasses. Now you're letting kids chuck things at him, like it's punishment–'

'No, no, no,' Hussein says, as if singing the word. 'A mistake, I promise.'

'I just hope they're all right,' Jody says. 'Some of them were taking a real beating.'

Hussein nods. 'I will investigate. Now, their wellbeing should not be your concern. May I suggest you come out on the terrace and relax?'

21

Sam reads Jody's expression, and says, 'No, thanks.' He hoists Dylan a little higher on his shoulder, hoping it's obvious how tired he is. 'We need to be leaving.'

'Are you sure?'

'The kids are worn out...' He looks at Jody again, sensing that more will be needed. This man Hussein has something of the salesman about him; won't take no for an answer.

'We've had such an amazing time!' Jody says. 'But yes, I do think it's best to get the children back.'

It seems to do the trick. Hussein bows his head. 'One moment, please.'

He enters the play room and unleashes a stream of what sounds like abuse. Jody blows out a sigh and gives Grace a hug. On Sam's shoulder, Dylan wriggles himself comfortable. Then Hussein is back, hands clasped together as if he's praying.

'Order is being restored. And your car will be just a few moments. May I invite you to wait somewhere quiet?'

He doesn't give them the option, marching halfway along the corridor and opening a door. Sam shrugs at Jody. He's aware that he's in no mood to go back and resume the conversation with Gareth and Michelle.

To Sam's relief, they enter some sort of lounge or meeting room, with an eight-seater table and half a dozen easy chairs. There's an opening along one wall, which perhaps has a bar behind it, but it's currently covered by panelling. Best of all, the room is empty. No other guests, no music, no chaos.

'I shall be back very soon,' Hussein assures them, and he closes the door softly behind him.

Jody sinks into a chair and cuddles Grace on her lap. 'Home in a minute,' she says, and Dylan twists round with a hopeful expression.

'Proper home?'

'Well, back to our hotel.'

'I wanna go to our *proper* home.'

'The hotel is our home for now,' Sam gently reminds him. 'Just for a few more days. You like it there.'

'Don't.'

Somehow Sam grins, though by now his patience ought to be wearing thin. Jody matches the smile, but then she frowns. 'I wonder how he knew we were English?'

Sam thinks about explaining his theory, but the door is opening. A waitress enters with a tray of drinks, ice cubes clinking as she sets it down.

'Some fruit juice,' she says, turning quickly to leave.

'Do you know when the car will be ready?' Jody calls after her.

'Uh. I find out.' An uncertain smile, then she's gone.

Sam rests his head back, closing his eyes for a moment. He prays that Jody won't have a go at him for not being more assertive. After growing up with people like Carl, people like his dad, in a pressure situation Sam is never sure how you gauge the difference between being assertive as in *getting what you're entitled to*, and assertive as in *doing something that'll get you arrested*.

Dylan slides off Sam's lap and makes for the drinks. Sam wearily follows, in case of a spillage. While he's there, he picks up a glass and takes a sip.

'What is it, orange?' Jody asks.

'Not sure. A bit of peach or something. Quite tasty.'

'Oh, go on then,' Jody says, and Grace doesn't want to be the odd one out. So they all take a drink, and it's quite pleasant to unwind, just the four of them, in this cool, quiet room.

'Did I overreact?' Jody wonders.

'Dunno. But it was definitely the guy. Our waiter.'

'You said "punishment". Do you really–?' She breaks off as Sam gives her a look, nodding at Dylan and Grace, both of whom, he knows, are only pretending not to listen.

Jody yawns, staring at the ceiling. 'I hope that car's here soon.'

Sam checks his watch but has to blink a few times before the numbers swim into focus. God, he's knackered. Worse than after a day scraping off woodchip in an Edwardian stairwell.

'Five minutes and...' The words come out thick and mangled. *Five minutes and I'll ring for a bloody taxi* is what he wants to say. *Even if we have to pay for it ourselves.*

He tries again but can't finish the sentence. There's a tightness in his chest. His head's swimming and he wants to get up because Jody has her eyes shut. She can't have fallen asleep that quickly – and yet she must have. Her glass has tipped over, some juice spilling out. Grace notices and leans over to pick it up, but her own glass drops to the floor with a thud and she collapses on to her mother's lap.

This isn't right, Sam thinks. We're all tired, fair enough – and yeah, Dylan is asleep, but he's only five, so that's understandable – but the rest of us, the rest of us should...

What?

Sam tries to snatch back the thought in his head, hiding far down in the dark, but nothing comes to him and the glass, now, is so heavy; his eyes, heavy, his legs his arms won't move and he

he can't...

they

can't–

Why?

PART II

ACTIVATION

22

(someone screamed)

... oh, but his head, and he's too warm, he's overheating, and it's making his head feel worse

(POUNDING)

and he wants to stay down, down in the dark where it's safe

(someone screamed)

but he mustn't, he has to come up: it's his du... his duty. Be the bigger man. Be the bigger man and wake up.

Another scream – and *oh Christ* it's Grace, it's his daughter screaming, and now Sam's awake and the pounding in his head comes after him as he tries to sit up, and when he cracks his eyes open the light coming in is burning dazzling *fucking terrible*, like it could kill him all over again.

But he's not dead, he just feels like death. And how he feels doesn't matter if Grace needs his help.

He can't sit up, so he rolls on to his belly. Placing one hand over his eyes, he spreads his fingers to control how much light can get in. There's a rushing noise in his ears, and beyond that a feeling of wide-open silence, interrupted every few seconds with the sort of lonely whimpering sounds that a child makes, woken miserable and scared from a long and disturbing dream.

'Dad...' Her voice is a rasping cry.

'I'm here. I'm here, Grace.' Those are the words his brain sends to his mouth, but he's not sure if that's what comes out.

His eyes are open, the light's shocking but bearable, and what he's staring at is sand. He tries to lift his upper body off the ground but his limbs are weak and juddery. There's a hangover tilt and swirl to every movement of his head, sending an urgent message to his stomach:

Unload. Unload.

And he does, spewing a foul green liquid onto the sand, his stomach clenching as though it's being parcelled up to fit somewhere smaller. Afterwards there's an acid taste in his mouth, a painful flash like a bulb firing in his brain, and within that flash there's a man flying through the air towards him–

No. It's not real. He shuts his eyes and lies still until the image fades. He can feel the heat from Grace's body as she shuffles closer. He manages to turn to her and she's sobbing, her face red, dribbles of vomit on her chin and her neck. They're both sick. Sick, hallucinating, wiped out.

Come on: she needs you.

He gathers his daughter into his arms and holds her tight. She buries her face in his chest; her hair tickles his chin and smells faintly of all the good things he associates with his little girl. They stay like this until her sobbing eases off and the big hitching breaths signal that she's calmer.

But when he looks over her shoulder, what he sees is still a beach. It's no hallucination. A long wide beach, sweeping outwards in a curve that ends with a ridge of higher ground, a natural breakwater formed of – limestone, is it?

'Where are we, Daddy?'

Gingerly he turns his head to check the other direction. It's just more sand, sea, rocks. Trees grow thickly along the top of the beach, almost down to the water at the opposite end of the bay. And there's nothing else in sight. No buildings, no boats, no sign of human activity at all.

He remembers something then, snatches at it like the corner of a comfort blanket. They were – they *are* – on holiday. Somewhere hot. Somewhere like this.

'It's okay,' he mumbles to Grace. 'We're not stranded.'

'But I don't... I don't know why...'

Me neither. Sam has never felt so off kilter, and it's all the worse because he can't think clearly with the throbbing headache, the burning in his gullet. It's like the world has swallowed them up in one place and spat them out somewhere else.

'Do you feel all right?' he asks. 'Are you hurt?'

'Just dizzy. And my tummy's a bit... *yuk*.'

He hugs her again, then studies her carefully. Her eyes are bloodshot, her face pale. She's wearing a black skirt and pink top. Sam checks his own clothing: chinos and a short-sleeved linen shirt. They look creased and grubby, as if he's been in them for a couple of days, but equally it could be from lying on the sand. And his watch has gone, he realises, leaving a band of pale skin around his wrist.

'Where's Mum and Dylan?' Grace asks, her voice cracking with emotion.

'I'm not sure.' Sam hates it that he has to ask this next question. As her dad, he wants to be the one with answers. 'What's the last thing you remember?'

Grace gives it some serious thought. 'We were in a car. A really big car.'

'A Hummer!' He can visualise it himself, and he's sure these are the clothes they were wearing. He manages to sit up, which feels like a minor achievement. Grace is massaging her temple, as if to tease out another memory.

'We were going somewhere. A hotel?'

'Yes.' He clicks his fingers. 'Con... Conchis?'

'Because we won a prize.'

He nods. Now he has more: the rep, Gabby, and a snobby couple who were all set to go in their place. Trevor and someone. Trevor and... Michelle?

No. She's part of another couple. He tries to picture them, but what he gets instead is bright flame shooting from a mouth: a woman breathing fire. *A man flying straight towards me–*

I'm tripping, he thinks. He has various friends and relations who have tried pretty much every illegal substance you could name. After a little dabbling in his youth, Sam decided it was a waste of time and money. No way would he ever *choose* to feel like this.

The party at the Conchis must offer clues, but all he gets are crazy images, like reflections in a broken mirror, which only make him more confused, more frightened – and right now, for his daughter's sake, he can't afford to be frightened.

So, three questions, none of them safe to ask out loud if he wants to keep Grace from panicking.

Where are we?

Why are we here?

What's happened to Jody and Dylan?

23

After helping Grace to her feet, they do some careful stretching to make sure they're not injured in any way. Sam's muscles are stiff with cold and cramp. Judging by the low sun, it must be early in the morning. Could they have been here all night?

He checks his pockets. He has a packet of mints and a couple of tissues. He's also got a small disposable lighter, which he's sure he hasn't seen before, but no cigarettes. Along with his watch, his phone has also gone.

They have a mint each, which helps remove the taste of the bile. 'I'm thirsty,' Grace says, and Sam realises that his mouth is as dry as an old chamois cloth.

'We'll get something soon. Back to the hotel for breakfast, eh?'

A nice try, but there's no mistaking her scepticism as she looks around. 'Where is it?'

'Good question.' He can't bring himself to lie to her. 'That's what we have to find out.'

While he's trying to get his bearings, he notices that the sand where they were lying is scuffed, but beyond that it's completely smooth in every direction. There are no footprints, no tyre marks, no sign of whoever put them here. It's like they just dropped out of the sky.

He examines the ridges at each end of the bay. One is much lower than the other, so he decides to go that way. Grace takes his hand and trudges along with him, saying nothing when Sam looks back – feeling idiotic as he does – to make sure they're definitely leaving footprints in the sand.

In a forlorn voice, she says, 'Were we naughty?'

'Why do you say that?'

'I don't know.' She clings to him suddenly. 'We had guns.'

'*What?*'

'Maybe it was a dream. Even Dylan had a gun, it was really big.'

Sam puts on a brave act, shaking his head and doing his best to reassure her. But the talk of guns has struck a chord. He can picture a scene of blood and chaos.

A sound comes to him, a low-pitched droning that at first seems like another symptom of his raging headache. Then he thinks to look up. High overhead, a passenger plane cuts the morning sky in half, a trail of white vapour spreading in its wake. The sight makes him feel ridiculously grateful: it means the whole world hasn't ended, at least.

The bay is a couple of hundred metres long and the lowest point of the ridge is close to the shore. Before he starts climbing, Sam has a moment when he's tempted to dip his face in the sea and fill his mouth: the idea of cool water is so appealing, even though he knows it's undrinkable.

He helps Grace clamber up. As they reach the top, where a few thin bushes are sprouting from dusty soil, they're able to see that beyond this breakwater lies another wide sandy bay. This one is bordered by a high cliff that extends far out to sea, ending in a stack of fallen boulders. Similar rocks are scattered across the beach, along with clumps of dark matted seaweed.

There is something else, but Sam doesn't realise until Grace, with a tiny cry, points it out to him.

A body.

Sam lets out a groan of such despair that it's probably as upsetting for Grace as if he'd screamed. He regrets it immediately. He's got to hold his emotions inside, no matter how much it hurts.

He starts forward, torn between telling Grace to stay put and wanting to keep her close. He needs to spare her, if it turns out that Jody

(*don't go there she isn't she can't be*)

won't wake up. But leaving Grace alone isn't fair either, and it might not be safe.

'Careful,' he says, as they slip and slide on the way down. He can hear Grace panting and knows it's not because she's puffed out; his own breath is coming in the same short gasps, his heart beating way too fast, blurring his thoughts into a single desperate stream:

Don't-be-dead-don't-be-dead-don't-be-dead

They're closing the distance when Grace points at something else, and Sam catches movement: what he thought was only a clump of seaweed has another body lying beyond it. The figure that kicks and rolls free is Dylan, and now they're close enough to hear him making a sort of mewling noise, as if he's given up hope that anyone will take notice.

'Dylan!' Although Sam roars his son's name, it's Jody he's running towards. She hasn't moved since he first set eyes on her. 'Can you get your brother?' he calls to Grace.

'Yeah. Is Mum...?'

'She's okay, I'm sure.' Turns out that he *can* lie to his daughter, if it's important enough. He's relieved when Grace doesn't argue, leaving Sam to make the horrible discovery alone.

He drops to the sand at Jody's side. She's lying face down, her head bent at an angle that doesn't seem natural. She's wearing the clothes he remembers from the car journey. Her hair is tangled and feels gritty with sand when he cups her head in one hand and with the other tries to ease her on to her back.

Her body feels cool but not cold. From the position of the sun he guesses she was lying in shadow until recently. But she's alive. She stirs when he moves her, eyelids fluttering, then seems to lapse back into unconsciousness.

Sam glances up to check on Grace, who is cuddling Dylan. Sam gives her a thumbs up, and her answering smile claws at his heart.

Leaning close, he gathers Jody in his arms and listens for the gentle whoosh of breath in her nostrils. The pause between each one is an agony in itself. He folds his body around her to lend her some warmth, whispering her name and telling himself that as long as she goes on breathing there's still hope.

24

Jody struggles into the world with the feeling that she is trying to escape many long and terrible dreams, unremembered but for one instance of supreme horror: she witnessed the death of her children.

The sense that she has lost them is so vivid that she's already crying when she wakes to find Sam's arms around her. He's crooning her name, just as he would if he needed to console her through the most unimaginable pain.

'I can't...' she manages to say, meaning *I can't go on. I can't go on living without them.*

It's all she can do to say their names, and when she does he responds at once: 'They're here. They're both here. We're okay.'

He's crying, too, as though it's *her* he's worried about. Confused, she open her eyes, squinting against the glare of the sun, and sees Grace and Dylan hurrying towards them. *Alive.*

Still sobbing, Jody gives a joyful laugh. Only now does she take in the fact that they are on a beach, so she looks round, expecting to see the hotel behind them, and other guests lounging on sunbeds, but there's nothing. They're completely alone. That can't be right...

'How much do you remember?' Sam asks.

It's such a silly question that she almost wants to laugh again. Her brain tries to shift back in time and immediately goes *bump*, as though she's turned to leave a familiar room and walked into the wall instead.

'We...' she starts, and then Grace and Dylan slam into her, hugging and weeping and clinging to her as though *they*'re the ones who had the nightmare to end all nightmares. Still ecstatic that they're alive, Jody is trying to comfort them when it sinks in that she has no idea what time it is – what *day* it is – and no recollection of how they came to be here.

Once she's sitting up, the children get comfortable, Dylan lying at her side with his head on her lap, Grace cuddling up next to her.

'Do you feel all right, physically?' Sam asks Jody. 'Any headache?'

'God, yeah. Like a hangover.'

'Same here. Grace and I woke up on the next beach along. It's like we've been...' – he mouths the final words – 'dumped here or something.'

'But that's...' Her spasm of fear sends a tremor through Dylan and Grace, and Sam winces, looking apologetic. A silent understanding passes between them: they have to be careful how they discuss this in front of the children.

'Do you remember the Hummer?' he asks. 'These are the clothes we were wearing for–'

'The party!' Things are coming back to her. 'At the Conchis. And the president's son was there.'

Sam's eyes widen. 'Oh Jesus, that's what it was.'

'What?'

'Didn't he have... a jetpack thing, strapped to his back? He came flying up towards us.'

'And there were women on stilts, breathing fire.'

'And they took the kids away...'

Together they patch up the holes in their collective memory, adding the mayhem in the soft play area, the tormented waiter from their own hotel. Sam and Jody had brought the children out, and someone agreed to arrange a car home.

'A man... Hussein, wasn't he called?' Jody says.

Sam nods. 'Yeah. They brought us drinks.'

'What time was that – about four or five?'

A tiny snore from Dylan: he's drifted off again. Grace, too, is heavy-lidded, and she has her thumb in her mouth; a habit they'd encouraged her to break three or four years ago.

'And now it's early morning, wouldn't you say?' Sam goes on.

'I suppose. Don't you have your watch?'

'It's missing. So's my phone. And your bag, by the look of it.'

'Oh, shit.' Jody looks around, then checks herself over. No handbag, no phone – and even their hotel's wristbands have been removed. But in the pocket of her cardigan, she finds a small tube of sun cream. 'I know I had this with me, but it was in my bag.'

'So someone put it there, like they wanted us to have it.'

'But why?' She can feel herself trembling; the idea that they must have been drugged, lifted up and carried, that unknown hands were on their bodies, going through their pockets–

She makes a loud retching sound and clamps her mouth shut, willing herself not to be sick. Sam gently rubs her back, then offers her the packet of Polo mints he'd brought to the party.

Jody takes one and places it on her tongue, grateful for a sugar hit. But she frowns at what else he found in his pocket.

'A lighter. Have you been smoking?'

'No. This isn't mine.'

'Then why is it...?'

'No idea.' Sam's voice is shaky, uncertain. He's every bit as scared as she is, and it makes Jody realise what an enormous challenge they're facing, simply to resist the ever present urge to panic.

Wearily, he scrapes his fingers through his hair. 'So we were waiting for a car. Did it turn up?'

'I can't get beyond us being at the Conchis.'

'Nothing else?'

She makes another effort at remembering; again there's that maddening *bump*. 'There must have been something in those drinks. The fruit juice.'

Deep in thought, Sam starts rubbing his chin. 'If it was four o'clock yesterday afternoon, and now it's, let's say, six in the morning? That's... fourteen hours. Do you think that's about right?' He seems to want her to hear the sandpaper rasp of stubble, and now she gets it.

'You mean how much your beard's grown?' She studies his face and agrees that it looks like a single night.

'I guess that's something,' he says, with a cautious glance at the kids. 'That we haven't been unconscious for a couple of days or longer.'

Jody shudders. She's been trying not to dwell on what might have been done to them. She can't feel any soreness or discomfort that would indicate a sexual assault, and she knows that even raising the subject is almost impossible. It would be cruel to put the idea into their heads.

She gazes into the distance for a moment, and notices something else. 'At our beach the morning sun was off to the left. Here it's more to the right. I think we're facing north.'

'Yeah, that's true.' Sam considers. 'So we could be a long way from our hotel – nearer the Conchis, maybe?'

'Maybe,' she agrees, only to add: 'That's if we're still on the same island.'

25

Sam hadn't even thought of that. They could be on a different island.

'I'm so scared,' Jody says. It's barely a whisper, but Sam still wishes she hadn't said it.

'I know.'

'We haven't done anything wrong. Why would anyone...?

Sam can only shrug. He feels like he should be taking charge, but he has no answers, no idea why they've been put here or how they should react. If there's a single positive, it's that the four of them are together and in one piece.

The sun is rising, throwing a fierce light across the beach. Sit here too long and they'll burn, and the heat will make them even thirstier. He realises that finding something to drink has to be their first priority. Water, then shelter from the sun.

Jody breaks the silence with a groan. 'This is insane. It can't be happening.'

'I know. One other thing I noticed, when I woke up, is that there weren't any footprints anywhere. It's the same here.'

She leans forward, still supporting a sleepy Grace at her side, and examines the sand. Then she eases free of her daughter, who sniffs and rubs her eyes. Dylan, too, is waking up. Jody asks Grace to keep an eye on him for a second.

'Where are you going?' she cries.

'Nowhere. Just along the beach a bit.'

'No, Mum, please–'

'We're not leaving you,' Sam assures her. 'We'll be right here.'

Jody is dizzy at first, and has to be supported. Grace and Dylan watch anxiously as they take a few steps towards the shore, where Jody points to a series of small, regular grooves in the sand, running in a neat semi-circle.

'Brush marks. It's been swept.'

Sam can only stare at her. It's almost too much to take in.

Jody says, 'So whoever it is, they left us here and then smoothed out the sand.'

'Is that to confuse us?' Sam wonders. 'So we don't know how we got here?'

They're both following the pattern of grooves towards the water. 'We must have come by boat. So we can't assume we're on the same island.'

Sam points towards the cliffs at the end of the bay. 'We need to find out what's over there.'

'We can't climb that.'

'I know. But if I swim out a bit, I should be able to see past it.'

She moves round to face him. 'I'll do it. You don't like swimming.'

'I'm crap at it, is what you mean. But the sea's calm, and I should be able to hold on to the rocks.'

He won't be persuaded to let her go in his place, though they both have to tramp over there, carrying a child each. When Sam kicks off his sandals, Grace gets upset and they have to spend a few seconds calming her down, promising that Daddy isn't going far, and he isn't doing anything dangerous.

At least I hope it isn't, Sam thinks. But his stuttering memory has thrown up that news story about the young couple who were said to have been eaten by sharks. *Sharks*, for Christ's sake. All he can do is tell himself they won't come this close to shore, but he has no idea if that's true.

He feels stupid rather than brave, stripping off to his pants, his blood running cold despite the heat. His body still has that classic British complexion: pale and pasty, with a few reddish-pink patches on his neck and his knees. Only his forearms are the sort of deep brown colour he hoped to be at the end of this holiday.

Now he couldn't give a toss about a suntan, or anything else. He just wants to get away from here.

The cliff, up close, is even more intimidating than they thought. As Jody finds a spot for her and the children to wait, a couple of birds take flight from the rocks, squawking in alarm, and she finds herself thinking, *Could we eat those, if we had to?*

Trying not to dwell on that repulsive idea, she wraps her arms around Dylan and Grace. Surely they won't be here long enough to get hungry? It's got to be a misunderstanding, or a terrible practical joke. There'll be a boat here any minute...

She doesn't want to watch as Sam wades in to the water. More importantly, she doesn't want the kids to watch. He's right that the sea looks calm, but what if there are strong currents beneath the surface?

Jody takes a sharp breath as his shoulders disappear, leaving only his head visible. He's still got his hands on the rocks, easing his way alongside them, bobbing up and down as if he can just about reach the bottom on his toes. It was how he swam with her in the hotel pool.

Grace clutches at her hand. 'Daddy's all right, isn't he?'

'Of course.' A choke in her voice; Jody pretends to cough. She feels ashamed that they've given in to sexist stereotypes. As the better swimmer, she should be doing this.

Sam glances back, comically spraying water from his mouth, but only Dylan laughs. At ten or fifteen meters out there's a sudden swell: like a living thing the sea rolls and rises, snatching Sam away from the rocks and into deeper water. For a moment he's floundering, then he turns and kicks his legs, splashing clumsily as he fights to stay on course.

Jody is plagued by images of a freak wave sucking him under. She'd have to go in after him – except there's also the children's safety to consider. Could she leave them alone here, with a chance that both she and Sam might perish? The idea of abandoning Grace and Dylan is even worse than the thought of losing Sam.

She is more terrified than she has ever been, but can't let it show. She settles for monitoring Sam on the edge of her vision while also gazing out to sea. Maybe she'll spot a passing ship and they can signal to it for help.

But would that be safe? Try as she might, Jody is struggling to accept that this is any kind of misunderstanding. A misunderstanding is being assigned to the wrong hotel room, or inadvertently taking someone else's sun lounger. There's no logical scenario where a family *accidentally* ends up stranded on a desert island.

Someone has put them here, quite deliberately. Someone who must *want* them to suffer.

'Daddy's a long way out.' It's a careful observation from Grace, spoken in a tone that sounds nothing like her normal voice.

'Not really,' Jody says, although for Sam it is. He's managed to swim clear of the rocks and now he's doggy paddling, his head turned towards whatever lies beyond the promontory.

'I wanna swim!' Dylan suddenly declares, and starts to get up.

'Not now, Dylan.'

'Let me swim, I wanna swim with Daddy!' He lashes out when Jody tries to restrain him, and they end up having a furious tussle, the sort that would get people tutting if it happened around the pool. At first Grace tries to help, but it does no good so she backs away from them, and by the time Dylan has calmed down Jody realises that she's forgotten to check on Sam.

He's gone.

She stares out at the water in disbelief. Beyond the rocks there is only glassy blue sea. It's like he was never there.

Her heart almost stops. She glances at her daughter, trying to work out how she'll deal with the terror, the grief... and yet Grace seems perfectly calm.

Hearing a disturbance close to the shore, she turns again just as Sam's head pops up. He climbs to his feet in the shallows and offers a grim smile.

In shock, Jody says, 'How did you do that?'

He shrugs, taking it as a compliment. 'Never liked getting my head under, but it's actually easier to swim that way.'

The relief comes in a rush. She jumps up and hugs him for a long time, but eventually she has to break away and ask what he saw.

When she does, Sam looks pained. It's not good news.

26

Sam suggests to his daughter that she could help Dylan search for a couple of shells.

Grace scowls. 'Why?'

'I fancy a couple to take home. Please.'

He and Jody return to where his clothes are piled up on the sand. He sighs. The pride he felt at overcoming his fear of deep water seems worthless compared to what he's got to tell her now.

'Nothing but sheer rocks. Even if you could swim round you'd never climb them.'

'What about inland?'

'Trees and more trees. It's like a jungle.'

From the way she shuts her eyes, Sam can tell how much she was praying for signs of civilisation: hotels, a fishing village, a harbour.

'So what next?' she asks.

'Try the other way, I suppose.'

She looks uncertain. 'Or should we stay here? Whoever did this might be planning to collect us–'

He cuts her off with a bark of laughter. 'Do you think that's gonna happen? Like someone's playing a joke on us?'

'I have no idea.' She lifts her arms and lets them collapse against her body. 'I keep going over it, and nothing makes sense. I've even started wondering if we could've, I dunno, *agreed* to this, and then somehow forgot.'

'Why would we agree to *this*?'

'We wouldn't, it's crazy. But so is every other explanation. I mean, perhaps it's some sort of challenge. Survive in the wilderness, like on that TV show.'

'What, *I'm A Celebrity*?'

'No. The one with that posh guy. Bear Grylls. They get a group of people and stick them on an island for a few weeks.'

'Right.' Sam's never seen the show, but it sounds bloody stupid. 'Except we didn't sign up for anything like that, and never would. We came on a fucking package tour. With our kids.'

'I know. I'm only trying to throw out ideas...' In tears again, Jody turns away from him.

'I'm sorry.' He pulls her close and they embrace. As they break apart, he says, 'Might as well try the other direction. We're gonna need to drink something soon, and there's nothing round here.'

'What do we say to the kids?'

'Dunno. Try not to scare 'em, obviously.' Sam hesitates, unsure how to put this. 'But I don't think we can keep everything from them.'

'You know this could scar them for life?'

'Yeah. But when we're in a mess as big as this, lying about it won't help them.'

The moody silence that follows has the feel of a standoff. They watch as Dylan spots something and drops to his knees, digging in the sand. Grace is behind him, hands on her hips; already she looks like a supervisor, Sam thinks. Maybe a manager of something, one day.

And then the real blow: the little stray thought that follows without warning.

Only if we get out of this.

Jody leads the way as they rejoin the children. Dylan has found a pretty white shell. He goes to hand it to his dad before deciding he wants it for himself.

'Okay, mate,' Sam says. 'I'll find another one later.'

'Wanna go home,' Dylan grumbles.

'Listen.' Jody has put on her proper Mum's voice. 'I know this is all very strange, waking up on the beach, but we've decided to treat it as a big adventure.'

'Don't wannoo,' Dylan says.

'Well, we are. And it's going to be really exciting.' She indicates the bay. 'Look how lovely it is here. And we have it all to ourselves, like we did the other day. Isn't that great?'

This time, nothing from Dylan, and Grace wears a blank expression, as though she's already resolved to dismiss anything they tell her.

'So now we'll take a walk along this way, and see where it goes. Okay?'

'I'm thirsty.'

'We don't have any drinks at the moment, Dylan, but–'

'Wanna juice! I'm thirsty, Mummy!'

'Here.' Sam produces the mints and offers them round. It's not lost on Jody that this is the only sustenance they have.

They climb the ridge over to the next bay, retracing Sam and Grace's original route. The scuffed sand where they'd woken is easy to make out, and on close inspection there are brush marks visible here as well. Jody waits until the children have drifted a few paces from them before she speaks.

'I was thinking about what you said, and you're right. We

didn't agree to this, and it's not a practical joke. We've been kidnapped. That means we're victims of a crime.'

It's no surprise when Sam grimaces. She knows that *victim* is a word he associates with weakness, while he – quite rightly, given his childhood – considers himself a survivor, not a victim.

'Okay,' he says, 'but I don't see what good it does to label ourselves...'

'We're not. What's important is that we know where we stand. I mean, supposing there's an accident, and one of us breaks an arm, a leg? You think paramedics are suddenly going to appear out of nowhere?'

'No,' he agrees with a sigh. 'We're on our own.'

The next ridge is a tougher climb, first over rocks, then a dry flinty soil dotted with unfamiliar looking plants. There are a few gnarled trees, with a greyish bark. Jody finds herself checking them for nuts or berries.

Then Sam stops abruptly, gasping with shock. Jody moves alongside him and takes in her first sight of yet another large sweeping bay: pristine yellow sand and blue sea, idyllic in any other circumstances. But Sam is pointing at something near the treeline. Four motionless figures.

'I thought they were people.' He sounds a little embarrassed. It makes no sense until Jody looks closer and works out what they are: four poles driven into the ground, with balls to represent heads. They're lined up at the highest point of the beach, as if staring out to sea. Two tall ones at each end with two smaller ones in between.

Like a family group, she realises.

Like us.

27

Sam remembers the moment when Dylan didn't want to get off the plane. The sight of these stick figures produces the same reaction: they remind Sam of that weird religion where people make creepy dolls to look like their enemies.

This has been set up for one reason: to freak them out. And it's worked.

Voodoo. He gets the word just as Jody points to what lies far off in the distance.

A wall.

'Oh, Jesus...'

The structure is perhaps two kilometres away, partially hidden by several more bays. More rocks and trees to overcome. This is an even bigger shock than the stick people.

Jody sighs. 'It looks like a prison wall.'

'There might be a gate,' Sam says, without much confidence. Dylan clutches his hand, making him jump.

'I'm so *thirsty*, Daddy.'

'I know, Dyl. We all are.'

Leading the way, Sam climbs down to the beach, lifting Grace and Dylan to spare them the last jump. After Jody's warning, he's aware that even a sprained ankle could become a major problem.

As they get closer to the strange little group, they see that the 'heads' are actually coconuts. The poles are simple wooden stakes, like fence posts. The outer ones are roughly two metres tall, the inner ones half that. Jody reaches out and gently prods one of the coconuts. It shifts a little but doesn't fall off. This new angle reminds Sam of the way he sometimes tilts his head after telling the kids a joke: waiting to see if he's earned the laugh.

With both hands, he manages to lift it clear. The head of a nail stands proud on top of the post, having sat inside one of the holes in the coconut. While they puzzle over what this means, Dylan is pushing the stake back and forth, as if wringing its neck.

Grace scans the beach, shielding her eyes from the sun. In a frightened voice she asks, 'Who put them here?'

'I don't know, honey.' Jody exchanges a glance with Sam, who shrugs.

The same people who put *us* here, he thinks.

Dylan, true to the destructive nature of a five-year-old boy, succeeds in wrestling one of the shorter stakes out of the ground before they notice what he's up to. The end that was buried has been sharpened to a point. Sam jokes to the kids about it looking like a giant pencil, but Jody can see what he's really thinking. It will make a good weapon.

He uproots the other smaller stake to take with them, and says, for Grace's benefit, 'They'll help us climb over the rocks.' But Grace only gives him another of her looks: *You must think I'm stupid.*

Dylan has never seen a coconut before. He's fascinated by the weight and texture, and downright sceptical when Jody explains what's inside. Sam tells him to leave it here, but Jody intervenes.

'We ought to take them.'

'They're heavy.'

'I know, but they're food. And the nails haven't pierced the holes, so there's liquid inside we can drink.'

Sam's eyes narrow, perhaps because he doesn't want to acknowledge how desperate they are. Later it occurs to Jody that he simply assumed they'd come back for them – that there was never any hope of getting out of here – but for now they agree a compromise. They'll take two.

Jody fashions her cardigan into a sling and wraps the coconuts up inside, to rest on her hip. They leave the other two in place, now with a lonely gap between them, like parents whose children have been taken away.

With the sunlight growing more intense, they are all flushed and sweating by the time they've climbed the rocks that separate yet another pair of bays. Stopping for a breather, it should be the most natural thing in the world to reach for a bottle of water, but they have nothing.

There's a distant rumble overhead. Sam points to a plane, way too high to be of any help. Jody imagines some of the passengers gazing down at them, seeing only glorious beaches and maybe a few tiny specks that they'll assume are lucky holi-daymakers. *Welcome to paradise.*

On and on they trudge, Jody keeping an eye out for boats. At one point she spots a large vessel on the horizon that could be a cruise ship or a ferry, but it's clearly not heading in their direction.

She estimates that it takes them about an hour to reach the wall, clambering over several natural promontories, stopping frequently to rest. On the beaches they walk in the lukewarm shallows, footwear in hand. There are detours, occasionally, to investigate strange objects half-buried in the sand, which invariably turn out to be nothing more than rocks draped in seaweed.

They've noticed a fair amount of litter – bottles and cans, fragments of fishing nets and other equipment washed up on the shore – but nothing of practical value so far. Jody feels it's important to keep checking, but Sam disagrees. He's impatient to get there.

The heat is putting a strain on their moods as well as their bodies. They pause to apply more sun cream to their faces, and Sam shares out the rest of the mints, but it's water they need.

Even when carried on his father's shoulders, Dylan is constantly grumbling. Finally it becomes too much.

'We're all thirsty, Dyl. Now be quiet!'

'*Sam.*' Jody scolds him, and he nods, crestfallen.

'Sorry, mate. I didn't mean that.'

'We'll open one of the coconuts in a minute,' Jody says. But there's a change of plan, because when they reach the final bay it isn't just a wall that's waiting for them.

28

Sam feels like a lowlife for snapping at Dylan. The poor kid is scared, exhausted and badly dehydrated. No way should Sam be taking out his own frustrations on his son.

The last ridge before the wall is quite low, and there are only a few scrubby bushes on top, making it easier to see what lies ahead. That's the good news.

The bad news is what lies ahead.

One more short curving bay of unspoilt white sand, and then there's another headland, extending far out to sea, with a cliff face that's almost as sheer as the one Sam tried to swim around. On top, the vegetation has been cleared to make way for the wall, which is about three metres high, constructed with large limestone blocks and topped with coils of razor wire.

His first reaction is despair. The wall is like a fortress. No way over it, and a hell of a long swim to get round the headland. Sam probably couldn't manage it, and neither could the kids.

Then he spots movement. In front of the wall there's a narrow strip of rocky soil, with a thin wire fence running along the very edge of the cliff. Within that strip there are dogs.

He counts three at first, sleek, black and dangerous-looking.

Then a fourth one appears: what looked like a shadow at the base of the wall must be a tunnel, allowing the animals to move back and forth. It takes Sam a second to understand what that means. Even if you made it round the headland, chances are the guard dogs would be waiting for you on the other side...

'*Shitting fucking shit fuck.*' This is from Jody, and it makes him jump. It isn't like her to swear in front of the kids, but on this occasion he can understand it.

As they press on, the dogs line up in front of the wire fence. If they break free, could the animals survive a jump down the cliff?

Sam doesn't want to find out. But he goes on striding across the beach, swinging a wooden stake in each hand like a cross-country skier. Jody is just behind, staying close to Grace and Dylan. They've seen the dogs but so far they haven't commented.

He stops when he's some twenty metres away. The dogs have clustered together and stare down at him, silent and still, like they're waiting for him to make the next move.

Sam looks to his right, trying to work out how far the wire fence extends, but once it enters the trees it's impossible to tell. The same is true of the wall itself, which follows the line of the hill, rising gradually away from the coast before vanishing into the woodland.

'Are you sure they can't get to us?' Jody asks.

'Pretty sure.'

'So we could call for help?'

He turns to look at her. 'Really?'

'It can't hurt to try.'

He says nothing, disturbed by a sudden vision of armed men appearing on top of the wall and opening fire. But Jody has taken his silence as agreement.

'*Hello!*' she shouts. The dogs immediately go rigid, backs arching in readiness to attack.

'*Mu-um,*' Grace moans, pulling her mum's arm.

'It's all right.' Jody turns back. '*Can someone hear us? Please! We need help!*'

The dogs are growling, snouts pushing at the wire, paws scrabbling at the dirt. Sam nudges Jody, urging her to back away. She takes the children with her, while Sam stands his ground.

Suddenly he's furious, and lets out a roar: 'WE KNOW YOU'RE THERE, YOU BASTARDS! NOW COME OUT AND FACE US!'

His outburst produces no reaction, other than to send the dogs into a frenzy, tearing up and down their narrow compound. It also upsets the children, and Jody gives Sam a sharp look as they retreat across the beach. He mumbles an apology, only for her to change her mind.

'No. I don't blame you.'

They move briskly until they've cleared the next ridge and put the dogs out of sight. There's some shadow here, at the base of the rocks, and Jody suggests they rest. Her skin is slick with sweat, especially where the makeshift sling is touching it. With a grateful sigh, she drops the cardigan to the ground.

Sam remains on his feet, monitoring the children as they sink on to the sand. Grace finds a brave smile for her dad, and says, 'It's cool here. Feels nice.'

'Good.' He gives a quick grin, but there's a look in his eyes that worries Jody. To her, he says quietly, 'One thing that wall tells us. This is private land. Someone owns it.'

'I remember the rep saying the north of the island has a nature reserve and a couple of estates.' Jody hesitates. 'She also said the president's son has a place on the island.'

'You think we're on his land?'

'I don't know. But the last thing we remember is being at the Conchis, where Borko was the guest of honour. And it was obvious how wealthy and powerful he is.'

They mull it over. Sam's attention drifts away, his gaze unfocused as he calls up a memory of something. 'Gabby,' he mutters.

'What about her?'

'I've been trying to think who'd miss us, at the hotel. And there isn't really anyone–'

'Trevor and Kay?' she suggests.

'Nah. They won't wanna hear us bragging about the party.'

'We wouldn't brag.'

'They don't know that,' Sam points out.

'True.' With a sigh, Jody reflects on that for a moment. 'Anyway, Gabby's got other hotels to look after. I can't see her noticing that we're not there, if that's what you're thinking.'

'It's not.' Sam wears a bitter half-smile. 'I'm worried that she *does* know we're gone.'

He checks on the kids, then eases a couple of steps away from them. Jody goes with him.

'Doesn't it seem funny to you that she was so desperate for us to take up the prize? All that stuff about how offended they'd be, and it was impossible for the Smugs to go in our place.'

Jody stares at him; her heart has begun to beat very fast. 'But that would mean all this was planned – for *us*, specifically.'

'Remember the welcome meeting, how relieved she looked when we turned up. And that's when we got entered into the draw.'

Jody cups a hand over her mouth. There's a cramping in her abdomen that reminds her of the early stages of labour; a feeling that her whole body is about to face an almost unbearable ordeal. She recalls the party, that moment when Borko gazed into her eyes as though he knew who she was...

'I might be wrong,' Sam says, apologetically. 'I hope I am.'

But Jody can only nod. 'If Gabby's in on it, she's not going to report us missing. And the hotel's so big, no one will realise until we're due to check out.'

'Yep. Which means we're well and truly *screwed*.'

He hasn't raised his voice, so it comes as a terrible shock when he snatches up one of the coconuts and hurls it at the rocks. There's an explosion that sends the kids diving to the ground, fragments of coconut flying out like shrapnel.

'Sam!' Jody is furious, tears blurring her vision as she grabs some of the larger pieces. 'Kids, pick up what you can. We can still eat this.'

They ignore her; too startled to respond. Jody can see wet patches in the sand, valuable fluid lost, and she rounds on Sam. 'This could keep us alive, for God's sake. We need every last drop of it!'

As Grace and Dylan rush into her embrace, Sam glares at her with real violence in his eyes, violence and fury and fear. Then he stomps away.

29

Sam hates himself, oh Christ does he hate himself for that. So much rage boiling inside him, but he knows how quickly it will fade and leave him nothing but shame; shame like acid, burning away at the idea of who he wants to be; leaving him to face who he really is.

But he's never been in a situation like this, has he? Where he's pushed to the absolute limit but still has to go on acting as if it's normal.

Jody's right, though. Without water they'll all die within a couple of days. For whatever sick reason, whoever's put them here is committing murder by neglect: a slow and agonising death. It brings to mind the news reports about parents not looking after their kids – cases that have always cut Sam deeply, because he knows he could have suffered a similar fate. His older sisters reckon they often fed him and changed his nappies when his mum was too hungover to bother.

He turns to look at Jody. The mother of his own children is a goddess, compared to that. And what kind of a fuckwit is he to lose it with her?

He heads back, desperate to be forgiven. Jody is kneeling on the sand, showing Grace and Dylan how to scrape coconut from its shell. She senses his approach, looks up and offers him a piece of coconut. 'Here.'

He meekly accepts it. 'Thanks.'

'The meat takes a lot of chewing. But at least it's food.'

'Meat?' Grace queries.

'That's what it's called, the white stuff. It's very nutritious.'

The effort she's making to keep their spirits up shames him all over again. Sam kneels down, gives Grace's back a rub and musses Dylan's hair. Then he rests his hand on Jody's arm. 'I was totally out of order. I'm sorry.'

'Don't worry. Better luck with this one, eh?'

Jody takes the other coconut and fixes it in the sand with its three tiny holes facing upwards, then wedges it between her knees. She picks up a wooden stake, gripping it in both hands with the nail pointed downwards, and jabs it into one of the holes.

'Genius,' Sam mutters. And he means it.

She repeats the procedure with the second hole. So the air can get in, she explains. 'I remember watching my dad do this, years ago.'

With the holes punctured, she lifts the coconut and carefully pours a few drops into her mouth. Shudders slightly. 'It's okay.'

'Grace next,' Sam says.

'I don't want to,' Grace mutters, and Dylan echoes her protest.

'We're all very thirsty,' Jody tells them, 'so we have to drink it. And we need to be careful not to spill any.'

Like stupid Dad, Sam thinks. Grace has a mouthful, pulls a face but swallows it. Dylan, to their surprise, declares that he likes it. Sam is reluctant to take any but Jody insists. He has a small sip – to him it's sweet and sickly – and then Jody finishes it.

'We'll open this when the first one's eaten,' she says. 'And I think we should go back and get the other two.'

They pick up their stuff. Sam offers to carry Dylan on his shoulders but the boy says he's okay to walk. He sticks his chin out a little, trying to show he can't be bossed around. His jaw's still working overtime on the coconut, white crumbs spraying from his mouth when he speaks.

Taking Sam aside, Jody says, 'I wonder if that's where we should stay – the beach with the coconut family.'

He snorts at the description, though inside it makes him shiver. Thoughts of voodoo dolls, and then an image from a fairy tale: the Pied Piper.

'Perhaps they were put there as a sign,' Jody says. 'It's not out of the question that someone'll come to collect us.'

'If you say so.'

After that they walk mostly in silence, gnawing at lumps of coconut. They don't hurry, because that will only make them hotter, thirstier. The sun is well above the horizon, and Sam guesses it's at least nine in the morning, maybe ten. If there's no way off the beach, what are they going to do all day?

Find water, food, shelter. *Survive*.

Easy peasy...

'Ha!' he mutters, and when Jody frowns he shakes his head. 'Nothing.'

But he shifts both the stakes so they're horizontal under one arm, then uses his other hand to work on the nail heads. If he can get them free, they could be quite useful.

It's a small relief to see the tall figures still in place; he'd half expected them to have moved. He also checks the beach for other tracks but finds only their footsteps from earlier. All that's different is the waterline: the tide has come in a little way, the water slip-slapping on the sand.

Jody helps him remove the other coconuts and extract the

stakes. These are hefty pieces of timber – valuable tools, given that their lives may depend on what they can build, or hunt. Jody has mentioned using one of the nails as a fishing hook.

'Mum.' Grace goes down to a whisper: 'I need the toilet.'

Jody nods. 'It should be okay in the trees–'

'No, Mum.' Grace is blushing bright red. 'Not a *pee*, okay.'

Jody leads her daughter into the woods, taking a couple of tissues Sam had in his pocket. It isn't lost on her that, unless they're rescued soon, all of them will have to deal with the problem of bodily functions.

But because she's the first to face it, Grace is mortified. Jody offers to give her daughter privacy, once they've found a suitable clearing, but Grace is too upset to be left alone. Jody tries to make it easier by claiming she needs to pee, though hardly anything comes out. She crouches next to Grace, using one hand to help her daughter balance. While she's glancing round, she notices what seems to be a dirt path through the trees.

Finally it's done. After Grace has cleaned up, Jody digs a hole for the tissues.

'We'll wash our hands in the sea,' she says, and tries for an encouraging smile. 'Actually, we could have a swim.'

'I don't have my stuff.'

'No, but underwear's okay.'

The look on her daughter's face says otherwise. Her hands tremble as they rise to wipe away tears. 'W-w-we're stranded here, aren't we?'

'No, darling...' Jody begins, but it's half-hearted.

'We are. They gave us something to put us to sleep, at that horrible party, and left us here on our own. There's no way back, and they-they don't c-care if w-we... if we d-die here...'

By the time Jody has comforted her enough to move on, she

can barely recall what foolish promises she's made. She understands now why Sam was concerned about lying to them: every false reassurance is simply stacking up problems for the future.

Back at the beach, Dylan has wandered away to investigate a half-buried rock, while Sam is hard at work. He's standing with two stones pressed between his feet and the fat end of the stake facing down, the nail enclosed within the stones. The idea is to wedge the nail so tightly that it can't move, then rotate the stake while also pulling upwards. In theory it's a workable method, but the pressure needed to stop the nail from slipping free is almost impossible to achieve.

'Any luck?' Jody asks.

'Shifting, slowly.' His gaze darts towards Grace. 'You?'

'Yes, thanks,' Jody says.

Even that causes Grace to moan. 'Don't talk about it.'

They wash their hands in the sea, then Jody tries to help Sam, adjusting the position of the stones to grip the nail more firmly. There's a tiny squeak as another millimetre of steel emerges from the timber.

Sam's face has gone bright red from the effort. When he stops to rest, she tells him about the path. 'We probably ought to see where it goes.'

He grunts. 'Dunno.'

'Imagine how silly we'd feel if we walk through the trees and find there's a road, or a café or something.'

'Oh, bound to be a café.' He glances at a non-existent watch. 'Wonder if they've stopped serving the Full English.'

They eye each other for a second, and could easily fall out, but choose to smile instead.

'Okay,' Sam says.

First they debate whether to open another coconut. They're all desperately thirsty, but Jody feels it's too soon. Sam calls to

Dylan, who has already ignored them twice. He's still hunched over, scrabbling in the sand around his rock.

'Dylan! Now!' Sam sets off towards him, and only now does the boy turn, eyes wide and saintly.

'Daddy, look!'

Sam falters. His posture changes. 'Jode.'

She picks up on the tone of his voice and hurries to see what's wrong, Grace alongside her.

Sam is pointing at the ground. 'What's that look like to you?'

Jody examines it, then laughs in disbelief. 'It's a prow.'

'*Prow*,' Dylan repeats, uncertain of the word but no less pleased with his discovery.

'What's a prow?' Grace asks.

'The pointy end of a boat.' Jody turns to Sam. 'Is that the right word?'

Shrugging, he kneels down and scrapes away some more sand before rapping his knuckles on it. The satisfying clunk of timber is unmistakeable.

'Definitely manmade. Those two pieces are joined together, see?' He gazes at it with an expression of wonder, then confusion. 'Who'd bury a boat in the sand?'

Jody only snorts. Surely they're past the point of asking questions like that.

30

Sam suggests using the sharpened ends of the stakes to loosen the sand around the boat. After that it's a case of digging by hand, ploughing their fingers in as deep as they'll go and flinging the loose sand over their shoulders. At first all four of them are at work – with varying degrees of efficiency – until Jody decides that the kids are too exposed to the sun.

They all take a few minutes to cool off in the sea, though Grace only paddles, still in her skirt and top. Then Jody finds the children a patch of shade just inside the trees, and she and Sam get back to work. His neck is starting to burn but he refuses sun cream: instead he drapes his shirt over his shoulders.

He digs feverishly, ignoring the thump of a dehydration headache, and gradually the boat is revealed. It's been buried face down, at an angle of about twenty or thirty degrees, so they don't have to go as deep as he first thought.

It's a classic old-fashioned rowing boat, probably three metres long. There don't seem to be any oars – and no attachments on the sides for the oars to fit into – but apart from that it appears to be intact. It's certainly big enough to carry them away from here.

He stops to wipe sweat from his forehead. The salt stings his eyes and makes it hard to see clearly. Jody, working on the other side of the hull, gives a small worried exclamation: 'Oh.'

Sam feels his heart sink as he comes round to look. She points to a thin black line, running for about thirty centimetres, right where the body of the boat curves towards the thin blade at the bottom. She rubs the sand away, using a fingernail to dig into the groove. When she swears, he understands what it is.

Not a groove. A crack. As she clears out the gunk, Sam can see where the wood has split. She turns to face him, cringing almost. 'I don't think it's seaworthy.'

He stares at it, tilting his head as he tries to visualise the boat when it's the right way up; whether the crack is definitely below the waterline.

It is. Once you allow for the weight of the people on board, there's no chance it'll float.

Sam stays where he is for a long time. His neck starts to ache and he thinks of the coconut, knocked into a crooked pose.

'Daddy coconut, that's me. Just not as bloody useful.'

It's a shock when Jody asks, 'What?' He hadn't intended to say it out loud.

He rises to his feet, the muscles in his back screaming as they straighten and stretch; then he stamps on the hull with all his strength, not caring if his foot bursts through the timber.

'Don't do that!' Jody cries.

'Why not? It's fucked.'

'No, Sam, it isn't.'

He doesn't really hear her, but she dives in front of him before he can launch another attack. Exhausted suddenly, he drops to his knees and falls forward, sprawling over the half-excavated boat like a mourner overcome at a funeral.

He's dimly aware of the kids' voices; Jody urging them to stay where they are. 'It's all right. It's all right.'

It's not all right! he wants to shout back. *It's not fucking all right, because we're going to die.*

Maybe he does say it. The next thing he knows Jody is behind him, her arms wrapped around his shoulders, her breath soft on his neck.

'Don't flip out on me again, Sam. I'm begging you.'

He's sure he'll sob, give himself away, but somehow he doesn't. He shuts his eyes and squeezes them tight. 'I'm so... *angry,*' is what he says.

I'm so scared, is what he can't quite say.

'I know. And I am, too,' Jody says. 'You're not the only one who feels like screaming. Our lives are on the line. The lives of our kids. After all these years, working our guts out, trying to make it a happy childhood. All the effort we put into staying together, so they wouldn't have the misery of their mum and dad splitting up. All that love and care, and it's being threatened by some... *bastard.* Some evil bastard who's trying to destroy us, and we don't know who or why.'

'Jode, please—'

'*No.* Listen to me. I can't tell you how much I keep hoping and praying that I'll wake up and find we're all back in our hotel, you and me a bit the worse for wear after that bloody party, the kids feeling sick from too much cake.'

Despite everything, Sam manages a little snort of laughter. So does Jody.

'But we aren't going to wake up from this,' she goes on. 'We're here, Sam. It's real. And we have to cope with it, the best way we can.'

Silence. Jody's holding him tight, but Sam doesn't say a word. He doesn't push her away. And yet Jody has no idea how he is going to react.

Is that a failing? Does it mean their relationship – almost eleven years together – is a sham? Would a couple that got together as adults, not kids, who didn't have to worry about pregnancy and a screaming baby virtually from the start, have a better understanding of each other?

No, she thinks, I'm not going to beat myself up about our past. How many people ever have to face something like this?

She feels Sam move and quickly releases him, shifting aside to try and assess his mood. There are wet streaks on his cheeks – tears or sweat, or both. He looks subdued, even guilty. That's preferable to anger, but still not ideal. Guilt, in her experience, mutates all too easily into self-pity.

She slaps a palm against the boat. 'To me, this is another sign, like the coconut people. Directing us to this specific beach.'

'D'you think so?'

'Someone's put this here. It would have taken ages to bury it, but they left a bit sticking out, which they didn't have to–'

'Unless it got uncovered by a storm?'

'That's true. But let's say it's here on purpose, for us to find.'

'Why? It's no bloody good.'

'Apart from the split, it looks okay.' She shrugs, glancing around. Grace and Dylan are huddled together in the shade, anxiously watching on. 'There might be some way we can repair it.'

'You'd need glue. It's gotta be waterproof.'

'What about tree sap? Or sometimes on beaches you get tar – like oil, you know? Plug the hole and we've got a working boat.'

'No oars.'

'The stakes?' She's excited, mapping it out in her mind: how they will paddle away from here, triumphant.

'Wrong shape. Oars have to be wide and flat to push the water–'

'We'll fix something to them! Come on, Sam.'

'I just don't think it'll float. If it's good for anything, I'd say use it as shelter.'

'Shelter?' She nearly chokes on the word. *How long are we going to be here?*

'Jode?'

'Yeah. Use it for shelter, then.' She stands up, reaching out to him. 'We need some time out of the sun. Let's check the woods, and find that café.'

He takes her hand. In a lazy, teasing voice he says, 'Maybe it'll have a bar. Cold beer on tap.'

They rejoin the kids and explain that they're going for a walk. Jody notices that Grace's lips already look dry and cracked. She moistens her own and realises how tender they are. Dylan's eyes seem slightly dimmed; he moves sluggishly as Sam helps him up. At home she's always so careful to avoid dehydration that she's never actually witnessed the symptoms. She has no idea how quickly the condition can progress; all she knows is that it's life-threatening.

She leads the others towards the path she spotted earlier. It's narrow and meandering, the hard earth scattered with leaves and twigs. They walk in single file, Sam bringing up the rear with the kids between them. Jody takes care not to trip on hidden rocks or tree roots; she's holding one of the short stakes, using it to beat down weeds or branches that intrude on the path.

There's a stillness in the trees that feels unnatural. No evidence of any human presence, and yet once or twice Jody is conscious of a tingling at the back of her neck. She wonders if there are guards or hunters out here; or could some kind of animal be tracking them?

Then a tiny snapping noise, off to her right. She freezes. Grace blunders into her, as if half asleep.

'What's up?' Sam hisses.

'Nothing.'

Jody stares at the undergrowth, wishing the shadows would transform into something she could identify. Although it's gloomy beneath the trees, it isn't any cooler. The air is hot and steamy, doing nothing to ease their thirst.

Another noise: this time Sam hears it. 'What was that – a bird or something?'

'I suppose so,' Jody says – though when she thinks about it, she hasn't heard any birdsong.

She quickens her pace, as a sign to herself that she's not afraid. Both she and Sam are crap at identifying things in nature, but she's pretty sure a lot of the trees are pines. The scent is very different in hot weather to the one she associates with Christmas. There's also a sort of musky smell, like vegetables left too long in the cupboard.

Then a bright colour catches her eye, a vivid unnatural orange. It's a plastic bag, snagged on a tree close to the path. She immediately spots the possibilities: maybe it could be used to repair the boat.

Hurrying forward, she has only a millisecond to register that the leaves beneath her feet are yielding when they should have crushed against the hard ground. Her foot sinks and she pitches forward, a whole section of the path giving way, and even as she falls she's pushing one arm out behind her, all her focus on trying to save Grace from the same fate...

31

Sam has been walking with his head down, guiding a fretful Dylan as he stumbles along the path. When it happens, the first thing Sam hears is a strange dragging noise, then a shriek from Grace. He looks up and Jody is gone, while Grace is teetering on the path, windmilling her arms as if trying not to fall.

Sam grabs her shoulder just in time. As Grace staggers back, he's able to see that the path has become an open pit, deep and black. There's a strange pattern over it, like a giant cobweb, and it isn't until he's moved the children back and taken their place that he understands what it is.

A net. It's well camouflaged, black nylon covered in leaves and small branches, and it's bowing inwards, stretched tight by the weight of the person caught inside it. Jody is lying face down in an awkward sprawl, one leg bent at the knee, the other stretched out where her foot has caught in one of the holes. Sam can hear her urgent panting and along with the shock there's also relief. She's alive, at least.

Then she sucks in a breath and screams. Sam leans closer, trying to work out how he can reach her without getting tangled up himself. The pit is about two metres square and a couple of metres deep, and Jody's in the centre, dangling just above the bottom–

Sam gasps. Did something move down there?

Jody is dazed, only half aware of what's happened. She feels bruised, and has had the breath knocked out of her, but doesn't think she has any broken bones. She's all twisted up in a net, and can't move. Below her there's darkness and a dank mulchy smell. As her vision adjusts, she notices the gleam of something alive, slithering through the rotted leaves. Must be a worm or a slug.

Except that more and more of it appears – too long and fat to be a worm. It's pale in colour, a kind of mottled brown, its body thick and sinuous, weaving from side to side as it moves.

A snake.

Jody screams. Snakes are one of her few real phobias. The previous summer the kids' big treat was a day out at Drusillas zoo, and in the reptile section – even with protective glass between them – Jody couldn't bear more than a few seconds before she had to get away.

Her body seems to shut down. The floor of the pit is only half a metre from her face. The snake is coming towards her. She shifts her head a fraction and sees another; this one is pale, thinner, with a strange little lump on its head, like a horn. It, too, turns in her direction.

She tries to scream again but her lungs are too constricted. A couple more snakes glide into view. One of them lifts its head off the ground, its yellowish eyes like buttons, zeroing in on her...

The net twitches. Her body reacts with a violent convulsion, as if she's already been bitten. Maybe she has. Maybe there are more, hidden in the trees, sliding over the edge and dropping on to her from above.

Something takes hold of her foot and at last she can draw in the air for another scream.

'Jody! Jode!' It's Sam, trying to calm her down – or maybe he's warning her that a snake has wrapped itself around her ankle?

She kicks her foot and the net dips and shudders. Then another shout. This time Sam's voice is clear and close. His hands are on her arms. He's got hold of her, dragging her away, using his own weight on the edge of the net to roll her towards him.

As she turns, she's able to reach out and make it easier for him. She tries to push with her legs but one foot slips through the netting and she almost faints from the terror. She'd gladly break an ankle if it means getting away from the snakes.

Then there's solid ground beneath her hands, and Sam is hauling her out. She's safe. But for a minute it won't compute, and she isn't able to stop shivering and crying until she registers the effect it's having on the kids. She has to draw on every bit of strength to appear calm and focus on giving them comfort, reassurance.

But Sam is still frowning as he stares at something beyond her, down in the pit.

'Oh, shit,' he mutters.

At first Sam assumed she was panicking because of the fall. It wasn't till he knelt down that he saw what was really freaking her out, and now he's managed to rescue her, he doesn't want to do anything other than get the hell out of there.

But when he glances back to make sure the snakes have stayed put, he sees what else has been hiding in this deep dark hole in the ground.

'Oh, shit.'

He doesn't hesitate: thinking about it will only put him off. He grabs one of the wooden stakes and leans forward, easing his body onto the net. He counts four snakes of different colours and sizes; he hasn't got a clue whether they're poisonous, whether some are more deadly than others. But he can't let that distract him.

There's a prize to be had here. A hell of a prize.

Jody is calling after him, confused and upset, and he can't spare her a long explanation so he tosses back a single word.

'Water.'

Two big bottles of the stuff. They're propped up in one corner, half covered by a pile of leaves. It makes him feel sick to think he might not have noticed them at all; and then he wouldn't be doing this.

Jody, disbelieving, says, 'What do you—oh God, *Sam!*'

He grunts, trying to concentrate on his balance and positioning on the net, and the movement of the snakes in relation to the water. The holes in the net are large enough to feed the stake through, but his arm scrapes painfully against the nylon strands.

He jams the stake into the ground a few centimetres from the bottles and uses it to lean on with his left hand. The nearest snake curls away. The others are at a safe distance for now

(nothing's safe they're lightning fast and they BITE)

so he forces his other arm through. His fingers stretch out and fumble the neck of one of the bottles, but it's not quite within reach. He needs to be further out on the net, so his weight forces it down a little more. But that also means coming closer to the snakes.

'Sam, be careful.'

'Yeah.' He can hear the kids whimpering, Jody trying to pacify them. The net makes a groaning noise as it sinks a little lower. His arm at full stretch, it feels like he's going to dislocate his shoulder... and then his fingers close around the bottle and it's his – just as one of the snakes comes nosing towards him.

Sam yanks his arm back, squeezes the bottle through the net and is going to throw it to Jody until he realises that it might burst. Instead he holds it out for her.

'I've got it,' she says. 'Come back now.'

'Nah. The other one.'

She says something else but he tunes her out, delving down before his nerve fails. One of the snakes is easing closer, slyly, as if hoping Sam won't notice. He can't afford to take his eyes off it, but that's okay: he knows where the bottle is and can reach for it without looking.

The relief when it's in his hand is a beautiful rush. He's picturing the ecstasy of a long refreshing drink as he starts to withdraw his arm. Nothing the snake can do, so Sam glances at the bottle to make sure he's holding it securely, and that's when he sees that there is a fifth snake, long and thin and bright red, wrapped tightly around the bottom of the bottle.

The shock is too much. A shudder of panic causes his body to spasm; his hand opens and the bottle falls back and lands on its side. The tiny snake, just as startled, vanishes beneath the leaves.

32

'Come on, get up,' Jody's taking a big risk, reaching out to grab his arm. Sam nearly loses hold of the stake but manages to pull it out, transferring his weight to her as she leans backward. His body lurches on the net as if he's on a bouncy castle, then he throws himself on to solid ground, collapsing at her feet and curling into a foetal position.

She crouches beside him. He's shivering, breathing far too quickly. His eyes are tightly shut, and the expression on his face alarms her. He's having the same reaction she did: in his mind he's still down there, amongst the snakes.

'Sam, it's all right. You did it.'

Finally he opens his eyes and straightens up. Jody urges him to move further away from the pit: she doesn't want the children coming too close. Then she beckons to Grace and Dylan, and as a family they embrace, and share their relief.

There's the feel of a religious ceremony, almost, when Jody holds the bottle up for everyone to see. Foreign writing on the label, and a plastic seal still intact around the lid. Two litres of pure water. After God knows how many hours without proper fluid, it's an unthinkable luxury.

Except that Sam goes on fretting. 'What about the other one?'

'Leave it for now.' *Get it tomorrow*, she thinks. Then: *Oh God, please don't say we'll still be here tomorrow.*

Jody breaks the plastic seal and carefully removes the lid. Dylan is almost wilting as he stares at the water, but Jody wants to test it first, to make sure it's drinkable. She has a single mouthful and savours the feel of it on her tongue, swilling it round as though it's a fine wine. She moistens her lips and gums, only now appreciating how dry and sore they've become.

Then she kneels to supervise while Dylan has a few sips, warning him to take it slowly so he doesn't choke. Grace is next. She sips once, twice, stopping sooner than she needs to.

After her, Sam takes an even smaller amount and insists that's enough for him. They debate whether to continue along the path, and decide it's too dangerous. But Jody points to the carrier bag. 'That could be useful.'

Sam wants to fetch it but Jody insists on going. She plots a cautious route around the pit, testing each step before she sets her weight down, scanning the trees for other lurking hazards. The bag looks so innocuous, snagged on a branch as if blown there, and yet it was the bag that had lured her forward, into the trap.

Just as they planned it? she wonders.

She unhooks the bag, checks there's nothing inside, then makes her way back. Staring at the pit prompts another thought.

'Should we take the net?'

Sam has had the same idea. He's studying the ground, trying to work out what's keeping it in place. It turns out there are half a dozen cables – bungee cords, Sam calls them – buried in soil and leaves and looped around the trees on each side of the path. As Sam unhooks each one, and the net begins to sag, Jody grows uneasy.

'What about the snakes?'

'It's not the net keeping them there. If they could climb up the sides they'd easily get through the net.'

'Yeah, of course.' She tries to focus on the net. 'Could we catch some fish with this?'

'I doubt it. Look at the size of the holes.'

He's right. And even if they caught one, how would they clean and prepare it? They've no tools, no utensils, and precious little expertise.

Sam gathers up the net and slings it over his shoulder. He's taking the bungee cords as well. A remark about building a shelter makes Jody's legs go weak at the prospect of being here at night. In the dark. Alone.

She lets out a sob – just the one – then crams all the negative feelings back inside. It's a brief moment of utter hopelessness, something to indulge and then regret, like a bitter chocolate.

Walking back, Sam takes the lead, frequently turning to make sure they stay close. He's wary of the possibility that there could be more reptiles loose in the woods.

There's a moment when Grace yelps, and Sam, imagining the worst, turns and raises the stake as if he's about to hurl it through the air. Grace is rubbing the bottom of her leg.

'Something stung me.'

Jody takes a look. 'There's a red mark. A bite, I think.'

Another problem to face in the coming hours. Jody was careful to bring all kinds of sprays and lotions, but out here they have no protection other than the sun cream, nothing to ease the pain of insect bites or stings.

Up ahead, the trees are thinning out before the wide sweep of the beach. Beyond it, the sea is as flat as a pool table, a million sparkles of sunlight dancing across the surface. Sam steps into the white hot glare and flinches, narrowing his eyes and turning away.

But not before he spots the boat.

Doubting his own eyes, he looks back. A sleek white yacht is gliding swiftly from left to right. Much closer than the ship they saw earlier, though still a fair way out.

'Hey!' he cries, as Jody eases past the children to see what's wrong.

'Is that...?'

'Yeah.' Sam drops everything and goes racing down the beach, yelling and waving his arms. Jody does the same, and at the water they splash into the shallows and jump up and down and scream.

'HERE! LOOK OVER HERE! HELP US! HELP!'

It does no good. The yacht doesn't alter its course. A couple of minutes and it's no more than a white speck on the horizon, but still Sam and Jody go on shouting, waving, *hoping...*

Until they don't, anymore.

And now they have to face the kids. After making so much effort to downplay the trouble they're in, they've just gone and shown how serious it is.

Sam takes Jody's hand and they walk back up the beach. Grace and Dylan are sitting by the rowing boat, knees drawn up, arms wrapped round their legs. Sad eyed and solemn, like a couple of grubby urchins from the olden days.

Jody sniffs. 'This is starting to remind me of that film with Tom Hanks.'

'Where he's stranded after a plane crash?' Sam tuts at the memory. 'Stuck on his own for years, with only a football or something for company.'

'Yeah.' She squeezes his hand. 'But he manages to get home at the end, though.'

'Only 'cause it's Hollywood. They wouldn't make a big movie

where he's alone all the way through, and then dies. Who'd want to see that?'

Wrong thing to say, he realises too late.

But Jody, in a matter-of-fact tone, says, 'In our case, someone *must* want to see it. Because they might have left us some water, but we shouldn't kid ourselves that they care whether we live or die out here. They don't.'

And on that happy note...

Rejoining the children, Jody says brightly, 'Who wants some more coconut?'

Grace is absently rubbing her leg and won't meet Jody's gaze. She knows exactly why they tried so hard to signal to the yacht. Dylan, looking tearful, shakes his head.

'Sure, Dylan? Aren't you hungry?'

'Want something else.'

'There isn't anything. Later we might try to catch a fish.'

'I wanna go home.'

'I know. And we will. But not yet.'

'I *want* to. I wanna go *home*. I wanna go home *now*.'

'Don't get whiny on us, mate,' Sam says. 'It won't be long.'

'Yes, it will,' says Grace, scratching at her leg.

'Ssh.' Jody frowns. 'Try to leave it alone. You'll only make it itch more.'

'It *already* itches, Mum. That's why I'm scratching.'

Jody takes a breath. *Be calm.* She'd love to suggest they have another drink, but she has no idea how long it's got to last.

Taking refuge beneath the trees at the top of the beach, they discover that a slight breeze has sprung up; it's cool and refreshing. With Sam's help, she cracks open the coconut she drained earlier and distributes more chunks of the white flesh. But Dylan shoves her hand away.

'Don't want it.'

Before he can get fractious again, Sam grabs him into an embrace that turns into a tickling competition. After a bout of near hysterical giggling, Dylan sits back in a better mood – for now.

Nibbling on a lump of coconut, he says, 'When are we going home?'

'Soon,' Sam tells him.

'Tonight?' Grace asks, her voice loaded with disbelief.

'No, probably not tonight,' Jody says. 'Tomorrow, hopefully.'

'Hopefully,' Grace echoes sarcastically, but Dylan is nodding as if a solemn promise has been made. His trusting nature is much harder to bear than his tantrum. At his age, Mum and Dad are still like gods: all knowing, all powerful. It breaks Jody's heart that his faith is so cruelly misplaced.

When their jaws ache from the effort of chewing, Jody passes the water round: two big mouthfuls each. Sam only wants one but she insists he has the same as them, to keep his strength up.

Then the children lie down on the sand. Jody helps them get comfortable, rubbing Dylan's back until he falls asleep. Once they're both off, she and Sam can rest. Jody shuts her eyes but sleep won't come. She settles for counting the seconds until she can feel the day slipping past, as indifferent to their fate as that big white yacht.

After a while she murmurs, 'Why us?'

'Uh?' Sam jerks a little; perhaps he was dozing.

'That's the one thing I can't make sense of. Why us?'

'There's no point, Jode. You're just torturing yourself.'

'No. *They*'re torturing us. Putting us here for no reason. Hiding water in a hole full of snakes.' She can hear her voice getting emotional; the tone of his sigh signals that he doesn't want to hear it.

'You're not gonna find answers by going round and round it in your head.'

'I can't help it. The idea that this might not be random, that we might have been chosen–'

'Can you leave it, Jode? Please.'

There's a moment of bitter silence. Jody wants to scream – or slap him. But either reaction will wake the children and make things worse.

Instead she looks away, stares at a patch of milky blue sky and asks, 'What are you hiding from me?'

She can almost feel the shockwave from this sudden change of direction. Sam has to swallow before he replies.

'Nothing.'

'You are. For weeks now. Months.'

'I'm not.' A big heaving sigh, but it sounds theatrical. 'Jesus, of all the times...'

'Okay, so when? *When* are we going to talk about it?'

33

Sam can't argue about this now – and he certainly can't discuss it calmly. He jumps up and marches across the beach. Running away, he tells himself. But so what?

To work out his frustration, he goes back to digging the rowing boat out of the sand, scraping away with his fingers until the sweat comes running through his hair and dripping from his nose like a leaky tap. His shirt is useless against the sun's raw heat. His back feels like a hotplate. His throat could be a tube of sandpaper filled with sawdust.

But the boat is virtually clear, and apart from that one crack along the side, it appears to be intact. Sam finds the long stakes and works them beneath the hull at a diagonal angle. Once they're in place he beckons to Jody, hoping there won't be a price for her co-operation.

She trudges over and gets to work in silence. Grace and Dylan wake and come running when they see what Sam and Jody are doing, pushing on the stakes to lever the boat out. It takes several attempts before the sand – with a comical sounding *sloop!* – gives up its prize.

After that, it's still a battle to flip it over. There's a lot of sand stuck inside the boat, hard-packed and slightly damp, sticking like cement in the voids behind the crossbars of timber seating.

The kids are helping to clean it out, laughing when it quickly turns into a fight, flinging handfuls of sand at each other – but mainly at Dad. Amazingly, despite the godawful trouble they're in, Sam is struck by the fact that there's still some pleasure to be had from being together as a family; no one on their phone, no one sloping off to watch TV. If only they were doing something like this at home, where they would be safe.

Jody can't see the point of testing the boat in water, but Sam insists that it's worth a try. If nothing else it's an easier way of cleaning out the last of the sand.

They drag the craft down the beach. Grace and Dylan are beside themselves with excitement, which Sam finds worrying. For all that he and Jody keep stressing that they're not going anywhere, the kids might well have assumed they're being deceived. It wouldn't be the first time, after all.

Sure enough, there's a bad reaction when the boat sinks in less than a metre of water. Dylan flings himself down and has a full-on tantrum, screaming and kicking his feet. Sam can't get cross: he feels like doing the same thing himself.

'It's still going to come in handy,' Jody says. 'We'll use it for shelter, probably.'

'Or firewood,' Sam adds with a snort. He's not serious, but it does prompt another thought. Just because it's sweltering now doesn't mean it'll stay that way. He suggests they find some wood to make a fire.

'For tonight?' Jody says, as if she can't believe what she's hearing.

'Yeah. Unless you have a better idea?'

Jody doesn't. And she's bitterly regretting what she said earlier.

However valid her suspicions, this wasn't the time to raise them. Now she has turned Sam against her, at the one moment when it's essential to be united.

Dragging the boat out of the sea is an arduous task. After filling so rapidly, it seems to take an age for the water to drain, and in the meantime it's all extra weight. But they do have to think about shelter, and the boat seems like their best option in that respect.

This, she finds, is the hardest part of the day: having to play the role of happy-go-lucky mum, smiling and joking, keeping their spirits high when inside she's burning, seething, ravaged by frustration and fear. Sam knows this – and he feels it too – but somehow he's allowed to be sullen. He's forgiven for snapping at them, for swearing, because that's just what men are like.

If a dad does his bit it's treated as something to be admired, worthy of applause, whereas with mums it's simply expected. Until today Jody had no idea how angry this makes her.

The sun is noticeably lower in the sky when Sam decides they've gone far enough, a few metres from the treeline. They prop the boat on its side to speed up the drying process. A swim to cool off, then back to the shade of the trees, where they're each permitted a mouthful of precious water.

It does little to quench their raging thirst, so Dylan and Grace are given another sip. The bottle is more than three quarters empty already. Jody finds it a struggle to replace the lid and set it down. Her tongue feels swollen, like some alien creature has taken up residence in her mouth. All she can think about is water. She obsesses over the second bottle, but every fantasy of sloshing it down her throat is countered by the horror show of a snake bite and a slow, excruciating death.

These images parade before her eyes, but it must seem to Sam as though she's merely gazing out to sea. He moves alongside her, a couple of metres from where the kids are nibbling, disinterestedly, on coconut.

'They aren't coming,' he murmurs.

'What?'

'They aren't coming for us. Not today, anyway.'

'I know that.'

'So why do you keep looking?'

'I'm not.' She isn't sure if that's true, but it feels too lame to admit that she can't quite give up hope. Because he's right, isn't he?

Sam shields his eyes with both hands and stares for long enough to give her heart a little jolt. What has he spotted?

'Look,' he says at last, and when she squints she sees it too: a thin line of cloud bubbling up on the horizon. 'First cloud we've seen all week, isn't it?'

Yes, she thinks. *But it's not a boat. It's not rescue.*

'What are we going to do?' she asks, in a tone that she never intended to sound so dejected.

He snorts. There's about half a second when it threatens to go seriously sour, the mood between them, but as it turns out he doesn't want that any more than Jody does.

'Stay alive,' is all he says, slapping his hands against his sides.

The long and the short of it. Stay alive.

Sam returns to the task of removing the nails from a couple of the stakes. Soon he's panting from the effort and swearing at the difficulty of doing this without tools. A claw-headed hammer and he'd have it out in seconds.

To spare the kids from hearing words they must never repeat at school, Jody suggests they take the net and try to catch a fish. It's an idea that meets with little enthusiasm, and she virtually has to drag them across the beach. Sam is glad of the chance to be alone; not having to wear a brave face for a while.

He tries to empty his mind of thought while he works away at the nails, the way he likes to do when he's painting with a roller. No stress or worry, just a sort of gentle *la-la-la* in his head while his hands do their thing. Meditation, of a kind, he supposes.

It's probably a good half hour before the first nail comes free. And what a sweet victory that is, even if he hasn't yet decided how it will be of use. A brief rest, then he looks for something else to do. Jody is chest deep in the sea, trying to sweep the net through the water like a bullfighter swishing a giant cape. Grace is off to one side, helping in a bored way, and Dylan is lost in a world of his own, swirling one of the stakes back and forth in the shallows. Sam hopes they'll get lucky, but it doesn't seem very likely.

After examining the point of the nail, an idea comes to mind. He's been trying not to dwell on Jody's little attack, but it still hurts.

There's a strip of metal fixed to the boat, some kind of ID tag with a number stamped on it. He studies it and finds that the tip of the nail will just about slot into the heads of the screws that hold the tag in place.

It doesn't take him long to get them out; then he uses the nail to prise the tag away from the hull, leaving a pale strip of timber, like a patch of skin after a plaster's been removed. The tag is made of steel, but thin enough to bend with just the pressure of his fingers. He's idly playing with it when Jody and the kids come trudging back, empty-handed.

'Forget that, then.'

She sounds desperately disappointed. Sam knows he must lift her spirits somehow, so he says, cheerily, 'Try again later. I'll give you a hand.'

Except that this earns him a glare, as though he's suggesting it won't succeed unless he's there to help. He shakes his head, then frowns, pointing behind her. 'See that?'

The clouds are massing like an army preparing to invade, their shadows darkening the sea at the horizon to a leaden strip. Off to the left – the west, it must be, just as Jody guessed – the sky has taken on an eerie orange glow. There's still a searing heat to the air, especially as the breeze has faded away, but this feels like something different. Something *powerful* is coming.

'Better get that shelter sorted quickly,' he mutters.

Jody goes on staring, distractedly, at the sky. 'You think it's going to rain?'

'Looks like it to me.'

'Honestly?' Still with that disbelieving tone, which has Sam wondering what he's missed.

'Yeah. A sky like that at home, you'd expect it to piss down.'

Now there's a big childish grin on her face. 'Oh God, can we be that lucky?'

'Jode, we're gonna get soaked.'

'Yes, we are.' She's laughing, delighted. 'With *water*.'

34

It's not all good news, of course; Sam has some valid points about the temperature dropping, the fact they have no warm clothes, no blankets or bedding. At the very least they'll have to find a way to escape the rain – but oh, to be able to drink as much as they want...

Jody takes the kids on an expedition to gather firewood. None of them are keen to venture far into the trees, especially with the shadows deepening. It's late in the afternoon, she guesses, and about fifty-fifty whether the rain or darkness will reach them first. Jody fights the urge to jump at every little sound, but she can't shake off a feeling that someone's watching them.

Grace has barely spoken since the abortive attempt at fishing, but when Dylan runs back to his father with an armful of kindling, she says, 'How do you know we won't be stuck here for ever?'

'Because...' *I don't*, Jody thinks, and for a moment the horror of that admission can probably be read in her face. 'We're not going to be, okay? If no one comes for us, we'll find a way out ourselves.'

'How?'

'I don't know yet. But we will.'

'I'm not a baby,' Grace says in a forlorn voice. 'You keep pretending it's going to be all right, but it isn't. You don't even know who's done this, do you?'

Jody, devastated by her inability to offer any solace, can only shake her head. 'No.'

'Or *why* they're doing it.'

'No.' She swallows. 'But we are going to find out. And the most important thing is that your dad and I will do everything we can to protect you and Dylan. You do know that?'

Grace nods, her eyes shining with tears, but Jody can read her mind. *It won't be enough.*

They return with more kindling and about a dozen large branches. With the inside of the boat having dried out, Sam comes up with an ingenious design for their accommodation. By driving the two longer stakes into the ground, he's able to prop the side of the boat against them at a forty-five-degree angle. It's a kind of clam shell arrangement, creating just enough room for the four of them to crawl beneath it.

She joins him while he's studying his handiwork and slips an arm around his waist. After a second, he hugs her tight and they gaze out to sea. The peachy glow of sunset is like make-up applied to the dark bruise of the sky.

'Wind's changing,' Sam says, with what might be a tiny shudder. A sudden chill in the air raises goosebumps on her arms. The storm is on its way.

Staring at their makeshift camp, Sam comes up with another idea. He wants to craft a ridge of sand around the boat to act as a windbreak. It might also help to divert some of the rain.

Here at last is a job for which the children are perfectly suited, building what is essentially a sandcastle – or a sand city wall, at least. They launch into the task with such energy, compared to their lacklustre support for her fishing idea, that Jody can't help feeling hurt. Out here, she realises, every disappointment is magnified tenfold, every emotion as tender as blistered skin.

By the time it's done, the cloud is stealing overhead and the sun has gone from the sky. It's cooler, if not exactly cold, and the air has a taste to it Jody can't quite identify. She keeps smacking her lips together, only to be reminded how dry they are.

Next up is the fire, a simple task thanks to the lighter – but even this makes her fret. *Why did they give us a lighter?* Using it feels strangely like cheating, perhaps because everything else has been such an ordeal.

'Might not last, if it does rain,' Sam says, blowing with expert care to help the flames take hold. Starting fires is one skill he *did* acquire during his turbulent youth.

'Don't you think it will?'

'Probably.' He sniffs the air. 'Thought it would've started by now.'

It's Jody's idea to use the fire not just for warmth, but as a way of making their only source of food more appealing. She skewers lumps of coconut on the hooks at the end of the bungee cords and dangles them above the flames. Hey presto: hot roasted coconut.

The kids eat with slightly more enthusiasm, probably thanks to the caramelised aroma. Cooking it has altered the taste, but not enough for Jody's liking. She has consumed enough to silence the hunger pangs. What she craves now isn't food so much as *flavour*: different tastes and textures. But more than that, of course – more than anything – she wants water.

It's a big decision to use up what remains. Jody argues that they are all dangerously dehydrated, and with rain on the way they should be able to replenish it. Sam agrees, despite some obvious reservations, but Jody takes the bottle and passes it round before he can change his mind.

'It had better bloody chuck it down,' he says. 'And we need to find a way to trap it.'

Another problem. Jody, in all honesty, hadn't looked much beyond cupping her hands and throwing water into her mouth.

They puzzle over the best way to refill the bottle. The darkness closes in, swallowing the distant bays and blurring the line between sea and sky. In amongst the trees it's pitch black; with every shiver of wind the branches stir, setting off a chorus of rustles and crackles and creaks. Anything could be prowling around in there, she thinks: predators both animal and human.

Jody has never regarded herself as being scared of the dark. At home she'd barely register this transition from day to night. Why would she, when she can simply switch on lights and draw the curtains? Doors and windows are effortlessly shut to keep the world at bay; within seconds they are cosy, warm and safe – whereas out here they are mercilessly exposed.

She turns away from Grace and Dylan, knowing her emotions will be all too easy to detect. The self-interrogation is up and rolling again, a form of torture made worse by her pitiful response to her daughter's questions.

How long will we be here? Why is this happening? What will become of us? How long will we be here? Why...?

It's little wonder that they've all been edging closer to the fire, enticed by the hypnotic motion of the flames, the lively pop and hiss of burning wood. When there's no true sanctuary to be found, no hope other than what may be conjured from your own resilience and courage, the warmth and light of a fire must be the most ancient form of comfort on Earth.

A tiny noise makes Jody flinch: the tap of a fingertip on the hull. None of them are anywhere near the boat. Could someone be creeping up on them...?

Then it happens again, followed by a scattering of soft explosions in the sand.

The rain.

Sam can't think of a system for funnelling the water into the bottle. He feels sick and weary with frustration at his own failings. Why isn't he *better* than this?

Even the idea of a funnel was prompted by a throwaway comment from Grace. It makes him impossibly proud: eight years old and she's way cleverer than him.

He watches her, staring at the fire with an expression he knows well from his own childhood: sad and angry, hopeless and determined, all jumbled up in a hot turmoil that can barely keep the tears at bay. He remembers pulling his scabby duvet over his head, stuffing the material into his ears to block out the sound of his mum and dad going at it: screaming, fighting, sometimes fucking; the interfering cow next door yelling that she was dialling 999, even though she never did.

Sam's insides shrivel to see his daughter like this. All he's ever wanted is for her and Dylan to grow up without feeling the way he did: scared, lost, alone.

'All right?' he asks.

Grace jumps, blinks away the pain and nods, but it means little. Then her eyes light up. She holds her hand out, palm up, as if asking for something. Sam has nothing to give her but she goes on smiling.

'Did you feel that?'

Jody, too, is looking around. There's a *plunk* as a fat raindrop hits the boat. Sam's still far from sure that this is anything to celebrate, but their mood infects him and he grins, turning to look upwards and catching a drop right in his eye.

'Ow!'

The kids are giggling when Jody claps her hands. 'The plastic bag!'

'What?' Sam asks, but she's thinking hard and won't explain. She wants them to strip to their underwear.

'Ugh! Why?' Grace wants to know.

'To have dry clothes to put on.'

Sam nods. 'It's worth it. No one'll look, I promise.'

'You can keep your top on,' Jody tells her, 'and wear mine later.'

They do as she suggests, then Sam stashes their clothes inside the upturned boat, using the central seat as a shelf. He finds Jody digging frantically in the sand, while Grace has fetched the plastic bag. Dylan is standing by, grasping the empty bottle in both hands. The rain falls as they work, soft in their hair, hard and stinging on their skin. It's cold but somehow pleasant; for now they're warmed by the effort, the excitement.

When the hole is deep enough, Jody sinks the bottle into it and replaces the sand, forming a tightly-packed bowl shape around the top. She uses a nail to pierce a hole in the centre of the plastic bag, which she lays over the bottle, smoothing the rest of the bag against the sand. As the rain hits it, tiny rivulets run down to the centre and drip into the bottle.

'It's working!' Grace cries, and Jody claps her hands and throws herself onto her back, thumping the sand with her fists as she shrieks with pleasure.

'*Yip-pee*! *YIP-PEE*!'

Sam copies her, lying back with his mouth wide open. The kids look on in disbelief, as though their parents have lost their minds, then they too join in. It's a delicious, delirious moment, going crazy in the rain, the sand turning dark and damp around them, the sea pitted and fizzing under the onslaught, and even a single distant flash of light does little to break the spell.

35

Jody forgets to count, but she thinks it is several seconds before they hear a low-pitched rumbling. It goes on for so long that she starts to wonder if it could be something other than thunder. Gunfire?

'Bears,' says Dylan, with a frightened moan. He has a grim fascination with the beasts, inspired by a nature documentary where a grizzly bear was standing face to face with a man; Sam, not very helpfully, remarked that the bear could take the man's head off with one swipe of its paw.

More lightning out at sea: not just flashes this time but jagged purple bolts.

Dylan clings to his dad, burying his face in Sam's chest. 'Don't like it.'

'I know, Dyl. But it's nothing to worry about.' Sam exchanges an uneasy look with Jody. 'We ought to get under cover.'

It's true that the novelty of drinking the rain has quickly faded; for the first time Jody is aware of how cold she feels. The fire is dying before their eyes.

'Should have stashed some wood in the boat,' Sam says ruefully.

They crawl under, Jody and Sam lying with the children between them. They use their clothes as both a groundsheet and a blanket, but the only real warmth comes from their bodies.

The noise is extraordinary: a constant angry drumming on the wood, the torturous *plop plop* as water drips off the sides; the boom and suck of waves against the shore. Raising her voice to be heard, Jody works at keeping their spirits up, pointing out how exciting this is, and won't it be great to tell their friends about it? Absurd to think there's any chance of sleeping in these conditions, but that's what she urges them to do. *In the morning we'll light another fire, and guess what's for breakfast, kids? Well, it ain't bacon and eggs, and it ain't Coco Pops...*

Now they're lying down, they realise they are all sore from sunburn. Grace keeps fidgeting, scratching her leg, and Jody can't think of any way to distract her or lessen the discomfort. They discuss the early part of the holiday – the lovely hotel, the kids' club and a chance to try archery – until Grace starts to cry.

'We'll miss the boat trip. I was really looking forward to that.'

If not for the conversation earlier, Jody might have been tempted to pretend it was still a possibility. Instead, she says, 'I know you were, darling. I'm sorry.'

She's lost for words when Grace, after wiping her eyes, says, 'You don't have to say sorry. I know you're doing your best for us.'

It's mostly dry under the boat, but for how long Sam isn't sure. The crack in the hull is leaking slightly, and the sand wall is taking a pounding from the rain, lumps of it collapsing into sludge and dribbling towards them. He feels cold, drained, clinging to his son just as much as Dylan is clinging to him.

Sam keeps thinking about the fire. So bloody dumb not to

have stored some dry wood ahead of the rain. Christ knows how long it'll take to get another one going tomorrow.

He starts idly fantasising about setting the whole forest alight. Surely people would come to investigate, and they'd be rescued?

Lightning blasts the sky. The thunder is an instant behind, so loud and close that they all wince. It really does sound like something splintering, as though part of the world is being cut into two.

Sam isn't sure what makes him leave the shelter. There's the reason he'll give to Jody, but he'll wonder later if it was sheer panic, more than anything.

He eases free of Dylan's embrace, wriggling past the stakes that hold the boat in place; then rolls and jumps to his feet, hearing Jody's question turn into a cry of alarm.

'The water,' he yells back, as if that's any sort of explanation. Right now, to him, it makes sense.

This will only take a second. There's no real danger.

As he kneels to move the plastic aside, there's an explosion overhead, stunningly loud. A bolt of lightning strikes the beach, a shower of blue sparks sizzling at its base. Sam rocks back from the energy of it, his skin prickling with static. There's a weird electrical smell in his nostrils. The image stays burned into his vision for a few seconds, white hot in the darkness as the echoes of thunder roll away across the sea.

It could have hit me, he thinks. *It's that close.*

He lifts the bottle: more than half full. He dashes back to the boat, skids on the wet sand and comes down hard on his arse. But he doesn't drop the water. *Result.*

Jody is gaping at him, her face bleached of colour in the last of the light. 'What are you doing?'

He holds out the bottle. 'Gotta make the most of it. I'm still gasping. Aren't you?'

She nods, and offers it first to Grace. It's not easy, trying to drink when the four of them are crushed together, and they can't sit up without hitting their heads on the boat. But eventually they've shared it out. Sam takes the empty bottle from Jody's hand.

'I'll put it back. Fill it up by morning.'

For a moment she's ready to beg him not to go out there again; he can read it in her eyes. But she doesn't. The water is keeping them alive. It's worth the risk.

This time it takes longer. He has to make sure the hole in the plastic bag is centred correctly, otherwise the water will run into the sand instead of the bottle.

When it's done, he stands up and hears a loud buzzing noise. He can feel the tingling on his skin, the hairs reacting to the electricity in the air a split second before–

BAM!

Then he's lying flat on his back and has no idea how he got there. Sam opens his eyes and quickly shuts them again, one arm shielding his face from the needles of rain. His head is fuzzy, confused. The echoes of another massive thunderclap slowly die away. Only then does he hear Jody screaming his name.

He twists on to his side and is able to rise a little. His frightened family are peering out at him, sheltering like mice in a shoe – *is that some kind of fairy tale he once read to Grace?* – and behind them, in the woods, there's a tree blazing in flame. For a moment he wonders if he went through with his mad idea: the nuclear option.

No. Must have been another lightning bolt. It looks like the rain will soon extinguish the fire.

Climbing to his feet, unsteady at first, he realises he was

thrown several metres by the strike. No wonder they look worried. He raises a hand to signal that he's okay.

In fact, against all the odds, he feels a hell of a lot better than okay. He might be standing in a storm, cold rain streaming down his body, but the pain and discomfort are lost in an overwhelming rush of energy. He feels more alive than he's ever been, as if the lightning has rewired his brain. With a dream-like certainty he understands that he is as much a product of this earth as any tree or rock, as much as the sand or the sea. His existence as an individual human being is practically worthless, but that's fine. What matters is that he is part of the universe, no more or less important than any other part.

His veins seem to be coursing with all the power of the storm. Clenching fists as heavy as hammers, he throws back his head and lets out a bestial howl of emotion. This is the payoff for cheating death by a matter of centimetres. He has come up against the raw might of nature and survived, and this brings him strength, a sense of calm – and even confidence.

We're going to get through this, he declares to himself.

We will survive.

36

The children appear to sleep quite soundly, but Jody is awake for long stretches of the night, and so is Sam. At best they manage only the sort of restless nerve-jangling slumber that she remembers from when the kids were newborns: part of her brain always alert to the tiniest movement or noise. The best thing she can say is that they are at least resting, conserving some energy for the coming day.

She'd imagined that sleeping on sand would be fairly comfortable, but it's agony. There's constant torment from whatever kind of bugs or lice make their home on the beach, and then there's the emotional torture: the compulsion to revisit the many terrible experiences of the previous day. The wall, the snakes, the dreadful thirst.

The lightning strike that blew Sam off his feet.

At first she thought he was dead. That memory alone is bad enough; worse is how she reacted. To her eternal shame, she shut her eyes, unable to bear the sight of his body.

But Sam wasn't killed, and when he came back to the shelter there was a manic gleam in his eyes. He was keyed up, vibrating with energy. After kissing Jody on the lips, he held his children close and promised them that they would all survive.

'We just have to stay strong. Stay strong and believe in ourselves, okay?'

His fervour scared her a little, to be honest, but what choice did Jody have but to nod and smile?

Eventually the storm moved off, and the intensity of the rain gradually eased. For a time, until the clouds began to break, there was utter darkness. You could hold your hand in front of your eyes and not see it.

Now, waking suddenly, Jody is aware of a weak light filtering into the sky; enough to illuminate several layers of wrung out clouds. She can hear the lonely echoing cries of a seabird circling overhead.

Her whole body is stiff and aching, her skin itching from insect bites and sore where the sand exfoliated her as she writhed in her sleep. The stuff has worked its way into her ears, nostrils and just about everywhere else. The realisation that they are still trapped, with no proper food or drink, makes her want to sob.

She lies there for a while, fighting the apathy, the despair. The other three go on sleeping, Sam twitching and moaning, Dylan and Grace nestled together on the clothes that form their bedding. Jody is squeezed in tight against the edge of the boat, so the only way to move without disturbing them is to crawl upwards, wriggling over the rain-sodden sand.

She makes it out, collects her sandals but stays on her hands and knees until she reaches the hole. She lifts off the plastic bag and discovers that the bottle is full to the brim. It's a wonderful sight, although realistically there still isn't enough water to keep the four of them hydrated for more than a few hours.

After putting the lid on without taking so much as a sip – she'd feel too guilty to drink it alone – she stands up and stretches until her limbs come back to life. There's a freshness to the air, with the day's heat yet to build, and it's a bit chilly to be wearing only her bra and knickers. But she can't retrieve her dress or cardigan without disturbing the kids, so she'll just have to put up with it.

The equipment they'd gathered is lying nearby. Jody studies it with a thoughtful gaze.

She already knows what she wants to do. The question is: can she do it?

She picks up the net that failed to catch them any fish, folds it into a manageable size and slings it over her shoulder. She also takes four of the bungee cords and one of the shorter stakes. Once she's equipped, she glances again at her family. Restless but still asleep, as far as she can see. That's good, because the temptation to wimp out is growing by the second.

The tree that caught a lightning strike is a mangled wreck, one side charred and twisted. It makes her shudder, realising how close Sam came to a similar fate.

She's ultra-cautious on the path through the woods, fearing the presence of other traps that the day before they might have missed by sheer chance. Realising she needs to pee, she works out that this will be the first one since the previous morning. But the urine that dribbles out is dark and pungent, and accompanied by a dull ache from her kidneys.

All the more reason to do this.

Today there seem to be a few more signs of life. Birds are chirping in the trees and insects buzz and whine. Here and there she spots dragonflies and bright shiny beetles, and once a plump lizard races across her path–

Some of these things are probably edible.

The thought produces three reactions: first the inevitable

growl from her stomach, followed by a shudder of nausea, and finally a nagging impression that an important idea hasn't quite crystallised: some connection she ought to be making.

She pushes at it for a while but gets nowhere. She's virtually tiptoeing, probably more from reluctance than caution. The trees are still dripping from the storm, creating a surround sound performance – *plop*! *tap*! *plunk*! *splat*! – that reminds her of those arty modern symphonies where the musicians use hose pipes and car parts and God knows what else.

But now she's here.

Back at the pit.

She swallows. It hurts her throat. Her mouth is drier than ever, like a cave lined with salt. Peering down, she counts three reptiles and then waits, waits a long time before she spots the tip of what might be the fourth – the pale one with the horn or whatever it is.

Four. She goes on staring, searching, and doesn't find number five. What to do?

She can't wait forever: her nerve will fail her. And the sun's coming up. She imagines Sam waking and finding her gone. If this goes wrong, he might not discover her body until the hidden life of the forest has begun to consume her–

'So don't fail!' For the final time she runs through the plan she formed while lying under the boat. The pit is slightly deeper than she figured, but it still ought to work.

She kneels down, then has an image of the missing snake gliding out of the undergrowth behind her. Turning, she kicks away the leaves so there's a clear patch of earth between her and the nearest trees. Probably won't help much, but it makes her feel slightly better.

Now for the pit itself. She lays the net down and unfolds it until it's a couple of square metres in size. She uses two bungee cords to hook the corners together, drawing them up to construct a makeshift basket. A third bungee cord is tied around the other two: this is the handle, enabling her to lower the net into the pit.

She lies flat on her belly. The ground beneath her is cool and damp, with a rich organic smell that makes her think of food: mushrooms especially.

Oh, yes: pizza loaded with mushrooms. And pepperoni, and thick strings of gooey cheese...

Her stomach lurches with desire. Some sort of bug goes scurrying past and Jody imagines her tongue snapping out to collect this tasty treat. Once again, along with the hunger and revulsion, she's tormented by the sense of something she's not seeing.

She dismisses it and moves forward, placing her head and both arms over the edge of the pit. The net is a lot heavier than she expected. Lowering it with her arms outstretched, it's all she can do not to let go of the cord. To get more control, she shuffles forward. Now her chest extends over the pit. Her toes are pressing into the earth, but they make for a poor anchor.

Topple over the edge and you're dead, you'll never see your kids again...

There's a little relief when the bottom of the net sags against the ground, only a few centimetres from the bottle of water. She gauges the strength she'll need to keep hold of the net with one hand, the hook of the bungee cord biting painfully into her palm. Then she twists round, reaching for the wooden stake with her right hand.

When she turns back the thin red snake, bolder than the others, is probing at the edge of the net. In a spasm of shock she almost lets go, recovering just in time. She brings the stake thudding down like a spear and the snake retreats, curling up in disgust. She can see the horned one in the far corner, apparently not interested, but the others are hidden among the leaves.

She has to forget them. This next bit is tricky enough even without the distraction. She wriggles forward again and jams the stake into the ground, using it like a crutch, the way Sam did. She's poised at the absolute limit, and the net is resting next to the water. She has to joggle it round to get it flatter, then she lifts the stake and tries to bring it across in tiny hops. With each one there's a gasp from the effort. From the fear.

She's done this all wrong. She's now reliant on the stake for her balance, but she also needs it to push and prod the bottle into the net.

'Fucking hell!' she growls, easing back a little; not too much, because she'll drop the stake or pull the net too high for the bottle to go in. If I was a bit taller, she thinks. If I had longer arms...

If I was Sam.

But she's not Sam. And she can't expect him to take all the risks. The bottle is there, right next to the net. It's doable. She needs to focus, use the strength in her hips and shoulders to keep her upper body rigid; then her arms can work freely.

She moves forward again, only this time the soil at the edge of the pit crumbles and collapses beneath her.

37

Sam wakes in a rush and tries to sit up, hitting his head with a *clunk*. Where the hell is he?

Settling back in a daze, he rubs his head and wipes his eyes. Everything hurts: his skin is gritty with sand and it feels like he's covered in bites. That's when he remembers – they're prisoners on the island. And last night, a huge storm; he was hit by lightning, almost, but afterwards he felt...

How did he feel? The memory doesn't seem reliable; more like a dream. Wasn't he strong, confident, optimistic?

Huh. That sounds insane.

There's a body pressed against him: Dylan. He's asleep but his sister isn't. She's propped up on one elbow, frowning. Sam smiles to reassure her.

'It's fine. Just bumped my head.'

But Grace casts a glance over her shoulder and then looks back at him, no less anxious.

'Where's Mum?'

Jody is sliding forwards, helpless; already she's thinking about how she can fight off the snakes once she's down amongst them. Then it dimly registers that she still has the wooden stake in her hand.

It can hold her up. It can save her.

She shifts on to her side, losing hold of the net because all that matters is staying out of the pit. She tightens her grip on the stake, painfully flexing her wrist as she drives the timber into the earth and at the same time pushes herself backwards. There's dirt and debris raining down, agitating a thick brown snake that has been hiding directly beneath her. Sneaky bastard.

Now she is safe – she thinks – but to bring the stake out she has to grip the edge of the pit with her free hand, trying to find the solid rock beneath the soil. The ground has been softened by the storm: that's what caused it to give way. Otherwise she might have succeeded.

Once she has a firm hold she's able to lift the stake, then retreat and get on to her knees. She stares morosely at the pit. She doesn't want to go back empty-handed. No water – and worse still, she's lost the net.

Desperate measures, she thinks after pondering for a minute. Taking the remaining bungee cord, she loops it twice around her ankle, then fixes it to one of the trees close to the path. There's enough play in the cord to reach the pit, but it should prevent her from falling in. Why hadn't she thought of that at the start?

She finds a drier spot, testing the ground carefully before lying flat once more. This time it's easier to manoeuvre because she can grip the stake in both hands, wielding it like a golf club. At full stretch she's able to nudge and roll the bottle on to the net. A bit of finessing to make sure it's caught in the folds, then she eases the stake under the bungee cords.

Every time she thinks she has it hooked and gently starts to lift, the stake slips free and the net drops back. She's reminded of a fraught afternoon in an amusement arcade when Grace was four or five: burning through nearly ten quid trying to win her a toy rabbit from one of those claw-grabbing machines. Jody failed then. She cannot, *must not* fail now.

Sweat pours down her face as she leans over for what must be the eighth or ninth attempt. This time she stretches to the limit, the bungee cord taut and burning around her ankle. She hooks the net again, twitches and joggles until the cords are more secure on the stake, and then she lifts, she lifts, ever so carefully – *gotta land this prize without it slipsliding away* – and at last the net comes up, and the bottle comes up inside the net, and the snake, the snake comes up along with it...

Sam can't believe he's leaving them alone. His children, so precious that he'd give his life for them in an instant: literally without a second's thought. But what choice does he have?

Jody might be in trouble. If she is, he can't have the kids tagging along while he searches. He can't bear the thought of them witnessing... whatever it is they might witness.

So he has to trust them. He instructs Grace not to leave the shelter of the boat. Dylan is still asleep, and Sam prays he stays that way. Depending on his mood, the boy will either obey his big sister or throw a paddy and do the opposite of whatever he's told.

Grace, understandably, is worried about the responsibility. 'If he wakes up and you're both gone, he'll scream his head off.'

'I'll only be a few minutes, I promise.'

'Where's Mum? Why did she leave us?'

Sam doesn't want to think too much about that second question. But at least he can point to the tracks in the sand.

'She's gone into the woods. Maybe needs the toilet.'

'But there are snakes!'

Sam gives Grace a hug and repeats his promise that he'll be

back soon. Everything's all right, he assures her. But he doesn't believe that, and he suspects Grace can see the truth.

He knows he ought to take the path slowly, but the need to find Jody is far too powerful. He's sick with fury that she went off without telling him; even sicker at the thought of what might have happened to her.

In places the ground is sticky with mud and mushy leaves. It gets him thinking about puddles, maybe even a stream somewhere deeper in the woods. Water they could collect and boil up to drink.

By now he's guessed where he'll find her. Some of the anger fades, but the anxiety is still there. He feels his chest tighten, then he's metres away from the pit and through the trees he spots Jody flat on the ground, a wooden stake in her hands, wobbling under the weight of whatever it is she's trying to lift out of the pit.

'Jode,' he says quietly, not wanting to startle her.

'*Unh*,' she says, too focused to reply.

Sam edges closer and gains a clearer view of the net, wrapped up and bound together with the bungee cords. Jody's almost brought it up to ground level. Nestling within it is the second bottle of water. *What a star*, he thinks.

'Let me help.' He crouches down to grab the water, and that's when he sees a fat brown snake coiling through the wide holes in the net. It's facing away from him, its head only centimetres from Jody's hands, which are white-knuckled and trembling with the effort.

She hasn't noticed it. By the time she does, it will be too late.

Sam's reaction is completely spontaneous – something that, if he thought about it, he could never, ever make himself do. He grabs the snake somewhere near its tail. There's an immediate shock that it feels so different to how he expected: cool but not cold, and not at all slimy; instead it's dry and firm to the touch, and unmistakeably alive. Its movement revolts him, and he knows he should be holding it near the head, but that wasn't possible so all he can do is snap his wrist like he's tossing a Frisbee and fling the creature as far as it'll go.

His arm jerks outwards and his body bends at the waist, trying to put even more distance between them, but the snake's head whips round and something – a tooth, fang, whatever – grazes the back of his hand as it reels away. The snake lands on the far side of the pit and is lost in the undergrowth.

Jody is flagging, the net still not quite on firm ground. Sam gathers it in, making sure the bottle is safe. She lets out a juddering sigh as he takes the weight. There are tears in her eyes, sweat on her face, her hair tangled and dirty. As she stands up, he sees that her underwear is grubby and stained; she's covered in bites and sores and there are muddy smears on her stomach that look like war paint. Like some brave warrior queen from the olden days.

The breath catches in his lungs. He reaches for a posh word to describe how she looks to him, and settles on... *magnificent*. She *is* magnificent, and in that moment he has never felt as much love or desire for anyone as he does for Jody.

38

She did it. And Sam helped, appearing out of nowhere as she was about to drop the net. Now there's an odd expression on his face. Jody's expecting fury but it's not like that at all.

'What?' she says, bewildered.

'You. You're... amazing.' His voice is breathless. There's a familiar gleam in his eye that's ridiculous in these circumstances. She's caked in mud and covered in bites and bruises. She must look dreadful.

'I didn't see the snake. Thank God you were here.'

'You did most of it.' Embarrassed, Sam glances at the back of his hand. Jody feels her stomach cramp in horror.

'Did it bite you?'

'It's all right, I think.' He points to a pale pink scratch below his knuckles. It doesn't seem to have broken the skin but she examines it to be sure.

'Can you feel anything?'

'It's fine.'

'Really?' They're standing close, probably in a cloud of sweat and grime, and yet he's gazing into her eyes as though they're on a balcony in Paris or somewhere.

'I love you,' he says, his voice boyishly sincere.

'I love you, too.'

'I don't want to lose you.'

'You wo–'

He cuts her off with a kiss. His arms go round her waist and pull her close. The kiss gets deeper, more urgent, and Jody realises she wants him with the same reckless fervour that Sam wants her, no matter how filthy they are. But they can't, and it's for the usual reason.

She breaks away. 'Where are the kids?'

'I left them at the boat.' Sam looks disappointed, but says, 'Guess we'd better get back.'

Nodding, Jody takes a step and nearly goes flying. She'd forgotten the bungee cord around her ankle. At least it provokes a laugh from Sam.

'Well, if I'd known you couldn't get away...'

'Funny.'

She kneels to remove the cord, and a couple of insects come zig-zagging across her path. That's when she gets it: the connection she should have made.

'You know we talked about reality shows?' She indicates the pit. 'Having the water hidden among snakes, it's like one of the trials on *I'm A Celebrity*.'

'Yeah, but it can't be. We didn't sign up for–'

'I hardly think they care about that. The point is that you don't set up something like this if you can't observe how it plays out.'

Sam looks lost, then stunned. 'They're watching us?'

'They must be. Otherwise why go to all this trouble?'

He says nothing. Jody unhooks the other end of the bungee cord and leans back, craning her neck to look into the higher reaches of the tree. Any camera has got to be positioned with a clear line of sight over the pit.

It takes her a while to spot it – or rather, to make sense of what she's seeing – but there appears to be a small black circle, or ball, nestled in the V shape between the trunk and one of the larger branches. About the size of a golf ball, with leaves carefully positioned all around it.

She motions at Sam to come and look, but he lets out a low growl, like a warning.

'Come here, Jode.'

'But I've found–'

'Ssh! Listen.' He edges towards her, and murmurs, 'We shouldn't let on that we know.'

'Why not?'

'It's better to act normal, while we give ourselves time to think it through.'

That seems like a wise move, so they say nothing more until they're heading back along the path. Keeping his voice low, Sam points out that there are probably more cameras at the beach, and perhaps microphones as well. 'If you're spying on people, you don't just want to see them. You want to hear what they say.'

I'm A Celebrity isn't a show they watch regularly – she and Sam tried one series out of curiosity and decided it was stupid, cruel and ultimately quite boring. But even as a non-viewer, the overexcited media coverage means it's impossible to ignore when the series rolls around each year – the endless discussion about who's in, who's out, who's a wanker, who's surprisingly calm and inspiring...

Her dad claims that the producers write scripts for all these reality shows and then assemble the footage in a way that presents the story they've already decided to tell – she's a diva, he's a creep – and never mind if it's only a few seconds taken out of context from thousands of hours of footage. The punters lap it up as the gospel truth.

So what's our story? Jody wonders. In the past twenty-four hours she's been brave, cowardly, clever, stupid, angry, calm, dithering, decisive, a good parent, a terrible parent: often many of these things at the same time. And Sam, too.

Is the footage being used to tell a story about them, and if so, who's telling it?

And *why*? Always that heart-rending, energy-sapping, unanswerable question.

What is the purpose of this hideous experiment?

Now he's on a bit of a roll, Sam outlines his idea about finding water they can boil up. To make a fire they'll have to gather some branches and leave them to dry on the beach. And collecting firewood gives them an opportunity to search for more cameras.

Jody grins. 'Sneaky.'

'That's what we've gotta be like from now on. Us against them. It's war.'

He can't quite bring himself to ask why Jody took such a big risk, going off on her own, but when he congratulates her again she makes an embarrassed comment about how much he did the yesterday: swimming out to check the headland, venturing into the storm to refill the bottle.

'Getting struck by lightning,' he adds drily.

'Yeah, that was too close for comfort. You could have had a heart attack.'

'Nah, not me.' He pats her bum. 'I'm much too young and fit.'

He wants to kiss her again but through the trees comes Grace's voice, high and scared. 'Dad! Is that you?'

They run the last few metres, and mum and daughter have an emotional reunion.

Dylan hangs back, looking uncertain, even shifty. It's the sort of expression he wears when he's broken one of his toys and hidden it so they won't notice.

'I heard a noise,' Grace says finally. 'It was like a boat.'

Sam and Jody stare at her. 'Are you sure?' Jody asks.

'I think that's what it was. You know the small ones that have the little engine fixed to the back? That sort of noise.'

'But you didn't see it?'

Grace shakes her head. 'It was over that way.' She points to the west, in the direction of the impassable headland.

Sam heaves out a sigh, aimed at Jody. 'Bloody typical. Just when we weren't here.'

Grace winces. 'Should I have gone to look?'

'No, darling,' Jody says. 'That's not what Daddy means.' To Sam, she whispers, 'Perhaps it wasn't a coincidence, given what we've found?'

Sam narrows his eyes as it dawns on him. If they're under surveillance, the watchers could have seen them go into the woods and timed the boat to come by in their absence.

'Better check it out,' he says.

Jody agrees, but first they all need some water. 'And coconut for breakfast.' She gazes thoughtfully at the sea. 'No, a swim to freshen up first. Plus sun cream on our faces.'

Sam expects Dylan to protest about the sun cream, but there isn't a murmur from him. In fact, he hasn't said a word since they got back.

'You okay, Dyl?'

No reaction. Jody kneels at his side, putting her arm around him. 'Probably tired, eh?'

Still nothing. Grace looks awkward, shifting her weight from one leg to the other. 'Don't start again,' she mutters to her brother.

Jody frowns. 'What do you mean?'

'Ask him.'

'We had a fight.' Dylan glares at his sister. 'Because of the lady.'

Now Sam is lost. 'What lady?'

Dylan gives a pantomime shrug: *How should I know*?

'No, come on, Dylan,' Jody says gently. 'Please tell us.'

His bottom lip wobbling, Dylan manages to say, 'The angel lady!' Then he bursts into tears.

39

While Jody comforts her son, Sam decides to open the second bottle of water from the pit. After testing it, he passes the bottle to Grace and asks her what Dylan is talking about.

'He said he saw someone. I told him he was making it up.'

'But you were meant to stay together!'

It's a fierce response, but Grace only sniffs, defiantly, and says, 'After he woke up, he wanted to get out from under the boat. He didn't *go* anywhere.'

Sam nods. 'All right, sorry. So he might have seen someone?'

'No. Because I had a look, and there wasn't anyone.'

'Sure?' Jody asks.

'*Yes*. I'd tell you if someone was there.'

Once Dylan has stopped crying, Jody encourages him to show them where he saw the woman. He indicates the ridge between their bay and the next.

'And what was she doing?'

He looks blank. 'She was on the rocks.'

'Did you see her walk along, or climb up?' Sam asks.

Dylan shakes his head. 'Just standing.'

'What do you mean by "angel lady"?' Jody asks.

Dylan bows his head, presses his palms together and holds them in front of his chest, as if praying. Jody and Sam exchange another mystified glance.

'Why didn't Grace see her?' Sam asks.

'Are you sure she wasn't moving?' Jody says. 'She didn't wave to you or anything like that?'

But Dylan won't answer any more questions. It's turned into an interrogation, and all they're going to do is scare him.

'Well, it doesn't matter now,' Jody says. 'Let's have a swim before it gets too hot.'

She falls in with Sam as they walk down the beach. After the turmoil of the last night's storm, the sea is almost deceptively benign, flat and calm and a pure deep blue.

'Think I spotted another camera,' Sam whispers. 'Up in the first line of trees, facing down over the boat.'

'So we're right about the stick figures. The boat. It was all put there so we'd choose this beach as our base – and then we could be watched.'

'Yeah. But we have to act like nothing's changed.'

Jody still isn't sure what this will achieve, but decides not to argue. She indicates Grace, tentatively swishing her toes in the shallows. 'Do you think there was a boat?'

'No reason to doubt it.'

'So this...' – Jody can't say *angel* – 'this woman Dylan saw, it could have been someone from the boat?'

'Maybe. But I can't see why she'd be standing there.' A pause, before he says, 'What do you reckon?'

Jody runs a hand through her hair. 'I don't know what to think anymore.'

Sam can't help marvelling at how Jody manages to shrug off her doubts. Once they join the kids in the water, she's acting as though this is just another ordinary day. It's a great achievement – and it's definitely the right thing to do, for the sake of the kids – but at the same time it only adds to his anger and resentment at whoever's put them here.

They shouldn't have to *pretend* anything.

They swim in their underwear, then it's back to the boat, where they dry off and dress. With all the salt and sweat, their clothes feel rank, but Jody insists they have to keep covered up. It's going to be another scorching hot day, and there's only enough sun cream to protect their faces and necks.

She opens the third coconut and carefully shares it out. While he eats, Sam can't help casting frequent glances towards the western ridge. With salt in his eyelashes, his vision keeps blurring, and for the second or two until it clears, he almost believes that he might see her – Dylan's angel lady.

But is she a good omen, or bad?

The knowledge that they're being watched won't leave him alone, and he worries that it's making their conversation sound false. He thinks again about his lunatic idea of setting the woods alight. That would show up on camera soon enough – and on a hot dry island you'd take a forest fire pretty seriously, wouldn't you?

As Sam ponders, his hand finds something unfamiliar in the pocket of his chinos. It's the thin metal tag he removed from the boat. He hasn't yet found a use for it, though an idea comes to him now. Smiling to himself, he files it away for later.

He notices Grace wincing as she rakes the bottom of her leg with her fingernails. 'That bite still hurting?'

'It's horrible.'

Jody crouches down and takes a closer look. Sam sees a flash of worry in her face, gone before Grace can pick up on it.

'A bit inflamed,' Jody says, but that's an understatement. Sam can see a bright red lump with three or four scabs where Grace has made it bleed. 'Try to leave it alone,' Jody tells her. 'I don't have any antiseptic, but the salt water should help.'

Grace looks unconvinced. It's only a few seconds till her hand is creeping towards it again. Sam suggests they take a walk along the tree line, collecting up wood for another fire.

First they agree on a couple more mouthfuls of lukewarm water. That's two thirds of the second bottle gone already – and they can't bank on it raining again this evening.

A few minutes into the search there's a welcome discovery. After catching her foot on a bramble, Jody delves into the trees and finds a whole clump of them, loaded with blackberries. She emerges with her palm full of the plump black fruit.

'There isn't much I can guarantee that's safe to eat, but these definitely are.'

Sam takes one. It's not something he's normally keen on, but after twenty-four hours with nothing but coconut, to sample a different flavour is mind-blowing. And this isn't only food: it's juice.

Thankfully the kids like them, and they spend a long time stuffing their faces. Dylan ends up with the juice smeared all over his cheeks, leading Grace to christen him Ribena Boy.

Then it's back to the search for firewood, though as they get closer to the ridge, Sam can't help drifting away from the others. With a subtle nod to Jody, he follows the rocky path towards the water, stopping every couple of paces to examine the ground.

A short distance from the sea there's a kind of bulge where the rocks slope out and upwards for a few metres. Sam decides to climb it, wondering if he might spot some evidence of a boat having come ashore. He doesn't hold out much hope of seeing anything, but he's wrong.

.   .   .

Jody tries to keep the children focused on the hunt for fallen branches, though Grace isn't easily fooled.

'What's Dad doing?'

'Nothing.'

'I don't think she was there. Dylan made it up.'

'That's not what he's...' Jody tails off, because Sam has climbed to the top of a sharp limestone crag. She watches him go up on tiptoe, craning to see.

When he returns, his face is grave. Jody moves to intercept him while they're still out of earshot of the children.

'No footprints, as far as I can see. The ground's hard and dry, but I couldn't find any marks on the beach either side.' Despite that, he is giving her a meaningful look.

'But you saw something...'

He nods. 'On the next beach but one.'

'What?'

'Can't really tell from this distance, but it looks like a cage.'

'A cage?' A worried glance at Grace and Dylan. 'Could you see what's inside it?'

'Not really. But this means there *was* a boat, so maybe Dylan did see a woman up there.'

Jody sighs. 'This is our next "trial", isn't it?'

'Probably.' He starts to move towards the kids when she grabs his arm.

'Aren't we going to check it out?'

'Later.'

'Why not now?'

'Because that's what they'll expect us to do.'

Accepting the logic of his argument, Jody helps to gather a bundle of kindling and a few more hefty branches. Back at the boat, Sam lays the wood out to dry while the kids lie down in the shade. A brief rest, Jody says, and then they can pick some more blackberries.

'Do we have to?' Grace asks. She can't leave her leg alone. 'I'm tired.'

'I know, but it's important. We don't want the birds to eat them.'

Sam snaps his fingers. 'That reminds me. An idea I had.'

'Oh?'

'Tell you later.' His cryptic tone is a reminder that she failed to prise out the secret he's been keeping. In a lower voice, he says, 'Found another camera. Top of the beach, set into a rock next to the path we've been using.'

Jody casts a nonchalant glance in that direction and spots a dark circular patch on the rock. It reminds her of Sussex flint, except it's far too uniform in shape.

'Sneaky bastards.' She sidles closer to him. 'I've been thinking about these tests. Leaving the water for us. It's like they want us to survive, at least for a while.'

He grunts. 'I s'pose.'

'They could easily have sent a boat by now, but they haven't. So there must be something else they've got in mind.'

'Yeah. Which is why I don't want to check out this cage until I'm good and ready.'

'All right, but what I'm trying to get at is: why us?'

'Jode, we went through this yesterday–'

'I know, and I want to go through it again.'

'We'll just drive ourselves mad.'

Ignoring him, she says, 'It feels like we were chosen at random, because we certainly haven't done anything to deserve this. But if that's the case, why couldn't the Baxters have gone in our place?'

'I dunno.'

'And like you said, Gabby seemed so relieved when we made it to the welcome meeting. That must mean we'd already been selected. The four of us, not the two of them. But why?'

He stares at the ground, idly carving a furrow in the sand with his toes. 'Trouble is, we can talk about it all day, but will that get us out of here? No. So what's the point?'

'We have to think of something, and if this helps us to... to brainstorm, then it's worth a try. What *will* get us out of here? that's what we need to ask.'

Sam laughs, a harsh and unexpected sound, and says, 'Dying.'

Jody flinches, seeing that there's no sense trying to discuss it when he's in this mood.

'Sorry, but that's the only sure way that comes to mind.' There's no humour in his voice this time; not even a trace of sarcasm. 'Dying.'

PART III

COMPLICATION

40

Borko wakes early, to a cool grey light beyond the shades. He pulls on a robe and pads along the hall to the edit suite, where he is disconcerted to find that, along with the sole technician on night duty, one of his guests is present. Jesse Cayner is twenty-eight, and a recent elevation to the billionaire set, following the IPO of the tech company he founded while still at Berkeley. This is his first invitation to one of Borko's gatherings, and so far the childlike exuberance for which he is famous has proved to be more irritating than endearing.

Like slurping his buckets of Coke through a straw.

Several of the chairs in the edit suite have trackwheels set into the arms, enabling the user to manipulate the images on one of the half dozen screens. Jesse is toying with the footage from the previous night, rolling back and forth to re-experience the spellbinding moment when Sam Berry was blown off his feet by the lightning. Each time, Jesse lets out a little whoop, bucking gleefully in the chair.

Borko watches silently, unable to shake off the sense of intrusion. His guests should be here only when he permits it.

'*Ka-boom!*' The American throws out a long, thin arm and snaps his fingers several times, like rifle shots.

'Top-class entertainment,' Borko says, enjoying the startled jerk his words provoke; a mini-avalanche of ice cubes as Jesse nearly drops the Coke.

Actually, *startled jerk* just about sums him up.

As Jesse spins the chair round, Borko addresses the technician. 'You're putting together a highlights reel for those who missed it?'

The man nods rapidly, but the image on screen in front of him, frozen in place, shows something else: the woman, Jody, leaning precariously over the snake pit.

'What's this?' Borko asks in their native tongue.

'Sir, Mr Hussein wanted you to see.'

As if responding to the mention of his name, a door opens across the room and Naji Hussein appears, bleary-eyed but otherwise immaculate in his Savile Row suit.

'They're proving to be quite inventive,' Borko says, in English.

'Nah, you made it too easy for them,' Jesse chips in. 'A kid could figure out some of these traps.'

'It's a delicate balance.' Borko's tone remains mild, as though he is perfectly relaxed about being contradicted. 'Last year we had three young men from Denmark. PhD students, no less. We expected creative co-operation, but within twenty-four hours one of them had strangled his friend after a disagreement about how best to light a fire. What followed was anarchy. The killer and the third man raged at one another for hours before going their separate ways, moping alone at each end of the compound as if content to waste away.'

'And–' Jesse stops to clear his throat. 'And did they? Waste away, I mean?'

Borko gives him an enigmatic smile. 'In a manner of speaking.'

The technician brings up the footage for Borko to view. It shows the woman wrestling the second bottle of water from the pit, helped in the final moments by the arrival of her partner.

'The children?' Borko asks.

'On the beach,' Naji says. 'It was a good opportunity for us. The boat went in as planned. The next stage is all set.'

'What's the next stage?' Jesse asks.

Borko shakes his head. 'No spoilers.'

The American makes a sound like *Awww* as Naji directs Borko's attention to the screen. 'Watch carefully, and you'll see how the woman examines one of the trees.'

'Searching for fruit?'

'It's possible.'

'Or they found the cameras, dude,' Jesse says.

'Can we hear them?' Borko asks.

'I regret not. The sound quality around the pit is unreliable, because of the storm. And we have three cameras malfunctioning. But we shouldn't rule out that they have detected the surveillance.'

As Borko ponders, he is aware that the other men are anxiously awaiting his reaction. Enjoying the tension, he shuts his eyes.

It was the small boy he saw first, at the airport on Tuesday. Dylan had run free of his parents, drawn by the presence of the armed guards on the apron. From his position in the control room, Borko observed the stragglers from the Gatwick flight and zeroed in on the family: mum and dad, brother and sister. 'Perfect symmetry,' he'd remarked to Naji, who was fending off complaints from the airport director about the somewhat hasty nature of their landing.

'A family, sir? Is that wise?' Borko's aide, a worrier to the last, had been imposed upon him more than a year ago. A human choke chain, by order of the President, though Borko still pulled for all he was worth.

'Why not? You see how young the parents look? I have a feeling that life has hit them hard. But has it taught them to cope?'

Naji said nothing. In his view, Borko had already pushed his luck with the unscheduled landing. His early departure from the mainland had been prompted by a violent argument with one of his girlfriends, a nasty little problem that another of his assistants had been tasked with cleaning up. But who cared if the British airline lodged a complaint about the intrusion into their airspace? He'd find a way to buy them off.

As for this family, he told Naji that he intended to listen to his instincts. 'And my instincts say that my luck isn't going to run out yet. Not this year. Not with them.'

Now a throat is cleared, apprehensively, and Borko opens his eyes, surveying the men who are waiting upon his word. He nods briskly.

'We should be prepared for them to surprise us,' he says. 'Sabotage, even resistance, of a sort. After all, is there anything in nature stronger than a family unit? The parents will strive against hopeless odds, endure any suffering for the sake of their offspring.' He smiles at Naji. 'My choice has been vindicated, wouldn't you agree?'

41

Sam has to remind himself it's not personal, this tension between him and Jody. It's got nothing to do with their current relationship, or their past history – it's only about the situation they're in right now.

He wants to make it up to her, but even though he's ninety-nine percent convinced it's what he should do, that one percent of stubbornness holds out on him.

Later, he vows to himself. After they've both cooled off.

In any case some time apart will probably help, so he doesn't say a word when she announces that she's taking Dylan and Grace to gather more blackberries.

Once they're gone he sets to work on his project. It's either a very clever or a very stupid idea: he can't decide which, but he's in no doubt that Jody will tell him bluntly one way or the other.

The conversation they had earlier keeps intruding on his thoughts. How did they come to be chosen for this? You stick a family on a deserted beach and leave them to get on with it. Why?

To see how they cope.

Badly, of course. Because modern people don't know how to

survive in the wild. So you give them half a chance, setting tests to win food and water, like in the reality shows. And to make sure you don't miss any of the fun, you put cameras and microphones all over the place. So far, so good.

Sam rests for a moment. He's burning hot but hardly sweating. He feels all dried out inside, like a piece of fruit that's been cut open and left in the sun. He has so little saliva that it's painful to swallow, and he keeps sending longing glances at the bottle of water from the previous night – the one he risked his life to fill up with rain. It's still full, untouched, and he could guzzle it down and so what if Jody went ballistic?

'Fucking no!'

He springs to his feet and takes himself away from temptation, flopping down on the sand close to the shore. The sun is climbing fast, the sea glittering beneath it, the mad darting flashes that suddenly, today, make him think of piano music, the work of some famous old composer, all classical and frantic.

Huh. Where the hell has *that* come from? He wonders if the lightning frazzled his senses and he's going to start seeing music or hearing smells, like some bloke in a documentary he saw once...

Anyway: *think*. Something's gonna go wrong, isn't it. You give the family a chance, but it's a bloody slim chance in the end. Sooner or later one or more of them is going to die.

How do you dispose of the bodies?

How do you explain away the deaths?

He gazes out to sea, losing himself in the endless view. Jody's dad Michael was a skilled machinist for most of his working life; obsessed with politics and union stuff, always doing night classes to improve his education. For the past few years he's had a part-time job on the checkout at their local supermarket, and to the whole family's amazement he's really enjoying it. With that, and Jody's mum working as a receptionist at a GP's surgery (plus a lot of careful saving over the years) they're doing quite nicely these days – a lot better than Sam and Jody, anyway. They own a three-bedroomed semi in Seaford, the mortgage long since paid off.

And Michael's own dad, Jimmy Lamb (Jimmy Greatgramps, to the kids) is still hanging in there at eighty-six. Widowed, and not in the best of health, he lives in a retirement home in Ramsgate. Jimmy was also a big union man in the sixties and seventies; now, prompted by his son, he's taken to the Internet with an enthusiasm that surprised them all. The last time they visited he was going on about the sites he'd signed up to – Avaaz and 38 Degrees, Amnesty and Greenpeace and the Good Law Project – and how proudly he was adding his name to various campaigns: fighting for a living wage, getting rid of tax havens, saving the glaciers and the bees and the rainforests.

Jimmy treated them to tea and cakes in the grand lounge at the home, which has stunning views over a huge marina, and laid out his theory for why people so often choose the coast when they retire. 'It's the limitless horizon. When you stare out to sea, it's like a glimpse of infinity.'

At the time, Sam vaguely recalled how the astronaut in *Toy Story* was always talking about 'infinity and beyond', so he guessed *infinity* must be the name of a planet or a distant star. Then, a few days later, Jody mentioned it to her dad, who snorted and said, 'Infinity? It's, what, twenty miles and there's a bloody great continent in the way. Silly old bugger!'

After that, Sam looked up the definition of the word and felt a bit stupid. But now he has a sense of what Jimmy G was getting at. This is *infinity* right here: the blank blue sea and the blank blue sky, like two gigantic sheets of plastic pressed together but never quite touching. And with that, it *does* come back to him, the way he felt last night. How enormous the planet is, how tiny we are upon it. A drop of water, a grain of sand, a human existence—

His head lolls then jerks; he's dozing off in the heat. His tongue feels like an off-cut of carpet. He slaps it against the roof of his mouth, trying to find enough moisture to swallow. *I'm all out of spit*, he thinks, and it makes him laugh. Dangerous, punch-drunk laughter.

'What are we celebrating?' says a voice behind him. 'A penalty competition, is it?'

Jody has switched to autopilot, too shaken by the risks of conflict with Sam to think straight about anything. After leading Grace and Dylan back to where they found the blackberry bushes, she allows Dylan to hold the carrier bag open while she and Grace pick the fruit and place it inside.

Every few seconds, like a late-night billboard, a vital message flashes in her brain: *I love Sam!*

I do love him, yes. But what does it mean if I have to keep reminding myself?

She thinks of Kay Baxter, and her quiet desolation when she was asked whether she regretted not leaving Trevor. *Every single day.* How horrific, to reach middle age and realise you no longer want to be with your partner. It hurts to admit that Jody has had similar fears herself, although never to the extent that she considered doing anything about it.

Perhaps she should have. After all, at the age of twelve or thirteen she'd never imagined ending up with someone like Sam. He was one of the rowdy kids, the disruptors, whereas she was always a diligent, conscientious student. At the back of her mind lay the assumption that when she got married it would be to someone with the same mindset, someone who'd worked hard and gone to university – as she had hoped to do – before settling into a well-paid white-collar profession.

She hadn't thought too closely about her ideal future partner – other than in terms of shallow things like looks and body – but as with most of her friends, a prosperous lifestyle was taken for granted. Otherwise why dream of a future at all?

A smart spacious house with an en suite and a decent garden; the mortgage manageable and always paid on time. Kids, eventually, once they'd seen a bit of the world... At twelve or thirteen, Jody couldn't imagine anything worse than getting pregnant before her education was complete.

Now she blinks a few times. Dylan snaps into focus, rustling the bag as he peers inside to see how much they have. A couple of metres away, Grace is standing like a flamingo, raking her lifted foot back and forth over the swelling on her leg.

Jody feels a crushing shame. Okay, so her life didn't exactly go to plan, but what does that matter when she's been blessed with two such beautiful children?

If Sam leaves me, I might have no choice but to start again.

Lately Jody's been tormenting herself with the idea that he has found someone else. The possibility of losing him has made her see how much she values their relationship – even if she hasn't yet found a way of expressing that to him.

Perhaps she should be glad she's not in her fifties, weary and defeated like poor Kay Baxter. At twenty-six she could start over, if she really had to. She hopes it won't come to that. Patch things up, and who knows what the future might bring? Sam's no City hotshot, but thanks to his uncle he's learning a lot about running a business. It's possible that one day he'll strike out on his own.

And then there's her job at the shoe shop. The manager,

Carol, is always encouraging her to look ahead to when the kids don't need her so much. 'It comes round sooner than you think. And you could run a store like this with your eyes closed.' So maybe, if she and Sam can stay together and work hard, they'll one day earn enough to buy that house of her dreams.

First, though, they have to get out of here.

Grace suddenly falters, a handful of blackberries falling to the ground as her shoulders slump. A sob escapes from her throat. Jody moves towards her and sees a streak of blood running down her leg.

'Darling...'

'I feel sick.' Weeping, she accepts her mum's embrace. Dylan backs up a couple of steps, watching with big solemn eyes. His lips wobble. *Not you, too*, Jody prays. Because if both her children break down, there's a fair chance she will collapse with them.

'It's all right. It's all right.'

Grace is suddenly angry, pushing her away. 'Stop saying that, Mum.' Another sob, then a brutal swipe of her nose against her forearm. 'I w-wanted to own up but I couldn't, and now I'm being punished.'

'What do you mean? This isn't punishment, and I'm sure you haven't–'

'I have!' Grace insists. 'It was Keeley's fault. Keeley and Liv. They were making fun of Jalilah, because she's just joined the school and she's from Syria, and Keeley said her family were terrorists, and it made Jalilah cry and I didn't want to join in, I honestly didn't, but if I'd told Keeley to stop she would have said stuff about me, and I was... I was too scared not to do it.'

The torrent of words runs out, and for a moment Jody has no idea what to say. Bullying is a constant worry, but only in terms of her children being on the receiving end. It has never crossed her mind that one of them might victimise someone else. She feels shocked, and disappointed – until she recalls some of the tricky compromises that became an essential part of her own survival kit at school.

'Don't worry, I'm sure Jalilah understands. Maybe we could invite her to tea when we get back?'

'She won't want to come.'

'She might. Anyway, I'll speak to Keeley's mum–' Jody breaks off, because Dylan has been edging away from her. She waggles her finger in a *Come here* gesture but he's looking past her, off to his right. All the colour has drained from his face.

'The lady...' he says.

Gasping, Jody spins to look, even while she tells herself that it's silly to indulge him. This isn't a real person and it's certainly not a ghost: it's just the product of his vivid imagination. Though that's enough, perhaps, to fire up her own imagination – because doesn't she see, through the trees, a thin and pale blur, moving deeper in the undergrowth? Her gaze flicks past it and back, but by then it has vanished.

42

Sam turns to see Jody trudging towards him with a bag of black-berries, the kids bumping along beside her, clinging to her dress as if afraid to break off contact.

'What do you mean, "penalty competition"?'

'This.' She gestures at his construction. 'It's a goal, isn't it?'

He looks again, and can't help laughing. He used two of the stakes plus a couple of sturdy branches, driven into the ground to form a rectangle. Then he draped the net over them, pinning it down with rocks on three sides but leaving it open at the front. Seeing it through her eyes, he has to admit it does look like a goal.

'It's a trap,' he says.

'What for?'

'Birds. We put something in as bait – coconut, I suppose.' He points to the bungee cords attached to the stakes, trailing away across the sand. 'Soon as a bird goes in after the bait, you pull on the cords and bring the net down over it.'

Her sceptical expression hasn't changed, so he adds, 'Once I get a fire going, we can cook what we–'

'Dylan saw the woman again,' Jody cuts in, as though she's already bored with his idea.

Sam makes a choking noise as he tries to swallow before speaking. 'Wh-where?'

'In the trees – I was with him,' she adds quickly.

'And you saw her, too?'

Before she answers, Jody eases herself free of the kids. Both of them immediately crumple to the sand.

'I'm not sure. I've asked him again about the first time, and I think she might have been wearing a cloak, maybe, with a hood.'

'And that's what you saw?'

'It did sort of look like someone in a white cloak. But it was a glimpse – could've been my mind playing tricks.'

It feels to Sam like she's backtracking. He squeezes one hand into a fist and thumps it gently against his forehead. He can't make sense of this at all.

'Why would there be a woman in a cloak, hiding herself so that she's only seen by Dylan?'

'I don't know.' A glance at the kids, sitting miserably a couple of metres away. 'Shall we try putting some bait in this trap?' Jody adds in a brighter voice. 'And these two need some more water.'

They settle the children in the shade of the boat and feed them berries, coconut and a few sips of water. The sun is high and punishingly hot; not even the hint of a breeze to bring them relief. Grace has to be persuaded that her leg will feel better if she can leave it alone. She looks doubtful, but curls up on her side and shuts her eyes. Within a few minutes she's dozing, sucking on her thumb.

Jody shakes her head. 'All the time we spent building up her confidence, getting her ready to face the world, and it's been undone in the space of two days.'

'It's horrible, but I still don't see any point in lying to them.'

'When have I lied?' Jody asks sharply.

'Pretending it's a game, then.' He lets out a long sigh. 'Have you thought about how this is going to end?'

'You said there was no point in going over it.'

'I know, but I can't help it. Neither can you.'

She says nothing, so he goes on: 'Maybe they'll let us go, maybe they won't. But I reckon there's one thing that'll decide it for sure – and that's if something happens to one of us.'

'Like what?'

'If one of us dies.' He mouths the words, because he's not convinced that Grace and Dylan are properly asleep. 'If that happens, they'll have to kill the rest of us. But if we can all stay alive, there might be a point when they plan to stop the game.'

'How can they let us go, after what they've done?'

'Once we're back in the normal world, what can we do to hurt them? You think their police will care?'

'No, but when we get home. There's the UK police, our MP–'

'What proof will we have? We've got no phones to take pictures or videos. We don't even know where we are! They'd laugh at us, Jode.'

She nods, and slowly traces her fingers over her dry, chapped lips. 'I see what you mean.'

'But that's if we're all okay. If one of us... you know... then all bets are off. Four people go on holiday, only three come back? No chance of keeping that quiet.'

'But we couldn't just vanish. Not a whole family.'

'We wouldn't *vanish*, exactly. You know that boat crash last year, the one Gabby was asked about? It wasn't the only bad accident over here.'

'How do you know?'

'I found out some stuff on the internet.' Embarrassed, he tells her of his plan to organise a boat trip, and describes how he stumbled across the news items about a couple of other tragedies. 'As long as they don't do this too often, they could easily explain it away. I mean, look how often you see something on the news about a tourist falling off a hotel balcony, or drowning, or killed by carbon monoxide while they sleep. Accidents happen all the time. No one's gonna question it, are they? It's just bad luck.'

'Bad luck?' she repeats with a hollow laugh. 'Oh, it's bad luck, all right.'

After first being wounded by the charge that she lies to the kids, any relief that Jody could feel at knowing why Sam went online is wiped out by this horrific scenario. It seems grimly plausible, and for a while neither of them can find anything to say. They're sitting within touching range but Jody can't bring herself to reach over and hold his hand.

What's happening to us?

Then, out of nowhere, Sam says, 'You know all the political stuff your dad and Greatgramps go on about?'

'The stuff you reckon is bullshit?'

'Yeah, but I dunno anymore. Spend a bit of time thinking about it, and you realise they've got a point. I mean, we've had years of prices rising, while wages stay flat or go down. No job security anymore. Fucking zero-hours contracts. Property prices are insane, and rents are a rip-off even for a shithole. Everyone's being screwed to the bone.'

'Not the one percent. That's the point Dad's always making.'

'I know. But even *they're* gonna suffer, in time, for the damage we're doing to the planet. I admit I feel guilty for taking the piss when Greatgramps was going on about fracking and bees and Christ knows what. But he's right. We're heading for disaster – not just you, me and the kids, at the level of one family, but almost everyone else is in the same mess. The whole planet, basically.'

Heavy stuff, and it causes her to look at him through narrowed eyes and find a glint of humour. 'If I didn't know better I'd say you were on drugs. Or maybe it was the lightning?'

He grins, which is a welcome sight, but he seems quite serious when he says, 'Maybe it was.' A self-conscious shrug, and then he goes on: 'Anyway, it seems like crazy bad luck, that out of all the time humans have been around, things will fall apart for *us*, for our generation – and the kids'. But then you think... well, it *is* going to happen one day, so why not now? It's like we're sleepwalking towards the edge of a cliff, and nothing's gonna wake us up in time.'

A gloomy silence follows. This subject is far from new to Jody. Most of these arguments have been put forward by her dad and her granddad, with both men subscribing to the theory that the children of the forties and fifties were possibly the most fortunate in the history of the working class – at least in the rich nations of the west. The baby boomers have had decent education, healthcare, affordable housing, unemployment benefit, free universities, as well as all the luxuries and delights of the modern technological age: from dishwashers and computers to cheap foreign travel.

'Work paid, that was the thing,' her dad likes to remind them. 'So we had a chance to realise our dreams through hard graft, with the knowledge that there was a proper, robust safety net if things went wrong. After just two generations that's winding down fast. It's the bloody eighties that did for us. Financial deregulation, ushering in the Great Greed. Banks that won't lend money to a thriving business because they can make a hundred times the profit by betting on the price of grain. And now you see the homeless dying on the streets, and kids coming to school hungry in a country where someone'll pay a million quid for a wristwatch. We're facing inequality on a scale that would make Caesar blush, and yet what are most folk worried about? The result of *Strictly Come Dancing*, or whether someone made an off-colour joke on Twitter.'

Usually such discussions ended with her mum prodding Dad with a rolled-up newspaper and telling him not to be such a miserable git. Jody always tried to take a more positive view, arguing that it's natural, as you get older, to feel that things are getting worse, but that doesn't make it true.

Right now, though, it's difficult to argue with Sam that they – and almost everyone like them – are on a downward spiral, no matter how hard they work. Once or twice they've skipped meals themselves to ensure that the kids would have enough, when an unexpected bill wrecked their budgeting for the month, and there was an occasion when Jody came close to approaching the local food bank, but stopped for fear of Sam's reaction – that and her own crippling sense of shame.

Drawing in a weary breath, she says, 'Are you saying there's no point in trying to survive here, if everything's so hopeless? Because I don't think I can accept that.'

He makes a grunting noise, as though he's not sure one way or the other. 'Is your dad wrong, then?'

'All I mean is that I can't bring myself to care about politics at the moment. The future out there in the world has got to look after itself. I'm talking about *here*, *now*, and whether we... surrender.'

'I'm not saying we should, Jode, but–'

'Last night you were so fired up. It was amazing. Inspiring.' She reddens. 'I admit it also scared me a bit. But at least you had the energy, the will to go on fighting. We have to stay strong and believe in ourselves, that's what you said.'

'Did I?' He looks surprised. 'Amazing what a lightning bolt can do.'

They both grin. Some of the tension has eased, and Jody knows she must seize this opportunity and ask what it is he's been hiding from her: whether their future, if they get out of here, is together or apart.

But at that moment, Sam squints at the sky and says, 'Midday now, don't you reckon?'

'Later than that, probably.'

'Can't put it off much longer, then.'

'What?' Lost in the track of her own thinking, her heart stutters. *He's going to tell me. But what if it hurts too much, on top of everything else?*

'The cage, remember?' He looks confused by her fearful expression. 'You were saying we should go. So let's go.'

Sam's feeling weirded out by Jody's behaviour. It's like she's with him one minute and gone away the next. Probably it's the heat, the dehydration, which is likely to be having the same effect on him. He keeps telling himself to make allowances but then, when they start to disagree, he forgets all about it. Like some part of him is itching for a fight.

There's another tussle over who should go to investigate the cage. Jody says she'll do it: he can stay here with the kids. Sam won't hear of that. It's bad enough that she went to the pit on her own.

'We both need to go,' he says. 'And Grace and Dylan will have to come.'

'They're exhausted. And it's the hottest part of the day.'

'I know. But you said yourself, we shouldn't put it off too long.'

Her lips are so tight that they almost disappear. He tenses, knowing she's going to tear into him for not going earlier.

'But, Sam–'

'No. Let's just do it, and not bloody argue about everything.'

'You think I want that?'

He shakes his head. 'It's what *they* want.'

She looks pissed off, but doesn't say anything. They go to rouse the kids. When Jody shakes her shoulder, Grace mumbles and groans, not wanting to wake up.

'She's burning hot.' Jody rests a hand on her brow. 'I think it's a fever.'

Sam feels his insides go watery with fear. He can see that Jody, as she stares at him, is thinking about what he said earlier.

If one of us dies, we all die.

43

Gabrielle Marchant is a two-faced bitch.

That was the verdict of her supposed best friend, overheard by accident when they were at sixth form together. To this day, Gabby suffers a little punch to the heart when she recalls that moment, even though she has good reason to be grateful for Marianne's assessment.

It could have destroyed their friendship, but Gabby decided instead to embrace the accusation. She gave no sign that she'd heard anything, and continued to act the part of soulmate for another fourteen months, until the optimum moment arrived – the night of Marianne's break-up with her first serious boyfriend.

'Why would I give a fuck?' was Gabby's cool retort when Marianne rang her in tears. 'I'm a two-faced bitch, remember?'

Gabby is from a well-off but not filthy rich family in the East Midlands. Educated at an excellent grammar school, she was an above-average student who excelled at many things, including drama (wearing a whole lot more than two faces) so it seemed inevitable that good A levels would lead to a top university and then, perhaps, to a lucrative and fulfilling career.

It started off that way, but after a term and a half of an English degree at Southampton, Gabby's vague plans and her family's far more concrete expectations were blasted off course by a combination of boys, debts, drugs, an unwanted pregnancy (terminated) and a brush or two with the law. Bailing out, she fled to her sympathetic grandmother in West London and staved off boredom with a part-time job at a travel agent's. Within weeks she was sleeping with her boss, a good-looking man in his mid-thirties, married with kids, who often reminisced about the fun he'd had repping at the start of his career and thought she should try it.

'With your wild side, you'd love it. And I mean, jeez, you've got all the assets.' *Snicker snicker*. It was a suggestion that owed more to a fear that his wife was going to discover their affair, but Gabby soon realised it was precisely what she needed. The fact that her family would be horrified only added to its appeal.

From the beginning she was Gabby, not Gabrielle. *Hi guys, I'm Gabby the rep!* It means a conscious change to her voice, roughening the accent and injecting a cheery, upbeat tone. *Bubbly* is what she aims for, because bubbly girls – especially if they're also pretty and not intimidatingly bright – don't get as much grief from the customers. *The poor lass is doing her best for us*, she wants them saying to themselves. *It's not Gabby's fault the hotel / food / resort / weather isn't up to standard.*

The dumbing down has proved to be a smart move, earning her a sky-high rating in her performance reviews. The face she presents to the clients and her colleagues is well-received and almost always taken as genuine. Very few of the people she interacts with would guess at her middle-class origins – the property mogul father and brittle gym-and-shopping mother – but there is one exception, one person who suspects that she belongs a little higher on the social scale than she lets on. And because of that – because of *him* – she has landed herself in a very tricky situation indeed.

She times today's mission to coincide with the long lunch session – tourists at the trough: *gross!* – when the hotel's reception area is likely to be quiet. Unfortunately it's the luck of the draw in terms of the duty manager, a sour-faced woman with onion breath and a large nose peppered with blackheads. She hands over the passports and attends to the paperwork without comment, but insists on accompanying Gabby to the room.

She doesn't offer to help pack the cases; just stands by the door with a sullen expression. Once or twice Gabby catches the woman staring at her cleavage; she can't work out whether it's jealousy, disapproval or desire, but it's making her uncomfortable – and God knows she's feeling jittery enough as it is.

It's tempting to throw the clothes and toiletries into the cases in a messy heap, but that wouldn't show the appropriate respect for their possessions – something the duty manager might later remember. During her final sweep of the room, Gabby spies a small plastic figure under one of the beds – a superhero of some sort – and feels the unexpected prickle of a tear. Silly Gabby, she scolds herself.

She leaves the toy where it is.

In the lobby the duty manager sets the case down as though it's radioactive and plods away. A porter comes over to help – Viggo, a good lad, with bright green eyes and magnificent pecs beneath his tight shirt. He takes the second case and a rucksack from Gabby, insisting he can manage them all himself.

She's following him towards the exit doors when footsteps

quicken on the marble floor and someone calls her name. There's no point pretending she hasn't heard.

It would have to be these two, wouldn't it? Their names are lost to her, despite the unpleasantness that nearly ensued when she asked for the invitation back. Generally it's only the heavy-duty troublemakers whose names lodge in her brain like shrapnel.

No, she's got it: the Baxters!

'Hi guys, holiday all good? Soaking up plenty of sun?'

It's a reflex question: these two belong firmly in the category of middle-class apparitions who inexplicably take hot-weather holidays, only to spend the whole time sheltering in the lobby, complaining that it's too hot, too noisy, too crowded – when usually what they mean is *too common*.

'It's about our, er, friends,' Mrs B says. 'Jody and, er, Sam.'

'They won the prize,' says hubby, addressing Gabby's right nipple. 'We were all set to go in their place, until–'

'Ah, yeah. Sorry about that.' Gabby tries to look bereft, but Mrs B shakes her head, coldly dismissive.

'The thing is, the family... we've not seen hide nor hair of them since Thursday.'

'Oh, really?' *Gotta sound totally nonchalant here, Gabs.* 'Well, it is a big hotel!'

'Medium-sized, I would say,' Mr Baxter corrects her. 'But I'm not sure whether they actually returned from the party.'

There's a painful silence. Gabby can't decide if lying will dig her deeper into a hole, but put on the spot, she really has no choice.

'I'm afraid there was a slight accident. Their little boy fell and broke his ankle.'

A microsecond's delay before the wife clasps a hand to her mouth. 'Oh my word! Trevor, didn't we say there might be something...?'

'He's fine now, don't worry. But the hotel felt so bad about it, they offered them a suite for the rest of their holiday.'

'At the Conchis?' Trevor Baxter's face is glowing like an over-ripe tomato.

'Yeah. Everyone wants to keep it kind of low key, you know? I'm just delivering the rest of their stuff now.' A pointed look at Viggo, waiting by the taxi, but the Baxters fail to take the hint.

'We were so looking forward to hearing about it,' Mrs Baxter says. 'Though I suppose we may see them at the airport.'

'Yes,' Gabby squeaks, and clears her throat. 'Maybe you will.'

'It's very odd.' Trevor is frowning deeply. 'The Fischers didn't mention a thing about any accident.'

'Fischers?'

'The other winners,' his wife says. 'A German family.'

Trevor's frown has taken on the look of an accusation. 'You were there to see them off.'

'Oh... yeah. I didn't know their names. The, er, accident happened quite late on, so perhaps they'd already gone.' She gestures at the taxi. 'Gotta rush, sorry.'

Allowing them no chance of a comeback, Gabby dashes out of the hotel. It's all she can do to dredge up a smile for Viggo as she jumps into the taxi and collapses on the back seat. She suspects the Baxters are watching from the window so she digs out her phone and pretends to be reading a text.

Except she doesn't have to pretend. There's one waiting for her: *Where are you?*

'Fuck,' she mutters to herself. She texts back: *I'm coming.*

She pauses, thumb wavering over the screen, then adds: *There's a problem.*

44

Jody encourages Grace to sip some water. The poor girl is listless, sleepy and confused. She ought to be lying on clean sheets in a cool, shaded bedroom, not hustled along a beach in the sweltering heat. Although her face is flushed, she doesn't appear to be sweating, which worries Jody all the more. She suspects the fever is a consequence of the bite on Grace's leg. The flesh around it is horribly inflamed; the slightest touch causes squeals of pain.

They bribe Dylan with a few berries and some water, and then they're ready to go. The bottle Jody rescued from the pit is empty, so Sam suggests they bring it along. He's still talking about finding a puddle or a stream, although up till now they haven't spotted anything resembling a source of fresh water.

Jody wants to take some tools with them. It seems like a better choice of word than 'weapons', but that's really what she means. Sam agrees, collecting up the bungee cords and the two shorter wooden stakes.

'Means taking your goal down.' Jody is only gently teasing, but the look he gives her could strip paint from a wall.

They set off across the beach at an ambling pace. Grace's

lack of energy is in stark contrast to her brother, who seems to have perked up after his sleep. The reason, he announces, is the angel lady.

'Who?' Jody asks, with a sense of dread weighing heavily in her stomach.

'The angel lady. She spoke to me.'

This comes as a relief: Dylan hasn't been out of their sight.

'It was a dream, darling.'

'I know,' he says, with a withering glance. 'She wanted to take me away.'

'Where?' Sam asks.

'I dunno, but it was better than here. We had chocolate.'

'That's a nice dream, then.' Jody leaves it at that. She hopes it means the other sightings were imagined, too. But, in that case, what did she see through the trees?

Nothing. You're just spooking yourself.

They negotiate the first ridge and drop on to the neighbouring beach. It's as they climb the rocks at the far end that the cage comes into view. It's been placed about midway around the bay, some ten metres up from the shore. There are no other signs that anyone has been here, the sand once again brushed smooth to preserve the illusion that this object has materialised from nowhere.

The cage is about the size of a child's play pen. It has what looks like a steel frame, with the sides covered in thick wire mesh. The holes are too small for them to see what's inside, and yet Jody has an impression of rapid movement: small dark shapes zigzagging in a fast haphazard fashion.

The closer they get, the slower they walk. The reluctance weighs heavily on them both. When they're fifteen, ten meters away, Sam knows for sure. He thinks Jody does as well.

'Right,' she says to Grace. 'I want you and Dylan to sit down here. Can you do that?'

'Where are you going?'

'To have a look at that...' Glancing at Sam, she gestures at the cage.

'What's in it?'

'Don't know yet,' Sam says, with the same guilty look that Jody just gave him.

They have to physically plant Dylan down on the sand. At the worst possible time he's turning hyper.

'Your sister is poorly,' Jody says. 'You need to stay together.'

'Yeah, Dyl,' Sam adds, 'you have to guard her.'

'Like a soldier?'

'That's right. Good work, sergeant!' Sam salutes him, then hurries away before Dylan has other ideas.

Jody runs to catch up. The inhabitants of the cage are well aware of their presence; some freeze for a second, in a twitchy kind of way, before rushing from side to side even more frenetically than before.

Up close, they see that one side of the cage has a removable panel, set into a recess and fixed in place with half a dozen thumbscrews. The holes in the mesh around the panel are slightly larger, and the screws are positioned very close to the edges of the panel.

In the centre of the cage there's a large plastic container, white with a red lid held on by metal clasps. It looks heavy, solid, and tightly sealed. The kind of thing you might take on board a yacht to keep your supplies from getting wet or spoiled.

The task is clear enough. After the pit, they know what to expect. The panel, once removed, would leave a space large enough for one of them to reach in and grasp the container.

The problem is the rats.

. . .

Jody counts at least twenty of them: hungry-looking creatures with a greasy sheen to their fur, as though they've just crawled out of a sewer. Their tails are long and slimy, like thick pink worms grafted on to their bodies. At any one time about half of them are trying to clamber up on to the container, but the plastic is too slippery.

Grimly, Sam says, 'What's the betting there's food in that pot?'

'I think so, looking at how the rats keep going back to it. Something's driving them mad, and it's not just because they're in the cage.'

'They've been starved.' Sam dangles his fingers a few centimetres from the panel. A couple of the rats leap into the air and cling to the side, their razor-sharp teeth clamping on the mesh. 'Those screws are fiddly. It's gonna take a while to undo them.'

'You can't. Rats carry all kinds of diseases, and we have no medicines. One bite, or a scratch...' She shudders.

'So maybe I could wrap something around my hand?'

'We don't have anything strong enough. Anyway, we can't risk opening it up.' Jody feels sick, picturing the rats swarming out of the cage and heading straight for Grace and Dylan.

'So what, then? Do we just walk away?'

'I don't know. There must be something in there worth having.'

Sam's shoulders have slumped. Lowering his voice, he says, 'You're right. But you know we're gonna be giving those bastards another cheap thrill.'

A glum silence follows, Sam scraping his palm over the bristles on his chin. Jody aims an encouraging smile at the children, though Grace's eyes are half-closed and Dylan is marching in circles around her, singing or chanting to himself.

The hopelessness hits Jody like a slap, an assault on her

previous good intentions. 'This is pure torture. Mental, physical, emotional torture.'

Sam is nodding vehemently, and Jody immediately regrets having lit the fuse.

'I'm gonna kill someone for this,' he growls, then turns and kicks the cage. There's a loud metallic clang and the rats leap and run in frenzied circles. Clenching his fists, Sam looks up at the sky and roars: 'DO YOU HEAR ME, YOU FUCKERS? I'M GONNA KILL SOMEONE FOR THIS!'

Jody knows how much it'll upset the kids but there's no way she can say that to him. Better that he purges the rage from his system.

She hurries over and assures them that Daddy's fine; it's nothing to worry about.

Dylan, in a tremulous voice, asks, 'Is he c-cross with us?'

'No, darling. He's not cross with any of us.'

'Who, then?'

'The people,' Grace says simply. 'The people who stuck us in this shithole.'

It's the first time Jody's ever heard her eight–year-old use such a term, and for a moment she has no idea how to react. Then she does the only sensible thing in the circumstances: she laughs and gives her daughter a kiss.

45

Sam has one arm folded across his chest as a support for his other arm, which is bent at the elbow, enabling him to prop his chin against his jaw. He'll stand like this when he's figuring out how to fold wallpaper around the corner of an uneven wall, or blend in new paintwork when it turns out that the shade of one tin doesn't quite match the others.

They can't ignore the pot if there's any chance it contains food or drink. But they can't open up the cage while it's full of rats. Jody's right. A bite from one of them, out here, could be fatal.

So: kill the rats. That seems to him to be the only option. But how?

He studies them for so long that Jody grows restless and comes over. Several times he senses her preparing to speak and then think better of it. The sun is white hot and blinding above them; stand here much longer, he thinks, and I'm going to keel over.

'Can't poison them.'

'What?'

He was thinking aloud; now he indicates the trees. 'I dunno if there's any plants or berries that might poison them.'

'No idea. Aren't rats meant to be able to survive anything?'

'I bloody hope not.' He considers breaking off a long splinter of wood from the stake, feeding it through the mesh and jabbing away at the rats. But the speed those things move, he'd be lucky if he killed a single one. Getting them all would take hours.

'Sam, we need to be in the shade. And the kids–'

'Yeah, yeah. You go.'

She doesn't move, perhaps because she's worried about what kind of dumb idea he'll come up with. He looks around, praying for inspiration. All he gets is sand, rocks, trees. The sea slapping against the shore. A few gulls off in the distance, whirling and swooping. One of them takes a kamikaze dive towards the water...

He grins. The phrase that's popped into his head is the one Jody uses to describe herself and the kids if they've walked home from school in a downpour.

He assesses how to move the cage. It doesn't look particularly heavy, but their fingers will be juicy targets for the rats. He starts to undress.

'Sam...?'

'Help me with these.' He hands her one of the bungee cords and explains that he wants to hook them at each corner of the cage, on the side that faces the sea. 'And keep your fingers well clear.'

'Don't worry, I will. So what are we doing here?'

He gives her a cheeky look. 'Drowned rats.'

'What?'

'Come on.' Like him, she strips to her underwear. Once the hooks are in place, they take up the slack in the cords and drag the cage across the sand. Inside, the container wobbles but doesn't fall over. Jody isn't reassured.

'What if it breaks?'

'It won't.'

'What if it's not waterproof?'

'It looks like it is.'

'But if it's not?'

'Do you have a better idea?' He doesn't intend to snap, but that's how it must sound to her. 'Never mind. Sooner we do it, the sooner we'll know.'

She puts more effort into it, and they wrench the cage so hard that this time the container topples over. It doesn't break, though Sam's heart nearly stops for a second, imagining all kinds of food tumbling out and being gobbled up by the rats.

The little bastards are going crazy, some of them clinging to the roof of the cage, their tails swinging like whips. Maybe they know what's coming, he thinks.

At the shore, a line of half-buried rocks brings them to a halt. It's Jody's idea to wedge the cage against them and pull until the whole thing flips over. By now she seems to have accepted that the container is strong enough to take such a battering. But it means they have to go into the water first and drag it towards them.

'The kids...' she says, when they're in up to their knees. She's afraid Grace and Dylan will panic at the sight of their parents disappearing into the sea.

'Good point. I'll take it from here.'

He can see her fretting.

'You sure?' she asks.

'Yep. This is the easy bit.'

Not quite true, but thankfully it's mostly smooth sand underfoot. As the sea penetrates the cage, the rats respond by climbing the sides. Too heavy to float, the big plastic container bumps and rolls in the shallow water sloshing around it. Sam pauses to study the seal on the lid. If that cracks, it's all been a waste of time. But so far, so good.

Jody is sitting with Grace and Dylan, her hands cutting and diving as she explains what Daddy's trying to achieve. Or maybe she's just spinning a load of bullshit to keep them calm.

Sam hauls the cage into deeper water, to the point where he's struggling to keep his feet planted on the ground. The rats fight for space at the top of the cage, some of them floating, others hanging from the mesh like bats. For this to work he'll have to get it completely submerged. That means taking a breath and allowing himself to sink beneath the water, crouching for a better angle so he can pull the cage the final few steps.

He springs up, breaks the surface and spits seawater from his mouth. There's a horrible temptation to swallow some, until he realises how disgusting it tastes. He swims round to the opposite side, still gripping the bungee cords. Now all he can do is wait.

He can't see the rats clearly but he can sense the disturbance underwater; bubbles spurting up in tiny streams. He knows they're swimming and fighting, desperately clinging to life. Like every living thing on the planet, they don't want someone else to come along and wipe them out.

If Jody's right, and this is all about tests and trials, did their watchers imagine Sam coming up with this solution? Did they expect him to be ruthless enough to destroy these animals in cold blood?

He stares at the treeline. Bound to be cameras up there. No way of knowing exactly who's watching, though he has a pretty good idea.

He remembers how the president's son looked in his jetpack: the superhero, the man of steel. Strutting through the crowd like a rock star. Talking down to them as naturally as any silver-spooned royal. *Well.* It's a pleasure to select that image from the Conchis and place it inside the cage: Borko in a dinner suit, drenched and drowning, kicking and punching while his cheeks suck in and almost implode, eyes bulging because it's so painful, it's such a slow and terrible way to die...

And Sam smiles at the thought. Like a true psycho, he thinks. Way worse than his brother.

Drown, you tosser, for what you've done to us. Drown. Drown. Drown.

46

It's like the agony of waiting for a medical test result. When her mum found a lump in her breast, she confided in Jody but swore her to silence; not even Jody's dad was allowed to know. 'He'll go to pieces, and that's no help to me.' As it turned out, thankfully, there was nothing to worry about. *This time*, said the look in her mother's eyes.

It feels like there's nearly as much riding on this. Jody can feel the heat radiating from Grace, but the poor girl is shivering. Dylan won't stop with the questions. What's Daddy doing? Can I go and see? Will the big mice swim away?

'Rats, stupid,' Grace mutters, to Jody's dismay. But at last Sam is moving again, dipping his head below the water to take a look. He gives her a thumbs up, then motions her towards him.

'I need to help Daddy, okay.' She has to fight her way up, Grace begging her to stay, Dylan pleading to go with her. Sometimes Jody doesn't know how she resists the urge to scream.

Sam is trying to shift the cage on his own when she joins him. He's gripping two of the bungee cords in one hand, but his other hand is holding the cage itself.

'Are they all dead?'

'Yup.'

There's a savage gleam in his eyes that Jody tries to ignore. She says a silent prayer: *Don't let the container be broken or split. Don't let it be empty, or full of acid.*

Together they wrestle the cage out of the water, stopping in shock at the sight of the wretched corpses. Many are bloodied and torn, as if the creatures turned on each other in their final moments. *Better them than us,* Jody thinks, but it's a sad, disturbing sight. They didn't ask to be starved and placed in a cage.

Gingerly, Sam unscrews the plate and has a careful look inside. The container has come to rest with bodies piled around it, so he uses one of the stakes to prod them out of the way. Then he reaches in, cupping his hand around the container, trying to ease it towards the opening. He ends up at full stretch, his head pressed against the metal frame.

'Do you want me to do it?' Jody asks.

'I'm fine.' He mutters something else that she thinks is, *You wouldn't want to.*

Eventually he has it, and Jody quickly shoves the panel back in place. She's sure that one or two of the rats are still twitching.

Sam sets the container down between his knees and plays out a little drum roll on the lid. 'If this is empty, I guess we'll have to eat the rats.'

'We can't. They're diseased.'

'If we put 'em on the fire, wouldn't cooking make them safe?'

'Not necessarily.' Jody has no idea, but she doesn't want to encourage him.

'I mean it. If we don't catch any fish, or trap some birds, this might be all we have.'

'Mm.' She wants to scream: *Open the bloody thing!* Instead, she says, 'Better to use the rats as bait, in your trap.'

'I guess.' A snort, and then – thank God – a smile. 'Let's see what's in here.'

Sam will only admit it to himself, but he's afraid to open the container. Given how things have played out so far, there's got to be a chance it's booby trapped.

He warns Jody to keep back, then flips up the metal clasps and tests the lid. He turns it slowly, anti-clockwise, and it moves easily. Three, four turns and there's no sense of pressure. Nothing about to spring out at him.

Then his stomach burbles, reacting to the smell before his brain can catch up. It's like walking into a bakery.

'Bloody hell,' he mutters, and takes off the lid. He and Jody lean forward at the same time and nearly bump heads.

'Is it food?'

'God, yeah.' He brings out the contents one by one, setting them down on the sand for Jody to see.

Four cans of soda, with foreign writing and an unfamiliar logo. Four energy bars, also foreign. Then a slab of cake, wrapped in cellophane. It looks similar to the cake in the break-fast buffet at the hotel.

Jody lets out a moan of desire. 'Oh my God...'

He's not finished. Next comes a bag containing four bread rolls, so fresh that up close the smell nearly makes him pass out.

'Wow.' Jody stares at Sam, a broad smile on her face. 'Thank you.'

'What for?' Suddenly he can't share her enjoyment. In fact, he feels sickened. *We're supposed to be grateful for this, when they're treating us like animals in a zoo?*

As he moves back, Jody tips the container towards her and goes rooting around inside it. Sam thinks of that cartoon – *Winnie the Pooh*, is it? – where he's searching out every last drop of honey from the pot. There's a packet of antiseptic wipes and a single foil strip of pills. Jody holds them up as if she's found a stash of diamonds.

'Painkillers. These might help Grace.'

There's a clunking noise as she sets the container down. It isn't quite empty.

Once again she feels inside, and brings out an old-fashioned iron key. Sam takes it from her, flakes of rust coming off on his fingers.

'What the hell is this for?'

'Looks like it ought to open a treasure chest.' She doesn't sound particularly interested. They have food, drink, medicine. Who cares about an old key?

He's inclined to leave it, then changes his mind. He pulls on his chinos and shoves the key in his pocket. Jody refills the pot and they gather up the bungee cords while discussing what to do next. She thinks they should share two of the cans straight away.

'Isn't that too much?'

'We're all exhausted, Sam. We need the calories.'

She's right. A decent drink, along with some fresh food, would build up his strength before he goes in search of more water.

They rejoin the kids, who react with delight. Jody opens one of the cans and takes a cautious sip. It's some kind of lemonade. She pops out a painkiller and encourages Grace to swallow it with a drink. That becomes a mini-drama, because Grace isn't used to pills: at home the kids have liquid Calpol. Sam watches their tussle, trying not to get uptight about all the lemonade Grace is using up.

He shares a can with Dylan. The drink is sweet, lukewarm and gassy, but it does at least ease the pain in his throat.

Then Sam takes out the bag of bread rolls. Normally he'd

want to add butter, he'd have ham or cheese and tomato, but here just a plain roll is a feast. The saliva's almost dripping off his tongue in anticipation.

He tells himself it's okay to be first – he and Jody have to test everything, after all – but still it feels more like naked greed than a safety precaution. He takes a small bite and it's everything he hoped it would be: the outside dry and crisp, the individual flakes snapping against his teeth, the soft fluffy innards swelling a little with the moisture on his tongue before slowly dissolving, creating waves of pleasure to rival an orgasm.

He's aware of the other three looking on, wide-eyed and thrilled, sharing his experience the way as a family they'll stop to watch each other open presents on Christmas morning. *It's my turn soon.*

He hands the bag to Jody and nods: go ahead. Then takes a second bite, much bigger and if anything even more delicious than the first... but Jody's expression is changing, looking worried, just as he feels a tickle on his upper lip, a bitter tingling in his mouth.

And movement. Something crawling on his tongue.

He jerks the roll away and sees ants spilling out from a hole in the centre. They're scrambling over his wrist, running along his top lip. And they're still in his mouth.

'Shit!' He drops the roll, clawing at his face while spitting frantically, but he can feel some of them mashed against the roof of his mouth. He has to hook his little finger in to scrape them out.

Then he's sick, more from the shock than anything. That's the fizzy drink wasted. He leans over, stars exploding in his head, aware that Grace and Dylan are sobbing, and Jody as ever doing her best to calm them down.

'Oh, the bastards...' he moans, 'the evil fucking bastards.'

His hand is stinging from where the ants must have bitten

him. His tongue feels numb. He doesn't think he's ever felt so repulsed, so full of disgust and anger and violence. Whoever came up with this idea, put them in front of him right now and Sam could kill them – with his bare hands, if he had to.

Yeah, that's big talk, says a voice inside his head. *But only because you know you won't get the chance.*

47

First, Jody is distraught, then heartbroken. How much more of this sadism will they have to endure?

'Let's get back to the boat,' she says, and Sam meekly agrees. His temper has flared and died down in its usual firework manner.

He takes over the duty of comforting the kids while Jody kneels to examine the half-eaten roll. It's covered in sand, the last few reddish brown ants crawling from their hiding place inside. She's tempted to salvage what she can, until Sam says, 'Forget it.'

She spins the neck of the bag to seal up the other rolls and puts it into the container. The ingenuity of this sick practical joke makes her want to weep. Like a doughnut, only with ants instead of jam. Who does something like that? And what if one of the kids had eaten it?

She can't quite believe how the joy at having secured this food has soured so quickly. She barely says a word on the way back. The only bright note is that Grace claims to feel slightly better. Jody had given her one of the wipes to press against the back of her neck, promising it would take her temperature down. She was relying on the power of suggestion to do the rest, and it seems to be working.

What she's come to think of as their home beach is just as they left it. They sit to the side of the boat that's coming into shadow. Jody empties the container, takes another of the rolls from the bag and holds it at arm's length before slowly tearing it open.

There's nothing inside. The other two rolls are also empty. They look, feel and smell normal. (No, they smell ridiculously, insanely delicious!)

'So how's that for odds?' Sam says.

'It was on top,' Jody points out. 'That was the idea. A cruel shock, but the rest of them can be eaten.'

She goes ahead and proves it, but the kids remain stubbornly resistant. They don't want any of the 'nasty bread', as Dylan puts it. He notices the key, which Sam is idly tapping against his knee, pesters for it and then aims it at his dad, like a gun, and fires: '*Pw! Pw! Pw!*'

Normally Sam would play along, pretending to be shot and firing back, but this time his reaction is only a heavy-lidded look of despair.

'All right, guys,' Jody says quickly. 'The rolls later, I think.'

Her suggestion is to eat the cake, because it's perishable, saving the energy bars for last. She upends the container to use the base as a table. The cake is wrapped in cellophane, which she unpeels as cautiously as if defusing a bomb. She leans forward and sniffs, stifling a groan of pleasure, then breaks off a corner and dabs it on her tongue. It has a sweet vanilla flavour, maybe with a hint of honey.

She savours the taste before swallowing, then breaks off a larger section, ready to jump back if more ants should pour out. But there are no ants, no maggots or worms. The cake crumbles easily, though towards the centre it gets a bit sticky. The smell alone is enough to bring on a sugar rush.

'Come on,' she says, using the mum-in-charge voice. 'We're all having a piece of this, but not too much in one go. It's quite sickly.'

Sam and Grace take her advice but Dylan is still reluctant. He's retreated into a world of his own, jabbing the tip of the key into the sand, carving out shapes with such vicious intensity that she wonders (and not for the first time, if she's honest) whether he doesn't have a little of his Uncle Carl's aggression.

'Dylan, put it down. It's time to eat something.'

'Don't wanno.'

'Oh, come on. You're "big greedy Dylan", remember? The cake monster!'

'Not a cake monster.' He's stabbing the sand, over and over. *Oh God, he's a serial killer in training.*

In a low growl, Sam says, 'Do as you're told, Dylan.'

Do it for the angel lady, Jody nearly says. But Dylan has picked up on the threat in his dad's voice, and in a fit of petulance he hurls the key towards the trees.

'Hate you!' he shouts, and Jody has to put an arm in front of Sam to stop him lunging at his son. He ought to know the boy by now. This is simply the last act of face-saving defiance before he gives in.

'Please don't fight,' Grace cries.

Glowering, Sam takes a lump of cake and then turns his back on them. Jody picks up the wipes and keeps her voice light but authoritative. 'Right, Dylan, you'd better clean your hands. Then you're having some of this cake. It's lovely.'

He slumps on to his knees in front of her, sullenly holding out a palm. She gives him a few small pieces of cake, pinching it between her fingers to make sure it contains no hidden perils. Grace has already had enough, and announces that she intends to take a nap. Without a word, Sam follows her round to the other side of the boat. Either he's seeing her safely into their little den, or else he's had enough of Jody's company.

'Daddy doesn't mean to be cross,' she says to Dylan. And when that gets no response: 'We're all a bit tired and grumpy.'

'I'm not,' he barks, and Jody can't help laughing.

By the time she's wrapped up the cake and put it back in the container, Dylan has curled up on his side and shut his eyes. Jody watches him for a few seconds, knowing she ought to get him to join Grace. But he already looks so peaceful, on the brink of sleep, and the boat's shadow is slowly spreading out on this side...

Her head slips down and snaps back up, the way it sometimes does on the bus home from work. She blinks a few times, unable to believe how easily she began to drift away. She has barely enough energy to lie down and wriggle close to Dylan. Is it any wonder, after such a stressful morning, and so little sleep last night?

There's no shame in surrender, she tells herself. The sugar overload is probably a big part of it: their bodies need time to digest the food.

She's almost gone when the possibility occurs to her that it's something more sinister – they've been drugged again – but by now she feels so mellow that she dares to believe this might be a good thing. They were brought here under sedation, after all. It's quite possible that the same method would be employed for the journey home.

Oh yes: cling to that idea, Jode.

We're going home, home, home.

48

It's mid-afternoon when Gabby arrives, having first returned home to shower, freshen up, settle her nerves.

This season she's been staying in an apartment on the edge of the largest town on Sekliw's south coast. The place is a dump, frankly, but it's conveniently placed between the seven or eight hotels she services on behalf of Sheldon Travel. She shares with two other reps but Gabby barely sees them – when they aren't on duty they'll invariably be on the beach or in a club.

It's a full-on lifestyle, exhausting but exhilarating; not something she can imagine doing much past her mid-twenties. This is her second season on Sekliw, with only six weeks left to run. She's already decided that next year – if she remains in the job at all – she'll go somewhere else for the summer.

The day is stunningly hot. Stepping from the air-conditioned car, it's like being dropped into a hot bath. She feels the prickle of sweat on her back, a flush of heat where the sun catches her neck.

This is her second visit to Borko's mansion; the first is one she'd rather not dwell on, not least because it was when she signed up for all this. There was quite a crowd on that occasion, including a dozen or more girls who she regarded as far more attractive than her – truly beautiful, some of them – but still she had a very narrow escape.

He's a frequent visitor to the island and has been pursuing her, when the mood takes him, for most of the season. The problem is that, by resisting, Gabby has presented him with a challenge – and Borko is a man who feasts on challenges.

The other problem is that, leaving aside what she knows about him (the facts and rumours both) she can't deny that she finds him attractive. *Very* attractive.

Borko wants her body, and pragmatic single-minded Gabrielle fears very much that, if she doesn't leave the country soon, her alter ego – that pleasure-seeking, impulsive tart Gabby – will give it to him.

She spent the journey trying to get into character. There's zero chance of feeling like she belongs at such a mega-exclusive gathering, and she can't really understand why he's invited her (yes she can it's completely bloody obvious) but in this country you don't get to say no to the president's son.

She has opted for low heels and a simple black skater dress: mid-thigh, sleeveless, a hint of cleavage – in her case, *no* cleavage is practically impossible. She knows the effect it has, whether she wants it to or not, but frankly that ought to be the least of her worries.

The main living room is like a smaller version of the grand balcony at the Hotel Conchis. A wall of glass opens on to a long terrace, with tables and easy chairs inside and out. A buffet and a bar at one end, and big cinema-style screens at every turn, broadcasting from the hidden cameras on Borko's ultra-private estate.

The room isn't anywhere near full. She counts twenty or so

guests, most of them middle aged or older. Billionaires, she guesses, almost to a man – or woman, for there are three or four females among them. None that would interest Borko, Gabby notes with regret.

She feels marooned, the only muggle in a gathering of wizards and witches. It's almost a relief to pretend to be absorbed by the images on screen, a montage in the style of a news bulletin that brings her up to date with recent events. Sam and Jody retrieving a canister of supplies from a cage full of rats. A bread roll laced with ants. From their faces, it's evident that the family bonds are being stretched to breaking point.

After a minute Naji Hussein ghosts to her side, taking pretend sips from a glass of champagne. 'Borko sent me to enquire why you are playing the part of a wallflower.'

Gabby shrugs, her senses already tuning in to that electric gaze from across the room. Borko is wearing a beautiful light grey suit and a black silk shirt. He avoids eye contact, though. As if to tease her, he is feigning interest in an elderly couple who appear to have been made out of wax and sprayed with mahogany paint.

On screen the little boy is throwing something away in the midst of a hissy fit. The gesture catches Borko's attention, and he sends a frown in Hussein's direction. The aide responds with the tiniest of shrugs, causing Gabby to wonder about the significance of what she has seen – and what she might have missed.

There's no opportunity to ask because Naji hastily takes her arm, steering her to meet a bloated Hungarian politician who grips her hand in his own sweaty paw for rather too long. He draws her attention to the live feed and taps the side of his nose.

'They sleep now, but soon there will be...' Here his English deserts him, so he makes fists and grinds them together with theatrical menace.

Gabby nods, and manages only a rictus grin. She gets the message.

More introductions follow, Borko working the other side of the room as though they're bride and groom at their wedding reception. Naji says nothing of Gabby's lowly occupation, though he does mention that, as a close friend of Borko's, she played a part in arranging 'our magnificent entertainment'. Inside Gabby is cringing. She wants no credit for this.

For a time she's deposited with a pair of thickset men – Qatari brothers, awash in oil and property – and a Canadian couple in their fifties, both tall and thin, elegant in a cold, theoretical way. The wife is clearly the dominant partner, a swan-necked, fleshless woman with porcelain skin and the eyes of someone who drinks the blood of virgins. In the kind of grating voice that cuts through hubbub, she's telling the Qataris about her ambitious plans for the human race. Gabby hears the word 'eugenics' and feels she ought to know what it means.

'Therapies to extend life are only one side of the coin. I'm determined to live until I'm a hundred and fifty, at least – but on a planet of ten, fifteen billion? No, thank you!' The woman's laugh sounds like a machine gun clogged with gravel. 'I believe a virus to be the best solution, something along the lines of myxomatosis, although they tell me that nanotechnology offers great potential.'

They are joined by a hollow-chested, gawky man with unkempt red-blond hair and an overbite. He looks about fourteen, but carries himself like a boy emperor. In a nasal American accent, he says, 'How'd you plan to direct it to the right targets? You can't single out according to ethnic groups, or even IQ. Just not feasible.'

The woman treats the youngster to an imperious sneer. 'I am told there could be a genetic marker.'

From nowhere Gabby hears herself say, 'For what, exactly? Poverty? *Bad luck?*'

There are gasps from the little group around her. Gabby realises it's the word 'luck' that disturbs them. Before she can be dragged out and stoned for this unforgivable breach of etiquette, she feels gentle pressure on her shoulders.

Borko turns her to face him. As usual, the scan of her body is so thorough it's like walking through one of those machines at the airport. His hair and skin immaculate as ever, his eyes a provocative gleam of danger and delight. He kisses her on both cheeks and deftly leads her away from the gathering. Most of the guests get the hint, but not the young American.

'Gonna introduce me here, Bork?'

Bork? From the shadow that crosses his face, Gabby wouldn't be surprised if Borko pulled out a gun and shot the American on the spot. It's something his father is rumoured to have done once or twice back in the bad old days – days that the international community have to come to agree were greatly exaggerated, if indeed they happened at all.

But Borko recovers his good humour and makes the introductions, only for Jesse to interrupt with his own résumé'. He's permitted a couple of minutes to brag about the 'world-changing apps' that he invented, before Borko breaks in, saying lightly, 'Who would have thought when it started that social media could turn out to be so important?'

'I did,' Jesse says flatly, and there's another moment when an on-the-spot execution might be the answer. 'Hey, this is the era of toys. Toys and games – like this.' He sweeps a hand at the screens, and then fixes his gaze on Gabby. 'No one grows up anymore, and kidults make the perfect product for social media. You happily tell us everything about your lives – things that businesses used to spend *billions* trying to extract from you. Now we get it for free, and we take that information and use it to sell you stuff, and even more importantly we tell you who to vote for and what to believe.' He stops, his mouth bubbling with saliva, and laughs. 'Can you tell how much I love it?'

'More than life itself?' Gabby asks drily, but Borko is already speaking over her.

'Jesse has suggested that next year we introduce drones.'

'Wouldn't that be the coolest thing? I hear Bork's dad is already using them for, like, surveillance and stuff. Get a couple and modify them. *Weaponize* them.' Jesse cackles, and lets off a couple of explosive finger snaps. 'Imagine every time a drone flies over, and they don't know if it's gonna drop a food parcel or, like, napalm or something!'

Borko laughs with what might be genuine enthusiasm, while Gabby smiles politely.

A minute or two later, the American is palmed off on an intense young man with a huge and prematurely bald skull, introduced only as, 'One of the whizzkids from Tufton Street.'

And then Borko has Gabby to himself, muttering as he leads her away: 'Can you believe he's one of the richest men in America?'

'Really?' Gabby reacts with a kind of double-take, which Borko obviously misinterprets.

'You are interested in him?'

'No,' she hisses. 'Of course not.'

He isn't convinced, taking a careful look into her eyes that causes her stomach to churn. Then he tuts. 'Oh, Gabby, if you were to choose Jesse over me, I don't know what I would do.'

49

It was at a more conventional party a couple of months ago that he had taken her into his confidence, hinting at some unorthodox entertainment put on each summer for the delight of a hand-picked group of VIP guests. He might want her help, he said, but first he needed to know she was capable of complete discretion.

Totally, she'd promised him, because this was fun-loving Gabby in charge. So he sketched it out, and Gabby was duly confused, stunned, sceptical, horrified, amazed and all the rest of it – as anyone would be in the circumstances. But then, with characteristic boldness, she set aside the more diplomatic questions and went instead for the jugular: 'Why do you do it?'

Borko had been genuinely taken aback. She guessed that no one had ever asked him this question – perhaps, she realised later, because no one dared.

His explanation, such as it was, drew on a number of comparisons. He spoke enviously of an Indian businessman whose purpose-built home in Mumbai was a *twenty-seven* storey building – his very own tower block – which cost at least a billion dollars to construct and offered nearly forty thousand square metres of living space. When he summoned up a picture on his phone, it looked to Gabby like an unevenly piled stack of shipping containers. And she said as much.

'That's your opinion, truly?' Borko said, with spluttering laughter. 'What about all that marble? All that glass?'

'Yeah, okay. A stack of *vajazzled* shipping containers.'

Then came other comparisons: the super-rich moguls pouring billions into space exploration, often with the aim of getting into space themselves, or cryonic preservation, because they were determined to cheat death. He spoke of an Australian who'd flirted with the possibility of bringing real dinosaurs back to life before settling for a vast theme park full of animatronic creatures. The same man had ploughed money into building an exact replica of the Titanic, while an American oil billionaire had recreated an entire Wild West town on his Colorado ranch, solely for his private entertainment.

Borko was rambling somewhat by this point, and his eyes kept flicking towards her chest, distracting them both. But Gabby felt she had got the gist. She could sum it up in three words, in fact. *Because I can.*

Why do you go to all this time and trouble? Why do you spend all this money? Why do you treat other human beings as your personal playthings?

Because I can.

They move to a discreet corner, where he enthuses over what he considers to be the important scientific integrity of his project. To Borko, this is far more than a spectacular piece of entertainment. It is a groundbreaking study of human nature in the raw, and as such he believes its data should be available for review by experts in the fields of psychology, anthropology and sociology.

Gabby knows from their previous conversation that it is Naji who vetoed such involvement. At first it puzzled her that Borko hadn't gone ahead regardless, but now she considers whether the aide is using Borko's father as leverage. Is it possible, she wonders, that the president has no idea what his son is doing on Sekliw?

If so, it's a dangerous game. Another very good reason for Gabby to get the hell away from here.

The super-rich guests are handpicked, he tells her, men and women of jaded appetites for whom genuinely original thrills are increasingly hard to come by – though as yet there hasn't been much excitement for them, not on the live feed, at least.

Borko is fuming about various technical difficulties, particularly a lack of sound coverage around the family's makeshift camp. 'We're reliant on the camera mikes in the trees, but the slightest breeze and we lose them completely.' He sighs, then remembers more bad news. 'Your text?'

Fearfully, Gabby says: 'A couple of the guests were asking after Sam and Jody. I gave them the cover story, but I wouldn't put it past them to phone the Conchis...'

She's expecting fury but Borko is already shaking his head. 'It's nothing. Forget them.' And he moves on to Jesse's suggestion of drones, revealing that he has a much better idea: 'Hunter robots. There's a firm called Boston Dynamics who have produced some remarkable devices...'

Gabby is lost for words. For Borko, problems are like snowflakes, destined to melt within seconds of contact with the burning force of his personality.

It takes him a minute to register her astonishment. 'What?'

'Doesn't any of this worry you at all – the risks you're taking?'

'No. Because those risks are carefully managed. We do this no more than once a year, and each time I choose a different nationality, from a different hotel, a different tour company.'

'Even so, something's bound to get out sooner or later. So many people must be aware of it.'

'Only people I trust,' he says coldly. 'The numbers are kept low for good reason.'

'I don't mean the guests. But the staff–'

'My staff are not so foolish that they would betray me.'

Gabby doesn't like where this conversation is going. Fortunately Naji comes over, signalling that Borko is wanted. The aide looks concerned – and Gabby has a moment to reflect, as she watches them conferring on the terrace, that perhaps it is Naji's role to worry for them both.

Retreating to a safe vantage point, she notices how the guests tend to form small groups where they chat for a minute or two, looking vaguely bored, then break up and drift away to repeat the process. Like some sort of high-status animals in search of nourishment. Sharks, perhaps.

She smiles to herself, with no discernible humour: of course, sharks.

As Borko comes back inside, the main screen shows movement at bay three: a small dhingy is gliding towards the shore. Borko claps his hands together like a pistol shot, and in a room devoid of bodyguards many of the guests flinch or duck.

Pretending he hasn't noticed, Borko says, 'Ladies and gentlemen, the afternoon's entertainment is about to begin.'

The dhingy glides ashore and half a dozen figures spill out, all but one of them dressed in black. The exception is a slighter form, female, wearing a long white robe. She and two of the men hurry in the opposite direction to the other three, who are carrying tool bags and equipment of some kind.

As the figures recede, the camera cuts to a view of the sleeping family. They are in pairs: Sam and Grace under the boat, Jody and the boy on the far side. In the distance the afternoon sun glitters on the water. The woman in the robe approaches slowly, the men appearing to hide behind her. She reaches the sleeping figures and stands over them, hands clasped together and head bowed, her face hidden by the hood.

Gabby shivers, just as Borko materialises at her side. 'She's a dancer and a mime artist, from Latvia. Very accomplished.'

Gabby can hear the unmistakeable note of possession in his voice: *conquest number eight thousand and whatever*.

Then the screen goes blank. Gabby assumes it's another technical glitch but Borko wears a sly smile, assuring his guests that the transmission will resume imminently. The last thing they see is the shadow of one of the men behind Jody, moving towards the bodies.

Not bodies, Gabby corrects herself. *People*.

They're still alive.

50

It takes Sam a while to wake up. He's woozy, nauseous, but unlike last time there's no confusion. He knows the deal straight away.

He's lying on his side, facing away from the boat, but he can feel the heat of another body behind him. He rolls over. Grace is fast asleep or unconscious, but her breathing is quiet, regular; it doesn't seem as though she's in any distress, which is one small comfort.

So why did they–?

He climbs to his feet, peering over the boat because he remembers that's where Jody and Dylan were when he left them. He just has time to note that the sun is slightly lower in the sky. And then he sees her.

He runs round the boat, stamping and skidding on the powder dry sand. He's gasping for breath, the air coming out in a kind of desperate growl. His fists are clenched so tight they're making his arms shake. A lot of anger welling up, but Jody's still out cold. It's not her fault. They've all been drugged again.

He kneels by her side and grasps her shoulder. 'Jode. Jody. Wake up.'

'Uh?' Her eyes flutter.

'Wake up, quickly!'

That does it: the alarm in his voice. 'What is it?'

'Dylan's not here. He's gone.'

Gabby tries to subdue her fears while she waits for the live feed to resume. She's beginning to appreciate how much she's been misled – to put it mildly.

Borko has played her for a fool, and this poor family are suffering as a consequence.

Several times she catches Naji giving her a stern glance. From her first acquaintance she regarded him as a total slime-ball, but more recently she's learned that he was originally recruited from the Syrian republican guard to work as chief interrogator for Dragan Radić, back in the days when Borko's father was a ruthless, ambitious warlord. There's a rumour, gleaned from a fellow rep, that Borko himself was expelled from one of his posh schools – Charterhouse, she thinks – when a couple of boys in his House were caught sharing the video he'd given them, showing a journalist being forced to eat his own excrement. It was Naji doing the forcing.

Borko calls for their attention. The screens are broadcasting again. 'They are awake.'

Sure enough, Sam Berry is now crouched over his partner. Gabby can't make out much more than a shadow beneath the boat, which is where Grace had gone to sleep. Her brother had been lying next to Jody, but there's no sign of him now.

Watching more closely, she sees that Sam is tense, agitated, while Jody looks confused, her movements sluggish.

It's the boy, then, Gabby understands.

Dylan is the next party piece.

. . .

Dylan's gone.

The strange thing, Jody will realise later, is that she never actually felt she was unconscious. But she does recall plenty of vivid dreams, and the most disturbing of them featured a woman in a white robe. The angel lady.

She was here, on the beach, standing over them. Hands clasped together, head bowed in prayer. Her absolute stillness contrasted with what felt to Jody like a flurry of movement all around her. In the dream the intense glare of the afternoon was so ferocious that it had the same effect as darkness, cloaking the activities of the wraith-like figures in the background.

Then Sam is at her side, urging her to wake up. The dreams don't matter; not when... not when Dylan...

'Sam, stop.' Her head feels like it's swelling, about to burst. Afraid she'll vomit, she clamps a hand over her mouth. But nothing comes up; there's only a sour taste in her throat, a pounding in her head and heart and of course the constant desperate craving for normality. For her family to be *safe*.

'Jody, listen. They must have drugged us again. That fucking food. And Dylan's disappeared.'

Sam paces up and down. She can feel his impatience, his fury and fear.

'Maybe he woke up and... wandered off?' she says.

'There are tracks.'

Jody manages to sit up, then rises to her feet. Sam makes no move to help her: too intent on studying the mess of footprints. From more than one person, by the look of it.

They exchange a glance, understanding the significance. No sweeping the sand this time. They're supposed to follow the trail.

'It's another frigging test,' he snarls. She can hear something in his voice: not just disgust but a longing to refuse. *I'm not playing this game anymore.*

But he can't do that, and neither can she.

Jody takes a deep breath, wishing her head would clear. Then the dream comes back: dangerous wraiths.

'The angel lady.'

'What?'

'Maybe she was...' *This is unhinged, but she's going to say it.* 'Wh-what if she was... a vision?'

'A *vision*?'

'Of... of his death. An angel, like he said.'

'Ah, Christ.' The scorn in Sam's voice is actually a relief. She'd welcome any degree of contempt over the possibility that she's right. 'You don't believe in any of that crap,' he mutters.

'No, I don't – or I didn't, not when we lived in a world that was...' She shrugs. 'Sane.'

Sam can't believe what she's just come out with. As if there wasn't enough to worry about.

What's clear is that this was all planned. The food or drink had something that knocked them out. Now, like obedient pets, they're supposed to go running off to find Dylan.

Sam examines the footprints and decides one set might belong to a woman. So maybe this *angel lady* is real. Perhaps Dylan really did see someone earlier.

'I'll go,' he says, noticing how pale and ill Jody looks. She's unsteady on her feet, utterly drained. But she shakes her head.

'You were right before. We have to stay together.'

'What about Grace?'

'It can't be helped. We don't know what we're up against.'

They rouse their daughter. She sits up, her face streaked with dust and tears.

'How are you feeling?' Jody asks.

'Bit better.' Grace looks round. 'Where's Dylan?'

'We're not sure,' Sam says.

'We have to look for him,' Jody adds. 'I'm sorry.'

Grace only nods, fighting back tears. A quick sip of water from the second bottle, and then they set off. Grace's leg is still red and swollen, but her temperature seems slightly lower than it was. She walks hand-in-hand with Jody, a few paces behind Sam. He's holding one of the shorter stakes, while Jody has a couple of bungee cords.

The footprints fade out as they reach the harder ground of the ridge. There's no sign of a detour towards the woods, so Sam decides to keep going. All the time there's a voice in his head, begging him not to think too much about what might have happened to his son. He can't imagine how he'll react if–

And then Sam hauls himself over a rock and spots a tiny figure on the beach, about a hundred metres away.

'That's him!'

'Is he all right?' Jody shouts. Sam doesn't respond. He needs to be sure before he raises her hopes.

'Sam! Tell me if he's–'

'I think he's okay. Come on.'

Jody and Grace scramble up. The trail resumes below them and leads straight to Dylan. He's lying on his back, his body twisted slightly, one arm across his face. Not the sort of position he'd normally sleep in.

Then his leg twitches. Jody groans as if she's been punched in the stomach. 'Why have they left him there?'

That's what Sam is wondering. He notices something at Dylan's feet, long and thin, snaking through the sand between Dylan and the sea.

But it's not a snake. It's maybe a rope, or a chain. When Dylan's leg twitches again, there's a disturbance in the sand and more of the chain is exposed. It seems to begin at Dylan's feet and lead all the way to the water.

'What's that?' Jody asks.

'Dunno.' Their son is alive; that's all Sam can focus on for now. He starts to move but Jody snatches at his arm.

'Watch out for traps.'

Good point. He checks the beach as he climbs down. Once on the sand, he crouches low, trying to spot any trip wires or patches of ground where a pit might have been dug and covered over. By the time Jody and Grace join him, he's satisfied it's safe to move forward.

'Stay behind me,' he says. 'Let's go carefully.'

But he ignores his own advice almost immediately, speeding up when he sees another movement from Dylan. It's a strange jerking motion, his arm wobbling above his face. Sam can't understand why the boy hasn't cried out, or looked round at them.

Then he gets closer, and sees that Dylan is still unconscious.

The chain is thick and heavy and clotted with rust. It might have come from a boat: an old anchor chain. What the hell is it doing here?

The answer comes a few seconds later, as he closes the distance and sees that the chain is attached to a pair of metal cuffs around Dylan's ankles. Maybe it's his imagination, but Sam seems to hear a low grinding noise, then the rasp of metal on sand. The links take a little jump towards the sea, and so does Dylan, his body pulled a few centimetres down the beach.

Sam collapses.

51

When Sam falls, the room is briefly quiet. Before that, there have been gasps, whistles, even incredulous laughter.

Listening in to several conversations, Gabby learns that it took four weeks and cost more than three hundred thousand dollars to modify a marine winch and place it underwater. The power source had to be hidden half a kilometre away, and fed through cables sunk deep in the sand. To Gabby it seems an obscene waste of time and money; not to mention the sadism involved. Then again, what does she know? No doubt the guests here would regard such expenditure as trivial compared to space rockets, dinosaurs and a twenty-seven-storey home in a city where millions live in poverty...

They're told that the scene is covered by four cameras, two in the trees overlooking the beach, the others set into rocks at each side of the bay. A powerful zoom lens allows them to see the fear and desperation in Jody's face. She's gripping her daughter's hand. Grace looks bewildered, and pitifully afraid. Dylan is unconscious, the chain tugging him slowly towards the water. Sam is sprawled on the sand beside him.

'He faints?' asks an elderly Israeli man. 'Or is it cardiac arrest?'

To laughter, someone drawls, 'Not gonna save his kid by taking a nap!'

They can hear the girl screaming her father's name. The sound quality is noticeably better here. Borko explains that a microphone was secreted in the boy's clothing.

For some reason, Gabby is revolted by this small detail. She turns away, only to find Jesse easing into uncomfortably close range.

'There's a tide here, right?' he asks Borko.

'Yes.'

'But you couldn't know exactly when this was gonna happen – the parents finding him. So how d'you calculate the clearance needed to stop the kid from drowning?'

Borko doesn't respond, which is answer enough.

Jesse's lips slowly curl into a smile of rueful admiration.

'Oh, jeez. That's harsh.' He's laughing. 'That's, like, really harsh.'

Jody drops alongside Sam, even as he rolls over and opens his eyes. It looked as though he passed out, though he insists he didn't.

'I'm fine. It's just...' He gestures at Dylan. Another twitch of the chain and their son is dragged closer to the sea.

Grace has slumped on to the sand with her head down on her knees. Cocooning herself. Jody kneels beside Dylan and whispers his name. When he doesn't respond, she carefully lifts his arm clear of his face, yelping as his body is jerked by the chain. His eyes remain shut, his expression peaceful. He doesn't seem to be hurt.

She leans closer to make absolutely sure he is breathing.

Sam, meanwhile, is holding the chain in one hand, testing its connection to the shackles around Dylan's ankles. They're made of heavy iron, each one circular apart from a straight section that appears to be hinged at one end. Old and rusted, like something out of a pirate movie.

That prompts a dim memory from earlier – a remark about a treasure chest? – and then Sam says, 'They're locked.'

'Locked? You mean they need a key.'

'Yeah.' As he makes the connection, there's a flare of panic. 'Dylan! Wake up!'

He reaches for Dylan's pocket but Jody stops him. 'He threw it away, don't you remember?'

Sam's eyes lose focus as he goes back in time. Then he lets out a roar: '*Shit!*'

Again the chain jumps and moves. Dylan bumps over a buried rock and lets out a sleepy moan. Jody and Sam have to shuffle down the sand to stay level with him.

Jody says, 'He was digging with it, and...' *You lost your temper* '... we got cross.'

Sam stares deep into her eyes. It feels like they're reading one another's minds with ease, but not in a good way.

'Which direction?'

She does her best to picture it. 'Top of the beach. Near the trees.'

'Right.' Without another word, Sam is up and sprinting. She understands at once: they have so little time. Looking at the grooves in the sand made by Dylan's body, he's been hauled a metre or so in the couple of minutes they've been here.

But Grace is staring in horror at what appears to be her father running away. 'He's fetching something to help Dylan,' Jody assures her. 'Don't worry. We'll get him free.'

'We won't. They want us to die.'

'No, it's just silly games they're playing.' Jody smiles, marvelling at this placid voice that bears no relation to how she's really feeling. 'While we wait for Daddy, let's both try pulling on the chain, as hard as we can.'

Grace, to her credit, does as she's told without protesting. But there's too much tension in the chain to lift it off the ground. They're forced to lie on their backs and wriggle beneath the chain, wrapping their feet around it as though they're clinging to a zip wire. Flakes of rust drift down on to Jody's face. Blinking and spitting, she grips the chain in both hands and feels a grinding vibration through the links.

She digs her heels into the sand, using all her strength, praying it will be enough to foul up the mechanism that's reeling it in. But the metal slides through her palms as if meeting no resistance at all. There's a squeal of pain from Grace as the friction burns her hands.

Jody tells her to come out; she's done her best. But she makes another attempt herself, aware that it's probably futile, knowing she still has to try. As she turns her head to avoid the glare of the sun, she spots a white streak across the sky: a jet passing overhead. For a second she wants to shout and wave, but it's a ludicrous idea.

Can anyone see what's happening down here? Can they tell the trouble we're in?

Of course not. And with a bitterness that's entirely new to her comes another thought: *Even if they could tell, why would they care?*

'Hurry up, Sam,' she whispers, but the plea is lost in another tug of the chain; another twist of the knife in her heart.

52

Sam jumps down on to their home beach and sends a spray of blood over the sand. He was vaguely aware that he'd crunched his knee against a rock as he clambered over the ridge, but hadn't realised it was bleeding, or that his trousers had ripped.

He runs on, a fog of panic in his brain. All that comes through clearly is the ticking clock, the chain moving every ten or fifteen seconds; the slow drag of it that will, if it isn't stopped, take his boy beneath the water.

If Sam had paid attention at school, he'd probably be able to figure out how long they have: how many centimetres per minute the chain is moving. But he'd dicked around, hadn't he? He remembers backchatting the maths teacher: 'What's the point, Miss? I'm never gonna use any of this stuff.'

How she would laugh, eh? She was Scottish, a right miserable cow. Kept stressing how hard they had to *wurrk*. Well, he's *wurrk*ing hard enough now, isn't he?

He reaches the boat and positions himself at the spot where Dylan was sitting earlier. A few precious seconds to kneel down and twist the way Dylan would have twisted – he can't remember for sure, that's the problem – and then act out throwing the key towards the trees.

He thinks he has the basic direction, but he keeps a close eye on the ground as he moves up the beach, sometimes using his foot to sift through piles of dry sand. With his head dipped, the sweat runs off his nose like a waterfall. A taunting voice in his head is saying, What if an animal's come and taken it away? A bird could have swooped down and carried it off in its beak...

Then he sees it, just lying there. Almost too easy. Imagine if Dylan had thrown it in the sea?

'*Fucking stop it!*' Sam shouts at himself, snatching the key and running back like he's Usain frigging Bolt. As he's climbing the ridge he notices the wound on his knee is clogged with sand, which has stopped the bleeding, at least.

He's shocked by how much further Dylan has moved: surely it's only been a couple of minutes? But the scar in the sand above Dylan's head has lengthened by a metre or more. Jody is kneeling by the chain, holding it in both hands. It jerks again and takes her and Dylan with it.

Grace is first to see Sam. She says something to her mum, who looks up and waves. Sam lifts one arm, hoping she can see the key. Jody's body seems to slump – from relief, he guesses. Grace frowns, then turns to look at her brother. As Sam gets closer, he understands why.

Dylan is waking up.

'I've got it, I've got it,' Sam calls.

Dylan opens his eyes and automatically twists away from the glare of the sun, only to be wrenched by the chain. He lets out a frightened squeal, which Jody smothers by throwing herself over him.

'Baby, it's okay, don't worry.'

'Here we go.' Sam kneels at Dylan's side, wipes the sweat from his face and takes hold of one of the shackles, lining up the key to fit into the lock. The chain moves again and Sam has to manoeuvre himself to stay with it. All of a sudden the gentle wash of the waves against the shore seems louder. They're, what, two or three metres away?

Plenty of time. He tries to calm himself, keep his hand steady and get this done. Then it's back to the camp and they're gonna drink the bottle of rainwater to celebrate, and sod the consequences...

The key slots in, but nothing happens. He pushes it a little harder, expecting to hear a click and feel something give.

Nothing.

The chain cranks forward. Dylan starts writhing, trying to kick, but the chain is too tight and he can't bend his knees. Grace is wailing in sympathy, and all this noise is making it even harder to concentrate...

In a panic, Sam fumbles the key out and tries the other shackle, knowing deep down that he's got to release them both if he's to save his son.

Jody turns, frowning at him. 'Come on.'

'It won't unlock.'

'*What*?'

He tries to be slower, more delicate; sometimes you can push a key in *too* far.

But it still doesn't open. He looks at Jody and feels his face go slack, as if something inside him is dissolving.

'It won't...'

Jody already has her hand out. She snatches the key and they switch places, Sam stroking his son's forehead while Jody tries one lock, then the other. Between each attempt there's another crank forward. As if to taunt them, a slightly bigger wave pushes in, foaming on the sand before slowly retreating.

'It doesn't fit.' Her voice is tiny, scared.

'Must be the wrong key.'

She shakes her head. 'Why, Sam?'

'Why? Because they enjoy fucking with us, that's why.'

Jody stares at the key like she's willing it to be the right one. The chain moves again, another link disappearing into the sea.

'What are we going to do?' she asks. It sounds like she's begging him but Sam doesn't know, he truly doesn't, he's useless–

Another jump: Christ, did he drift off or is it speeding up? He glances to his left, the water almost close enough to touch.

'Sam! What are we going to do?'

He shakes his head. He has no answer, and Jody shouldn't be putting him on the spot – not when Dylan can hear them.

How is Sam supposed to admit that he can't save his own son?

53

The tension in the room is palpable, but only Gabby seems appalled by what's happening. *You didn't say it was going to be this dangerous*, she thinks. But does she dare confront Borko?

The guests are clustered in their little groups, and in some there are wagers being made. She hears a Russian man declare: 'Half a million that he dies,' and the men with him cackle and take the bet.

'Cliffhangers,' Jesse says. 'Corny but effective.'

Acting as though the American has said something perceptive, Borko adds, 'We know our emotions are being manipulated, but we can't resist.'

He catches Gabby's eye, as if seeking her opinion. She nods politely and eases away, signalling to Borko that she wants him to follow. Once they're alone, she says, 'Tell me you're joking? You won't really let that boy drown?'

Borko opens his arms in a gesture of helplessness. 'The solution is there, with the parents.'

'You could switch it off. You must be able–'

'Sadly, no. The remote activation doesn't allow for that.'

'But they found the key and it didn't work.'

'Ah. That was rather wicked of me. But they still have time.'
They turn to look at the nearest screen. Dylan's feet are less than
a metre from the water's edge. 'Let's see if they have the
resourcefulness to meet the challenge.'

'This isn't a game of *Sims*.'

'No,' Borko agrees, looking vaguely offended. 'It's much more
interesting than that.'

Gabby wilts, knowing full well that he wants her to beg.
'Please, Borko. Don't do this to them.'

'It's a test, remember. A test of their character, their courage.
If they fail – and I hope they don't – then it has to be said that
the world can probably do without passing on their DNA to
future generations.'

A series of gentle waves are followed by another larger one. It
splashes over Dylan's feet and covers the shackles for a second
or two. Jody rears back in panic and hates herself for it. She's still
holding Dylan's hand but it's not enough. He senses her fear and
stops crying, regarding her with a strangely adult expression. It's
as if, all at once, he fully comprehends what's happening to him
– and not only that, but he accepts it.

The chain slips into the water, link by link, and it feels like
only Jody cares. Sam is barely moving: he seems to have gone
into shock. Grace is lying face down on the sand, her body
quaking with quiet sobs. The next wave hits Dylan's foot and
hardly retreats. Jody can feel all her hope and strength slithering
away.

Then Sam says, 'The other end.'

He's staring at the water. The shallows are clear enough to
see the chain running along the seabed.

She holds up the key, the hope growing inside her like a sly and deceitful companion. 'Could there be a lock at the other end?'

Sam's already taking off his shirt. Another pull on the chain and the water creeps up to Dylan's shin. As Sam extends his hand, she remembers how he struggled yesterday.

I should be doing this. I swim better than him.

'Sam–'

'Just try to keep his head above the water. If I can't find a lock I might be able to jam it up, at least.'

She gives him the key. He steps out of his chinos and wades in up to his shoulders before slipping below the surface. There's a splash as he dives down, his feet briefly reappearing as he scissors his legs and kicks towards the bottom.

'Won't be long,' Jody mutters, though she has no idea who she's trying to convince. Dylan is staring at her, open-mouthed, and she's nearly broken by the memory of holding him as a baby, his dark eyes solemnly roaming her face; how she was so often spellbound by the deep, unknowable curiosity of his infant gaze.

The chain tugs him again, the water lapping at his knees. In a snap decision prompted by the memory, she helps him to sit up and then backs into the water herself so she can lift him into her arms. To get enough clearance it means wading in up to her waist, but this at least creates some slack in the chain.

By holding him tight and taking the burden of the chain in her hand, she's hoping to fool Dylan into believing there's nothing to worry about. But the weight of the shackles is a shock, and the chain is still being reeled in. She'll have no choice but to step into deeper water, all the time straining to keep his head clear of the surface.

Could she float, if necessary, while bearing all this weight? She knows she'll have to try, but it's impossible to overcome the remorseless pull of the chain. She is tormented by an image of

Dylan being dragged from her grasp and slipping under the water.

Even then she won't give up. When he was ill with meningitis, she told herself she'd swap places with him in an instant, and now she will breathe for him if she has to, taking gulps of air and diving down to blow that air into his mouth. *The kiss of life.*

Except that it sounds ridiculous. She probably saw it in a movie and of course it would have worked a treat; not so likely in the real world.

But if it doesn't work, she can't let him die alone. Dylan is her baby, her little boy. She'll have to sink beside him and accept that she's saying goodbye to Sam, and to Grace, open her mouth and let the water flood her lungs and end it, finally; this wicked, wicked game they're being forced to play.

Sam swims four, five strokes, and still the chain leads nowhere. Up ahead the seabed slopes into darkness. Tiny fish dart away from his clumsy approach; on the bottom there are plants with long crinkled leaves, weaving back and forth like tentacles. Hiding among them is a crab the size of his hand. *Food.* He could come back and catch it once Dylan is free.

The pressure in Sam's lungs quickly becomes unbearable. Lightheaded, he rises to the surface and sucks the air in desperate gasps. He's further from Jody than he expected. She's now in up to her waist, holding Dylan in her arms, whispering in his ear the way she does to get him back to sleep after a nightmare.

Sam plunges back down, flipping over to dive head first. It takes him a moment to get his bearings and find the chain. Once again he's surprised by how much easier it is to swim underwater than on the surface, and that gives him hope.

He can do this. He *will* do this.

After a few strokes his lungs are protesting, but this time he's determined not to go back up until he's located something. Another couple of metres and finally he sees it. His first thought is that it's like a giant version of the commercial cable reels he uses every day at work; only this is metal not plastic, and the giant drum is winding up a chain instead of electrical cable.

He swims closer, using the chain to fight his body's natural buoyancy. He's wondering about the power source when he notices a thick black lead trailing off to his right. Presumably it connects to a generator somewhere onshore. Far too late to go searching for it now.

And there's another problem. The chain is already wrapped around the drum at least a dozen times. The drum is boxed in with heavy steel plates, so he can't see where the chain is attached. There's nothing here to suggest that the key would be any use at all. Even unwinding the chain would be almost impossible, because of its weight and the difficulty of working underwater.

So what, then? He needs a weapon if he's to jam the mechanism. Immediately the wooden stake comes to mind. Why didn't he bring it with him?

And swim underwater with it? While also holding the key?

He's desperate to breathe. Has he got time to swim back to shore and fetch the stake? Maybe not, but he has to try. He lets go of the chain and pushes upwards, just as he notices the small red box on one side of the apparatus.

It's too late to change direction; in any case, his chest is about to explode. He propels himself towards the surface in a stream of bubbles, releasing the dead air from his lungs in anticipation of a fresh breath, a second or two away. The image of the box stays fixed in his mind. Maybe it has a switch inside: a simple on/off that could bring this nightmare to an end.

Then he's out, bobbing and gasping, not checking on Jody

and Dylan this time because he can't afford to lose focus. A few quick breaths to recover, then another lung filler and back down he goes. Straight to the box, grabbing the chain in one hand to keep him steady – though at that very moment it winds on, almost trapping his fingers against the drum.

The box is made of metal, about the size of a cashbox. It requires a key, of course. But this time there's no trick: the key fits and the lid pops open.

No switch or button inside. It appears to be empty. In desperation Sam feels around... and discovers something taped to the top.

Another key.

54

The chain pulls relentlessly, scraping against Jody's skin when she tries to trap it between her knees. She's holding Dylan as high as she can but the sea is up to her chest, which means it's around his waist. Dylan's face is pressed against her shoulder. She can feel the heat of his tears as he weeps in wretched silence.

Another tug. Jody takes a step back, trying to test the ground first but misjudging how much it shelves. She stumbles and nearly loses him, a wave catching them both. As they retch and spit, she hears a loud splash and turns to see Sam waving the key as if he's got something to celebrate.

The chain pulls again, dragging Dylan down, and in that moment she hates Sam almost as much as the rest of them, and that hatred, that resentment is in her voice when she screams: 'It's still moving! You haven't stopped it!'

He looks stunned by the outburst, but he's gasping for breath and can't speak. He swims frantically towards her, creating a wash that threatens to engulf her son.

'*Fucking stupid idiot*–' She breaks off only because the fury is draining too much energy from her. In a steadier voice, she says, 'I can't do this for much longer.'

Sam nods as though he understands. 'Key,' he says, the way a toddler would – because he's trying to swim and talk and spit water from his mouth.

Key?

'Will you listen to me?' she yells. 'It *hasn't. Bloody. Worked.*'

'Another, there's another...' He waves it at her again. To Jody it looks identical to the one they've already tried, and it crosses her mind that he's had a breakdown, convincing himself that he's found a different key.

He comes closer, wading rather than swimming, and with both hands free he lifts them to show her that he has two keys. Then he's dropping, bending his knees to sink beneath the surface. She feels him bump against her as he reaches for the shackles. Dylan's body spasms and she does her best to calm him, but she has no idea whether he's able to take on board what she's saying.

The water has reached his neck. She's crouching to hold him, trying to use her arms to shield him from the tiny waves. If she could, she'd scoop out all the water that keeps swirling around them – a mad thought that prompts a memory of her childhood, her dad with a bucket and spade, striding across the beach at Camber Sands. *I'm off to dig a hole in the sea, anyone wanna help?*

Something changes in Dylan's posture. She feels a kick.

Sam's head bursts up, water spraying from his mouth. 'It works! One of them's off.'

'Thank God. Do the other–'

He's already on his way back down. The chain pulls. This time it's even harder to hold Dylan because he's using his free leg to kick and fight. Jody can't stop him wriggling because she feels the panic every bit as keenly.

A few seconds. Only a few more seconds.

But she's watching the top of Sam's head, clearly visible in the water, and suddenly it drops away.

He's let go of Dylan's leg, but the chain is still in place.

Still pulling.

The key slipped in easily on the first shackle. Sam felt it slot into place in a way that the other one hadn't. A gentle turn and the lock released, the bracelet around Dylan's ankle snapping open.

The second one should have gone the same way. With Dylan kicking out, it took a little more concentration, but it was doable. And yet, somehow, as Sam nuzzled the key against the opening and thought it was lined up, he pushed a bit too firmly and the key struck the outer plate and slipped from his grasp.

He saw it fall, the descent so slow and lazy it should have been easy to catch. But the sunlight cutting through the water was playing games with his perspective, causing the world to shift and shimmer. He snatched at the key and missed, and it has landed on the bottom among the sand and weeds.

Sam plunges down in what he's sure is a straight line. He feels around but doesn't find it. He can't stay much longer; his throat is being crushed. A couple of seconds and straight back, okay?

Except that Jody is calling his name.

He'll have to tell her.

'I dropped the key. I'm so sorry. I dropped the key.'

The words come spilling out as Sam rises from the sea. Jody stares at him, too distraught to find words. One of her hands is cupping Dylan's chin, trying to stop the water from reaching his mouth.

'I swam down but I couldn't find it.'

He sounds broken. Jody realises he's crying. He opens his mouth wide to take a gulp of air but she shouts: 'Wait!' A moment's hesitation, which gives Jody her chance. 'Take Dylan.'

'But–'

'You're stronger. Take him!'

Sam does as he's told, flinching when the chain moves again. Jody drops into the water, and sees that Sam has stood on the chain, hoping his body weight will slow it down. Why didn't she think of that?

It's hard to relax enough to sink. She ends up having to swim properly, folding over and kicking her legs to reach the bottom. The water has become cloudy with all the sand they've raised, and now she understands why Sam failed to find it.

She tries to visualise a falling key – would it turn and spin, or drop like a stone?

Then she notices how the clumps of weeds are swaying gently to her right. The current might have caused it to drift from where they're standing. She moves a metre or so from Sam's legs, but not before she sees him stumble; the chain jerking beneath his feet.

She gropes in the sand, her vision almost useless in the murky water. It's so hard to focus, so hard to hold her breath and be strong when she wants to kill her own partner for being so cackhanded; wring his bloody neck and scream: *HOW COULD YOU DROP IT?*

'Come on, mate. Just hold on. Be brave for me, yeah?'

Sam is holding Dylan the way the vicar held Sam's niece at her christening last year. Cradling his head as it rests on the surface of the water. Sam has his feet jammed against the ground and he's trying to straighten his legs, but the tension in the chain is too powerful to fight. He's determined not to loosen his grip on Dylan's body, so what's happening is that the poor kid's leg is being stretched, like in one of those torture devices from the Middle Ages.

When Dylan lets out a howl of pain, it's met by an echoing scream from Grace. She's on her knees, hands clamped to her face. None of them have ever experienced terror like this. If Jody doesn't find the key in the next twenty or thirty seconds, Dylan's mouth will be under the water. And if Sam goes on resisting, his son's leg is likely to be wrenched out of its socket.

Should Sam let that happen? Let Dylan suffer terrible injuries in order to keep him breathing?

If I had a knife right now, he thinks, I'd have to cut off his foot to save him.

And I would.

55

Gabby is aware of a change in the mood: a growing air of disbelief. Perhaps some of the guests had secretly assumed the whole event was staged. But if they genuinely hadn't expected to see something quite this harrowing, there's little sign they object to it.

On the contrary, this is what they want.

The underwater camera on the seabed offers little more than a view of thrashing legs and swirling particles of sand, clouding the water just as things become excruciatingly tense. And the microphone hidden in the boy's clothing is failing – Borko's already growled his displeasure at the fact that it isn't fully waterproof, as promised – though they do catch a few words here and there between the crackles of static. A couple of minutes earlier they heard Jody jabbering something about 'kiss of life' and 'my baby, I'll go with you' – said in a way that suggested she didn't even know she was speaking.

Then Jody shouted at Sam to unlock the other one. Hearing this, Gabby dared to believe it was going to be okay. They'd found the second key and unlocked one of the restraints.

Except for Sam's awful admission: he'd dropped the key. A few people hadn't understood; some clearly had issues with Sam's accent. She heard rapid translations; then one man threw back his head and roared with laughter, as though this was the funniest thing he'd ever heard. 'The dumb fuck dropped the key!'

Now there's only fast, desperate breathing. The image of Sam's distress fills the screen as his son is about to be consumed by the sea.

Gabby can't stand it any longer. She clutches Borko's arm. 'You've got to save him.'

'Impossible.'

'Send in the boat.'

'It's too late.' A shake of the head that might signal genuine regret. 'I'm sorry, Gabby. I thought they could do it.'

Down here the water's quite cold, which has a numbing effect on Jody's fingers. Because of this, and the fact the key is covered in a thin layer of sand, she is unaware of her discovery until she moves her hand and feels something shift beneath her fingers.

She scrabbles in the sand and rejoices when a sharp nub of metal jabs her palm. She grabs the key and rises, becoming aware that, while Sam is still shouting, Dylan has fallen silent. She can see that his head is submerged, his eyes wide open, staring blankly at his father.

She takes hold of the shackle and this time Dylan doesn't struggle. His body is limp in Sam's arms, but Jody can't let herself consider what that means – what it *might* mean – until she has freed him. She slides the key into the lock and opens the cuff, roughly pulling Dylan's leg out. The tension in the chain whips the shackles towards the bottom.

'Lift him, lift him!' Jody cries as she surfaces. Sam is already striding towards the shore, propping Dylan high on his shoulder with his head flopping downwards. Jody moves behind to get a better look, sees water running from Dylan's slack mouth

(*he's dead he's drowned we failed we failed*)

and then he vomits, little more than a thin yellowish gruel, but it's the most wonderful thing she's ever seen. It means he's alive.

Jody calls out to Grace: 'He's okay! We're all okay, I promise!'

On the beach, Sam starts to lie Dylan down but Jody says no, sit him up. The boy is coughing and spluttering. Jody slaps his back, encouraging him to spit. Dylan, after all this trauma, still manages a frown.

'I know spitting's bad,' she says, 'but this time we don't mind.'

'You get special permission, mate,' Sam adds.

Jody gives Grace a hug and feels guilty when her daughter clings on and won't let go. She wants to be holding Dylan as well. But she gets her turn when Sam suggests he have a cuddle with his mum and sister.

Dylan stands, weakly, his clothes drenched and clinging to his skin. That's when Jody notices something in his pocket, a squarish lump.

'What's that?'

Dylan shrugs. Sam slips his hand into the pocket, bringing out what looks like a memory stick. He holds it on his palm for Jody to see. It has a mini-USB socket at one end and a tiny red light in the centre.

'Is that what I think it is?' he says. 'Some kind of spy equipment.'

'They must have put it there when they took him.'

At this, Dylan gives a solemn nod. 'The angel lady,' he says. 'I don't like her anymore.'

'Me neither,' Sam mutters. Standing, he turns away from them and bellows into the microphone: 'YOU EVIL WANKERS! I HOPE YOU ROT IN HELL!'

And he hurls the device into the sea.

56

Sam's fury blasts through the speakers and nearly takes their heads off. Only Gabby guessed what he was about to do and braced herself.

The sound is quickly muted. Once they've recovered, most of Borko's guests can smile at Sam's outburst, as if indulging a naughty child, though the Russian who's just lost half a million dollars looks moderately pissed off. There's a general air of disappointment that they won't get to witness the parents' response to losing their son.

Watching Sam throw the bug away prompts a memory: Dylan threw something earlier, and that was when Borko and Naji started to look concerned.

The first key. They knew it was missing, and still they went ahead.

Desperate to be away from them all, Gabby hurries out to a long hallway, making for the nearest toilet. She barely reaches it before she's violently sick.

She kneels on a cool marble floor, head tipped over the sink. Her thoughts drift back to the day the family arrived. When she greeted them at the airport she had no idea Borko had already made his choice. The call came through later that day, meaning they had to be at the welcome meeting.

If they hadn't shown up, would he have changed his mind? She doubts it. Another way would have been found to get them here. What Borko wants, Borko gets.

As if she needs further proof, after cleaning up, Gabby opens the door to find him standing outside. She rears back in alarm.

'Something wrong?' Borko asks.

'No. No, I'm fine.'

'You will be staying tonight.' It's not really a question. Then he catches the anxiety in her face, and adds, 'Your own room, of course.' The smile broadens, finally reaching his eyes. 'The door has a lock.'

And you have a key, she thinks. But she's exhausted, so she gives in and thanks him for his hospitality. At least here she's close to the action, though it seems unlikely she'll be able to influence what happens to the family.

She starts to move towards the living room but Borko stands his ground. 'Tell me,' he says.

'You know what it is. This has gone *way* beyond what I thought would happen. It's just... it's *wrong*, treating them like this.'

'I disagree. Once the parameters of the experiment have been set, it wouldn't be right to change them. This isn't like those cheap TV shows, where all the danger is faked.'

'But they're human beings, not lab rats.'

'Gabrielle, there are over seven billion people on this planet. Do you really believe they can all be treated with equal respect? Or guaranteed a life without hardship, tragedy, pain?'

She's biting her bottom lip; it's only when Borko mentions pain that she realises how much it hurts. This, perhaps, is a warning from her own body: *Be careful here, Gabrielle.*

But Gabby the rep has a fiery spirit, and she's too angry to leave it there.

'When I asked you before if anyone had been hurt doing this, you said there had been a couple of incidents over the years...'

'Regrettable accidents, yes.'

Accidents like this – being dragged into the sea to drown?

The question has formed when she suffers a flash of memory: someone at the Adriana welcome meeting asked about a boat crash the previous year. Three young men died and the bodies weren't recovered for days, by which time they were battered and ruined by the sea. She recalls a few mutterings about the circumstances being a bit odd, but on an island dependent on tourism it was in no one's interests to ask too many questions. In fact Gabby, with a cynicism she now regrets, used the incident to push the company's official tours as a safer bet than going it alone.

'But there wasn't anything... deliberate?'

His eyes narrow, and then she gets a politician's response: 'What happened was unfortunate, but I'm confident the family will emerge unscathed.'

'I hope you're right,' she says hotly.

'I'm always right.' Borko chuckles. 'Oh, Gabby, you Brits do love to portray yourselves as morally superior. A hangover from your empire days – teaching us "savages" how to behave. But do a little research and you'll find that the elite of most nations consider themselves to be above the law – usually with good reason.'

He offers her a surprisingly gentle smile and ushers her along the hall. 'We shouldn't forget that for practically the whole of human history, ninety-nine percent of the population – people like Sam and Jody – were peasants or slaves, at the mercy of emperors and kings. The egalitarian world of today is a brief anomaly, already overdue for correction. Surely *you* would agree with that?'

Gabby's mind is in disarray; the unexpected emphasis snaps her out of a daze. 'Would I? Why?'

'Come on.' He touches her arm and she shivers. 'Even at a modest estimation, your father's portfolio is worth around eight million pounds. That surely excludes you from the common herd?'

Gabby swallows hard. It isn't just the fact that she had no idea of her father's true worth, but that Borko has been snooping into her family's financial affairs.

How? she wonders. *And why?*

Picking up on her confusion, he says, 'Papa kept it from you?'

'No, he... I mean, it wasn't...'

Borko frowns. 'I'm disappointed. Your background is one of the reasons I felt you could be trusted to assist me.'

There's no mistaking the threat, and it takes all of Gabby's nerve to steady her voice and say: 'But that's not an issue, is it? Because you've just told me the family will come through this – and you're always right.'

Borko gives her a thin smile, acknowledging that this particular verbal bout has ended in an honourable draw. 'Of course.'

57

They return to the camp. After a couple of attempts to lift the mood, Jody falls silent. Grace and Dylan are worn out, and quietly tearful. Sam has withdrawn into himself, and Jody doesn't have even a fraction of the energy needed to bring him out.

The water is passed around. Jody has to intervene when two thirds of the bottle has gone. Sam just shrugs at the suggestion that they must save some for later. His idea of searching for more seems to have gone by the wayside.

She considers the remaining supplies. 'I think it was the cake that was drugged. The energy bars have proper wrappers, so they ought to be okay.'

Again Sam barely reacts, so Jody decides to open one and take a small bite.

'Let's give it a few minutes. If I don't flake out, we can share these between us.'

'Whatever. I'm not hungry.'

She gazes at him for a moment, a silent appeal, but it has no effect. She stands and draws him away from the children.

'Please, Sam, don't do this.'

'What?'

'You know what.'

A curt shake of his head. His face is contorted with pain. 'I dropped the key, and he nearly died. I'm a fuck-up.'

'That's not true. You saved him.'

'*You* saved him, Jode. You found the key.'

'No. I found it the second time, but you were the one who swam down and got it in the first place.'

Sam doesn't argue. There's a small breathing space before he says, very quietly, 'They were gonna let him die, weren't they?'

Her jaw is clenched too tightly to speak. 'Mm,' is all she manages, and a nod.

'Up till then, I thought... maybe it *is* just a game. That if things got really out of hand they'd turn up and help us. Because we've got kids, and no one kills little kids for fun. That's what I was clinging to. But I was wrong, wasn't I?' He asks.

And all Jody can do is agree with him.

Sam feels like a spare part, watching Jody at work. Sharing out one of the energy bars. Soothing Grace and encouraging her to swallow another painkiller. Cuddling Dylan as he whispers to her in a solemn voice, then massaging his back until he falls asleep in her arms. Sam knows he would never do these things as skilfully, as naturally, as she can.

The truth is, he feels much the same at home. He's always been enthusiastic about helping with the kids, but reflecting on it now he understands how hopeless he's been. Nappies that Jody had to reattach after he'd put them on wonky or loose. Clothes she would change because he'd chosen outfits that were totally unsuitable. The food he burnt – even simple things like chicken nuggets and potato waffles – when he was asked to make their tea.

He's known plenty of blokes over the years who got someone pregnant and then buggered off. Now he wonders if that was the right thing to do – not only for them but for the families they helped to create. His own dad was a complete waste of space, and maybe Sam's no better.

He sits on the sand and fiddles with the metal tag he removed from the boat. The sun is falling slowly, and he can think of various things he ought to be doing before it gets dark – set up that trap, collect some firewood, search for water – but he can't find the energy to start. So he does nothing instead and considers how he can tell Jody that he's given up. He can't deal with this anymore.

She already knows, of course. That's why she's ignoring him, taking on all the parental duties without a word of complaint. Once Dylan is asleep, she sits with Grace, talking quietly, secretively. Grace's leg is hurting again; even from a few metres away, Sam can see how swollen it is. Poor kid needs antibiotics, and soon. But it isn't going to happen.

What *is* going to happen, he knows beyond doubt, is that they will be left here to suffer.

And suffer some more.

And then die.

Grace won't settle. The ibuprofen has possibly reduced her fever, but not the irritation around the bite itself. On a hunch, Jody gets up and searches among the undergrowth for plants with broad flat leaves. What she finds doesn't really fit the bill, but since she knows nothing whatsoever about herbal medicine, one type is as good as any other.

Returning to the camp, she shreds the leaves and uses a couple of small rocks to mash them to a pulp. She moulds that into a ball and places it against the inflamed skin. If nothing else, it might draw out some of the heat. She has no idea if it will work, but her daughter's gratitude is so humbling it makes her want to cry.

As it is, she's been cut to pieces by something Dylan confided to her while she was getting him to sleep. After encouraging him to look forward to getting home and going back to school, he declared he didn't want to do painting anymore.

'Why not?' she asked. 'You love painting.'

'Don't like it now.'

It took her a couple of minutes to coax out the reason. In one of the last lessons of the summer term, two other boys had sneaked up behind him and yanked his trousers down while he was standing at a bench in the art room. It was only his trousers, not his pants, and he'd quickly pulled them back up, but the incident had obviously left him embarrassed and ashamed.

'Why didn't you tell me or Daddy?'

Dylan wouldn't answer that.

'Was Mrs McGoochan cross with them?'

'She didn't see. But they were laughing at me. So was Elsie.'

Although Jody wanted to smile at this, she had to maintain a serious expression. Elsie is the classmate for whom Dylan has, on several occasions, expressed his undying love.

'I'm sure everyone will have forgotten by the time you go back.'

'Will they?'

'Yes. I promise. And painting will still be great fun, you wait and see.'

This seems to cheer him up, but afterwards, as she reflects on the conversation, what disturbs her is that Dylan has kept this episode to himself for the whole of the summer holidays. Five years old and he's already capable of keeping secrets from them.

It mortifies her to recall that earlier she was comparing him to his Uncle Carl, when really he is a sweet, sensitive, good-natured little boy. Not a thug at all.

With Grace finally asleep, Jody summons the nerve to talk to Sam. He's barely moved for what must be an hour or more. As she sits beside him, she notices that he's fiddling with that metal tag again. It's his version of a comfort blanket.

'Could do with making a fire,' she says, by way of a greeting. *Subtle, eh?*

He sighs. 'In a bit.'

Then a long silence. They could almost be Kay and Trevor, sitting mutely while their relationship crumbles.

Jody rests her fists on her knees, shuts her eyes and takes a deep breath. It shouldn't be this difficult. It shouldn't take such effort to ask a question when you're desperate to know the answer.

Unless the answer is something you're dreading.

'This has been, without doubt, the shittiest day of my life,' she says. 'And I'm pretty sure I can't feel any worse than I do now, so you might as well tell me what it is you've been hiding for the last few months.'

Sam gives a start, but there is guilt as well as shock in his eyes. 'What are you on about?'

'My guess is an affair, though I can't work out who with. Anyone I know?'

She stares fiercely, determined to get a response. As she expected, he looks sheepish, downcast.

'I wouldn't do that.'

'Sam, be honest–'

'I am. I wasn't sleeping around. But I have screwed up. Again.' Another big sigh. 'It's money.'

The instant he says it, Jody knows two things: he's telling her the truth, and she should have guessed it ages ago.

'What have you done?' This is probably better than yelling: *How much*? But you wouldn't think so from the look on his face.

'Ian at the builders' merchants got a tip on a horse, said it was as close to guaranteed as you can get. Fifteen to one. So I borrowed some money–'

'How much?'

'Five hundred quid.'

'*What*? Who from?'

His shame is so transparent, so childlike, that for a moment he looks younger than Dylan. 'One of those online companies...'

'Payday loans?' She winces. 'You know my dad warned us about them. They're pure evil. What is it, a thousand bloody percent or something?'

'I know. But I thought I'd be paying it off straight away. Five hundred quid at fifteen to one, that would have been seven-and-a-half grand. Enough for a wedding.'

This stops her short. Many times they've discussed marriage; always deciding it's not worth the money. Not when there are so many other priorities. And Jody, if anything, has been more adamant on this issue than Sam.

She can't help narrowing her eyes. This could be a ploy, to take the sting out of her fury. 'You've never been that bothered...'

'I thought it would be nice. It's the right thing to do.' He sees the doubt, leans forward and places his hands over her fists. 'I'd have done it years ago if we had the cash.'

She nods, a little briskly, to make it clear he's not yet off the hook.

'When was this?'

'Seven, eight months ago. I was trying to make the repayments out of spare change here and there–'

'But we had the savings for this holiday.'

'I couldn't have used that, not when we'd paid the deposit.'

He shakes his head. 'I didn't want to say anything, because it would have been something else to worry about.'

'And I'd have torn your head off.'

'Yeah, that too.' He manages a rueful smile. 'Anyway, Paul noticed something was wrong, so I ended up telling him. He settled it for me, and I agreed to work extra hours to pay it off.'

Jody frowns, remembering numerous times when Sam had vanished on a Saturday afternoon with some vague excuse about helping his uncle with a bit of DIY. One time when he wasn't home till nine in the evening, she'd complained that Paul ought to be paying him.

'You still should have told me.'

'I know.'

'The two of us getting along is a lot more important than a wedding. Or money. And we can't be happy if we don't trust each other.'

She starts crying. So does Sam. They move together and share a long embrace.

Jody wants to believe this will begin to heal the rift between them, but she can't shake off the sense, even as she holds him tight, that the man she adored and fell in love with is no longer present.

58

Sam feels slightly better as a result of this conversation. In all the time he was hiding the debt from her, he never imagined she'd think he was having an affair.

In an effort to make amends, he gets busy with the trap. For bait, Jody has the bright idea of using some of the cake. If it knocked them out, it should do the same to the birds. A lot easier to kill them that way.

His next task is to build a fire. The timber ought to have dried out from the previous night's storm, but it stubbornly refuses to light. After half a dozen attempts the lighter is empty. He throws it down in disgust. No fire means no way of cooking what they catch – not that a single bird has gone near his trap.

Dylan and Grace wake up as the sun is dropping towards the horizon. The heat is nowhere near as brutal, and he and Jody agree that they have to make the best of the next couple of hours. They use a few wipes to freshen up, then share the energy bars and more coconut, plus the remaining cans of drink. Still no one wants the bread rolls.

Sam takes Dylan into the trees to have a pee, but all he can manage is a few drips. Then it's the girls' turn, but on the way back Grace is sick, bringing up all the precious food and drink she's just consumed. Afterwards she's feverish again, and hardly seems to know they're there. Jody insists on using a few drops of water to cool her down. Sam can't argue with that decision, but it feels like another nail in their coffin.

By tomorrow morning the water will be gone. What happened to Dylan is proof that no one's coming to rescue them. Another twenty-four hours – forty-eight at the most – and they'll be finished. Dead.

Perhaps it's the prospect of darkness that makes him feel so bleak, but whatever the reason the despair falls on Sam like an avalanche, crushing every last trace of energy and hope. He wanders back and forth along the treeline, brooding over the question Jody *ought* to have asked – the one that's never stopped haunting him.

What if there hadn't been someone to bail you out?

Sam knows people whose whole lives have fallen apart because of something like a failed MOT. Can't afford to fix the car, and that makes getting to work impossible, so then you lose your job. No job means you can't pay the rent, so you're out on the street, begging the council for help, and if you're lucky you end up with your family in some shitty B&B, your kids so far from home that they have to go to a different school or not go at all.

He shudders. This depressing line of thought seems, in the end, like a slow, bitter way of justifying to himself what has to be done. He's on the brink of selfish tears, his stomach gassy with pain and fear.

How's it going to end? That's really the only question that matters.

And he thinks he has the answer.

. . .

Jody lies between Grace and Dylan, holding hands with them both. She's got them playing a competition called Find a Star, which basically entails lying very still and staring up at the sky, and the winner will be whoever spots the first star.

She marvels at the almost imperceptible change from blue to purple, each shade rich and yet subtle, glowing with the soft light of a sun that has fallen out of sight. Every day this happens, every day a miracle of beauty and grandeur. Why have I never really noticed this before? she wonders. Why don't I take more interest in the world around me?

Because the world around me is Dylan and Grace.

Jody keeps up a cheerful mood, though she dreads the coming night. She imagines herself back in a world where humans lived without fire, and she can't understand how they survived for long enough to evolve into *us*. Were they worshipped as gods, the people who first found a way to banish the darkness, to turn wood into warmth and light?

She doesn't want to dwell on Sam's failure to get a fire going (or the fact that he dropped the key). But a mean and spiteful thought keeps creeping into her mind: *He isn't husband material.* It was a phrase her mum used once, a long time ago. She's apologised many times since, but Jody has never forgotten it. And until now she's never dared to consider that her mum might have a point.

No, that's unfair. She believes what Sam told her about the debt, and it's nowhere near as serious as if he'd been cheating on her. In time they'll pay Paul back and then perhaps start saving–

Ha! Who is she kidding? Making plans as if life's going to merrily roll along as it had before. *Look around you, Jody. You're trapped. You still have no idea where you are, or who put you here. And you can't discuss it with Sam because he's so volatile, so on edge all the time.*

His state of mind is becoming a huge concern. She senses

what it took out of him, to admit to his mistakes, but there's a lot more to it than that. She doesn't know how to help because she has no idea where he's going, inside his head.

Nowhere good, that much is for sure.

When he returns, the sky above them has an indigo sheen. The kids want to go on with the game but Jody sits up to gauge how he is. Sam greets her with a smile so shy and hesitant it reminds her of the first time he asked her out, in a busy school corridor. She turned him down that time – and also the second time, when he caught up with her walking home from school.

The third time, outside the chip shop in Fort Road, he got lucky. Or – if you wanted to be a bit cynical about it – she gave in.

He positions himself directly in front of her, then goes down on one knee. His hands tremble as he takes out the strip of metal he keeps playing with. It's been shaped into a circle.

A ring.

'Jode–' His voice chokes. 'Will you marry me?'

At first she can't believe what she's heard. It only sinks in when Grace jerks upright, her eyes wide in astonishment.

'Dad?'

Jody shushes her. 'Sam, please...'

'No. We should. Right now, in fact.'

'Here?' She wants to laugh, but equally she wants to cry. She covers her mouth with her hand, knowing either reaction could be dangerous.

'You need someone to do it,' Grace points out.

'Normally, you do,' Sam says. 'But the main thing is to have witnesses, and we've got you and Dylan. That's all we need. It's all we want.'

He holds Jody with his earnest gaze, seeming to plead with her to agree. She feels confused. Delighted. Trapped.

'It would be an honour,' she says.

They come up with a ceremony of sorts. When she was eleven or twelve, Jody had practically memorised the entire oath. At the time it seemed important to know it by heart, so she wouldn't stumble over the words in front of her family and friends.

Now, with the four of them kneeling in a circle, she guides Sam through the service, supplementing her memory with phrases from TV and films, noting the irony that she is having to lead even though it's Sam's idea.

Bless him, though. She thinks she understands his reasoning. And as dreadful as it is, she can't dismiss the blush of pride, the thrill when he eases the band of metal on to her finger and kisses her respectfully on the lips. The doubts she has harboured guiltily for years are banished in that instant: hopefully never to return.

'I do,' she says – because it sounds more definite, more immediate than *I will*.

'I do,' he says back. There's no ring for Sam, but he's never been one for jewellery.

To conclude, he suggests they all link hands and sing a song. Jody is wondering whether to go with that favourite ballad of her mum's from *Dirty Dancing* when Grace breaks off contact, suddenly enraged.

'I know why you're doing this.'

59

Sam had banked on this lifting the mood for an hour or two, at least. But the ceremony is over far too soon, and it's Grace who shatters the illusion that they have anything to celebrate.

Jody reaches for her hand, saying, 'Darling, come on...' But Grace won't be fobbed off. She twists free of her mum while staring fiercely, almost hatefully, at Sam.

'You think we're going to die.'

Jody gasps. 'No. Grace–'

'It's true. Dad knows it.' The words have a vicious sting.

Sam wants to turn away but he can't. 'Look, I thought it would make everyone feel better. I'm sorry if it hasn't worked. But I love your mum, and I don't tell her that enough.'

It's a cheap move, he's aware of that – getting emotional to deflect Grace's argument – but he's going to do whatever it takes to end this conversation on his terms. Jody jumps in with some warm reassurance, and although it sounds a lot more convincing than anything Sam could say, he can see that Grace is too smart to be fooled.

Thankfully Dylan comes to the rescue as only he can, jabbing a finger at the sky. 'Stars! I win!'

They all gaze up at the tiny pinpricks of light. To Sam they only emphasise the darkness, settling over them like a cloak.

While Jody gets the children to sleep beneath the boat, Sam sits a few metres away, staring at the glitter of moonlight across the blue-black sea. This time last night the storm was coming in. Tonight, by the look of it, will be clear and dry, which isn't really the good news it might seem.

Without water there's no hope. No reason to change his mind. He's made a plan and he's going to stick to it.

Jody comes over to join him. She looks exhausted, and sunburnt, but still beautiful. Squirming in his admiring gaze, she says, 'Don't. I'm a horrible mess.'

'You're perfect, Mrs Berry.'

Her grimace isn't the reaction he'd hoped for. 'Still don't know what I think about that. "Jody Berry".'

'Well, I could take your name and be Sam Lamb.'

They both snort. Jody shakes her head. 'Do you know what, Mr Berry? Despite all this other stuff we're dealing with, I feel like I could burst with happiness. I'm so proud to be with you, so proud of what we've achieved through the years.'

He smiles sadly. 'No one thought we would last, did they?'

'You can't really blame them. I mean, getting pregnant at seventeen isn't exactly the best of starts.'

'They never gave us a chance, though.' His tone is a little too aggressive; Jody tenses, before nudging against him.

'My mum and dad have come round. It took them time, that's all.'

'But they didn't think I was good enough.' He sniffs. 'And they're probably right.'

It's not the conversation either of them wants to have, so they sit in silence for a minute, before Jody indicates the beach, and the silver flakes of moonlight sprinkled over the water.

'Wouldn't this be the perfect place for a wedding? Trouble is, my mum would be devastated if she missed out. And in her version we'd have aunts and uncles we've never met, silly posh food for the catering, a fortune spent on flowers and table decorations and all that rubbish–' She breaks off, pressing both hands against her face, but still a sob escapes. 'I'm never going to see them again, am I? Mum and Dad.'

'I don't–' Sam tries. 'I can't say the words you want to hear. Not after what happened to Dylan. The bastards doing this, they've got cameras, microphones, they know how close it came–' He swallows. 'But no one stopped it. No one rescued us then, so why should they now?'

He does at least spare her his fear that they have days of this still to come. More tests and tricks and traps, and all that time they'll be expected to stay strong for the kids, pumping out false hope like living on the stale air from a tyre.

Jody, weeping silently, can't let it go. 'The way we suffered in January, not knowing if Dylan would pull through. But then he did, and it seemed like a miracle. Like we were blessed... only for this to happen.'

'I know.' He sniffs. 'But the two things aren't linked. This is just... more shitty bad luck.'

She reflects on it, then gives a little bark of laughter. 'And what's worse, somehow, is to know our families aren't even missing us yet.'

She's right. The holiday has a few days left to run. Until they fail to arrive home next Tuesday, no one will think it odd not to hear from them. By then, they could all be dead.

Better off dead.

With a shiver, Sam says, 'My mum won't miss us, I know that. And as for my dad – he's never given a toss about anybody.'

There's a curious silence from Jody. She slips her arm through his, a way of connecting that Sam has always regarded as a bit too grown-up for a couple of kids like him and Jode.

'No,' she says carefully, 'but Paul and Steph will be cut up.'

'Suppose.'

'They will, Sam.' She jostles him a little, to stress the point. 'Your uncle loves you like a father, there's no doubt about that. In fact–'

She breaks off, and he turns to look at her. 'What?'

'Don't you ever think... maybe that's what he is?'

It's the sort of thing you say and then immediately want to reel the words back in. Jody is so nervous, even her toes are curled up tight.

'*Paul?*' Sam says, as if he can't get his head round the concept.

Too late she realises that he can, but he's horrified by it. That much is evident from the way he draws his arm clear of hers and edges away.

She gabbles: 'Sam, I'm sorry. I know it's out of order. But from the first time I met him, it struck me how similar you are – as people, I mean.'

'So how come you never said?'

'Because I don't know, do I?' She makes a sweeping gesture with her hand. 'Sorry. It was a silly thing to say.'

'But Paul would've had to sleep with my mum. *His brother's wife*. And to cheat on *his* wife.'

'But he wasn't married to Steph then. I didn't think they got together till after you were born?'

As Sam pauses to work out the dates, Jody is praying he can view it the way she does: a scenario where Paul, fundamentally a decent man, takes pity on the wife of his violent waster of a brother.

'I dunno,' Sam says at last. 'It's so far back. But if they did do it...' He shudders. 'Dad would go mental if he found out, even after all these years. He'd kill Uncle Paul.'

She cringes in shame. Why hadn't she considered the implications before she opened her mouth?

'I'm really sorry. The only reason I said it was because of how often you compare your character to Carl's. I know deep down you worry about sharing DNA with him. This way it would mean you're only *half*-brothers.'

Sam seems confused. 'But me and Carl aren't the same, any more than Paul is like my dad.'

Jody can't admit that it's not just Sam she's thinking about, but Dylan. How much better it would be if kind, generous Paul was his grandfather.

'I know. Forget I said it, please.'

He stares at her for a moment, then turns away. All the effort they've made to re-establish a connection and now, thanks to her clumsiness, the distance between them is greater than ever.

What comes back to her is Sam's admission that he'd dropped the key. In that moment she thinks something fundamental changed in him, something that might never be put right. The fact that he had to stand there, gazing into his son's eyes as Dylan slipped beneath the water...

I should have let Sam swim down and retrieve the key. That was his chance to redeem himself. But supposing he *hadn't* found it, and then she had to watch Dylan die in her arms... Either way, their relationship was doomed, wasn't it?

She hears movement, Sam shifting closer again. 'Sorry,' he whispers.

'No. I am. I was such an idiot.'

He puts his arms around her, but before she can savour the relief, there's an anguished moan from Grace.

'I'll go,' Sam says, quickly kissing Jody on the cheek. His face, like hers, is hot with tears.

He has to feel his way on hands and knees because the beach around them is being swallowed by the night. Jody listens to Sam as he soothes Grace back to sleep. His body is in silhouette, crouched awkwardly beneath the boat, his head dipping to kiss his daughter.

'I love you, Grace.'

'*LoveyoutooDaddy*,' she mumbles in response.

Jody, moved by the exchange, crawls towards them.

'Listen to me, Grace,' Sam says gently. 'This is all a nasty dream, yeah? I want you to go back to sleep, and when you wake up you're going to be somewhere lovely.'

'Home?'

'If you like, sweetheart.' His glance at Jody is unreadable, and yet it feels significant in some way she can't fathom. 'Wherever you want to be, Grace. Wherever's the perfect place for you.'

'*Whataboutyou?*'

'Yeah, we'll be there too. We'll all be together, the whole family.'

He sounds so convincing, so very sure of his message. It's a remarkable transformation – and the polar opposite of what he's been arguing up to now: *Don't lie to them.*

One last word from Grace: 'Promise?'

'I promise. Now go back to sleep. I love you so much, remember that.'

He eases out from under the boat and almost collides with Jody. He gives a start, then takes her outstretched hands, allowing her to pull him close till they're face to face, their gazes locked and lit by the moonlight.

'How can you say that to her?' she whispers.

'I have to.'

'But it's not true.'

Sam just shrugs. 'Isn't it?'

PART IV

RETRIBUTION

60

Borko is aware that the party loses something when the family beds down for the night. Within an hour most of his guests have departed to their suites at the Conchis. Gabby, however, has been persuaded to stay. She made it clear that she must work tomorrow but will return in the late afternoon, to be present when Borko releases Sam, Jody and the children.

Gabby seems quite glad to see the back of his guests, but at the same time she grows increasingly ill at ease in his presence. Even now he cannot say to what extent she is deluding herself, but he will know soon enough.

In the absence of a working microphone at the family's camp, the evening's activities were frustratingly ambiguous. First there was Sam, pacing up and down and glaring at the trees, often looking directly at the camera. But he didn't come closer to investigate, so the assumption held that he hadn't spotted the surveillance.

When he returned and spoke to Jody, there was a solemn air about him. At one stage they were all kneeling together, talking in low voices. The microphones in the trees caught only a hum of conversation, and gave no clue as to what they were discussing.

After that, it was clear the family could do little more than sleep. They had failed to light a fire, and even with the rising moon, the darkness around the camp was oppressive. With very little water left, Borko agrees with Gabby that the mood by morning will be desperate.

She makes a spirited case for releasing them right away, but he can't agree to that. He does, however, confirm that the family will get a favourable deal by way of reparation.

The reason for the delay is that he has business to conclude with Jesse, who is also – regrettably – a house guest tonight. As Borko explains to her, the American refuses to sleep in hotels, and even his room here had to be fumigated, fitted with new furniture and, most specifically, a new bed.

'When he was a student travelling in the Philippines he developed a phobia of bedbugs. As soon as he became wealthy, he stopped using hotels and now he rents an apartment and has it furnished according to his needs.'

'Even when it's only for one night?' Gabby asks, incredulously.

'Why not?' Borko doesn't quite understand her disbelief, but in this instance he is greatly relieved that it *is* only for one night. He assures Gabby that their business will be concluded by midday; Jesse will be driven to the airport, and then, as he puts it to her with a devilish smile, 'You will have your way.'

Either she misses the innuendo, or skilfully ignores it. Later, once she has retired to a guest room on the second floor, he marvels at the extent to which he is enjoying this slow seduction.

He's already decided against making a move tonight. He considers it to be a test of his self-control.

But tomorrow, he thinks, is about right. Regardless of what happens to the family.

Regardless of what Gabrielle wants.

Gabby wakes to the sound of a tap on the door. Before bed, she made sure to lock it, not caring if Borko was offended. Even if he has a master key, the noise ought to wake her in time.

Her head feels cloudy, and judging by the taste when she swallows, something unpleasant has died in her mouth. Her hair has been pressed into sleepy folds across her face, and there's a line of dried saliva running from the corner of her mouth. It would take a brave or foolish man to find her sexy in this state.

She twists round to check her phone: ten to three in the morning. Jesus, what a time to choose.

Earlier she was weighing up the pros and cons of giving in to Borko, trying to decide if it will get her what she wants. She was taken aback when he agreed to release the family the following afternoon, but still isn't sure if she can trust him.

No, scrub that. She *knows* not to trust him.

After she'd pressed him for more details of how the family would be treated, he led her through an orange grove to a long single-storey outbuilding. There would be a transition period, he told her, during which time the family would stay here, under medical supervision, to be rehydrated and restored to full health.

Unlike the lavish guest suites within the main house, these bedrooms were small and plain, with minimal furnishing and the sterile air of a clinic. Gabby couldn't fail to notice that the doors were lockable from the outside. There was a living room with a TV, a coffee table and a couple of sofas, and a kitchenette dominated by an American-style refrigerator. Curiosity prompted her to look inside, though it was immediately obvious that Borko would rather she hadn't. As well as rows of soft drinks, there were several polystyrene trays containing vials of liquid. Tranquilisers, sedatives.

'They're not going to be drugged again?'

'I hope it won't be necessary. But there have to be safeguards; otherwise releasing them could be... problematic.'

Too right it could, she thought. *For you much more than them.*

Another knock, this one sharper. Gabby climbs out of bed and slips on the luxurious robe that was supplied for her. She creeps over to the door and listens for a moment, regretting the absence of a spyhole.

'What's the matter?' she hisses.

'This is Naji. Please open the door.'

Something in his voice sends a shiver down her spine, but she knows to stay on her guard. She unlocks the door. The first shock is the sight of Naji Hussein in anything other than his Savile Row suits. He's wearing tracksuit trousers and a white t-shirt, and his grey hair is uncombed.

'Borko wishes to see you.'

'Oh?'

He shakes his head: *Not that.* 'Come now, please.'

'What's happened?'

An impatient twitch of his eyebrows. He starts to move away.

'Hold on. I need to get dressed.'

She closes the door and makes a point of locking it again. Into the bathroom to freshen up, then she puts on the dress she wore the last night. She knows Naji will be pissed off by the delay, even if it's only a couple of minutes. Part of her is aware that she shouldn't be doing anything to antagonise these men, but she's in such deep trouble already that it has brought out the reckless side of her character.

He knows how much your father is worth, Gabby.

He thinks he owns you.

His promises could all be lies, and there isn't a single thing you can do about it.

61

Hussein is quietly fuming when Gabby emerges. In silence they hurry to the small viewing room at the back of the house. It's the nerve centre for the operation, although at present all the screens are blank. The single technician on duty is hunched low in his seat, as if hoping to go unnoticed.

Borko sits behind him, in a high-backed office chair, anchoring himself with one foot while swivelling restlessly from side to side. Gabby takes in his dejected air and knows at once that something bad has happened.

The girl was ill, she remembers. An insect bite, as far as they can make out.

Borko looks up. His gaze is distant, distracted. 'I wasn't sure whether to disturb you, but I decided you'd want to be informed.'

'Why? What's gone wrong?'

He waves her to a vacant chair, then signals to the technician.

'I'm sorry, Gabrielle. I don't think any of us could have anticipated this.'

The main screen blinks into life: an infra-red view of the

clam-shell shape of the family's shelter. But for the gentle shimmer of moonlight on the water, it could be a still picture rather than video.

They watch for thirty seconds. Nothing happens. Gabby wants to say something but the atmosphere of foreboding robs her of the will to speak.

Then movement. The camera zooms in, framing the boat and the indistinct shapes of the family beneath it. A slight ridge in the sand above the boat means the figures are not fully visible. It's a ghostly scene in infra-red: the dark grey sand, the lighter grey of the human forms. Gabby leans forward in her seat, identifying Jody on the outside, with Grace next to her and then Dylan. The children are lying on their sides, presumably asleep.

It's Sam who has moved, rising carefully in the confined space. He crouches over his son, his arms each side of Dylan's head, his face so close that he might be whispering in the boy's ear. Sam is bare-chested, and there's something in his right hand – a balled-up shirt, maybe. That hand appears to be touching Dylan's face.

Weird.

He stays frozen in place for what feels like a very long time, then moves across to Grace and assumes the same stiff pose. It brings to mind a vampire poised to strike. Again the bundle in his hand is right next to her face, and Gabby can only think of how it must reek of Sam's sweat.

'What's he doing?' The question slips out, regretted the moment she speaks. The men in the room ignore her.

Eventually Sam lifts himself over Grace and kneels beside Jody. They have a clearer view of him now. Gabby registers the tension in his body, the oddly blank expression on his face. He stares at the shirt for a few seconds then tosses it aside, leans over Jody and grabs her throat with both hands.

Gabby lets out a yelp. Finally she understands what she is witnessing.

The children first; now Jody.

She sinks back in her chair, afraid she might pass out. On screen, Sam is trembling with the effort he's putting into his task, the muscles in his arms and back standing out in rope-like cords. Below him, Jody hardly moves at first, then she spasms violently. One of her feet starts drumming against the sand; an arm comes up, flailing against Sam's body, but he is far too strong. A few more seconds and her arm flops back on the sand and she is still.

So that's it. In the viewing room there is a silence so intense that Gabby can almost hear the cold sweat popping from the pores on her forehead. She realises she isn't breathing, and has to make a conscious effort to start again.

To think she genuinely believed she could ensure their survival. After all, she'd made a deal with Borko. She'd stayed close, using her influence to argue in their favour when she could have sloped off and had nothing more to do with it.

This, she sees now, is simply what she told herself to counteract the guilt at betraying them in the first place.

Sam climbs off and rests back on his knees. His shoulders slump and his head droops forward, as if waiting for the executioner's blade. Then he rises to his feet and removes one of the wooden props, bearing the weight of the boat while he takes out the other prop and gently – almost tenderly – lowers the upturned craft, setting it down over the bodies of his family.

'Entombed,' Borko murmurs. He doesn't sound happy about it, but he doesn't sound all that troubled either.

Gabby knows she will require every atom of self-control to keep a lid on her feelings. In that sense it's almost a relief to go on watching, not having to face Borko or Naji until she's had time to compose herself.

Sam stands over the hull with his head bowed and his hands pressed together. The picture isn't clear enough to see if his lips are moving, but it's a safe bet he's saying a prayer. Then he picks up one of the stakes and sets off along the beach. The camera follows him until he disappears from its range, then clicks back to the upturned boat.

The tomb.

62

Borko has viewed the footage several times. On this replay his attention is reserved for Gabby. He watches her surreptitiously and notes how well she conceals her grief. After a suitable period of reflection, he clears his throat and says, 'I truly didn't think he would react in such a way.'

She exhales through her nose. 'As you said, it's just a lot of poor quality DNA that won't now get passed on.'

The bitterness stings, so he doesn't have to pretend to look hurt. 'Perhaps I was too harsh. The manner of their deaths has upset me, particularly as there are young children involved.'

'So you're admitting it was a mistake, taking a family and... *torturing* them, basically?'

Naji grunts in a way that communicates his displeasure at her insolence. Borko's calming gesture is intended as much for his aide as for Gabby.

'In the light of these events, I would have to say yes, it was.'

The admission throws her off balance. She nods vigorously, then looks back at the screen. 'So where is he?'

At Borko's command, the technician brings up footage from a camera on the next bay to the west. It tracks Sam as he climbs down from the ridge and staggers halfway across the beach before weaving towards the sea. He looks like a drunk on his way home from a party, gesticulating in a manner that suggests he is arguing with himself.

After stumbling through the shallows, he returns to the sand and makes for higher ground. Another camera follows him into the next bay, where once again he heads for the water. This time he trips over and is submerged for a few seconds, hauling himself out as if unsure where he is. On he goes, floundering across yet another bay. A final close-up shows him briefly turning back, his face contorted by what appears to be an agonised scream. Borko catches Gabby wincing at the sight, as if for a moment she can set aside what Sam has done and feel his pain, his grief, as keenly as if it were her own.

But that's impossible, of course. She can't begin to appreciate Sam's state of mind, any more than Borko can.

'We lose him after this,' he says. 'There are no more cameras at that end of the compound.'

'What are you going to do?'

'If he's intent on harming himself, there is little we can do to stop him.'

'Haven't you sent anyone in?'

With a sigh, Borko checks his watch. As much as he admires Gabby's strong character, he wonders if perhaps Naji is right. He's too indulgent where attractive women are concerned.

'Not yet. At first light we'll retrieve the bodies.'

'But what if... I mean, say one of the kids is still alive?'

Borko shakes his head. 'You saw the footage. Sam was a man possessed. He will have made sure.'

Borko's right. Gabby wishes he'd woken her earlier. Perhaps she could have persuaded him to dispatch a medic straight away.

She wants to rant and rave at Borko, but her attitude already has him bristling, and Naji keeps shooting venomous glances in her direction. Borko suggests she goes back to bed, promising to fetch her when the boat goes in.

There's no point in refusing. What she desperately needs is privacy. Sanctuary.

She returns to the room and locks the door, stands under a hot shower for several minutes and bawls her eyes out. And that's when it hits her – the reason why Borko brushed off her suggestion about the children.

After what's happened, there's no way that Dylan or Grace could be permitted to survive. If Sam hadn't done the job properly, Borko's men would have had to finish them off.

Gabby dresses again before lying face down on the bed. She doesn't sleep, doesn't want to sleep: she's too afraid of her dreams.

It's slightly less than an hour when she's roused again, this time by a softly spoken member of Borko's security team. No sign of Naji in the viewing room. Perhaps he's coordinating the clean-up operation, or perhaps he's just gone to bed, disgusted by the way his boss permitted Gabby to talk back at him.

The same technician is still cowering in his seat, but otherwise she's alone with Borko. She takes a seat to one side of the main console, leaving two empty chairs between them. Borko recommends a coffee to wake her up, and Gabby can't think of a good reason to refuse.

Outside, a few birds are chirping and squawking. The room's single window shows a pale sky, with a distinctive peachy glow to the east that she associates with the exhaustion of the weekly graveyard shift, the airport run to collect the bleary-eyed passengers from a Manchester flight that arrives at two a.m.

The surveillance cameras have switched to daytime vision, yet somehow the scene looks less real now: the beach cold-washed by the blue morning light; a raw image of churned-up sand and a few seabirds circling and always the dreadful stillness of the boat, like a coffin washed up on an alien shore.

One of the birds swoops down to land on the hull, where it nuzzles at the wood. If Sam hadn't thought to cover the bodies, the bird would be pecking at their eyes–

Gabby retches, swallows down bile. Borko regards her with concern.

'I'm fine,' she says. 'Something caught in my throat.'

A servant brings the coffee, to which Gabby adds plenty of sugar, and sips it with gratitude. On screen, the camera picks up the motorised dinghy as it races towards the beach. There are only two men on board, leaving plenty of room for the grim cargo which will accompany them on the return journey.

'What about Sam?' she asks.

'I've stepped up security around the perimeter, and sent another patrol to look for him.' A little shrug. 'If he ended up in the sea, it's possible he'll never be found.'

The men are dressed in boiler suits. They trudge up the sand, clearly not relishing the task ahead. Halfway up, one of them abruptly straightens, perhaps remembering that their boss will be watching on camera.

Gabby steels herself as they stand alongside the boat. She doesn't want to see them moving the bodies, but nor can she bring herself to look away. This feels like retribution for her part in their deaths. She has to face it.

The men squat and try to lift the boat, but it barely moves. They let go for a moment, seemingly puzzled. Is it stuck, somehow?

From Borko, a growl of displeasure. 'What's stopping them?'

As they set to it once more, a figure bursts from the trees, swinging a lump of wood which strikes one of Borko's men on the side of his head. He collapses against his colleague, who struggles to stay on his feet while also fumbling for something on his belt, but the attacker is in a frenzy, driving the fatter end of the club into his stomach and then butting him full in the face. The second man trips, falls, and takes another couple of blows while he's down, his hands raised in a plea for mercy.

When he is satisfied that neither of them poses a threat, Sam Berry turns to stare at the camera, slowly raising his arm and jabbing his index finger, several times, as though thrusting a knife.

Gabby isn't sure if it means: *You did this*. Or maybe: *You're next*. But what's clear is that everything has changed once again.

63

The red mist. Sam's brother has a way of making it sound like an excuse. *I can't be blamed for kicking some guy's head in, because the way he looked at me brought on* the red mist.

It isn't an excuse, but at least Sam now understands what Carl meant – and why his brother is currently serving a four-year prison sentence for grievous bodily harm. While Sam's in this mood he feels like he can do anything. There's no question of right or wrong, no limitations or laws that matter: just a crystal-clear purpose and a determination to do what needs to be done.

Well, now it *is* done – the first stage, anyway – and he can let that mist start to clear. There's still a good supply of rage inside, ready to fire up again when it's needed.

The first man took a hell of a whack. As Sam crept back through the trees, moving slowly in near total darkness for what felt like hours, he had plenty of time to weigh up whether he should use one of the stakes as a weapon. Swung with full force, he knew it was capable of killing a man, and by the look of it that's what has happened here.

He checks the other guy first. He's got a bashed up nose,

maybe a cracked rib or two; semi-conscious but not permanently out of action. Sam grabs one of the bungee cords, rolls the man on to his belly and ties his hands behind his back. The man starts whining and moaning, until Sam slaps him on the head.

'Shut the fuck up.'

The first man still hasn't moved. He's all twisted, a trickle of blood leaking from his ear. Sam doesn't even check for a pulse. He grabs the man's feet and drags him away from the boat.

Pausing a moment to catch his breath, he's aware of the adrenalin rush fading, leaving him exhausted – disheartened, even. He stares at the upside down boat and reflects on the risks he took. Has it been worth it?

Then comes a knocking on the inside of the hull. A worried voice calls out, 'Sam? Is that you?'

To Jody the fight is a succession of brutal, sickening noises, sending her imagination into overdrive. When it falls quiet, she has no idea whether it's Sam out there, or whether his plan failed. She pictures him being subdued by men with guns; after lifting the boat and finding her alive, they raise their weapons and open fire...

This terror only adds to the hellish quality beneath the boat. Sam had warned her it would be tough, that it could be hours before anyone came to investigate, but she never dreamt that the close confinement would affect her so profoundly.

A rehearsal of her own death, that's how it seemed. Try as she might, she hasn't been able to shake off the effect of being throttled. Sam kept his hands as loose as possible around her throat, but for the sake of realism he'd pressed down with all his strength, his face contorted with a viciousness that looked too intense to be faked.

Her last glimpse of him, before she shut her eyes and played dead, convinced Jody that he could be doing this for real.

Thankfully the kids stayed asleep during the charade. She had been desperately afraid that one of them would wake while Sam was pretending to smother them, ruining the illusion in the minute or two before the boat was lowered and they were hidden from view.

She had expected that to be a relief, but instead the claustrophobia gathered in her chest like smoke. It quickly grew stifling, despite another of Sam's clever ideas – earlier he'd nudged a couple of small rocks into position beneath the boat, keeping it propped a few centimetres off the ground at the lower end, where it couldn't be seen by the cameras. Jody was forced to waggle her feet to try and stir the sluggish air. She moved as much as the cramped space allowed, tormented by the insects that made their home in the sand.

Grace and Dylan were equally disturbed, writhing and itching in their sleep; whenever they started to wake, Jody did her utmost to send them back off before they could register where they were. It worked, just about, except for one occasion when Dylan briefly opened his eyes and grumbled: 'Don't like this room.'

'Ssh, your sister's asleep. It won't be for long.'

Sam's final brainwave was potentially the most important one. When Jody heard someone approaching, she was to wrap her arms around the seat above her head and place her feet on the seat at the other end. That way she was adding her body weight to the boat, making it heavier to lift. The idea was to disorientate whoever came to investigate, giving Sam a better chance of taking them by surprise.

But has it worked? Unable to bear another second, she knocks and calls out: 'Sam? Is that you?'

No answer; just a creak of timber as someone nudges against the boat, taking hold of it.

Then a voice: 'Jode, you can let go.'

'Oh, thank God!' But she's thinking: *Why didn't you answer straight away?*

She understands a little better when she catches sight of him. Sam looks a decade older, hollowed out with tension and fear. Groaning with the effort of lifting the boat, somehow he finds the strength for one mighty heave which rolls it right over, thudding down on the sand. Beside her, the children jerk at the noise, but neither of them is fully awake yet.

Jody sits up, brushing sand and bugs from her hair, and registers the two men lying nearby. One is tied up, conscious and muttering to himself. The other has a serious head injury. She moves nearer, cautiously, to examine the wound.

'What if you've killed him?'

'So?'

'It wasn't this guy's idea to put us here.'

She is feeling for a pulse when Sam comes to stand over her. 'No, but he works for whoever did. So he's the enemy, too.'

'All right, but–'

'No! It's not "*All right, but*"!' Sam shouts. 'It's them or us, haven't you got that by now? Them or us.'

Sam kicks at the sand, sending a tiny spray over her leg. He's almost angry enough not to care if he accidentally catches her with his foot.

It's all gone to plan. Why isn't she more grateful?

Jody bows her head, but not before he's seen the flash of fear in her eyes. It was there the last night, too, when he was pretending to strangle her. But hasn't he always said he'd rather kill himself than threaten violence against a woman?

348

'I *do* get it,' she says. 'But he's still alive. We ought to sit him up, at least.'

'I'm sorry,' Sam murmurs, kneeling beside her. 'That was out of order.'

She manages a weak smile. 'It's okay.'

He opens his arms and embraces her. Feels her tears on his cheek.

'I don't care if these two die,' he says, 'and I won't apologise for that. I don't care *who* dies, if it means saving you and the kids.'

She nods. Gently he pushes them apart, so he can look her in the eye.

'This isn't over yet. You realise we might still have to do some horrible stuff?'

'Us or them,' Jody agrees. By now the dinghy has caught her attention. 'Why don't we get away in that?'

'We have no idea where we are. Once we're out at sea, they could easily ram us in a larger boat – then this has all been for nothing.'

He can see her thinking it through for herself. His fury has subsided enough to recognise that it's an advantage, her refusal to take his word for it. Two heads are better than one.

'As a last resort, though?'

'Maybe. But it won't be easy.' He gestures at the men. 'We'd have to take at least one of these guys with us.'

Hostages, is what he means, but hopes he doesn't have to spell it out. Then there's a cough and Grace sits up, rubbing her eyes. Dylan is also awake.

'Better get to work,' Sam says briskly.

Jody tells the kids to stay where they are, and she and Sam roll the injured man on to his side before tying his hands with another bungee cord. The bleeding seems to have stopped, but the man doesn't react in any way. Jody checks his pulse again and says he's still alive, but deeply unconscious.

They strip him of his weapons: a knife and a gun. It's an automatic pistol, Sam thinks, though all he knows of guns is what he's seen in the movies. But the sight of the firearm turns him cold. This was to execute them, if need be.

'Hide it,' Jody hisses, nodding towards Dylan.

The gun is much heavier than Sam expected. Stuffing it into his pocket, he's aware of its weight, its bulk – and the fact that if it goes off by accident it could kill him.

The second man jabbers to them in his own language, his voice thick and phlegmy because of the damage to his nose. Then he switches to English: 'Please...' he says, almost weeping as he begs for mercy.

Stone faced, Sam makes the universal symbol for *Be quiet*, and to his surprise, the man obeys. Maybe it's the fact that Sam has the gun.

The children have stood up for a better view. 'Who are they?' Dylan asks fearfully.

With a glance at Sam, Jody says, 'Just some men who came to see how we were.'

'I don't like them,' Grace says. Her eyes are shining with tears and she's unsteady on her feet, using one of the stakes as a crutch.

'Can they help us?' Dylan asks.

'Not really,' Jody says.

'But if we ask them nicely?'

'Yes, Dylan, that's what I'm gonna do.' Sam plucks at Jody's arm, and when she leans close he whispers, 'Better take the kids away for the next bit.'

64

It's a request that ought to fill Jody with dread, but his outburst has brought it home to her. Their lives are at stake, and when it comes down to it she, like Sam, would sacrifice anything – anyone – for the sake of their children.

Grace and Dylan have to be physically manhandled away from the boat, both craning their necks to keep their gaze on their father. They can sense the prospect of violence in the air, as well as the fear and uncertainty, though their moods lift when they see the dinghy up ahead.

'Are we going on that?' Dylan asks.

'Maybe. But not yet.'

'Ohhh.' His body sags, dragging on her arm. 'But I wanna go home, Mummy!'

So do I, darling. So do I.

Grace is shivering. 'I don't like boats. And I don't feel well.'

Her matter-of-fact tone threatens to crush Jody's spirit. Her poor daughter is well aware that no one can relieve her suffering: she simply has to accept it, and she does, bravely and with remarkably few complaints.

And that, Jody decides, is more than enough to justify whatever action Sam needs to take.

They skirt the dinghy and wade into the sea, paddling while they wipe off sand and insects. They're all covered in fresh bites, and sore from sunburn, but after a few seconds Grace backs out. The water is too cold for her.

While Jody's distracted, Dylan manages to clamber over the side of the dinghy, and yells: 'Water!'

At first, Jody doesn't understand. She grabs Dylan's t-shirt before he tumbles into the boat, then spots two half-litre bottles of drinking water. One has been opened and there's a mouthful or so missing; the other is sealed.

'Well done, Dylan. I'll get them.'

As she leans over, she notices something else of interest: a walkie-talkie. She grabs the water, hands one bottle to Dylan and then picks up the radio. Her first instinct is to call to Sam, but he's busy leading the conscious prisoner towards the trees.

'Where's Daddy going?' Dylan asks.

'Nowhere much.' She forces a smile. 'Let's have a drink, shall we?'

In the viewing room they have watched, for the most part, in stunned silence. Naji joins them, gripping a two-way radio as though it's a stress toy. He and Borko are staring so intently at the screen that Gabby feels like she's been forgotten.

Which isn't a bad thing. When Sam lifted the boat to reveal that Jody and the kids were alive, Gabby wanted to whoop with joy. She had to settle for a discreet fist pump.

The family are unharmed. There's still hope.

One of the guards looks to be in a bad way, though Gabby is impressed that Sam and Jody have put him in the recovery position. It's more than she would have done if she was in their place.

The camera picks up Sam taking a knife from the guard, along with something she can't see clearly. She guesses its significance by the way he and Jody stare at it.

'Is that a gun?' Gabby asks.

'Yes,' Borko confirms.

'Why did they take a gun with them?'

'They always carry guns. It means nothing.'

Gabby doesn't respond, but she's even more gratified that Sam has turned the tables on them.

When Jody leads the children down to the shore, Gabby assumes they're going to use the dinghy to escape. But Sam hauls the other guard to his feet and heads towards the trees, stopping a couple of metres from the camera. The sound quality is far from perfect, but he's close enough for his message to be heard. And if there was any doubt, he puts a knife to his prisoner's throat.

'Whoever's watching this – is it Borko, you fucker? If you don't let us go, I'm gonna kill this guy here. Got that?'

Gabby is shocked to hear Borko's name, but the man himself barely reacts.

Naji says, 'We should notify the other patrol. They're still some distance away.'

'Tell them, but don't send them in.'

'But, sir–'

'We hold off for now.' Borko indicates the screen with a twitch of his coffee cup. 'First let's see what happens.'

'We want a safe way out of here!' Sam shouts at the camera. 'A proper boat, no more than two people on board. No guns or knives. You've got an hour.'

As he says it, he glances at his prisoner and spots a watch on the man's arm – thank God. He's making this up on the spot, and has a horrible feeling it shows.

It doesn't help that he has no way of knowing if his message is getting through. He has to assume there's someone listening at the other end, but he can't know for sure.

'Who's in charge?' he growls at his prisoner. When he doesn't respond, Sam shakes him roughly, then hooks his ankle, causing the man to stumble and fall.

'Please,' the man cries. 'No hurt. Is mistake. Mistake.'

'Too bloody right it's a mistake. Now tell me who's done this to us? Is it Borko?'

The man's eyes widen at the name, which is all the confirmation Sam needs. Feeling grimly satisfied, Sam turns towards the shore and sees Jody looking in his direction. The kids are beside her, sharing a bottle of water. The sight of it makes him forget everything else for a second.

Jody holds something up, and when he beckons to her she comes running, Grace and Dylan trailing behind. Not only does she have a second bottle of water, but there's a two-way radio.

'Found this, in the boat.'

'Have you tried...?'

'No. I thought you'd want to do it.'

He nods, and is about to take the radio when he has another idea. 'Not yet.'

65

Jody can see that Sam is in no mood for a debate. He glugs a couple of mouthfuls of water, then thrusts the bottle back at her. 'Stay with the kids.'

'Shouldn't we stick together? They might be sending reinforcements.'

Sam shakes his head. 'We have to show them we mean what we say. Otherwise we're not gonna get out of here.'

'We still have the dinghy,' she points out. For all Sam's objections, she's more and more inclined to take their chances out at sea.

'Not unless we have to. I don't reckon we'd last long out there.'

Grace and Dylan seem to have been revived by the water. They're holding hands as they approach, casting wary glances at the man on the ground. To Jody's dismay, they seem equally wary of their dad.

'Is he all right?' Grace asks. Picking up on her concern, the guard directs his pleas to her. When Sam wrenches the man to his feet, she gasps. 'You're not going to hurt him, are you?'

A warning glance from Jody prevents Sam from saying

something he might regret. Without another word, he takes off through the trees, crashing through the undergrowth with his prisoner stumbling at his side.

Jody decides to follow at a safe distance, while trying to construct an explanation for the children. Daddy, she says, needs to scare the man in order for them to leave the island – so they mustn't get upset.

It sounds feeble even to her own ears. How much better if she could tell them the truth: *These men don't care if we live or die. If we're going to survive, we have to be every bit as ruthless as they are.* But what kind of message is that to teach your children?

The correct one, Sam would probably say. Because that's how life is, once you strip away the rules and conventions designed to hide that reality.

Their destination, unsurprisingly, is the snake pit. It's the one other place where they know there will be cameras.

The guard understands quickly enough. As they get closer, his shoulders slump and his movements become sluggish. Sam takes him right to the edge, and once again turns to face the camera. He studies the walkie talkie for a moment, then presses a button and speaks into it.

'So it *is* Borko, isn't it? Your guy's just told me. I wanna speak to you.'

There's no response. Sam confers with Jody, who takes a look at the radio and agrees that he's using it correctly.

'Why don't I do it?' she says, and with a reluctant nod, Sam hands it over.

'Please, if you're there,' Jody says into the radio. 'This has to end now. Our daughter–' Her voice catches. 'Grace needs a doctor. We don't want anyone else to get hurt. We just want to leave–'

Sam grabs the walkie talkie, not roughly, but with purpose. This was his plan all along, she realises. Good cop, bad cop.

'You were quite happy to see one of us end up in that pit,' he snarls. 'You've got five minutes to answer – then your man's going in.'

Borko has mixed feelings about Sam's act of rebellion. There's admiration, certainly, and a grudging respect; he's conscious that his guests would have been thrilled to watch these events unfold, though he knows that part of their delight would stem from the fact that his extravaganza has gone so dramatically wrong.

In his own language, he says to Naji: 'Do you think he could kill them?'

'He's desperate enough, certainly.'

A huffing noise from Gabby: she's picking up some of what they say, but not enough to take part in the conversation.

He tells her: 'We were discussing the likelihood of Sam carrying out his threat.'

'He'll do it,' Gabby says immediately. 'Look at his face.'

Toying with her, Borko says, 'Do you think we should let him go ahead?'

Naji draws in a sharp breath. 'Sir, Luka is the nephew of Duravar's mayor. I don't think the president would approve of his death, given the strategic importance...'

It's a less than subtle reminder that he is answerable to his father, and Borko works hard to maintain his composure. Gabby has also picked up on the slight, which is unforgiveable.

'I think you should talk to him, at least,' she says.

'Negotiate?'

'Why not? The last thing you want is a bloodbath.'

Borko shrugs, resting back in his chair. Ignoring Naji, his steady gaze contains a question for Gabby.

What's it worth to you?

. . .

Sam has removed the man's watch and forced him to kneel facing the pit. Time's nearly up and there's been no response. Jody stands a few metres away, trying to keep the kids distracted.

'Looks like you've had it,' Sam mutters to his prisoner.

'Please, sir. Not do this, please, sir.'

The *sir* is a new tactic. Sam peers into the pit. He spots a couple of the snakes in amongst the dirt and leaves.

'Why not? No one minded if we died in there.'

More urgent shaking of the head. 'Snakes not kill. Snakes here to...' Running out of English, he goes wide-eyed, mimicking fear.

'Just to scare us, eh?'

'Scare,' the man repeats, then nods. 'Not kill.'

'But some people die here, don't they?'

The man looks confused. 'Sir...?'

'Don't give me that bollocks. I'm not *sir* to you, any more than you're *sir* to me. And you understand English well enough. This has happened before, hasn't it? People brought here and left to cope in the wild?'

The man shrugs, but it's half-hearted. 'Yes,' he admits. 'Others come.'

'You evil bastards.' Sam steps closer and places his foot on the man's shoulder. Keys the radio and says, 'I hope you're watching, cos he's going in.'

There's a sudden shout from Dylan: 'Has Daddy got a gun?'

Sam glances down at his pocket, then back at Dylan. In his excitement the boy has forgotten everything but his obsession with weapons; he springs forward for a closer look, and Jody only just grabs him in time. But now the guard is moving too; he's worked his hands free and he twists round, lunging at Sam, who tries to stamp down and push him over the edge. But he doesn't have the momentum; his body weight is shifting in the other direction and he stumbles as the man grabs Sam's ankle and shoves his foot into the air.

Sam goes down heavily on his back. The gun has slipped from his pocket. They both see it at the same time but the guard is quicker to react, launching himself at Sam, pressing down on his legs and punching him in the groin. It causes a gruesome muffled pain, deep and faraway but coming in like an express train; Sam can't help drawing his knees up as he turns, reaching for the gun...

He's too slow. The guard snatches it, rolls clear of another swiping kick from Sam and comes up on his knees, spitting blood as he lifts the gun and growls at Sam and fires–

66

The crack of the gunshot brings everything to a halt. Jody instinctively crouches, pulling Dylan down with her. Grace is wide-eyed, her hands clamped over her ears. They're all nearly deafened by the noise.

Jody fights a violent urge to be sick. Because of the trees in the way, all she can see of Sam are his legs. He's flat on the ground, not moving. She has a better view of the guard, up on his knees and aiming the gun as if to fire again. She'll never reach him in time...

There's a squawk from the radio, and a voice barks: 'Luka!'

The guard hesitates, then climbs to his feet. He glances at Jody, shifting his position so he can keep an eye on her. Slowly she straightens up. There's another gruff command over the radio, which is still clutched in Sam's hand. He's alive, conscious, and Jody can't see any blood. She feels incredible relief when she registers that the bullet must have missed.

'Sam! Give the radio to Luka.'

Jody gasps. Sam meets her eye and she knows he is thinking the same as her: that voice sounds like Borko.

But Sam looks in no mood to obey. Jody has a terrible feeling that he would rather die than accept defeat.

They watch the screen to see if Borko's intervention has come too late. Gabby is gnawing on her fist like an overanxious fan in the closing seconds of a cup final.

Sam looks beaten, which Gabby has realised is a bad thing in this context. It means he has nothing to lose. And the pause, while he weighs up his options, is sheer agony.

But it's Jody who makes the decision. That's clear from the way Sam turns to her, then drops his gaze and tosses the walkie talkie at Luka's feet.

Borko issues instructions, then his man motions to Jody and hands her the walkie talkie.

'Jody,' Borko says, 'I need you to go back to the beach. Help is on its way.'

She snorts, turning to find the camera. 'How can we believe anything you tell us?'

Borko replies smoothly: 'Please remember that Luka will shoot you if I ask him to. It's down to my goodwill that he hasn't already done so. Now go.'

He turns to Gabby. 'Satisfied?'

She knows better than to celebrate, but says, quietly, 'Yes. Thank you.'

'You're welcome.' There's a quality to Borko's smile that suggests she has just walked into a trap. 'And now I need something from you.'

They walk in single file, Jody leading the way with Sam behind her, then Dylan, then Grace. The guard who placed them in this order comes last, ready to shoot one of the children if Sam or

Jody cause trouble. Even with his poor English, Luka has made it plain that Grace will be the first to die.

Sam is fuming at Jody's insistence that they do as Borko says. 'We can't just roll over and surrender.'

'Yes, we can. Don't you dare get any ideas.'

Sam hasn't: that's the problem. But he can't bear to accept failure – not when the price of that failure is likely to mean their deaths. Jody, for some reason, can't seem to see that. She's choosing to place her trust in Borko – and how sensible is that, given what they know about him?

Back at the beach, they're made to sit in a tight cluster a few metres from the boat. Luka checks on his colleague while talking urgently on the walkie talkie. As far as Sam can tell the other man is still alive, just about. For the first time it occurs to Sam that he might end up guilty of murder – manslaughter at the very least.

In his own view, he's not guilty of anything. He was forced to take extreme measures after being put here against his will. But he doubts if the courts on Sekliw – Borko's courts – will agree with that.

They wait in a miserable silence. The children are trembling, their eyes blank with shock. A feverish heat pours out of Grace, while Jody is hugging Dylan close, singing to him beneath her breath. It's getting hotter now the sun is up, and they're all desperately thirsty. Jody asks the guard for some more water, but he only sneers in her direction.

It's probably fifteen or twenty minutes before there's another brief message on the radio. Luka stands up and peers out to sea, and a moment later they hear the low thrum of a speedboat. Jody exchanges a look with Sam, shaking her head as if he's just put forward some crazy idea. He answers with the same gesture, so it looks like they're both saying no to something.

He has no ideas left, crazy or otherwise.

The kids have sensed the tension and are staring at the sea as the boat comes scudding into view. Sam spots several figures on board. Suddenly he feels weak with dread.

He watches Luka, who has maintained a safe distance while monitoring the boat's approach. Every couple of seconds his gaze flicks back over his prisoners. No way he'll be distracted enough to give Sam a chance.

It's a suicide mission to fight back. But isn't that a better way to go, a more... *honourable* way to die than like this, helpless and afraid?

The engine cuts out, and Sam turns back as the speedboat drifts into the shallows. A man in shorts and t-shirt drops over the side, carrying a rope fixed to a metal spike that he drives into the sand at the shore. Another man climbs down, a medical bag over his shoulder, and unloads what appears to be a stretcher. He races up the beach, heading for the unconscious guard, and when he moves out of their sightline, Sam sees the first man helping someone else climb out of the boat.

He groans.

Jody has never thought of herself as remotely violent, but the sight of the rep threatens to unleash a whole new personality, a demented creature capable of tearing at Gabby's long blonde hair and gouging out her bright green eyes.

The rep is barefoot and wearing a close-fitting black dress, clingy where it's damp, as though she's here for a photoshoot. Jody tracks her progress up the beach. Gabby acknowledges Sam first, with a slightly pleading half-smile. Her gaze passes quickly – guiltily – over the kids, and then she greets Luka with a nod.

She doesn't look at Jody until she's only a couple of metres away. By then the man from the boat is behind her, a gun in his hand. Suddenly Jody's feelings about the rep seem trivial. Are they about to be shot dead, and their bodies dumped at sea?

'Guys, look.' Gabby raises a forefinger, squaring her shoulders as if to make it clear that she cares about their welfare but isn't going to take any crap. 'I can imagine how you feel–'

'You don't have a fucking clue!' Jody shouts. 'You sold us to him, didn't you?'

Jody looks at Sam, wanting him to agree that their theories have been proved right, but he only nudges his shoulder against hers and whispers: 'Later.'

Gabby looks shaken by the ferocity in Jody's voice. But Sam is right, and now she understands why his mood is less bleak than it was a few minutes ago. Gabby's presence might be a sign that they're not facing immediate death.

Sam indicates the man tending to the unconscious guard. 'Grace needs a doctor. Can he help her?'

Gabby nods. 'You'll all get checked over. There's so much to explain, but for now can you hold off on the questions and come with me? We're only minutes away from somewhere you can clean up and recover.'

'So the "game" is over, is it?' Jody asks, her tone still caustic.

'Like I say, I will explain. Let's get moving.'

As they stand up, Grace's bad leg gives out. Sam lifts her into his arms. The guard looks pleased that Sam is now less of a threat.

'Where are we going?' he asks Gabby.

'Somewhere safe, I swear.'

Jody cuts in: 'A town? A harbour? The airport?'

Gabby's smile is weak and condescending: *Now you're being silly*. Perhaps, to her, this is no different from fending off complaints about blocked toilets or lumpy beds, just scaled up a little.

Behind them, Luka and the doctor are preparing to lift the

unconscious man on to the stretcher. Jody watches them for a moment, then gazes at the battered old rowing boat, the wooden stakes and the netting, the remnants of the food they retrieved from the cage full of rats.

It might not be true, but she wants to believe that anywhere will be better than this.

67

Gabby hangs back, letting the guard, Zivko, herd the family down the beach. It's the same tactic she employs towards the end of an overpriced excursion: any hint of dissatisfaction from the punters and she'll make herself scarce, reappearing only when the coach driver has taken the brunt of the whinging.

She was petrified of how the family would react when they saw her. She tried to persuade Borko to send someone else – Naji, maybe – but Borko refused. Gabby was the one who wanted them spared, brought back to civilisation, so she has to play her part.

But they'll hate my guts for this, she wanted to tell him. As if Borko would care.

She can't really blame the family for their attitude towards her, but still she feels a little resentful. If only they knew how she's been advocating on their behalf... though of course she couldn't risk trying to explain or justify herself in front of Borko's men.

Luka and the medic carry the stretcher down to the shore. After a quick discussion they decide to transport their patient in the dinghy – it's easier to get him aboard, and a quicker landing at the other end.

Gabby wades into the sea and attempts to help Grace, who is struggling even to grip her mother's hands as she and Sam try to lift her into the speedboat. Jody gasps at the intrusion, but swallows back an insult when Gabby's assistance makes the difference.

Jody is next to climb aboard. For a second, Gabby is alone with Sam; just enough time to whisper, 'I'm on your side, remember that.'

Sam looks scornful but says nothing, and Gabby feels another stab of resentment. *If you understood what this is costing me.*

Borko told her that while she was doing this, he intended to rouse Jesse and turf him out. And he was scrapping their proposed business deal. 'Partly because I can't have him here while this is going on. And partly because I can't stand the man.'

Clearing the decks, in other words.

The speedboat has limited seating, so there's a tense atmosphere from the start. As Zivko gets underway, easing the throttle open, Gabby notices Jody toying with her jewellery and decides to make an effort to lighten the mood.

'Ooh, that's an unusual ring.'

Jody gives a start and lifts her hand. Peering closer, Gabby can see the ring has been crudely formed from a strip of metal that appears to have numbers stamped on it.

'My husband made this for me,' Jody says, and Gabby starts to frown – *she didn't think they were married?* – when Jody adds, coldly: 'Because we thought we were going to die here.'

Sam can't work out what Gabby's up to, but he's aware of an unexpected voice in his head, telling him to trust her. It's occurred to him that, up against someone as powerful as Borko, the rep might not have a lot more choice about this than they did.

When the boat picks up speed, it gets quite cold. Sam draws Grace close, and Jody does the same with Dylan, all four of them hanging on tight. The driver (or whatever he's called) isn't worrying too much about making it a pleasant ride.

They hit a wave and for a second they're airborne. Sam is stunned when Dylan gives a little yelp of excitement. That's cause for hope, isn't it? In time the kids, at least, might be able to put this behind them.

After racing out to sea, they turn right and run parallel to the shore for a few minutes before moving back in. They've passed the high boundary wall and are heading towards a wide sandy bay with a timber jetty at one end. The beach here is steeper, with a rocky cliff at the rear. There are steps cut into the cliff, and on top there are neat lawns and terraced gardens arranged around a house so large it might be a resort hotel.

Half a dozen men in uniforms are waiting on the jetty, one of them holding a stretcher. For Grace, it turns out, and it's badly needed. Although she's conscious, and even manages a brave smile as Sam prepares to lift her out, she can barely stand.

A couple of the men help to lift her from the boat. Sam then takes Dylan's hand, waiting while Jody clambers out first, determined to stay by her daughter's side.

Gabby says, 'We'll look after her, Jody. I promise.'

Sam thinks Jody hasn't heard, till she glances back at the rep and snarls, 'Your promises are worthless.'

Gabby seems more disappointed than upset. She meets Sam's eye as he prepares to climb out. 'Whatever you may think, I'm doing my best for you guys. But you have to stay calm.'

Sam scowls at her. 'Is that a threat?'

'No, but it is a warning. For your sake, please don't ignore it.'

. . .

Jody accompanies the stretcher across the beach. Instead of taking the steps, the men veer off to the left and move into a shadowy opening cut into the cliff face. Inside, to her astonishment, she finds a long marble corridor containing a couple of toilets, a changing room and an air-conditioned elevator large enough to take the stretcher and the three adults.

She looks back. Sam and Dylan are with Gabby, heading for the steps. She has to stifle her panic, tell herself the separation isn't for long.

Sure enough, they're soon reunited in a wide hallway with a series of archways on one side. Jody glimpses an outside dining area, a striped lawn as immaculate as the centre court at Wimbledon, and a long sinuous swimming pool that seems to form a figure of eight, complete with various bridges and slides.

As they climb a couple of steps, Jody finds that her feet are aching. She realises it's because she has become so used to walking on sand; these manmade surfaces feel hard and jarring.

They cross a palatial living room, filled with sumptuous furniture and dazzling modern art: paintings, sculptures, photographs. It's blissfully cool, almost cold, and yet there's no one in here. Jody is plagued by a sense of unreality: after the past few days in such a tough environment this is far too plush, too rich.

It feels like a trap.

68

In Sam's view, the property looks like it could claim the centre-fold in *Fuck Off Homes* magazine. They step inside, and with the cool wash of the aircon he's immediately aware that he stinks. They all do, probably. Their clothes are filthy, soaked with three days' worth of sweat, and yet he's barely noticed until now.

Gabby mutters something about seeing them later, then vanishes. The family is led through the house and across a tree-lined courtyard to a single-storey outbuilding. The door is opened by a woman in a nurse's uniform. She takes charge of the stretcher, ushering the men into a bedroom where a gawky young man is setting up some equipment next to the bed.

The man greets them, speaking English in a soft French accent, and gives each of them a quick appraisal while Grace is being transferred to the bed. Then she becomes the focus of his attention. Once they've been reassured for the sixth or seventh time that she's going to be okay, they allow the nurse to show them to another bedroom across the hall where they can shower and change.

Sam is gobsmacked to find their suitcases waiting for them.

Jody doesn't take it well, angrily kicking one of the cases over. She lets out a shuddering sob.

'What?' Sam winces, remembering Gabby's warning.

'This!' Jody shouts. 'All of this. What a fucking, fucking stitch-up.'

Jody knows that Sam doesn't get it. How could he, when even she can't really comprehend why she is so distressed by the sight of their cases? But it's Sam's job at the moment to be the calm one. No doubt, before long, it will be her turn again.

There's a sense of violation, she decides eventually. To know that Borko's people – or, worse still, that evil cow of a rep – went to the hotel and packed up the cases, pawing through their clothes and personal belongings; things they had no right to see or touch.

A hot shower calms her mood a little. Sam and Dylan go next. Blissfully clean, Jody dresses in shorts and a t-shirt and hurries back to Grace's bedside. The doctor has hooked her up to a drip – for rehydration, he explains. He is at work on her leg, explaining how a mosquito bite became infected because of dirt in the wound. He has started Grace on a course of antibiotics, and he gently cleans and dresses the leg while Jody holds Grace's hand and encourages her to be brave, promising that she'll sleep away the pain and wake up feeling much better.

'She will heal quickly now,' the doctor says. He's about their age, late twenties or so, with long limbs and a wispy beard. He has such an honest, open manner that Jody wants to ask whether he knows what has been going on here. But she's too cowardly. This friendly interaction with a stranger feels so refreshingly normal that she doesn't want to ruin it.

Soon Grace is asleep, watched over by the nurse. The doctor accompanies Jody to the other bedroom and gives Dylan a thorough check-up, then does the same for the adults: temperature, pulse, blood pressure and so on. Sam, in the doctor's opinion, is dehydrated to the point where a drip would be invaluable, but he flatly refuses. Jody guesses it's partly that being tethered to the equipment will make him more vulnerable.

Their cuts and grazes are treated, and painkillers doled out, along with creams to soothe the insect bites and sunburn. A maid brings a jug of a dark purplish liquid which, the doctor says, will help to restore their electrolyte balance.

Remembering the fruit juice at the Conchis, Sam and Jody have the same reaction – is it safe to drink? Noting their hesitation, the doctor gives a sympathetic smile and says, 'It contains nothing that it shouldn't.'

So he does know. Jody feels distraught that even this charming young man is part of the conspiracy.

At Sam's insistence, the doctor has to sample it first. Only then does Sam take a few sips. He grimaces – it's got a blackcurrant flavour, which he doesn't like – but signals that it's okay to drink.

The doctor recommends only a light meal to begin with; otherwise there's a risk of vomiting. But when they're ready, breakfast will be waiting for them in the living room at the end of the hall.

Breakfast. That seems absurd to Jody. It feels like they've been up for hours, but according to the clock by the bed it's barely eight a.m.

She frowns. The clock has reminded her of something.

Another maid passes by, wafting a smell of bacon that makes Sam moan with desire. Jody feels her stomach turning cartwheels in anticipation, but she ignores her hunger for a minute, flipping open the cases and digging through them. She finds her handbag, tossed in amongst the toiletries and clothes, and Sam's wallet and keys are there, but other items are missing.

'No phones,' she mutters. 'We haven't got our passports or tickets back, either.'

Sam just shrugs. Dylan is swaying like he's going to pass out if he doesn't eat. Jody checks the room. No landline phone, of course, and the window, shaded by a blind, turns out to be securely locked.

'Come on,' Sam says. 'We'll deal with this later.'

They take the drinks with them, check in on Grace one more time, then hurry along the hall to investigate the buffet that has been prepared for them. Tea and coffee, fruit juice, scrambled egg and bacon and hot toast, and a handful of delicious sweet biscuits.

It's heaven. With every bite, Jody wants to squeal with pleasure. She has to fight off the constant urge to be grateful. It might be a lot more comfortable here, but she can't let herself forget that their status hasn't changed.

They are still prisoners.

69

There are moments, while he eats, that Sam actually manages to relax. So does Jody, but each time they do it's quickly followed by a look of furious concentration. Neither of them can avoid the issue of what's going to happen next.

Sam thought about it while he showered and dressed. It was on his mind when he picked up the grubby torn trousers he'd worn on the beach and went to throw them in the waste bin. Then he remembered what was in the pocket, and quickly transferred it to the shorts he's wearing now. Luckily, Jody had already gone across to Grace's room. Better Jody doesn't know.

His conclusion, when he goes over it again, is that they were naive to think they might be driven to the airport or returned to their hotel. It's even occurred to him that the people who died before – the Danes and the Germans and whoever else – might have gone through this stage: rescued from the beach and promised it was all over, only to be taken somewhere else and killed.

There's no way of discussing it without upsetting Dylan, so Sam says nothing. After they've eaten, they return to Grace's room and sit around her bed, watching her sleep. Soon Dylan has dozed off in his mother's arms, and at the nurse's suggestion they lie him on the bed next to his sister.

They hear the main door open – Sam has checked and found that it's kept locked, with a couple of guards patrolling outside – and Gabby appears. She too has taken the chance to freshen up since they last saw her. With her hair and make-up in place, she seems to have regained her confidence. It's like being back on the coach from the airport: she's in charge; their job is to sit back and listen.

'Good breakfast, guys? That's brilliant. You all look so much better. And the children are sleeping – lovely! Now, Borko can't wait to meet you. He's so impressed by the way you handled this. Do you want to follow me? We can sit on the terrace–'

'We're not leaving the kids,' Jody says.

'But it's just across–'

'I don't care. We're staying close to our children.'

Gabby huffs out a sigh and shifts her weight from one hip to the other, like a teenager protesting at her curfew.

'Give me two seconds.'

'You agree, don't you?' Jody asks Sam when Gabby has gone.

'Course I do.'

He hugs her, as if to prove it, but Jody won't be mollified so easily. Sam doesn't seem nearly as hostile towards Gabby as he should be, and that makes Jody suspicious. Surely he hasn't been suckered by her charms.

The rep soon returns, accompanied by a severe-looking man in his fifties, dressed in suit trousers and a crisp white shirt. Jody immediately recognises him as the man at the Conchis who dismissed their concerns about the chaos in the playroom. Naji Hussein.

They agree to leave the children in the nurse's care and

gather in the living room. Naji orders more refreshments, and explains that Borko will join them 'imminently'.

He goes on to say, 'I'm sure you have many questions, but first let me congratulate you both. You met every challenge with tenacity and courage, and we wish to salute you for your performance.'

Performance? Jody is at first taken aback, then disgusted by his praise.

'You're talking as though we had a choice. We were dumped there and held against our will.'

Naji bows his head with regret. 'And we are here, now, to discuss compensation.' He peers at them, perhaps hoping to spot dollar signs in their eyes, like in the cartoons. Jody makes sure to glare at him instead.

He says, 'If you had been forewarned, it would not have had the same... validity. Or, to be frank, the same value.'

'Value?' Jody says. 'You mean as entertainment?'

He nods. 'Your exploits were shown to a selected audience of, er, quite exceptional individuals. Borko, as you saw at the Conchis, is a man with a vibrant imagination. It's just unfortunate that you could not be informed of the... *arrangement* from the beginning.'

Jody can see that Sam is struggling to understand. His frustration is expressed by a spluttering laugh.

'"Unfortunate"? You've treated us like slaves. Like animals in a fucking zoo. If you'd done this in our country you'd be in prison.'

Naji only raises an eyebrow, as though he's not so sure about that.

The conversation is interrupted by Borko's arrival. He strides into the room, looking around with a vague air of distaste. He is taller than Jody remembers, taller, leaner, and physically – though it sickens her to admit it, given how much she now despises him – very attractive. It's as if he comes enveloped in some tremendous force field, radiating energy at everyone around him.

He catches Jody's eye and she feels her face reddening with anger and embarrassment. But he seems not to notice, his gaze moving swiftly on to Sam.

'Incredible. An extraordinary family.' Borko turns back to Jody. 'I mean it.'

'I was saying the same thing,' Naji says in an oily voice. 'Naturally they have some, ah, *objections* to their treatment.'

'I expect they do.' Borko settles cheerfully in an armchair and slaps his palms on his knees. 'Some more good news: Anton has regained consciousness. It is hoped that both he and Luka will make a full recovery from their injuries.'

Jody can tell that Sam has got the message. With a defiant sniff, he says, 'I don't give a toss about them. You wanted us to die out there.'

Naji starts to protest but Borko silences him with a flick of his hand.

'I had faith in your abilities. I knew you would survive.'

'Oh, yeah?' Sam retorts. 'So what about the people before us? Did you have faith in *them*, too, before they died?'

70

Gabby is willing Sam to shut up. Earlier she thought she'd bonded with him, to an extent; made him see how important it was to stay composed and follow her lead.

Now there's an icy silence. Borko's friendly demeanour is still in place, but it's as delicate as the froth on Gabby's coffee.

'I think you must know something I don't,' he says. 'Who are you talking about?'

Borko sounds so genuinely baffled that Sam is thrown off balance. Gabby has to stifle a snort as the poor man sends his partner an uncertain glance, and he doesn't get a particularly supportive look in return.

'I read it online,' Sam says. 'There was a boat accident last year. Three Danish guys. And before that, a young couple disappeared while scuba diving.'

Borko tuts. 'How tragic. But these events have nothing to do with us.'

At last, Jody comes to her husband's rescue. 'You've done it before, though? Put other people in the same position?'

'Broadly speaking, yes.'

'You searched for these incidents on the internet?' Naji interrupts. 'When? You had no access...'

'Or did you find a laptop on the beach?' Borko adds drily.

'It was before all this,' Sam admits. 'I was looking for a boat trip.'

'So what reason do you have to believe there's a connection?' Borko asks, still sounding plausibly innocent.

Sam has gone bright red; his voice at first comes out as a squeak. '*What abo*–what about Dylan, that stunt with the chain? If he'd drowned, are you saying we'd still be sitting here now, talking about... compensation?'

Borko weighs up the question. 'We think very carefully about the nature of the challenges we set. Nothing you encountered was quite as dangerous as it appeared.'

Gabby remains impassive through this bare-faced lie, recalling the key that Dylan threw away.

'Easy for you to say,' Jody mutters, while Sam gives a disgusted sigh.

'Why us?' he asks.

For a moment Borko looks lost. Then he shrugs. 'I saw you at the airport. I was in the control room when your little boy ran off to look at the soldiers. My instincts told me that you – your family – would rise to the occasion. And you did.'

'So that makes it all right?' Jody sounds ready to explode, but Gabby knows she can't intervene without drawing unwelcome attention. It's crucial that Borko and Naji go on trusting her.

Looking slightly apprehensive himself, Sam tries: 'Jode, maybe we–'

'No, I'm going to have my say. This is what my dad was talking about – the great greed.' Staring straight at Borko, she says, 'There was a time when the rich and powerful used to at least make it look like they cared about laws, and rules, and decency.

Now, because you're *so* rich, *so* powerful, you don't even have to pretend anymore, do you? And why would you, when a... a Russian dictator can use radioactive poison to kill people on the streets of Britain, and the Prime Minister just shrugs and moves on. A Saudi prince can get a troublesome journalist dismembered – a man who worked for an American newspaper – and the American president just shrugs and moves on. And now, right here, the son of a warlord can capture and torture a family to give his friends a laugh... and afterwards? Well, we're expected to shrug and move on, because that's how it is these days. Crime after crime, in broad bloody daylight, and no one gets punished.'

There's a stunned silence. Gabby wants the ground to swallow her up – on Jody's behalf, at least – but Jody is glowing with righteous anger, and Sam, far from disapproving, looks like he'll faint with pride.

Borko remains relatively poker-faced; Gabby suspects the hint of amusement on the surface masks a profound fury, and a loathing for these 'little people' who would dare to dispute the limits of his power.

There's a long moment when she has no idea how this will go. Finally it's Naji, after flashing an unanswered glance at his boss, who clears his throat to catch their attention.

'You should know,' he says quietly, 'that the sum proposed for reparations is three hundred thousand euros.'

As the fury and frustration comes pouring out of her, Jody is aware of a burning hostility, barely held in check by the two men. And when she catches Gabby's eye, Jody can tell the rep is worried for her safety.

You've gone too far, she thinks. This is a full-on tirade, and a man like Borko won't stand for it.

But he still hasn't said a word, and now his sidekick has put a number on their misery. Jody can't pretend she isn't floored by it, but neither is she gratified. Her instinctive response is suspicion.

'And how would that work?' she asks. 'We can't get on a plane with a suitcase full of cash.'

'No, no.' Naji produces an unremarkable brown envelope. 'To avoid questions from the authorities, it will take the form of a lottery win. That way you can bank it in England without attracting any liability for tax.'

'Put some away for the children,' Borko suggests, in a lack-lustre tone. 'A college fund. The first car.'

'But treat yourselves as well, eh, guys?' Gabby says, though the words come out with a forced jollity that fools no one.

'Oh, maybe we'll splash out on a dream holiday?' Jody retorts, with a withering glance at Gabby. 'Can you recommend a resort where we *won't* get abducted and tortured?'

Borko sucks air between his teeth, and quietly says, 'It is a very fair offer.'

'And what are the terms?' Sam asks. 'I suppose we can't tell anyone?'

'Correct,' Naji says. 'But that is the only condition we impose.'

'What about our children?' Jody asks, even as she realises that the question could put them at risk. 'We can't force them to say nothing.'

Borko only shrugs, dismissively. 'They're kids.'

In other words, no one will listen to them.

Jody and Sam make eye contact for a moment before Sam abruptly looks away, shaking his head. Whether that means he's tempted to accept – or he thinks Jody is tempted but shouldn't be – Jody isn't sure.

'Lots to consider, so why not talk it over?' Gabby advises them. 'Best if you stay here while you recover, let Grace build up her strength. Then you can either resume your holiday, or we'll arrange a flight home–'

'*Home!*' Jody almost shouts the word, and this time they're in perfect agreement.

'We wanna get out of here as soon as we can,' Sam offers Borko a sarcastic grin. 'No offence, eh?'

Borko stands, eager to be on his way. He looks more bored than angry with them, Sam thinks, as if mentally he's already ticked this chore off his list.

Naji and Gabby are also getting to their feet, so it seems natural for Sam to rise with them, and just as natural to slip a hand into the pocket of his shorts.

He's had an eye out for a better weapon since they were shown into this building. He still hasn't ruled out using one of the heavy glass tumblers – smash it against a table and shove it into Borko's throat – but it's a risk, because you don't know how effectively the glass will break. He saw his brother do it once, in a pub, but the glass shattered into tiny pieces and left Carl looking like a twat.

It's decision time. There's a glass within reach, but Sam's hand is already closing around the nail he prised out of the wooden stake, back on their first day as prisoners. If he holds it between his fingers, he can punch Borko in the neck and drive the nail as deep as it'll go.

And then what?

Gabby says something about leaving them to rest. There's a flicker of alarm in her eyes as she registers how intently he's staring at Borko. Deep down, Sam knows this won't achieve anything – Naji and the guards will be on him in an instant, and there's enough medical expertise on hand to keep Borko alive, even if Sam gets a direct hit on an artery – but at the same time, what sort of man would pass up an opportunity for revenge?

He's a coward if he doesn't do it.

His hand slips free of the pocket, his fingers working the nail into place. He reckons it should penetrate a couple of centimetres at least, maybe deeper if he can flatten his hand out–

Then Jody's jumping up, saying, 'Give us a couple of hours.' She eases in front of him, and her hand brushes against his as if accidentally making contact – only to go rigid, her fingers splaying out to block his path.

No one else seems to have guessed what he was planning, although Gabby maybe has an idea. She steps aside for Borko and Naji to leave first, then follows them along the hall.

Jody turns on Sam, hissing, 'What were you going to do?'

Sam shoves his hand in his pocket. He's trying to come up with an explanation when Gabby hurries back, checking over her shoulder to make sure she's alone. She too glares furiously at Sam.

'Do you want to get yourself killed?'

71

All of Jody's instincts say she should defend her husband, but it's difficult when she is livid with him for the exact same reason.

'That's gonna happen anyway, isn't it?' Sam mutters.

'No, actually. It isn't.' Again Gabby makes sure they're not being overheard. 'Borko had two options here, and I worked my butt off to get you the good one. Three hundred thousand euros, remember!'

'What's the other option?' Jody asks, sure that her worst fears are being confirmed.

Gabby assesses her carefully before replying. Her tone becomes brisk, unemotional; all traces of the bubbly, superficial rep have vanished. 'If you don't play ball, you'll be put under sedation for several days. The drugs basically wipe your recent memory, and they'll probably use hallucinogenics as well, to scramble your brain and make it impossible to know what's real or imagined.'

Jody shudders. 'The children, as well?'

'All of you. Then you'll be moved to a private hospital. When you come round you'll be told that the whole family went down with a serious infection.'

'And they've done that before, have they?' Sam asks.

'At least two occasions that Borko's admitted to. And it works. Anything you remember will be dismissed as a bad dream.'

'Except we'd all have the same dream,' Jody points out.

'So what? Nobody will be interested, not when the paper-work supports the official version of events.'

It's almost exactly what Sam predicted last night. Jody tries to imagine how it would feel to wake after several days and find that her nightmares were identical to Sam's. The disorientation, the anguish could destroy your sanity.

A long sigh, then she squares up to the rep. 'That's what will happen if we don't accept the cheque? You're sure?'

'Yes. Can you understand now why I'm trying to keep every-thing on track?'

Sam looks doubtful. 'I still don't see why Borko would trust us. We could take the money and then go to the police once we're home.'

'Or the media,' Jody chips in.

'You could,' Gabby agrees. 'But you won't be able to prove a thing. And anyway, guys, let's face it – if you've got all that money, why risk creating hassle for yourselves? Why not just enjoy it?'

Gabby leaves the guest block believing she has averted disaster. Sam and Jody are bound to see sense and accept the money, so this time tomorrow the family should be on a plane home, and Gabby can look forward to getting her life back on track.

And yet the unease lingers. She crosses to the main house, expecting to find Borko in the living room, but it's empty. There seem to be far fewer staff in evidence today, she realises. *Fewer witnesses?*

Half the doors to the terrace are open, even though the

aircon is gamely working away. She moves closer and hears voices, hushed and fast, and in their own language, which is difficult enough to comprehend at the best of times.

Another careful step, and she manages to translate a few stray words: *boat* and *quick* or *quicker*. Then something about a flight – *first flight*? The gist seems to be that a boat is the best option to reach the airport.

There's a pause, during which she can picture them turning to check once more that no one is within earshot. Perhaps fearing one of the servants is listening in, they switch to English. Naji says, 'And Gabrielle?'

'She'll be with me.' A snickering laugh, and then Borko adds something she doesn't catch.

'You've shown great restraint,' Naji says with his usual smarmy admiration. 'Though, in truth, it wouldn't trouble me if she was on the boat with them. Kill all the birds with one stone.'

'We'll see. Perhaps if she fails to live up to her promise.'

Another laugh, and Gabby understands that phrase, *blood runs cold*. Her reaction ought to be to flee from here at once. But she can't abandon Sam and Jody...

Can she?

Gabby quietly retreats, thankful that she's had this vital warning. She creeps into the hallway, where she encounters a couple of the maids. They give her a slightly cool glance, but they seem to be aware that she means something to Borko, and therefore she's allowed the run of the place.

Her focus is on preparing for the worst. Survival mode. She takes a couple of minutes to explore, then pops to her suite to collect her bag before returning to the living room. She steps outside at the far end of the terrace, pretending to search for her host. Borko raises a hand while Naji only glowers, then strides away.

'The wife had a lot to say for herself, didn't she?' Borko issues a sarcastic little laugh.

Gabby shrugs. 'I suppose she had to get it out of her system. I wouldn't pay it much attention.'

'Oh, I'm not. Though it's perfectly true.' His eyes gleam, and he gestures at a chair. 'Are you going to sit down?'

'Uh, I need to get to work. I'm already late.'

He looks disappointed. 'I thought you'd want to see the family off in the morning.'

'I do.' She looks at her watch, notices her hand is trembling and quickly drops her arm. 'I'll be back this evening. Probably seven, eightish.'

He considers for a moment, as though he might not grant her permission to leave. 'Very well. And are you satisfied with the room, or would you prefer somewhere more comfortable?'

There's no doubting what he means, so she has to smile, flirtatiously, and give him the answer he expects.

'I wouldn't rule it out.'

'I hope not.' He ponders for a moment. 'You know we're going ahead with the apartment complex on Turtle Bay?'

'In the conservation area?'

'Mm. It turns out we don't need to conserve quite as much as everyone said.'

'That's lucky for you.'

'Isn't it?' He winks. 'The first stage will be complete by the spring. I'd like to put one of the apartments at your disposal, rent free, for next season.'

Her natural reaction is shock, which she can just about get away with – so long as Borko doesn't question *why* she's shocked. Gabby covers her mouth with her hand, hoping to seem overwhelmed by his generosity.

'It's months yet,' he says. 'Take some time over your decision. But know that you will be very welcome.'

'All right. Well... thank you.'

His body language is inviting physical contact, so she comes forward and gives him a quick embrace, a kiss on the cheek. Borko's arms enfold her and he doesn't let her go, waiting until she's made eye contact before kissing her gently on the lips.

Another long second before he releases her; a hungry look in his eyes.

'Tonight, then,' he says, as though it's a contract signed in blood.

72

The living room feels too public for the sort of conversation they need to have, even though they appear to be alone in the building. It's occurred to Sam that there might be cameras watching their every move, and he whispers a warning to Jody as they return to the bedroom.

They lie side by side and quietly discuss what happened. Sam admits, reluctantly, that Jody got it right. He had planned to attack Borko.

'What with?'

'One of those nails from the stakes.'

'How would that help, with armed guards everywhere?'

'I just felt I had to do something.'

'You'd have put us in far more danger.' Jody seems cross, until she rests a hand on his arm and says, 'It was unbelievably brave of you.'

'But stupid, as well.'

She gives him a gentle smile. 'No worse than me ranting at Borko about how evil he is.'

'You were amazing.' Sighing, Sam picks up the envelope. 'So what do you think?'

'It sounds better than the alternative, if Gabby's to be believed.'

'A big *if*, after all the tricks that were played on us.'

Jody agrees, tapping the envelope. 'And maybe this is fake.'

Good point. Sam slits it open. He's picturing something snazzy, like those big cardboard cheques they bring out on Comic Relief and Children in Need, but this one is a regular size and printed on normal paper. The lottery symbol means nothing to him, though the bank's logo is vaguely familiar.

'BNP Paribus,' Jody says. 'That's an international bank.'

'So it's legit?'

'Seems to be.'

Three hundred thousand euros, as promised. The payee is *Mr Sam Berry*. Jody makes no comment about that, even though Sam feels sure she must be reflecting on the debts he hid from her.

This would put him in the clear with his uncle, and pay for a hell of a lot more than a wedding. They could buy their own place, just about.

He groans. 'I'm already doing it. Dreaming about how we could spend it.'

'We can't let those zeros go to our heads. At the moment it's still only a bit of paper.'

'But that's what they're counting on, isn't it? That we're so hypnotised by the money, we accept what they did to us.'

The main door opens and they tense, but it's only the nurse. She looks in on them, then heads to the other bedroom. A minute later she returns to say that Grace is awake.

Jody springs up, and Sam follows her across the hall. What they find is a minor miracle. Grace is sitting up, the colour restored to her cheeks, her eyes clear and bright. She is bemused by their reaction.

'God, Mum!' she protests when Jody pulls her into a crushing embrace.

'You look so much better, I can't believe it.'

'I feel better, too.' Grace looks at the drip. The current bag of fluid is about half empty. 'How long do I have to keep this in?'

The nurse says she'll fetch the doctor to find out. The activity has woken Dylan, who announces that he's starving. He also looks to have benefitted from a nap. *Talk about resilient*, Jody thinks, and from that comes some cautious optimism.

Perhaps it's an overreaction to worry about the long-term effects?

Perhaps the money is a fair deal to keep their mouths shut?

The doctor recommends that Grace stay on the drip for another twenty minutes; after that she's free to get up, and she can eat whatever she wants, providing it's only in small quantities.

'Chocolate,' she says, and Jody's kneejerk reaction – *You're not having chocolate until you've eaten something healthy* – is stifled by Sam, who says, 'Sounds like a great idea.'

Lunch is a comfy indoor picnic. The maid rustles up a bar of Italian chocolate, along with crisps, pasta, salad, cold meats and a selection of bread.

That's the only bum note. As one of the trays is set down, Dylan recoils with a cry of alarm. No one can understand what's wrong until Sam points to a couple of bread rolls. Even he looks anxious as he tears them open, showing Dylan that there's nothing to be scared of.

So much for the cautious optimism, Jody thinks.

As they eat, she and Sam have to field off a number of questions from the children. Is this house owned by the jetpack man?

Is he the one who kidnapped us? And then, from Grace: 'Why is he being nice to us now?'

'He...' Sam begins, then stares at Jody, lost for words.

'There's a lot we still don't understand,' Jody says. 'He claims we were never really in danger, and it was sort of like a... a big practical joke.'

'That's horrible,' Grace declares. 'He should go to prison for doing something like that.'

Dylan nods excitedly. 'Can we call a policeman to arrest him?'

'Not... not really.' Sam is cringing, and so is Jody.

'They want to pay us some money,' she says. 'As a way of saying sorry.'

Grace only narrows her eyes at this; eight years old and she knows it's a squalid deal.

After lunch the kids are persuaded to watch cartoons on TV, so Jody and Sam can continue to discuss it. They see nothing more of Borko, or Gabby, but Naji drops in, apparently to make sure they're being well cared for.

'Are you closer to a decision?' he asks.

'I think so.' Jody is about to accept their offer, based on what she and Sam have agreed, when he drops a bombshell.

'It's not enough for what we suffered.'

Naji arches one eyebrow. 'Oh?'

'We want four hundred thousand.' There's a slight tremor in Sam's voice, but you'd have to know him well to hear it. Jody catches Naji's eye and nods firmly.

'Then I will consult with Borko.'

'And we don't have our passports,' Jody adds. 'We'd like them back right now, along with the other paperwork, our keys and our phones.'

Naji says nothing to this. The moment he leaves, Jody gapes at Sam. 'Where did that come from?'

'Just popped into my head. Besides, it's true, isn't it? Look at how Dylan reacted to the bread. None of us are gonna forget this any time soon. Anyway, it's small change to Borko.'

So it proves. Within ten minutes Naji is back, with a face like he's sucking lemons.

'Four hundred thousand. With Borko's compliments.' He takes the first cheque back and hands them a new envelope, along with a leather document wallet bulging with papers and keys.

'Everything but the phones. Those we cannot return until you leave here, for security reasons.'

It sounds a bit lame to Jody, but neither she nor Sam is in the mood to argue. Frankly, they can't believe the bluff worked.

'Should have asked for half a million,' Jody mutters afterwards, then has to stress that she's joking; otherwise Sam might start berating himself again.

'I wanted to test them,' he says. 'Half a million, they'd think we were getting greedy. This seems fair to me.'

She shuts her eyes for a second. Like Sam, she's caught herself idly making shopping lists, musing over gifts for family and friends, wondering about long-term investments so the kids have the money to put down on homes of their own one day.

It ought to be intoxicating, knowing they have a small fortune to spend. But it's not. It feels wrong.

73

Soon the kids are bored with TV. They want to go outside. Sam isn't sure at first, though he too is beginning to tire of the unnaturally cool air.

There are servants coming by every few minutes to see if they want anything, but also, Sam suspects, keeping an eye on them. He asks about the pool, and after a quick consultation with someone, they're told the answer is yes, go ahead.

It turns out there are actually several pools, on different levels, linked by a network of slides and chutes. And they have the whole thing to themselves. Ridiculous.

Sam takes the kids on the slides and does his best to look like he's enjoying it. Jody is a lot more reluctant to join in, or allow herself to relax. She needs some persuading even to lie and sunbathe, knowing Borko and Naji might be watching from the house.

'Does it matter?' Sam asks. 'The past few days they've seen every bloody move we made.'

After lazing away the afternoon, they shower and change. For an early dinner they're invited into the main house and decide to accept, though they're dreading the thought of small talk with Borko or Naji. They're waited on in a dining room groaning with chandeliers and oil paintings, at a marble slab of a table that could happily seat twenty people, but thankfully their host and his sidekick are nowhere to be seen.

Grace and Dylan are wilting by the third course, revive briefly for ice cream, then make a demand that's practically unheard of: they want to go to bed.

As ever, one of the staff accompanies them to the guest block. There's a single guard outside the building, a different one from earlier. He's sitting in a garden chair with a paperback on his knee, and barely gives them a glance.

Sam can't help snorting. *We're obviously not seen as much of a threat.*

It's a little after eight when he and Jody settle the kids and cross the hall to their own room. If they hadn't been so exhausted – and if they hadn't just argued – then a bit of fooling around might have been on the cards.

The argument was polite, conducted in careful whispers while Grace and Dylan were brushing their teeth. Jody wanted to tell the kids they might be flying home tomorrow, while Sam was concerned about raising their hopes.

'I already did that last night,' he pointed out. 'What if it doesn't happen?'

'If it doesn't happen, disappointing them will be the least of our worries.'

With that, he shrugged and let her go ahead. Jody kissed them goodnight and said, 'Get to sleep quickly, and in the morning we'll be making plans to go home.'

'Real home?' Dylan asked.

'Real home,' Jody confirmed. 'Won't that be nice?'

'You'd better not just be saying that,' Grace warned, pulling the covers up over her head.

'Can't fool 'em anymore, can we?' Sam says as they lie down.

'Unfortunately, no.' Almost immediately, Jody feels her eyes growing heavy. She forces herself up and into the bathroom.

'You're getting ready for bed?' Sam asks.

'Yeah. I'm shattered.'

She comes out to find him smoothing his hand across the sheets, an expression of sheer bliss on his face.

'Uh oh, it's a man with a bed fetish.'

'Too bloody right, after three nights on sand.'

He uses the bathroom while Jody adjusts the aircon, then slips into bed.

'Funny that your mate Gabby's not been round,' she says when Sam emerges.

'Huh. Probably glad to see the back of us.'

'How fake, pretending she cares about our safety.' Jody snorts, watching Sam closely. All he does is shrug.

He climbs into bed, stretches and sighs with pleasure, then they share a quick hug and a kiss and say goodnight. Within seconds the smooth cool support of the mattress is pulling Jody down into sleep.

Untold luxury, she thinks, and remembers how she felt that afternoon when she was lying by the pool, trying to savour her brief experience of the billionaire lifestyle. What she understood then was that it means nothing to live in such palatial surroundings if you're not safe, if you're not secure.

It all seems a bit foolish now, recalling how anxious she felt.

Because they *are* safe, aren't they?

74

A schoolfriend once said Gabby's mum reminded her of the character Margo from *The Good Life*, a classic 1970s sitcom about a young couple who opt out of the rat race and attempt a life of self-sufficiency in the unlikely setting of the Surrey commuter belt. Margo is the sharp-tongued, snobbish but essentially good-hearted next door neighbour.

Gabby could see what her friend meant, both in terms of looks and character, and for years she took it as an unkind comparison. She thought it meant her mum was seen as a snooty bitch. Nobody wanted to be Margo; they wanted to be Barbara, the elfin blonde goddess next door.

But now, as she returns to Borko's home hours later than agreed, she's hijacked by a sudden wave of love and appreciation for her mother. It doesn't matter that she vehemently disapproved of Gabby's decision to take this job; in fact, her barely-veiled contempt for the whole idea of package holidays seems a lot easier to understand now. After all, Gabby regularly jokes with her fellow reps that this would be a fantastic job – if it weren't for the tourists.

Something to ponder: not just that she is turning into her mother, but that she doesn't particularly *mind* very much.

It's her mother who misses her – or notices her absence, at least – more than anyone else. Her father, she's always felt, loves her more in theory than in practice. On the rare occasion he makes contact, it's invariably the result of a nudge from her mother, even though her parents have been separated for nearly a decade. Her eldest brother, Oliver, a derivatives trader in New York, hasn't given a flying fuck about her since she was six or seven. The middle child, Rory, has been trekking through Central America for nearly three years and sends brilliantly entertaining emails to the whole family, but rarely asks after any of them.

So it's her mother, undoubtedly, who will be burdened with the funeral arrangements if it all goes badly wrong tonight.

A member of staff escorts Gabby to the living room where Borko sits alone, nursing a brandy while watching what appears to be a highlights reel of Sam and Jody's tribulations.

'You are late,' Borko says, without looking round.

'Sorry. Work was a pig today.' Before she can lose her nerve, Gabby hurries forward and places a kiss on the top of his head. 'I'll never understand how people on holiday can end up being so miserable all the time.'

'I messaged you.'

'I've only just seen it. Sorry.' The breathless delivery sounds good; it doesn't have to be faked, because her heart is thudding like a jackhammer.

She collapses into an armchair, rests her head back and shuts her eyes. It's a vulnerable pose, allowing him to feast on the view. She's wearing her uniform of blue skirt and patterned blouse, but the top two buttons are undone. She hesitated over the third and decided that would be a bit obvious.

Come home, darling, she hears her mother imploring her. *Go back to university – whatever course you choose. Persevere with your studies and in time you'll see that the life I want for you is the best life there is.*

Gabby waits, fully psyched for the performance of her career. She can feel the tension in the air dispersing, like morning mist.

Time to move.

She opens her eyes and Borko's gaze is there, hungry and resolute. Gabby pushes herself out of the chair and walks towards him: three slow, deliberate steps. She places her hands on his knees and lowers herself to eye level before moving in for a kiss.

Afterwards, she sighs. 'I've wanted to do that for a long time.'

'And yet you resisted.'

'Couldn't have you thinking I was easy.'

'But what if you are?'

She laughs, swatting at his arm, but she's not sure if he's joking. 'How are the family?'

'Fine.'

'Have they decided...?'

'They've taken the offer. Why wouldn't they?'

'Good. Well, I ought to go and say hi.'

She straightens up but his hand whips out to encircle her wrist. 'Just when we're getting started?'

'I won't be long – and then you'll have my undivided attention.'

'I hope so.' He releases her and turns back to the screen.

Gabby exits on to the terrace and tries to steady her breathing. The smell of blossom is overpowering, like smoke in her lungs. The gardens are lit at night, in a subtle but complicated design that apparently cost a small fortune. Dozens of bugs flit across the bars and beams of multi-coloured light.

She turns a corner, changing direction the moment she's out of sight. She re-enters the main house through a door at the side, follows a narrow hallway past the kitchen and turns into a small office. She'd come past it this morning and noticed the family's personal items sitting on a shelf behind the desk.

She spots their phones and picks them up, but everything else is missing.

Disaster.

75

Why us?

Was that a memory, a dream, or a conscious thought? Sam isn't sure. All he knows is that he's now awake and alert, and the question that nearly tore them apart seems pointless, irrelevant.

The space around him is dark but there's a comfortable bed beneath him. They're at Borko's house. Tomorrow they should be going home.

A quiet hiss: 'Sam!'

He rears up, disturbing Jody who is sleeping close beside him, the room almost cold because of the aircon. They left their door open a little, so they could hear if the kids woke up.

But this isn't Grace or Dylan. It's Gabby.

In a croaky voice, Sam says, 'What's up?'

Jody's waking, clutching at him in panic as Gabby moves across the room and turns on a lamp.

'I didn't realise you'd be asleep,' she says. 'The plans have changed.'

'Wh-what time is it?' Sam asks, expecting her to say two or three in the morning.

Incredibly, it's barely ten o'clock. After rubbing his eyes, Sam gets a clear view of Gabby's face. She looks freaked out.

'I told Borko I was popping over to say goodnight. I can't find your passports.'

'We've got them,' Jody says. 'We asked for them back.'

'Oh, thank God!'

It's a sigh of such deep relief that Sam's stomach does a flip.

'Why...?' he and Jody ask in unison.

'You have to leave right away. No cases or anything heavy. Passports and phones, basically.'

Sam climbs out of bed, a little self-conscious in his jockey shorts, but Jody doesn't move.

'How do we know we can trust you?'

'Please, Jody, I'm risking everything here. It's not safe to stay.'

Sam pulls on jeans and a shirt. Jody was already wearing a t-shirt, and she gets out of bed on the other side, takes Gabby by the shoulders and turns her so they're face to face.

'Have you betrayed us again?'

Sam can only stand and stare. If Jody lashes out, he won't be able to reach her in time.

Gabby drops her gaze. 'I'm truly sorry about what I did. I swear I never knew how badly you'd be treated. That's why I'm trying to make it up to you. This morning I overheard something that makes me think Borko might not honour the agreement.'

'What's he planning?' Sam asks.

'I don't know for sure. But nothing pleasant.'

Jody says, 'So why not tell us earlier?'

'Because I had arrangements to make. It was better you didn't know – you might have given yourselves away. Now come on, *please.*'

With Jody looking like she's about to lose it, Sam quickly says, 'But we negotiated with them. Four hundred grand.'

Jody nods. 'We've got the cheque.'

'Right.' They can see Gabby's mind working. 'Did they put up any sort of fight?'

Sam feels his confidence evaporating as he makes sense of the question. 'Not really.'

'That's why, then. It could say ten million for all they care. They know you won't be around to cash it.'

It's clear from his face that Sam has bought the argument. Jody wants to hold out, but hasn't it been bothering her that Borko agreed so readily? Her dad reckons that the rich hate to give money away – as he says, that's how they get rich in the first place. But she didn't voice her doubts for fear that Sam would think she was belittling his achievement.

'Where are the children?' Gabby asks.

'I'll get them,' Sam says. Jody asks if they can take a rucksack, and Gabby nods.

'If you're quick.'

Jody opens the case and digs around for a pair of jeans, plus clothes for the kids. Fleeces, in case it's cold. She packs a rucksack with some basic toiletries, their phone chargers and a few other personal items.

'But what are we going to do? We're not scheduled to fly home till Tuesday.'

'I've called in some favours.' She picks up Jody's bag and asks to check their passports. This is a Gabby so sombre, so tense that Jody has little choice but to believe they're in danger if they stay here.

She's making an effort to adjust her opinion of the rep when Sam comes in with the kids, both of them grouchy and confused.

'We're going somewhere,' Jody says. 'It'll be an adventure, but nothing like last time.'

'Don't wannoo,' Dylan exclaims, far too loudly.

Sam takes hold of him, kneeling down to eye level. 'Dylan, listen to me. Do you want to go back to that beach?'

The boy's eyes widen in fright; he whips his head from side to side. '*Noo-ooo!*'

'Sssh! No, you don't. So that's why you have to be a good boy.' A glance at Grace. 'You too, okay? We all do what Gabby tells us, and we get away from here.'

Jody doesn't approve of how he's scared them into silence, but there was probably no better way. Gabby explains that the security presence around the house is fairly light. Borko's reputation is such that no one seriously expects his property to be targeted – and in any case the focus is on intruders trying to get in, rather than anyone wanting to leave.

'What about the dogs?' Jody asks quietly. 'There were guard dogs on the edge of the compound where they kept us.'

'That's a separate section. There aren't any in the grounds here. Borko has a phobia of dogs.'

'*What?*' Jody isn't sure whether to laugh or cry at the irony.

In the hall, Gabby hesitates for a moment, undoing another button on her blouse. Then she opens the front door, a big smile ready as she steps out.

The night air is rich and humid, a sauna compared to their rooms. There are crickets chirping and a constant hiss of water from the garden's irrigation system.

The same man from earlier is sitting in his chair, a *Game of Thrones* novel open in his lap. He glances at Jody as she and the others follow Gabby outside, but his gaze quickly returns to the rep.

She leans in a little, giving him a flash of cleavage. 'Just going to see Borko.'

The guard nods, leaning forward to unclip the radio from his belt.

'It's okay, he's expecting them.'

She straightens up and marches away as if the matter has been decided. Jody and Sam quickly follow, hustling the kids between them.

They reach the corner of the main building, and Sam mutters, 'I think it worked.'

Too soon to be relieved, Jody draws alongside Gabby and whispers, 'It's that easy to wipe a man's brains?'

'Ridiculous, isn't it? But right now we've got to be grateful for that.'

Sam moves to the rear of the line as they make their way round the house. He's haunted by a sudden vision of the guards opening fire and wants to shield his family as best he can.

They have to duck low beneath some of the windows at the front, then they're past the house and plunging into the gardens on the far side. It's not as well lit here, which means they have to slow down, picking their way carefully on the stone paths and steps that link several terraces. In the moonlight a tennis court gleams faintly, the white net reminding Sam of the snake pit.

They reach a small building that houses pumping equipment for the swimming pools. Gabby stops and checks her watch.

'I need to go back before Borko gets suspicious.' She instructs them to follow the path until it bears to the left. Another set of steps will take them to the boundary wall. 'I checked it from outside and you'd struggle to get over, but from inside the garden it should be okay. There are trees growing very close.'

Once they're over the wall, they have to turn right along a dirt track for a hundred metres to the road, where they should find a black Jeep waiting for them, driven by a man named Nick.

'What about you?' It's not lost on Sam that Borko might react violently when he finds out they've escaped.

'I'll be fine, don't worry.'

She doesn't sound totally convinced. Sam feels bad about leaving her here, but one glance at Grace and Dylan tells him he won't be able to do things any differently.

'Come with us.'

It's Jody who's spoken, and they all look surprised by her plea.

But Gabby shakes her head. 'Borko would only come looking for me, and then none of us would get away.' She puts on a brave smile. 'I need to go back in and... distract him.'

76

Gabby feels bewildered when Jody gives her a quick hug. If they were to have any physical contact at all, she'd have bet on it being a slap.

Sam shakes her hand but finds it hard to meet her eye. He too seems to have picked up on her euphemism – 'distract' – and what it means in reality. For Jody there doesn't seem to be any doubt: she's worked out how Gabby plans to save them, and she looks both sickened and immensely grateful.

Gabby rushes back, heading first to the outbuilding so that it looks as though she's crossing from there to the main house. This time there are guards by the orange grove, smoking and chatting. They jump at the sound of her footsteps, one of them reaching for his gun until he sees who it is.

Crumbling inside, Gabby manages to stroll past with a haughty look on her face. But the close call isn't lost on her: a couple of minutes earlier and she and the escapees would have been caught red-handed.

Borko hasn't moved, which is something. She's mindful of the extensive network of cameras that monitor the property and suspects that she wasn't able to evade them all.

He greets her with only a twitch of a smile. She crosses the room, trails her hand along his shoulders and perches on the arm of his chair. His silence is unnerving.

'Turns out I caught them getting ready for bed. They're exhausted.'

Nothing. She tries caressing the back of his neck.

'Hey, they're really pleased about the extra money. It was very generous of you.'

He grunts. *Bored with this.*

On screen, Sam is chest deep in the sea, battling to keep his son's head above the water while Jody dives for the key. Another thirty seconds and Dylan would have drowned, signing a death warrant for the other three.

Gabby says, 'Seems very quiet here.'

'I've given most of the staff the night off.'

She was right: *no witnesses.* Swallowing hard, Gabby shifts over, nudging her foot against his leg. That's when she notices a smear of fresh mud on her shoe.

'Naji not here?' she asks, knowing Borko is more likely to spot the mud if she moves her leg away too quickly. He'll think it odd because the paths close to the house are kept spotlessly clean.

'He has a meeting at the Conchis. One of my guests wants in on the Turtle Bay project.'

'Oh. Lovely.' Gabby knows how vacuous she sounds, but she can't care about that. She yawns and stretches in an exaggerated manner, at the same time twisting round so she can kick off her shoes. He watches her carefully.

'Nervous?'

It should be a flirtatious question, but it's not.

'Excited,' she says.

'So why the yawn?'

'Tired.' *Oh shit, she's making a mess of this.* 'And maybe a bit nervous. I want this to be special.'

'It will be.'

At last, Borko seems to relax. Taking her hand, he leads her up to his bedroom suite. She's seen it once before, when he gave her a tour of the house, but on that occasion there was a party in full swing. The room isn't as large or ostentatious as she'd expected: he told her he preferred bedrooms to be cosy. It's still huge by any normal standard, and there's a balcony with a hot tub, which he suggests they might want to use later.

'But the bed first, I think,' he says.

'Oh, beds are best. Definitely.'

He adjusts the lighting, unbuttons his shirt and sits down on the bed. She walks towards him, understanding that he wishes to watch her undress. But then, as she approaches, he undoes his belt and slowly pulls it free, wrapping one end around his hand.

'You know, Gabrielle, I really ought to punish you.'

It's caught her off guard, and she gasps. 'What?'

'You lied to me.'

Finally, Jody thinks, a lucky break. Because where the path runs out, there's a vehicle parked on the grass close to the wall. Some sort of maintenance buggy. There's no key to start it, of course, but by climbing on to the seat it's a lot easier for Jody to reach the high stone wall.

She waits on top while Sam hoists Grace up, then Dylan. She's astonished by the children's courage, the way they've managed to control what must be a desperate urge to panic.

The drop on the other side is a couple of metres. A long way down. Jody knows that if she thinks about it she'll chicken out, so she lifts both legs over, wriggles forward and lets go, trying to remember doing gymnastics at school: bend your knees and roll. The ground is hard-packed earth, but that's still better than rock, and she lands without any real injury.

Sam's on the wall, gripping it with his legs as he leans over to lower the kids down to her, one by one. Then he joins them, wincing as he turns his ankle on impact.

'All right?'

'Yeah.' He's sweating, visibly in pain, but insists it won't be a problem.

They walk briskly, jogging when the kids can be persuaded to speed up, stumbling sometimes in the dark. At any moment Jody expects searchlights and sirens, 4x4s with machine guns mounted on the roof...

Then a flash of red up ahead. Brake lights. She grips Sam by the arm.

'What if it's a trap?'

'If it is, we've had it.'

The vehicle swims into view: a black Jeep. The driver's door opens and a tall man in a grey t-shirt and shorts turns to greet them. Nick is about thirty, with bleached blond hair and a goatee beard. Australian, Jody thinks when she hears him speak, but later he mentions New Zealand. He turns out to be a fellow rep, albeit with a different tour company.

'You're the mates of the Gabster? Jump in, nice and quick. She says they probably patrol this road?'

That's all the warning they need. Sam takes the front seat while Jody and the kids pile into the back. The interior is pungent with a mix of diesel and cannabis.

Nick drives recklessly fast, which is all the more frightening when he doesn't turn his headlights on for the first couple of minutes. He's setting out the next stage of their journey, and here's another shock.

'*A boat*?' Jody says.

Up front, Sam has gone rigid, and Grace says, 'I don't want to go on a boat.'

'Sorry, guys, but it's the only way. Sekliw is Borko's island, yeah? You can't move an inch without him knowing, and you definitely can't get on a plane.'

Nick's driving them to a small village on the east coast, where another friend of Gabby's is waiting to transfer them to the mainland. The boat owner's brother will drive them to the nearest airport. Gabby has booked tickets on the last flight out at three a.m.

'To Heathrow, not Gatwick. Best she could do at short notice.'

Jody says nothing. It must have cost well over a thousand pounds for all four of them. And there she was, thinking of Gabby as nothing more than a phony double-crossing bitch.

Which she is, of course, for her part in luring them to the Conchis. But clearly that's not *all* she is, and Jody can't help but feel a pang of regret that the rep wasn't able to escape along with them.

77

'What do you mean? I haven't lied.'

So why do you sound so afraid?

But Borko doesn't say what Gabby is thinking. He makes a face that suggests he is willing to compromise, although the belt is still coiled in his fist.

'You were "economical with the truth", then.'

'Was I?'

'Gabby, please stop treating me like a fool. Nobody – *nobody* – treats me like a fool.'

Maybe you should get out more? The words almost make it to her lips. It's that giddy, reckless side of her character again. But what matters is that the family got away, and the longer Gabby keeps stalling, the more likely they'll reach the boat and Borko won't catch them–

'I offered you the use of an apartment. You pretended to consider it. Why didn't you tell me the truth?'

'Wh-what?'

'Naji spoke to your boss. Apparently you have no plans to return to Sekliw next season. You've specifically asked to go elsewhere.'

Gabby wants to scream with relief. Then common sense prevails: this is still dangerous.

'What can I say?' She takes a single step backwards, out of his reach, and starts to unbutton her blouse.

'I'm young, free and single. I want to see as much of the world as I can before I settle down. You can understand that, Borko.'

The blouse comes off, the room so quiet that they both hear the whisper of its progress over her skin. He's about to speak when he sees her reaching back for the clasp that holds her bra in place.

It silences him immediately: the expectation, the hunger, wiping his brain as effectively as a lobotomy. For a second, she is maddened by the power this has bestowed on her. Here he is, the son of a president, a billionaire – a killer, probably – and yet she can render him helpless simply by displaying two mounds of flesh designed to store milk for infants.

What a world.

She fumbles with the clasp, frees it, shrugs the straps off her shoulders, then deftly extracts her arms while keeping the cups in place. All the time she holds his gaze, her smile acknowledging the skill of the tease while inwardly she's astonished by the way his mouth has fallen open.

'So...' he gives a start, as if remembering who he is and what they were talking about, '... you want to leave here?'

'I'm afraid so.' Hands clamped over the cups. *Wait, boy, wait.* 'But not until I've fucked your brains out.'

'You–' A laugh escapes him. He leans back, eyes narrowed, as if studying her properly for the first time. 'Until *you've* fucked *my* brains out?'

'That's right.' Now it's time to open her arms, step forward and bend a little, dispensing with the lingerie as she reaches down and takes hold of him. 'Do you have a problem with that?'

. . .

The boat is used for tourist trips, and there are various items of scuba diving and fishing equipment on board. The owner, whose name sounds like *Lev* or *Lex*, is an older man, a native of the island with quite basic English. He is worryingly vague, sucking on a roll-up cigarette and seemingly baffled by the controls of his own boat.

They sit at the back, only partly shielded from the cold wind. When Lev notices how they're huddled together, shivering, he roots around in a locker and produces a couple of mouldy blankets. Better than nothing.

The journey takes just over an hour. Grace and Dylan sleep for much of it, lolling against their parents. At times they wake, scared and confused, believing they're back on the beach. Jody and Sam are quick to reassure them, but the effect is strangely disturbing: gradually their own words become harder to believe.

Perhaps this *is* just a dream, Sam thinks, and soon we'll wake up beneath the boat, to face yet another day in captivity.

Finally they moor up in a lively tourist resort, the water lit by dozens of harbour-side restaurants and bars. It sounds like a thousand parties are in full swing: there's music and laughter, shouts and whoops and car horns; dogs bark and doors slam and heels click on the cobbled streets. The atmosphere reminds Sam of Brighton – the Kings Road Arches on a Saturday night – and he understands that, oblivious to what he and Jody and the kids have just gone through, these tourists will feel they're in a kind of wonderland out here. *Life is good, the night is young, you only live once*: a holiday state of mind.

Lev's brother collects them. He's bearded and balding, and

he thrusts a flask of whisky at Sam. There's a fair chance he's had a few nips of it himself, but what are you gonna do?

As he leads them to a beaten-up Mercedes, Sam whispers to Jody: 'How did she get all these people to help her?'

'I bet they fancy her. Except Nick.'

'Why not Nick?'

Jody makes a face. 'He's gay.'

'Is he?'

'I might be wrong,' she says, with a little twist of her mouth that means, *I'm never wrong.*

He tuts. 'Imagine if we hadn't trusted her. We'd still be there.'

Jody has a distant look in her eyes. 'I don't think you can blame us for doubting her motives... but yeah.'

They get in the car, this time all four of them squashing together in the back. There aren't any seatbelts, and Sam has the impression that no one cares much about rules like that over here.

'Airport, yes?' the driver says.

'Please,' Sam says. *Oh Christ, yes.*

'I can't believe we're going home,' Jody whispers once the kids are dozing again. 'It makes me realise I didn't think we ever would.'

'Me neither.'

'I keep worrying about Gabby. Will *she* ever see her family again?'

'Dunno,' he says with a weary sigh. He thinks of how he'd looked at his children and knew there was no way he could risk their lives for Gabby's, no matter what she had done for them. If that makes him a bad person – selfish, cowardly, whatever – then so be it.

'Nothing we can do now,' he says, 'except pray she gets away with it.'

78

Gabby wakes in darkness and grabs her phone to check the time. Almost three a.m. – the family should be safe.

She's amazed that no one has raised the alarm. The guard outside the guest block must have assumed they're still with Borko. Or maybe the staff have strict orders not to disturb their boss when he's 'otherwise engaged'.

She has half a second to bask in relief, until she registers that she's alone in the bed. Then a light snaps on in the adjoining dressing room and Borko emerges, completely naked. She might have assumed that round two is on the cards, if not for the look on his face.

That side of it has been more enjoyable than she anticipated. It turns out he isn't nearly as selfish in bed as his everyday manner would suggest. But it wasn't easy to put her fears aside; several times she had to pretend to be suffering from perfor-mance anxiety, rather than fear of discovery.

His expression now is ominously stern. She sits up, not both-ering to cover herself, lifts her arms and fingercombs her hair into some sort of order. She wants his attention on her body as she subtly shifts a little closer to her bag, which is on the floor beside the bed.

'All right?' She allows her voice to slur a little, while inside her rib cage there's a heart beating itself into a frenzy. 'Something wake you?'

He nods, but doesn't say what. Like a prowling animal he crosses the room, coming to stand at the end of the bed.

'Did you know, Gabrielle, it was my father who inspired these gatherings?'

She shrugs, realises it's too sullen a response, then says, 'He did this as well?'

'Not exactly. He threw lavish parties for key people in our country. The purpose was to impress, or intimidate, or blackmail, and the focus was purely on the pleasures of the senses. Food. Alcohol. Drugs. Sex.'

He snorts, his gaze turning distant. 'Always sex. There were men, women, children on hand, who were required to copulate with the guests, and each other, and even with farm animals a few times. It was...' His face screws up, as if at a sour taste; Gabby interprets it as revulsion until he finishes with: '... insipid, after a while. But then, as we've seen here, jaded appetites tend to become ever more extreme.'

Gabby hardly trusts herself to speak. She considers snapping out a flirty remark, but knows he won't buy it. The vibe's all wrong.

'You're a smart cookie, Gabrielle. Perhaps you've gathered that I wasn't entirely truthful when I downplayed the dangers to the family? I assured you they would make it, but that was never what I expected... or wanted.'

'Right. So can I ask... why not?'

'Because a spectacle was needed. Those Danish students pulled from the sea? They were here, but quickly fell into conflict–'

'Then Sam was right? You lied about them?'

He nods curtly. 'One of them murdered his friend. Witnessed live, it was a spellbinding moment. My guests were ecstatic. I'd bestowed on them an experience they will never forget.'

'So this...' She swallows heavily. 'This year had to offer even more?'

'It's what I hoped – though always on the basis that the family were to be given a fair chance.' Borko's lips curl into a smile, but it's unlike any smile she's ever seen. 'I correctly foresaw that they would display great spirit, and might find a way to survive. But I was also ready for savagery, desperation – and yes, I was fascinated to see how my guests would react to the death of a child.'

'Dylan is only *five* years old. Would it really not have mattered to you if he'd died out there?'

Borko turns slightly and sits on the corner of the bed. He's close enough that he could reach out and touch her leg. Gabby wants to shrink away from him, but she cannot.

'The truth? Their suffering means nothing. I know it isn't what you wish to hear, but actually, if you were honest with yourself, you'd admit that you are no different.' He leans in. 'I realise nowadays it's important to make the appropriate noises, but at a fundamental level, none of us truly care about people we do not know.'

'Of course we do,' she says hotly. 'It's why charities exist, it's why–'

He cuts her off: 'All for show. A fleeting moment of sympathy, usually to assuage guilt. Nothing more.'

'No, I disagree.'

His sudden laugh makes her jump. The silence that follows is paralysing.

'I'm perfectly aware that you disagree, Gabrielle.' There's a weight to his words that at first she can't interpret, but she feels a vertiginous dread. Borko stares at the floor, then slowly raises his head to look into her eyes. 'No doubt that's why you spirited them away from here?'

They're at the airport soon after midnight, and collect the tickets Gabby purchased on their behalf. It's three hours till the flight, but they tell each other the time will pass quickly enough.

The driver won't accept a tip, any more than his brother or Nick had done. 'For Gabby,' they all insist. 'For Gabby.'

Inside it's far too bright, and disturbingly quiet. They attract a few inquisitive stares, and Jody half expects to find 'wanted' posters with their mugshots on them. It's only when they've checked in and gone through security that she dares to celebrate. They've taken another important step away from Borko.

'Can he reach us now we're airside?' Sam wonders.

'In his own country, I bet he can get anywhere. It's more a case of him not knowing where we are.'

'We hope.'

'Exactly.'

The harsh lighting keeps the kids awake, so the four of them end up slumped around a grubby plastic table in an overpriced cafeteria, listening to the near-constant chime and murmur of the PA system. *Sam and Jody Berry*, it's about to say, *you cannot run from Borko Radić. You cannot escape.*

But it appears they can, and they do. A couple of grimy, tedious hours later they shuffle along to the gate, show their tickets and join a thin queue of early-morning travellers boarding the bus that will drive them to the plane.

Jody isn't sure if it's her imagination, but it seems that the eastern sky is already starting to lighten. She gazes at the stars overhead and wonders how long it will be before she catches herself looking back almost wistfully on their experience of living life in the raw; when they were truly a family unit, working and surviving together, appreciating every sip of water, every morsel of food. That extraordinary intensity of living in the moment will be hard to beat. However perverse it seems now – for all the hardship and anxiety and pain – Jody suspects that she *will* miss it, just a little, once they start taking life for granted again.

She can't believe how nonchalantly Grace and Dylan have greeted the news that their ordeal is over. Of course, there's no way of telling what sort of long-term damage might have been done – and it could be years before the full effects are felt. But they seem to be remarkably adaptable, perhaps because they're accustomed to having their lives controlled by grown-ups.

The plane is barely half full, and a kindly steward suggests they spread out over all six seats in their row. It means the kids are able to stretch out, one at each window, while Sam and Jody sit across from each other in the aisle. During take-off, Sam gripped her hand. With the plane horizontal again, and the seat-belt lights out, he can relax.

First he releases a long and heartfelt sigh. Then gently, play-fully, he taps his thumb against her DIY ring. 'You don't have to keep that on, you know.'

'I want to.'

'I'll get you a proper one.'

'Oh, will you?' She turns to face him. 'Is that a proposal?'

'I already proposed.'

'So you did.' She smiles, reaches across the aisle to kiss him, then looks down at the ring. 'This one is fine.'

79

'Spirited them away?' Gabby tries bluffing. 'What do you mean?'

Borko is shaking his head. 'Your behaviour today has been quite odd, so I had the cameras monitored by a couple of my most trusted staff. The family went over the wall...' He glances at a clock by the bed. 'Around five hours ago. By now I expect they're on board the Heathrow flight.'

'You knew?' Gabby exclaims. Her next question – *Why didn't you stop me?* – dies in her throat. 'Have you... gone after them?'

Borko shakes his head. 'They pose no threat to me.'

Gabby can't believe what she's hearing. Relaxing a little, she leans forward and lifts the sheet to cover her breasts. 'But you *had* planned to kill them?'

He looks bemused. 'Where did you get that idea? Thanks to you, they will arrive home tomorrow and resume their lives. I don't expect to hear from them ever again.'

'Right. And you were happy to give them all that money?'

'Actually, no. The cheque has already been cancelled.' As she winces, Borko opens his hands. 'What are they going to do? A rough and ready working class family with no credibility, no leverage, no proof.'

She lets out a held breath. *Think, Gabby*. Where does this leave you?

The family are on their way home, and Borko's fine about that. It's cost him nothing, ultimately, and he's right: when the cheque bounces, there won't be anything Sam and Jody can do about it.

So it could be worse. Could be a hell of a lot worse–

Then Borko moves. First a punch, so heavy and brutal that it slams her down on the bed. Blood pouring from her nose, her brain scrambled, the pain as sharp as glass and the shock, the fear like an even heavier blow.

He bends down, reaching for something, and sprawls on top of her. She struggles and tries to fight him off but he's too strong, pressing all his weight on her legs and arms, and his breath is hot on her face, hot and foul, and he laughs.

'Your ingenuity was impressive, Gabrielle. Most devious.' He leans slightly, peering over the bed. 'And you even came prepared.'

He's staring at her bag, at the last component in her oh so clever plan. Although reckless Gabby gets a kick from danger, sensible Gabrielle prefers not to be quite as vulnerable, so during her earlier roaming she prudently searched for – and was fortunate enough to find, in the bottom drawer of a unit in the downstairs office – a small gun.

She left it nestled in her handbag, within easy reach, believing it could save her if the worst came to the worst.

She was wrong.

'Personally, I don't care for firearms,' he says. 'Too easy.'

And now she learns what Borko picked up from the floor. A silk necktie. As with the belt earlier this evening, he loops the tie around one fist, and then the other. It means her hands are released – with a pitiful lack of strength, she claws at his stomach, his chest, but even when she draws a little blood, he barely reacts.

'Borko, please.' Tears spring to her eyes. 'You've just said you don't care if the family get away. Let me go and I'll take the first flight out of here–'

'The family played their part. Whereas you, Gabrielle, only betrayed me. You lied to me. Made a fool of me.' He grabs her by the hair, lifts her head off the bed and slips the tie around her neck. 'You remember Jody's spirited outburst? How the rich and powerful no longer pay lip service to the rules that govern society?'

He crosses the ends of the tie and rests his fists on her shoulders, slowly extending his arms and increasing the pressure on her neck.

'I can confirm that Jody is entirely correct – and I speak as a man whose father is personal friends with the presidents she condemned today.'

The constriction is making her dizzy, making her nauseous; Gabby feels starkly terrified but she tries to persuade herself that it's a tease, a sex game. Any second now he'll let go...

Still pulling tighter, and coating her face with saliva as he speaks, Borko says, 'It's a world without limits, Gabrielle, for men like us. And in this world, people who betray me have to face the consequences. It's nothing personal, merely a standard I have to maintain. I hope you can appreciate that... Gabrielle?'

But Gabby can no longer hear him.

Jody tries to doze but can't. Too much on her mind. Should they speak out or keep quiet? Perhaps, after a few days at home, they'll be able to decide what's best.

The media, not the police: that's one thing she's clear on. Her dad has an old friend who works for the *Guardian*. A backroom job, but even so, he's bound to know some journalists.

At the airport, when she used the toilet, she discovered a folded sheet of paper in her handbag. Gabby must have placed it there when she was checking their passports. It contains a list of names, under the heading: 'Borko's party guests'. One or two seem vaguely familiar. Names a *Guardian* journalist might recognise.

Feeling restless, she opens the overhead locker and finds the envelope with the cheque. She shows it to Sam as she sits down.

'I've been thinking.'

'Yeah?' he says, in a tone that means, *Uh oh...*

'If we take this money, Borko's won.'

'How d'you work that out?'

'It means we're accepting that the world is how he wants it to be. Run by people like him, *for* people like him, while people like us just put up with it.'

'You're sounding like your dad again.'

'Good. From now on I'm going to listen to my dad a lot more.'

Sam sighs, but it's slightly half-hearted. 'We could buy our own home with this, Jode.'

'Except it wouldn't be ours. It would be Borko's house, and we'd remember that – we'd remember how he demeaned us, and terrorised us, and endangered our children – every time we stepped through the door.' She pauses, waits for him to say something, and then continues. 'When we buy our first property together, I want it to be truly ours. The home we worked for, saved for, *dreamed* of owning. Until then...' she nods at Dylan, snoring gently next to his dad, then presses back in her seat so that Sam can see Grace, sound asleep beside Jody, '... we're doing okay, aren't we?'

He's silent for a few seconds, but finally says, 'Yeah. We are.'

'Then it's our world too. It doesn't belong to him. *We* don't belong to him.'

He returns her smile. She opens the envelope, goes to hand him the cheque but he shakes his head.

'You do it.'

'We'll both do it.'

So they tear it up together: first into two, then each of them rips their half into many tiny pieces before sprinkling the fragments into an empty plastic cup. Nothing has felt this crazily good for years. *Liberating*, is the word Jody wants; a concept that's barely entered her head since she first peed on a stick and the blue line appeared.

The steward is approaching, pushing his trolley. More drinks and snacks. No one's hungry at four in the morning, and it's a dreadful time to contemplate alcohol, but they order champagne all the same.

EPILOGUE

All his life, Naji was a faithful servant. He did terrible things, unspeakable things, for unspeakable people. For years, decades, he had few regrets. He felt no guilt. No compassion.

And still he doesn't.

But he is a practical man. Pragmatic. He follows no ideology, and owes no loyalty.

Borko didn't know that, and neither did the president. They think they own him. In fact, they were merely leasing his skills, his diligence, his judgment.

The house is monitored by a network of cameras, but Borko ruled out coverage in his bedroom suite, even when his aide strongly recommended it on grounds of personal security.

So Naji installed them anyway, on a separate network, by a different contractor who was sworn to secrecy for the duration of the work. A contractor who regrettably met his demise shortly afterwards.

Naji watched the rep's murder and enjoyed every second. Enjoyed it more than the earlier fornication. He always regarded her as a cheap whore, no matter what her father was worth.

And now, even more importantly, he has the footage.

On the mainland, unrest is growing. Opposition to the president becomes bolder, more vocal with each passing day. A new leader has sprung up, and so far he has managed to stay alive. He is young, charismatic, wealthy and less overtly corrupt than anyone in the current regime. Word of his potential is spreading. In foreign capitals, a subtle courtship is underway. Ambassadors and business leaders have been briefed that change is on the horizon; a lucrative new era for those willing to pledge their support.

And when the time is right, this young man will step on to the world stage and call for the old order to be swept away and replaced by something fresh and vibrant and pure.

All he needs is a trigger point. An inciting incident. Proof of the irredeemable criminality of the current leadership.

And now Naji has obtained it for him. More than enough to destroy Borko, and through him, his father.

Borko, initially keyed up after his nocturnal exertions, is sleeping soundly. For a few seconds Naji observes him, not fondly, while he despatches a copy of the footage via a secure link to an account only he and his London-based lawyer can access. He places another copy on a flash drive and slips it into his pocket.

Call Naji a cynic, but he doesn't feel the new leader will do much to improve the country's fortunes; the problems are far too deep-rooted for that. But to Naji's personal fortune, the young man will make an *immense* difference, and that is really what matters.

Naji wears a broad smile as he leaves the house for the last time. The sun is shining, birds are singing, there are gentle waves lapping against the shore.

It's another beautiful day in paradise.

ACKNOWLEDGMENTS

Thank you to Betsy Reavley, and to Fred, Tara, Morgen and the whole team at Bloodhound, as well as to Hannah Whitaker at The Rights People. Special thanks to Sumaira Wilson for setting the wheels in motion.

And as ever love and thanks to all my friends and family, especially Niki, Emily, James, Lizzie and Theo.

PRAISE FOR THE AUTHOR

"Tom Bale is one of the best British thriller writers around."
Simon Kernick

"Bale keeps us guessing as our heroes edge towards a shocking climax." *Matthew Lewin, Guardian*

"This is a mystery and a thriller that is satisfying on every level."
Jon Jordan, Crimespree

"With strong characters, a fast pace and lots of twists and turns, this is a satisfying read, right to the shocking end." *Peterborough Evening Telegraph*

"This is a neat British gangster thriller written with élan and substance." *Geoffrey Wansell, Daily Mail*

"A rollercoaster of high-octane action that just won't let go. Highly recommended." *Kim Slater*

Made in the USA
Monee, IL
12 June 2020